LOYALTY

LOYALTY

By

JOHN A. CURRY

ISBN# 1-58721-097-5

1st Books-rev.03/02/00

About the Book

Loyalty is a psychological action novel of betrayal and revenge centering on three Boston-area Irish-American brothers during the period 1947-1982. Focusing on the oldest brother, Jack Kelly, the emotionally complex and deeply alienated protagonist, the cinematic narrative chronicles the conflicts between his Boston Irish crime family and Irish rivals on New York's West Side, Italian dons in Boston and New York, and Black gangsters in Roxbury. It also traces Kelly's existential struggles as he seeks to find his way in what he sees as an unfair and amoral world.

Shadowed by the early death of his mother and the abuse of his alcoholic father, Kelly plays the devoted father and protector of his brothers -- Tommy, a promising middleweight boxer and Jerry, a bright Harvard undergraduate who eventually establishes a legitimate business. Jack executes an elaborate plan to thwart a fight-fixing scheme initiated by Connie Ryan, leader of the New York Westies, thus protecting Tommy but setting off a decades-long vendetta by the Westies' leader.

Kelly's relations with women are undermined by a too deep attachment to the memory of his dead mother and by his own one-way brand of loyalty that denies any real place in his heart to Marjorie, with whom he fathers two sons before they separate; Courtney Stahl, a sexy lawyer who eventually becomes disenchanted with him; and Catherine Slattery, the widow of one of his lieutenants. Family relationships become more strained as Kelly's son and nephew are drawn into his crime circle. As the net of deflected threats from the FBI, seen and unseen adversaries, and an informer within his own organization tighten around him, Kelly moves to eliminate his enemies, particularly Connie Ryan, who has made known his deadly intentions toward Kelly, his son, and his nephew, the heir apparent to his fraternity of crime.

The novel is rife with inventive incident, is evocative of the political, social, and physical atmosphere of the post-war decades, and offers a rogue's gallery of interesting secondary characters. The presence of the sea and the city is keenly felt and intimately connected to the psychological action of the story. Always on the move, Kelly ends as he began, the existential outsider who thumbs his nose at an unfair universe and whose ultimate loyalty is to no one and no thing.

Acknowledgments

First thanks to Marcia and Susan for their love and encouragement in the dark hours.

Special thanks to my friends Jan Surette and Charles Coffin and to my agent, Frank Weimann, for their time, advice, and faith in my project.

My gratitude to all those who read the manuscript in different incarnations, especially Robert B. Parker and Gary Goshgarian.

For technical help on various matters I'm grateful to Jamie Dendy, Coordinator, Reference Services, Northeastern University Libraries; D. Joseph Griffin, Director, Public Safety Division, Northeastern University; and Michael Schaffer, Crime Prevention Officer, Public Safety Division, Northeastern University.

My thanks also to Alan Kort, Joseph Luca, and John Burns who each offered critical words at critical moments.

"LOYALTY is exciting, intelligent and a pleasure to read. The characters will stay with you long after you've finished the book."

-Robert B. Parker

"John A. Curry's LOYALTY is a smart, fast, and compelling chronicle of the rise of Boston Irish mobsters following the war years. It is also a powerful study of family--of characters related by blood and blood-letting, where the difference tests the meaning of the book's title. LOYALTY skillfully combines an intricate plot, a vivid sense of the period, and a rich cast of characters who evoke both our wrath and sympathy."

-Gary Goshgarian

Author's Note

Parts of this work are drawn from actual incidents yet <u>Loyalty</u> is a work of fiction.

1

Jack Kelly first heard the commotion twenty-five yards from their brown and cream triple-decker in the middle of Fayette Street. The screaming and yelling pierced the cold spring night air as he approached the large wooden structure. Reacting quickly, he bounded up the four steps to the front door on the left. Pushing the door open, he entered a small hallway which led to a living room fronted by a modest sunroom facing the street.

"All you do around here is eat, sleep, and shit," his father bellowed, hovering over the young boy picking his homework papers from the living room floor.

"Dad, I told you I finished the chores. They're done. I..." Jerry Kelly sobbed.

"What's going on here, Dad?" Jack interrupted.

"What's going on here, you ask? I'll tell you what's going on here. You boys better start showing me some fuckin' respect. I provide for this family -- past, present, and future. You and your two lazy brothers better remember that. This little prick sits there doing his homework, not even answering me when I ask him a civil question."

"You threw my papers around for no reason, you drunk," Jerry sobbed.

Joe Kelly advanced on his youngest son. "You need a God damn good back-hander." As he raised his hand, Jack stepped between them, grabbed his father's arm and shoved him away from Jerry.

"You touch him again now or ever, and I'll kill you," he said. "Wouldn't Ma be proud of you?"

1

Joe glared at him for a long moment as if deciding whether to advance or retreat and then turned and staggered toward the pantry just beyond the dining room. He reached above to the cabinets and brought down a pint of whiskey. He poured the VO into a shot glass and downed it in one swallow, wincing before he followed it with a water chaser.

"A fine bunch of boys they've turned out to be, huh, Luke?" During the past two months he had begun to communicate with an imaginary friend. Like a child, he would stare at the wall or at one of his three sons, hallucinating. "You hearing this, Luke? Peg would be ashamed of me? Me?" he shouted toward the small window. "And don't think I don't know you bastards are stealing from my wallet. Why don't you take my bones, too?" he shouted as he flung his wallet from his back pants pocket to the pantry floor. At the height of his tirade, he paused, suddenly becoming quiet. "I'm tired. I don't need this aggravation. I'm going to bed. Get your own fuckin' supper," he slurred as he crossed the dining room to his bedroom.

"Are you all right?" Jack asked his brother. At fourteen, and now a ninth grader at Lynn English High School, Jerry could have served as poster boy for the stereotypical Black Irish look - - flowing dark black hair coupled with soft blue eyes, a low forehead, full mouth and straight nose. A mirror image of his older brother, he possessed the same lanky runner's body, standing almost as tall as Jack.

"I'm fine. He didn't touch me this time."

"What set him off?"

"Nothing. When he's drinking, he's just mean, looking for a fight."

"Where's Tommy?"

"At the Boys' Club with that boxing coach."

Jack nodded and bent to help pick up the papers. "Finish your homework. He acts up I'll be out on the porch for a while. Okay?"

"Okay." Jerry smiled at his brother.

He would have to quit the track team in this his last year of high school, Jack thought as he sat on the top step and surveyed

2

the neighborhood. He could not leave them at home together. Either his father would hurt Jerry, or Tommy would hurt him.

Jack looked around the street. Neighborhood was everything. It was family and friends -- almost all Irish-American -- bonded together as their grandparents and parents had been in the old country. People comfortable with their own, feeling they were God's chosen ones, oblivious to outsiders, prejudiced against those not of the faith or not of Irish-American blood, or both.

Triple-deckers lined Fayette Street with an occasional single cottage interspersed among the apartment dwellings. To his left, west along Fayette Street about a mile away, the small Negro neighborhood sat close to English High. To the east about a similar distance, Fayette Street crossed to the Jewish neighborhood and then to the ocean.

Located just ten miles north of Boston, Lynn offered the best of two worlds. Jack marveled at its urban attractiveness. Downtown, there were five large restaurants and three huge department stores, nine different movie theaters, including the majestic Paramount Theater complete with a Wurlitzer organ, and a hundred small businesses from ice cream parlors, to stamp and coin shops, to neighborhood corner markets where you could dip your hand into an icy chest of Coca Cola. Yet the city also sat on the Atlantic, its long coastline featuring endless stretches of sandy beach, a virtual paradise of enjoyment and exploration.

He loved Lynn for its vibrancy, and especially for its people -- over 100,000 residents united in a love of country, yet rigidly divided into neighborhoods, most of them feeling that life now, post-depression and world war, was decidedly better. Triggered by the three General Electric plants in the city, its residents had contributed to the winning of the war by producing jet engines. And now the Korean War, as well as new threats from Russia, meant jobs would remain plentiful. Dreams could be realized. The city pulsated with the confidence brought on by the stability people now felt in their lives.

Looking toward the east, he saw Tommy walking toward him, a duffel bag at his side. As he approached, Jack observed him carefully. In contrast to his own thin frame, his sixteen-year-old brother possessed a strong upper body and unusually large hands. An outstanding football player at English, he lived for the competition. As a ball carrier, he could punish the older boys by squaring his shoulders and running over them. As a linebacker, he tackled aggressively, with complete confidence in his abilities.

"What's the matter?" he asked Jack as he reached the steps.

"I had to separate Dad from Jerry. He's in his cups again."

"Jesus, he touches Jerry one more fuckin' time, I'll..."

"No. You won't, Tommy," Jack interrupted him. "Ma would want us to show him respect. Remember that."

Tossing the duffel bag onto the porch, Tommy sat next to him on the top step. "You want me to respect him? Does he show us any respect? He doesn't care if we eat or starve to death. If it wasn't for you cooking for us, seeing to us, where would we be?"

"I promised Ma I'd look after him as well as you guys. You know that."

"He keeps it up he's going to lose his job," Tommy said.

"We'll be all right anyway. I graduate in a few weeks and I've got the job at Cushman's Bakery right after that," Jack replied. "And you're working part-time at the drug store."

"That's no future for you. You should go to college."

"Nights. I can do it nights, Tom. Maybe Saturdays too. Hey, what's happening at the Boys' Club?" he asked, anxious to change the subject.

"You know the coach there -- Tony Parelli? He thinks I have some potential. I love it, Jackie. The team's going to move out, take on some teams from Revere, Lowell, Salem, some of the other cities. Pretty soon I'll have my first fight."

Jack nodded. "Good. I'm looking forward to seeing you compete. Now, how much homework's been done for school tomorrow?"

Tommy frowned. "I'll do it now. That is if the boy genius in there can make some room at the table for me."

The next morning Jack rose early. Since their mother's death a year before, he slept in the small sunroom fronting the street or on the living room divan, his father in one bedroom and his brothers in the other. One day a week he allowed time for a heavy breakfast, and as he lay in the warming early morning sun he planned for sausages and fried eggs, orange juice, toast, and tea.

He stood and slipped on his trousers and walked toward the kitchen. For some reason he hadn't heard his father rise and so was surprised to see him sitting at the kitchen table facing the pantry, a copy of yesterday's <u>Boston Post</u> shaking in his hands.

For Jack, the drying out process was the most difficult to deal with. The belligerent, loud alcoholic of the previous night was now reduced to a shell of a man, his hands quivering, his face hidden behind the paper. Both he and Jack knew he had no intention of reading the paper, as he sought only to hide his pale, clammy features. His self-confidence on this and on so many other days following his heavy drinking was shot, non-existent.

"You want some eggs and sausages, Dad?" Jack asked.

Slowly Joe Kelly lowered his newspaper a few inches and peeked over the top. He was not an imposing man. Of medium height, he had gone to fat. His light blond hair was parted exactly in the middle. Because of his hair, his size, his slightly upturned nose and, in his earlier years, his ruddy complexion, he reminded Jack of the actor James Cagney.

"No. I don't want any."

Jack knew the answer almost before he asked the question, for there was no way his father could easily hold a knife and fork.

"That was a bad scene last night, Dad. I'm going to tell you again -- before Tommy and Jerry get up -- you need help. Why won't you see Father Dolan at St. Joseph's?"

His father hid completely behind the paper once again. "Fuck Father Dolan. I don't need any help from him or you or anyone. Peg is gone. What can anyone do?"

Jack moved to the refrigerator and took out the eggs and sausages. He could feel his father's eyes following him across the tiled kitchen but never once did he lower the paper.

"I'll tell you one thing. I talked to Luke this morning. We're going to do something about that fuckin' GE."

"What are you talking about, Dad?" Jack asked gently.

"I didn't tell you last night? Can you imagine them letting me go? After all these years. I went in early, stayed late. Gave them all I had, the dirty bastards," he railed, finally dropping the paper on the table. "Eighteen fuckin' years as a jet engine assembler and they can me."

Jack placed the orange juice on the table alongside the bottle of Hood's milk. He sat down slowly, deciding as he did so that it would do no good to express either the anger he felt or the sympathy he did not.

"Dad, you have to listen. You can't work anywhere with this problem. We have to get it and you straightened out."

"NO! Like I said, Luke and I will straighten those cocksuckers out." He stood slowly, beads of perspiration inching their way down his brow, wetness covering his T-shirt, the smell of an unwashed body overtaking the room. He walked to the pantry, his brown chino pants wrinkled from his having slept in them.

Jack thought back to the mid '40's, to a time when his father wouldn't even touch a drink, wouldn't even think of appearing slovenly. That was a time when the anchor of his life -- his mother -- was alive to care for them all. Somewhere in the '40's his father developed the ulcer that caused him so much suffering. On more than one evening his father would return from work, skip supper, and then writhe in agony on his bed or on the living room couch, hoping that the milk he drank or maybe some ice cream would temper the burning pains.

Then just a few months before Jack's graduation from St. Joseph's in 1948, his father had half of his stomach removed.

That spring the boys began to experience the downside of their father's new-found good health. His drinking began, largely confined to weekends when he would stand in the pantry downing straight whiskey. And when that occurred, the boys learned to keep out of the way. Drink largely transformed their father from a quiet, strict, reasonably fair man into a crude, ugly personality. Woe be to the one who caused any problem, neglected any assigned chores, or even looked the wrong way whenever Joe Kelly was in his cups. But whatever his condition, his relationship with and behavior toward his Peg never changed, never fluctuated from that of the loving, concerned husband. But in 1949 she had become ill with cancer. Her brave fight weighed heavily on all of them, as they watched the pretty woman with the long, angular face grow old and deteriorate right before their eyes. From that time on, Joe Kelly was never the same.

"What are you doing, Dad?" Jack asked as his father reached above the pantry doors.

"I'm getting a fuckin' drink is what I'm doing. I need to calm my nerves."

Jack stood and closed the half open cabinet gently. "No, you're not, Dad. Not at 6:30 in the morning you're not. I'll make some coffee for you."

His father glared, obviously debating in his head whether he wanted a fight. A man who never swore in front of his family now did so regularly, and, increasingly would physically accost one of them, usually Jerry, the youngest, the most vulnerable. His father had become a coward.

Joe Kelly avoided Jack's stare. "Fuck you guys. I'll get my drink somewhere where I'm appreciated." He turned toward his bedroom, his bare feet slapping the kitchen tiles as he crossed to his room.

Jack lit the stove and placed three eggs in the frying pan next to the three sausages. He stared at the mix as the heat reached them, evaluating his situation. He was eighteen going on forty. God had taken his mother, and his father relied now completely on the bottle for solace. From Jack's view God and the Church had failed him when he most needed their help. For all intents and purposes he was now head of the family -- responsible for them all. He had only distant relatives to assist him, Tommy, and Jerry. Because of his shame at their situation, he had few friends, but curiously, he felt no need for them. His brothers were his friends, and he didn't need any others. He felt cold and unemotional, determined and bitter, all at the same time. In three weeks he would graduate. But to what?

2

The huge lot on Sanderson Avenue was filled with black and white vans with the Cushman's Bakery logo prominently displayed. Cushman's of Portland, Maine, and Lynn, Massachusetts, provided New England families with door to door service, moving their variety of delicious baked goods from the two production facilities all around the six states.

"I'm Jack Kelly, here to begin work on the 11-7 shift," he said to the receptionist, on entering the bakery sales division office adjacent to the production facility.

"Just a minute, young man," a stout, diminutive older woman replied as she picked up the phone and dialed. "Ray, the Kelly kid is here. Can you come and pick him up?"

As she set the phone in its cradle, she said, "He'll be right here."

He thanked her and moved toward an immense plate glass window that provided a view of a major part of the large production area. Throughout the plant, conveyor belts raced in rhythm, moving away from massive ovens toward sorting stations. Some carried trays of bread, others donuts or cakes. Racks of packaged bread and donuts were stockpiled around the perimeter of the floor, eventually to be moved onto the waiting trucks and vans.

"You Jack Kelly?" inquired a handsome young man with an extremely agreeable smile. Perhaps seven or eight years older than Jack, he was broad through the shoulders and tall. His eyes were gray and gentle under heavy black brows. With the humidity his hair was limp, falling in a cowlick over his left eye.

"Yeah," Jack replied firmly.

"Well, I'm Ray Horan. I'm one of the assistant foremen. You ready to work today?"

"That's why I'm here."

"Come on, we'll go over to the line, and I'll explain the various steps. This your first job out of high school?"

"Yeah. I graduated from English last week."

"I've been here for three years now. The work's tough, but you look like you can handle it. Ever work in a bakery before?" Ray asked as they entered the large room.

"No, but I know how to work. I worked in a drug store part-time through high school."

Ray smiled. "Well, that's a light touch compared to this shit. You ever see Jackie Gleason chasing those conveyor belts on television? It ain't any fun, believe me."

They paused in front of the ovens, the intense heat overwhelming them.

"Someone will place these dollies of bread dough right here. Take two trays at a time like this guy's doing and place them in the ovens as the planes rotate. Got the idea?"

Jack nodded.

"You do that for a forty-five minute cycle and then take a fifteen minute break. Believe me, you'll need it. When you're back on the floor go to the second station." He moved about ten feet across the face of the oven to a conveyor belt. "Next, grab the bread as it comes out of the oven. Use the gloves and bang the bread out of the trays. Watch this guy," he said, pointing to a thin older man.

Jack noticed that the gloves he used were nothing but pieces of cloth that protected the worker's palms. Huge welts covered the back of the man's hands.

"Throw the trays on this rack. They're red hot. And be fast here. You have to keep up with the conveyor. Then take another break and report to the sorting area over here." Ray walked to an area thirty yards down the conveyor belt where a middle-aged man, again with only cloth pieces looped around his wrists, straightened the loaves of bread prior to their entering the packaging machine.

"Here again, the bread's still hot. Use the gloves and move fast. That's it. Three cycles, three breaks. Any questions?"

"No, not for now," Jack said.

"Good," Ray smiled. "And by the way kid, I'm just an assistant. There's a prick named DeLeo who's the main guy. Keep your guard up with him. He thinks he's King Shit. See that room in the corner up ahead? That's where you change into whites. I'll see you later." With that, he extended his hand and then walked away.

A minute or two before 11 P.M. Jack walked toward the first station, the noise of the machines deafening, almost making conversation impossible. An unsmiling figure cut into his path.

"Hey, kid! You the new guy?" asked a short, stocky middle-aged man with pock marks dominating his face.

"I'm Jack Kelly," he replied, extending his hand.

The man did not accept it. "Yeah, right. I'm Ralph DeLeo, foreman. Do me a favor and don't fuck this job up. And then you and I can get along. Ray fill you in?"

"Yeah, I'm on my way to the first station."

"Good. Try to get your Irish ass there without falling in a pile of shit on the way," DeLeo said.

Fuck you, Jack thought. He could kick the dink right in the ass, but that wouldn't be politic. He would just watch the guy, focus on him, be sure he read him right – what was important to him, what irritated him. Once he knew those answers, he would know how to handle the guy, how to play him.

After a week, he also knew he could handle the job. His hands were red and blistered, and his legs ached from the long sessions at each station. The heat from the ovens sapped his energy, but he kept up with the pace of the clock and the conveyer belts, and the urgings of the foreman. And the challenge seemed to give him confidence. He needed the job, and he was not going to fail. He felt an inner strength, a determination to succeed, a love of hard work that fueled him. Above all, he felt proud bringing home a paycheck each week. They all depended on him and that check. It was now clear that his father was not going to work again, as with each day Luke became a more prominent figure in his life.

And in the early fall, he felt like a proud parent as he witnessed his brothers' progress. An All-Scholastic at English in both his sophomore and junior years, Tommy excelled as a tailback in the Red and Gray's single wing offense and as a linebacker on defense. Tommy had no particular interest in school, but in the evenings Jack insisted they go through Tommy's homework assignments together. With Jerry, now a sophomore at English, there was no such need. An A student, he loved to read and was naturally inquisitive.

Every night Jack would cook supper for them. In fact, he had become a pretty good cook, trying to prepare balanced meals featuring meat and potatoes – the traditional Irish-American meal, he laughed. If this stuff causes cancer, we're all dead, he often thought. He assigned chores to his brothers, who obviously worshipped him for providing some form of stability in their lives. Together they cared for their father, kept the apartment clean, assured that all family debts were paid.

"So are you coming to see your hotshot younger brother, Jackie?" inquired Tommy, one September night while they all washed dishes together.

"See my brother do what?"

"Fight, brother. Fight. Remember? At the Boys' Club on the Common on Friday. The amateurs. Tony Parelli says I'm ready for my first fight."

Jerry chimed in, "Jackie, you have to see him box. He's good."

"I'll be there, Tommy." Jack said. "What time?"

The front door closed slowly as their father moved unsteadily into the living room. "Well, boys, do you have any supper left for me?"

"Sure, Dad," answered Jack. "Sit yourself at the kitchen table, and I'll warm up some hamburg and potatoes."

"Forget it. I'm going to bed."

Despite their efforts to help, Joe was distancing himself from them, avoiding contact as much as he could. In the early evening when they sat together to eat, he would visit the Red Fox Café at the corner of Fayette and Essex Streets. Most nights he missed supper with them, and if he did participate, would quickly pick a fight, feign disapproval at whatever the conversation, and walk toward his bedroom with his normal comment, "I don't have to listen to this bullshit."

Neither friends nor Father Dolan nor the boys made any difference in his outlook. One night, Jack had mentioned the idea of his father asking a neighborhood woman out.

"Mrs. Hogan? The widow on Trinity Avenue?" Joe exploded at the idea. "I want nothing to do with another woman. How can you suggest such a thing? You know what your mother meant to me. What the hell are you thinking?"

"Dad, it's just that you should do something with yourself. Look at you. Your appearance. Your clothes."

Joe glared at him. "Look, you little prick. I'm not seeing her or any other woman. And keep people away from me. I'm happy with me, even if you people aren't. MYOB."

Jack's insistence that their father be treated with respect was a difficult proposition for Tommy, in particular, who sneered at the idea and very reluctantly followed Jack's lead. "Isn't he just a pisser?" Tommy sighed as Joe slammed the bedroom door closed.

"Be respectful."

"If Ma could see him now..."

"If Ma could see him now, she would tell us exactly what I'm telling you. She loved him," Jack retorted.

"Well, I don't love him. Not the way he's left us in the lurch. I'll do what you say, Jackie -- because you're asking -- and that's the only reason."

"What time's the fights on Friday?"

"I'm going on about seven o'clock, the second fight. We're going against a team from Lowell."

"I'll be there. A couple of the guys from Cushman's are going over to the dog track around eight, so the timing is good."

3

During the summer months he had become very friendly with Ray Horan. The job was always difficult, the pace hectic, but he liked Ray and most of the crew. Together they snickered or giggled at DeLeo, most particularly when he screamed at them about productivity, an assault almost always uncalled for. They kept up with the conveyors, met their targets -- so there was no reason for the heat. Actually, there was heat enough already. Jack had lost ten pounds in three months working around the ovens.

During one particular break early in the week of Tommy's fight, he and Ray sat smoking in the employees' rest area, drinking coffee and flipping newspaper pages, scanning rather than reading. "I'm going over to Wonderland Friday night. Want to go?" Ray inquired.

Jack looked up from the newspaper. "You got the money to gamble? I'm not sure I can afford to lose. We're not rolling in dough at home, you know."

"It's no big thing. I set a limit, lose a little bit on the puppies and leave. Besides, there's a couple of friends I want you to meet."

Jack looked up. "Guys from Charlestown?"

"Yeah. One's a friend from my neighborhood and the other's a friend from Mission Hill. Come along, and have a little fun."

"Okay. I'll be there. I always wanted to see what the track looks like."

On Friday night he and Jerry walked to Central Square and then west to City Hall Square and the Boys' Club next to Lynn

Classical High School. In the main hall, a regulation boxing ring sat in the middle of the large room that functioned as a gym for basketball, as well. Across the ring they spotted Tommy in blue boxing trunks and a white robe, waiting his turn to enter the ring. At sixteen he was developing by the day. Thick black curly hair and hazel green eyes contrasted with his rather pale skin. Yet one noticed the body first -- hard, muscular, and taut. He waved at them, winking as well, bouncing on his toes, throwing lefts and rights into an imaginary opponent's mid-section.

"Ladies and gentlemen," a squat, middle-aged announcer boomed without benefit of a microphone in the center of the ring, "our next bout features middleweights at the 160 lb. limit. From Lowell, in the red trunks, meet Petey Lorenza." A tall, angular young man walked up three steps, extended his feet through the ropes, and entered the ring. "His opponent, from Lynn, in the blue trunks, Tommy Kelly. Three rounds." From the other set of steps Tommy ran into the ring, his eyes concentrating completely now on Lorenza.

Jack and Jerry moved toward the three rows of chairs surrounding the ring, most of them filled by family, friends, or members of the teams themselves. They sat as close to Tommy's corner as they could.

Both boys, wearing protective head gear for the three round bout, moved toward the center as the bell for Round One sounded. With no hesitation, Tommy moved straight into his opponent, unleashing a left hook to the jaw and a short right under the heart as the surprised young Italian moved back.

"Hit him in the la bonza, Petey!" implored an enthusiastic sixty year old from across the ring.

As Petey bicycled, Tommy barreled ahead quickly, aggressively, throwing punches in combinations, with lightning speed and with real effectiveness. A left to the mouth drew a trickle of blood and a following right cross staggered Petey for a second. As Tommy moved in, the bell sounded, saving Petey after three minutes of intense pressure.

16

Tommy winked at them on his way back to his corner, but before he reached the stool, the referee intercepted him and brought him back to the center, simultaneously raising his hand in victory. Lorenza did not argue this decision, instead moving to the center to embrace Tommy and offer words of nodding encouragement.

Tommy exited the ring, glided down the short stairs, and stopped at their seats. "What do you think, big brother?"

"Not bad, Tommy. Robinson had better watch out."

A thin, frail, middle-aged man with scar tissue around his eyes appeared next to Tommy and uttered, "Sugar Ray he's not. At least not yet. But he's got real promise if he keeps at it. I'm Tony Parelli."

Jack shook the extended hand, "How are you, Mr. Parelli. I've heard a lot about you."

Jerry embraced his older brother, "Great job, Tommy. You were all over him."

"And I've heard a lot about you from Tommy. He thinks you're..."

Tommy interrupted him. "Never mind. I'm going to take a shower."

Jack stood. "And I'm catching the bus to Revere. Nice to have met you, Mr. Parelli. Be sure he doesn't get hurt, huh?"

"More likely he'll inflict a lot of hurt if he dedicates himself."

"See you guys back home," Jack said, tapping Tommy with a light left to the head, extending his other hand to Jerry as he moved away.

Outside on North Common Street he boarded the Boston-Haymarket Square bus which would follow Route 107 through West Lynn into Revere. As with any late summer or early fall evening, the bus was jammed with teens heading toward Revere Beach and its two miles of beachfront funland complete with ferris wheels, dodge 'em cars, carnival games, and pizza parlors. A number of men stood, holding onto the overhead straps, studying racing forms.

Just below Bell Circle Jack stepped down from the bus and along with thousands of others dropped a quarter into the automatic coin collector and entered Wonderland Park. He strolled through the vendors hawking programs and walked up the grandstand steps. Turning right at the top of the grandstand, he faced a huge scoreboard in the middle of a large grassy knoll forming the inner portion of an oval. A circular dirt track surrounded the infield. Across the field, eight greyhounds paraded on their route to the 7/16 of a mile starting boxes and their eternal pursuit of Swifty, the mechanical rabbit.

Scanning the crowd, he noted Ray in deep conversation with two men, waving their programs and studying the changing odds on the giant board. "Three minutes to post time," brayed the announcer as Jack descended the steps toward them.

"What do you say, Ray?" Jack asked, moving into the vacant end seat.

"Hey, Jack. Meet some friends of mine. This here is Leo Slattery," he said, indicating the tall, thin man probably in his late twenties sitting next to him. Leo carried an overt intelligence in his eyes. His hair was already beginning to recede. Jack extended his hand which Slattery readily accepted. "And Vinnie Sullivan," Ray said, indicating the rubbery-faced, burly man to Leo's right. He had the look of a bully, his apple red cheeks bubbling under angry eyes.

Jack again extended his hand, which this time was left hanging in mid-air.

"Who the fuck is he?" Sullivan asked Ray, hardly looking at Jack.

"He's okay. I vouch for him. He's good people." Ray responded, too defensively.

"I don't need any vouching for, Ray," said Jack, glaring at both of them.

"You need vouching for if I say you do," Sullivan retorted.

"Look, Ray," said Jack, looking directly at Sullivan, "You asked me here. If this asshole doesn't start acting a little more friendly, I've got better things to do."

"Take it easy, Jack. This guy likes to yank people's chains, that's all. Calm the fuck down, Vin. Ray says he's all right," Leo urged.

"Well, let me know ahead of time next time okay, Ray? I don't like surprises. First, I wheel the seven for a fuckin' payoff of a lousy $24 on the double, and then this chippy bastard shows his nose," Vin complained.

"One more fuckin' ugly remark out of you, shitface, and you'll get a real surprise," Jack responded.

Vin snorted, "Kid, you want to show me you're okay? Here take this. Go up and get me a $50 ticket on number six to win the third. Got it?"

Leaning forward in his seat, Jack stared at him. "I got it but I'm not getting it."

"Suit yourself, kid." Vin replied.

"Shut the fuck up, Vin," Ray said, standing.

"Hey, we're all friends here. Ray says you're all right. That's good enough for me. How about we all calm down and enjoy the puppies? I don't need any more aggravation. You want a fucking ticket, Vin? Then get it yourself. And while you're at it, get me a win ticket for $50 on the three dog," Leo commanded.

Vin stood, glaring viciously at Jack, and moved to the rear of the grandstand.

Leo said, "I should have told him you were coming. I forgot to mention it to Vin. Jack, it's a pleasure to make your acquaintance. My short-peckered friend there has a perpetual hard-on to prove he's a man. But he's a solid guy. Dependable, and a real friend. After we clean out the track, let's go into Boston for some beers or something. Get to know you a bit. Settle this bad beginning down."

Jack immediately liked this friendly guy dressed in black slacks with an open necked red sports shirt. "Fine with me," he responded, gazing at the board. "So what looks good tonight?"

"Well, that was a wonderful evening. $150 down the fuckin' drainpipe," Leo sighed as his '52 Chevy coasted down

Huntington Avenue heading west from Copley Square. They passed the Mechanics Building, the twenty-eight acres of railroad yards, the Uptown Theater and Brigham's ice cream parlor opposite Symphony Hall. Leo stayed in the inside lane and then reversed direction at Gainsboro Street heading back east, stopping almost immediately outside the Lobster Claw at the corner of Huntington and Gainsboro.

They walked to a table in the back of the restaurant, moving through groups of college kids and a mix of middle-aged to elderly neighborhood regulars at the bar.

The waitress was young, brunette, very attractive. She delivered the shots of whiskey and bottles of beer and smiled at Leo. "Anything else for now?"

"We're all set," Leo said dismissively. "You're from Lynn, Jack?"

Jack nodded, fingering the glass of Budweiser.

"Well I live up on Mission Hill, about a mile from here -- on Horadan Way," Leo said. "Great Irish neighborhood. No fucking interlopers in the area. That is so far, but with that fuckin' mayor Hynes and his urban renewal plans God knows what's coming. Good families, most attended Mission High like I did. Vin here, now, he's from Charlestown like Ray. You play any ball in Lynn, Jack?"

Jack shook his head. "I ran some track. My brother Tommy's the athlete in the family. He made the <u>Boston Traveler</u> All-Scholastic football team as a sophomore."

"Lynn's where the Agganis kid's from, right?" Leo inquired.

Jack replied, "That's right."

"Imagine him playing in the Red Sox system this year. That's unbelievable. The Greek was a great football player, and now he's on the way to being a fuckin' major leaguer. Great story," said Leo, raising his shot glass.

"So you guys are still sweating your balls off at that bakery, huh, Ray?" teased Vin.

"It's a job," Ray replied.

"What do you two do?" asked Jack.

Vin glared at him after first looking quickly at Leo.

"We both work on the docks," answered Leo, signaling the waitress for another round. "I'm a bookkeeper for the union and Vin's a loader." He changed the subject quickly. "Ray tells me you're taking care of your family. Now I admire that."

"There isn't too much choice," Jack responded. "We have to eat."

"You like the bakery work?" Leo inquired.

"It's okay. Not much of a future, but that night work differential helps."

"Look at that DeMarco kid," Vin interjected, pointing to the television set above the bar. "He'll be fighting top notchers in the Garden next. The kid's good."

Jack turned in time to see Tony DeMarco being interviewed by a Channel 4 sportscaster, the Old North Church serving as a backdrop.

"His real name's Leonard Liotta. I know him," Leo said. "Great kid from a hard working family over on Fleet Street in the North End."

"My brother's doing some amateur boxing," Jack said.

"No shit," Leo said, downing his second boilermaker.

"Lots of luck to him and the Red Sox," Vin snickered. "Good way to get your brains scrambled."

"Well I admire what you're doing, Jack. Family is important. It's everything. Without family there's no foundation for life. The Church help you to understand that?" Leo asked.

Jack lowered his beer glass. "I don't have much use for the Church. The Church didn't help me understand much of anything," he replied bitterly, "except maybe that the Lord helps those who help themselves."

"Amen," Leo responded. "Your other brother is a top flight student Ray tells me."

"He's a straight A student," Ray said.

"Will he go to college, Jack?" Leo asked.

"He has a couple of years of high school left. I'll find a way to get him there." Jack glanced at his watch. "I appreciated meeting you guys, but OK if we head back? Speaking of family, I need to check on a few things back there."

Leo said, "Sure. We're outta here," as he placed a twenty dollar bill on the table.

"What's my share?" Jack asked.

"My treat, Jack. Nice to meet a friend of Ray's. He and I go all the way back to Mission High. Hope we see you again. We hit the track most Friday nights," Leo said.

A half hour later, after they had driven him back to Central Square, Jack walked up Union Street reflecting on the meeting. What was that all about? he wondered. Why did Ray want him to meet those two? He liked Leo. He was smooth, considerate, friendly. He did not particularly like Leo's probing about his family. Yet he liked the man, his style, his demeanor.

Leo had not reacted to his comments about the Church. He should probably keep his opinions concerning sensitive topics to himself, he thought. But he more and more resented what he perceived as an uncaring, unfeeling Church lost in tradition, prejudiced against Jews and Protestants, incapable of ministering to its local constituents, led by a God who chose to take his mother and render his father helpless.

As for that loudmouth with Leo, he could have killed him. He caught himself as he walked past St. Joseph's Church. What was he thinking? He could have killed him? Yes, he could have for a moment, he thought. But why? Because he didn't care much about anyone. He felt detached from anybody who was not family. He didn't need anybody, except Tommy and Jerry.

He walked up the steps of the triple-decker close to midnight. Jerry sat at the dining room table with books spread out over the table.

"How you doing?" he inquired.

"Fine. I'm working on a composition for English class. How did the puppies treat you?" he asked, looking up.

"You're working on a Friday night? Jerry, maybe I haven't said it right. I'm very proud of you. You keep up those grades, you'll be the first in the family to go to college," Jackie said, as he scrubbed Jerry's head.

22

"If you weren't keeping this family together, I wouldn't have time for studying. I should be working along with you and Tommy."

"You let Tommy and me worry about money. You just finish these last two years with the kind of grades you've been getting. You'll have plenty of time to work later. Tommy home yet?"

"He went to bed early. Gee, he really looked good tonight, don't you think?"

"Yeah, he looked good. But fighting's a tough business for him or anybody. I'm hitting the sack, too. See you in the morning, Einstein."

4

On the ride back to Boston, Leo Slattery rode his '52 Chevy through Revere continuing on Route 1A, and entering the Sumner Tunnel in East Boston. "So why so quiet, Leo? What did you think of him?" Ray asked.

"I'll tell you what I think of him," interjected Vinnie. "If Leo wasn't there, I would have taught him some manners."

"That's the big trouble with you, Vin. Along with too much mouth, you're stupid. I'm trying to get a line on this kid, and you're all ready to deck him," Leo admonished. "Some day someone is going to permanently close that mouth of yours if you don't start wising up." Vin flinched in the passenger seat and sat quietly, turning his attention to the West End neighborhood as they headed toward Scollay Square and the Casino Theater.

"Yeah, I liked him, Ray. He knows when to talk and when not to. He showed some balls back there with this dope. He's old world Irish. Everything for the family. He reeks of loyalty. He's a loner. Yeah, I liked him a lot," Leo said.

"So, what's next?" Ray asked.

"I'll talk to Jimma. See if an approach is all right with him. My recommendation will be positive. We need guys like him," Leo answered. "But in the meantime, I want you to suggest nothing to him. If everything is okay with Jimma, I'll personally visit Kelly. Nothing's to be said, got it?"

Ray replied, "Well, not from me anyway. I told you you'd like him. He's smart, close-mouthed, and hard."

Leo parked the car on Canal Street and the three walked to the burlesque theater where huge placards announced that Irma the Squirmer would follow Sally Rand next Monday.

"Hey, Jack, did you enjoy Friday night?" Ray asked, easing himself into the wooden chair in the employees' lounge at Cushman's on Sunday night.

Jack stirred his black coffee as he simultaneously reached for one of the plain donuts, not too long out of the ovens. "What was that all about, Ray?"

"What do you mean?"

"I mean I felt I was being evaluated for one thing."

"Just some friends I thought you might like. They catch the puppies almost every Friday, down a few drinks, and just enjoy each other's company."

Jack smiled. "Yeah, sure."

"I go back a way with Leo. He and I went to the Mission elementary school up on the Hill," Ray continued. "My family moved to Charlestown, but I kept going to Mission High. Leo went on to Boston State College and later took up bookkeeping. A real smart guy, highly regarded by the union on the waterfront."

"What about the mug with him? You telling me he's not trouble?"

Ray laughed. "Vin? Vin's okay. Likes to play the hard case to impress people. He lives near the Bunker Hill Monument a street over from me."

Jack said, "If he's not a legbreaker, I'm Clark Gable."

In the distance a whistle blew signifying the end of the short break and the return to Hades. Jack sighed. "Come on, let's go back to chasing the conveyors," Ray said. "We're just like the dogs chasing Swifty. We're never going to catch up."

On Thursday morning about 6:45 Leo swung his '52 Chevy around the Nahant rotary, following the coastline by Lynn Beach as he headed toward Swampscott. A cloudless sky greeted the early commuters weaving their way toward Boston in the crowded lanes opposite Leo and the few cars moving north with him. In just hours the first arrivals would descend the walkways to beaches and settle on the mile long stretch of sand called

King's Beach near the Swampscott line. But at this hour only a few elderly people walking their dogs dotted the sidewalks to his right. Not even a good-looking broad to observe at this hour, he thought.

Just before the Swampscott town line he turned left onto Eastern Avenue and a half mile later took another left onto Sanderson Avenue. He parked almost directly across from Cushman's so that he could see Jack coming when the shift ended. On his left Kiley Park, with its acres of open fields and basketball courts, sat in stark contrast to the claustrophobic setting of the giant bakery.

At exactly 7:00 Jack came out the front door along with forty or fifty others, almost all men, heading towards cars parked along both sides of the street. "Hey, Jack!" Leo shouted through the rolled down passenger-side window. "Ride home?"

Jack separated himself from a small group and walked toward the parked car. "Hey, Leo. What brings you to Lynn?"

"Enjoying the beach views early in the morning for one thing. For another, I want to talk with you. Any place we can get some coffee and talk in private?" Leo asked.

Jack said, "Sure. Let's go back to Lynn Beach. There's a place at the Nahant rotary."

At the rotary, Leo eased into Christie's parking lot. Owned by the same Greek family for generations, Christie's served the beach crowd, principally with grilled food and soft drinks. They ordered two coffees and two muffins to go and returned to the car.

Leo bit into his bran muffin, balancing the coffee in one hand and the muffin in the other. Jack blew on his cup, foregoing the muffin for the moment.

"Will you look at that water coming over the sea wall?" Leo marveled. "What a sight the power of the sea is, huh Jack?" Across the rotary, with the high tide running, majestic waves of green pounded the sea wall, sending the few walkers scurrying toward the grass, away from the walkway.

As a boy, Jack had come here or to King's Beach a mile up the road, every summer day, usually with both Tommy and Jerry

-- all three boys armed with peanut butter sandwiches and a nickel to purchase a soft drink at Christie's. Gazing across to the ocean, Jack thought of the time he was here at this beach with Tommy alone. From the shore he had been running into the onrushing waves, riding them back to shore, while Tommy, then about age six, watched him from the water's edge. Suddenly he heard Tommy yelling at him. "Jackie, I'm bleeding," he screamed, looking down at his foot.

Racing from the water, Jack examined the severe cut on the bottom of his brother's right foot. He had stepped on a broken Coke bottle buried in the shallow water. Jack remembered helping Tommy to the towel they had stretched out on the beach, wrapping his own T-shirt around the foot as a tourniquet, and then carrying him on his shoulders the one and a half miles back to Fayette Street. Once they were home, their mother had staunched the bleeding and Dr. Judge had stitched the wound.

"What a view!" Leo continued, shaking Jack back to the present.

Leo turned to him. "Jack, the other night I told you what I did for a living and asked you about your situation. Like I said then, I admire a guy who cares about and takes care of his family. It shows me commitment, it shows me loyalty, it shows me some character. And character's what separates the winners from the losers." Leo paused, sipping from the steaming cup. "Look, money has to be a problem for you, right?"

Jack grinned, "No argument there."

"Then listen carefully to my proposition. And whatever your answer, I've got something else to tell you," Leo said. "Jack, like I told you, I work for the union on the waterfront. But that's not my only job. You probably want that kid brother of yours to go to college, right? And how about the one you mentioned is taking up fighting. What's his future? And you? You going to break your balls pushing donuts into ovens the rest of your life? And I understand your father..."

Jack interrupted him, "Never mind my father. Get to the point, Leo."

Leo threw the empty coffee cup out the window, turned to Jack, annoyance in his voice. "The point, Jack, is that there isn't much of a future ahead. A smart guy like you must see that.

"The point, Jack, is that I'm as big on family as you are. I value what you value -- the family, its protection, loyalty, a set of values, caring for each other. At home there's just me, the wife, and the kid. But I have another family as well -- Vin, Ray, and a dozen other guys who care about that other family, nourishing it, protecting it, taking care of each other."

He lit a cigarette and exhaled slowly. "We're all Irish. We're like a fraternity. Just like the guineas band together to provide for and protect each other, so don't we. Sort of like an Irish Mafia.

"We do things together. We work for an organization and a head that expects the same loyalty as the guineas do. Except there's no formal initiation ceremony on the way in. There may be on the way out, though. A bullet between the eyes if any one is ever disloyal to or informs on the group. You can leave if you want to at any point, but not ever as an informant. In that way we're not too different from the boyos in the old country." Leo started the engine, eased the Chevy away from the beach, heading toward downtown and Central Square.

As he absorbed Leo's words, Jack was pleased that he had guessed right. The need to fend for himself, two brothers, and a distraught father had built in him a maturity, an insight into human behavior, and an instinct to see things coming beyond his eighteen plus-years.

"What do you guys do? I mean, what exactly are these things you do together?" he asked as Leo turned from Central Square moving north on Union Street.

"Lots of businesses provide us with money to protect them, and lots of guys borrow from us. Sometimes they both forget to pay and have to be reminded of that little oversight. We also operate the numbers rackets in our neighborhoods --Southie, Charlestown, Cambridge, here on the North Shore. We work with the union guys on the waterfront, which provides kickback money, that is if guys want to work down there.

"There's good money, Jack. You'll average close to $300 a week for sure to begin. And we promote. No shit, just like regular work. You do good work, you advance over a period of time."

They passed St. Joseph's at the same moment that Jack said, "I'm in."

"You're in?" Leo repeated. "Like no other questions? Like is this for me? Maybe before 'You're in,' I should point out a couple of other items. Number one, you work with me. At some point soon you'll meet the boss. He'll want reports on how you're doing before you meet him. Number two, you keep your job, either the bakery job or another one. But you always have a legitimate job. And number three, remember, you can drop out at any time, and maybe, if you don't cut it, we drop you out. But there must never be any trace from you to the authorities. You understand that, right? So just don't say 'I'm in.' Make sure you understand the rules."

"I said I'm in, and I understand," Jack responded firmly.

They moved onto Fayette Street and stopped in front of his house. "So what's next?" Jack asked.

"I'll pick you up in Central Square at the Waldorf Cafeteria next Tuesday night about 7. Be there. You don't go to work until 11 right?" Jack nodded as he stepped out.

As Leo drove down the street, Jack stood on the porch watching the car move toward Laundry Hill on its way over to the beach. A way out, he thought. A way to a new life. A way to provide for his family. He did not feel any ambivalence at all. As he entered the living room, his father, sitting in the sunroom with Jerry, looked up and asked him if Luke had come home yet.

5

Tommy countered the left lead with a right cross under the heart. The pasty-faced kid across from him staggered, caught himself and lunged toward Tommy. Avoiding the charge, Tommy moved counter-clockwise and peppered three quick jabs into his opponent's face. Displaying grace and skill, he unleashed a hard right to the stomach sending the kid from Salem to one knee. The referee quickly stepped in, pushing Tommy toward his corner, signaling the fight was over. Tommy threw his arms skyward in triumph, pointing a glove at Jack and Jerry as he received Tony's congratulations.

In the locker room a few minutes later, Tommy embraced his brothers as they sat on the rubbing table on each side of him. "What do you think, Tony? What if we turn pro and make some money, huh?" he teased.

Tony frowned. "You know and I know you're a long way from that, Tommy. Stick with me for a year or so, then you'll be ready. There still is a lot to learn right here with the pures, kid. Don't get too ambitious too soon," Tony said, unwrapping his hands. "This time next year you'll have your high school diploma, a full-time job or college -- things under you before you chance the pros."

"Listen to the man, Tommy," Jack said. "Keep this in perspective. You're going to be offered a football scholarship somewhere. Get an education through football. Make something of your life."

Tommy winced. "We'll see, Jack. We'll see. You're working. I need to help, too. Dad's never going to work again."

Jack jabbed him kiddingly with his left hand. "Listen to your older brother. You and Jerry get educated. Money won't be a big problem. Let me worry about it."

Tommy grinned. "Sure, look at you. You've left twenty pounds already in the ovens. What do you weigh? 150 and falling?"

"160, wise ass. Same as you. I'm lifting weights at the Y and running still," Jack replied. "You better be careful, or I might take up this racket."

By sitting at a table facing Central Square, Jack would be able to see the car as it approached. He looked around the Waldorf Cafeteria, with its mix of lost elderly singles just passing time sipping coffee and noisy high schoolers sitting in large groups trying to impress one another.

Outside, people lined up for buses to take them into Boston, and across the square other commuters waited for buses bound north for Swampscott, Salem and Marblehead. He thought back to VJ Day and the wild celebration that had erupted in Central Square that night in August of 1945. Confetti had rained down from the Boston and Maine railroad station elevated above the square on the thousands gathered together in joy and happiness to celebrate the peace.

During the war years, the center of the city at night had bustled with window shoppers, lovers holding hands, high school boys pushing other boys into teenage girls. The effects of television had changed all that. In its early days, television had brought people together, but as the novelty wore off, people drew back into themselves, and socialized less. The crowds in the square were much lighter, the various businesses catering to much smaller numbers of customers. Lynn was changing, and so was he.

Leo beeped to get his attention. He left the quarter on the table and moved toward the street.

As he approached the Chevy, the passenger side back door opened and he stepped inside. Leo wheeled away from the curb, introducing a guy he'd never seen sitting in back with him.

"You know Vin. Jack, this is Paulie Cronin. Paulie, Jack Kelly." A heavy set young man, maybe twenty-five, squeezed his extended hand, "Nice to meet you, Jack." Jack noted his heavily freckled face and hands.

"We're going over to Revere Beach, Jack. Son of a bitch of a welsher owes us $4,000. Ray's been tailing him and, if he's right, the guy's in his apartment down a ways from Kelly's Roast Beef right now," Leo said.

Leo exited Lynn on Route 1A, crossing the General Edwards Bridge into Revere five minutes after leaving the square. Maintaining an even pace, within the speed limit, he turned left onto Revere Street, and headed toward the beach.

Across from Kelly's Roast Beef, Ray sat on a bench, the black ocean behind him, watching lines of patrons ordering from five or six people working energetically inside the long wooden stand that was Revere's favorite eating place.

Leo stopped at the bench, and Ray approached the car as Vin rolled down the passenger side front window. "He's there, and he's alone," Ray said. "Two houses down from Kelly's, Apartment 2B."

"Jump in," Leo commanded.

Leo drove along Revere Beach Boulevard another thirty yards and then tuned right into one of the parking spaces that fronted the beach. From here all the way to the end of the boulevard three out of every four parked cars, Jack guessed, contained young lovers petting, and in almost as many cases, a cautious young woman willing to pet but in dreadful fear of becoming pregnant and being ostracized from family and friends.

"Let's go," Leo ordered as he cut the lights. "Jack, you stay by me. Just observe. Let the rest of the guys do what needs to be done. There shouldn't be any problems. Paulie, you stay with the car. Get behind the wheel and be ready. Okay, you guys move. Jack and I will follow."

They stepped from the car, walked back toward Kelly's, and crossed the Boulevard, passing around the lines of folks ordering hot dogs and clam plates, Jack and Leo ten yards behind Ray and

Vin. The white-stuccoed, two-story facing the ocean needed a coat of paint, Jack thought as they moved to the entry, and once inside, up a short flight of stairs to the door marked "2B."

Leo eased past the others and pounded loudly on the door. "Larry, open up and make it fuckin' quick. This is Leo. We know you're in there."

A second later, a bolt moved and a tall, well-built man, probably in his late forties, opened the door, a warm smile on his tanned face. "Leo. Leo, my friend, come in. Come in," he gestured. "What's this, the shore patrol with you? Why don't you bring a few more reinforcements next time?"

Larry Cally was dressed in blue trousers and a white T-shirt. He held a half empty beer bottle in his right hand.

"Never mind the bullshit, Larry," Leo cautioned. "Jimma wants his money -- $4,000 cash. You remember, Larry? You remember it was due a week ago?"

"Ah, yes, of course, Leo," Larry said, moving to one of two swivel chairs surrounding a newly reupholstered couch in the middle of the room. "Sit down, relax, Leo," he said, pointing to the couch.

Jack scanned the three-room apartment, noting the small kitchen and bedroom off the living room. In the corner opposite the couch on a small RCA television set a Texaco gas station chorus line sang about the merits of servicing cars.

Larry said, "You guys ever watch Milton Berle? The fuckin' Jew is funny. You got to give him that."

"Never mind the fuckin' hebe, Larry. Where's Jimma's money -- and the vig?" Leo said.

Larry put the beer bottle on the coffee table in front of the couch and started to stand.

"Sit down, Larry. Sit the fuck down. Where you going?" Leo asked belligerently.

Jack stationed himself at the window overlooking Revere Beach, watching Vin and Ray move around the apartment.

"Jesus, Leo. I want to get my fuckin' wallet in the bedroom, that's all. I've got $2,500 for you toward the $4,000. Why are you so up tight?"

Leo sat back on the couch. "I'll tell you why, Larry -- why I am so up tight. You know why, Larry? Because at Mission High the nuns taught me something. Now granted I was thinking of planking Gail Rafferty while the nun -- what was her name, Ray? - Sister Christina? - was talking about algebraic equations, geometry and shit like that -- but I did listen a little bit. One thing I learned, Larry. You know what? $2,500 is not $4,000. Some shit about the sum of the parts is not necessarily the whole. I learned that."

"Leo, give me a break." Larry fidgeted with the beer bottle, lifting it for a swig, putting it back on the glass table. "I've got $2,500 in the bedroom and I'll have the other $1,500 by Friday. Honest to God. Jimma doesn't need to worry."

"Larry, listen carefully," Leo said, standing. "Jimma is not worried, not at all. He knows you'll pay the $5,000."

"$5,000!" Larry raised his voice. "What $5,000? Jesus, it's $4,000, Leo."

"No, it's not, Larry. It's $5,000. You keep being late, the vig jumps some more. Now get the fuckin' $2,500. Vin, you go in with him to the bedroom."

Leo sat quietly until Vin returned with Larry. Larry passed a wad of dollars to Leo and sat on the couch.

"Larry, do I need to count this?" Leo inquired.

"Jesus Christ, Leo. We've known each other for five years. Am I good for this or am I not?" Larry pleaded.

Leo picked up the now empty beer bottle, lifting it close to his face. "Larry, let me tell you something. I'm coming back here Friday night to see $2,500 on this fuckin' table." He lowered the bottle and abruptly smashed it against the edge of the table, leaving jagged edges exposed as it split in half.

"I'm coming back with a bottle like this one," he said, raising the jagged edges near Larry's left eye, "to cut your handsome face if the money isn't on the table. You understand?" Leo asked.

Leo dropped the broken bottle on the floor, stood and walked toward the door, the others following. A quivering Larry sobbed, hyperventilating on the sofa as Leo reached the door.

"See you Friday night, Larry. And you better be here with the fuckin' money," he emphasized.

Crossing the boulevard, Leo turned to Jack. "I watched you in there," he said as they trailed behind the others. "You observed, that's good. Did you notice the lead man does the talking? The others back him up, case the place, be sure there are no interruptions. We don't need nine guys yapping at the mark.

"Now next time I'll pair you with Vin, Paulie, Ray or one other guy. Usually just two guys make the visit. You'll make maybe three or four calls a day or night to guys like him, bars, pimps, bookies, liquor stores, numbers runners we think are stiffing us, union guys that didn't kick back. Results are what counts. That's how you're evaluated."

He slowed while the others climbed into the Chevy. "Another thing -- I suppose you're wondering whether I would cut him? Right?"

Jack replied evenly, "Wrong. I think you would."

Leo stopped at the sidewalk. "You're on target. Saying it has to be the same as doing it. Never hesitate to do what you said you would do."

"Come on. Let's go over to the Ritz Cafe on Revere Street. Get some pizza before you check in at the bakery," Leo said.

6

Throughout the fall of 1952 and into 1953 he usually paired with Vin or Ray, occasionally with Paulie or Leo himself. In the early visits, one of them would always take the lead role and he provided support. But as weeks went by, he assumed his share of the major responsibility.

And in those weeks that followed he learned his lessons. Whether in visits to Bloomingdale Street in Chelsea, Glendale Square in Everett, L Street in Southie, or wherever, he observed the behavior of the others in tense situations. He felt involved, excited by the events streaming by him, and yet in control of himself at all times.

He could smell the fear of those they approached. From his view they all owed his new family money. For one reason or another, they hesitated to pay their debt.

On the Saturday following the visit to Larry Cally, Leo had accompanied him to the Maine woods, about an hour above Portland, where he familiarized him with weapons. Deep in the woods they placed targets on the trees and practiced the proper use of firearms.

"Despite what you see in the movies, Jack, we don't like to shoot people. If it happens, it happens infrequently and it is carefully planned. The threat of violence should be more effective than the violence itself. Remember that. In 95 percent of our transactions, we want to collect what is due us, and in the other 5 percent to teach some stupid shit he can't fuck around with us." Leo balanced the .38 and the .45, one in each hand as he spoke.

"Now see the target? If we shoot someone, it's bound to be from close up. We're not the fuckin' Rifleman, what's his

37

name? Chuck Connors? We want to be within a few yards of the other guy. Now, let me explain the differences between the pieces."

In his early months he carefully evaluated the techniques the others used. Vin would straight out move toward physical intimidation, which worked 80 percent of the time. But when it did not, Vin was done, cooked, out of options unless he murdered the debtor, a practice strictly forbidden by Leo, unless sanctioned by Jimma himself. In contrast, Ray was a cajoler. His easy manner, soft voice, and smiling countenance often gave the target a feeling that the matter was not that serious, leading to miscalculations on both their parts, and an extended process as well.

When it was his turn to take the lead, Jack varied his approach depending on the situation. He waited for his own personal read of the method that would get the desired result. Initially, he would strive for eye contact, seeking in the first minute or two an understanding of the target's mind set. And if softness could bring the result, then he was all for a soft approach. If moderation would win the day, God bless moderation. And finally, if only a hard approach would work, then he was ready to implement it and willing to follow through as Leo had said. Above all, he tried to convey the impression that he was in full control.

And sometimes the approach he chose didn't matter at all. One September night, Jack and Vin parked Vin's '51 Chrysler Imperial in front of an apartment on St. Botolph Street, near the intersection of Massachusetts Avenue, around the corner from the Boston Arena.

As they walked along St. Botolph Street, Vin asked, "Hey, Jack, you ever been to the Arena? The Celtics play there, you know."

"No," replied Jack, feeling behind his back for the .38 he had begun to favor in recent weeks.

"Well, Jesus," said Vin, "You should see that fuckin' magician, Bob Cousy, particularly when they're playing the Knicks or Syracuse."

"Vin, let's pay some attention to this situation right here, OK? Leo fill you in?" Jack asked.

"Jesus Christ, Jack. Relax. All I'm saying is we should go over to the Arena sometime. Good fights too, Tommy Collins is fighting tonight."

Jack stepped on the sidewalk. "I don't give a shit what's over there. Let's concentrate on this deadbeat. Leo says he's dangerous."

At 172 St. Botolph Street, they climbed the steps leading into a vestibule. A bank of mail boxes was mounted on the right wall. Peering over the list, Jack said, "He's on the first floor, James Donovan, Apartment 1C." He pressed the bell.

"Yes?"

"Mr. Donovan, I'm Jack Kelly. Here to see you on behalf of Leo Slattery. I..."

"Okay. Hold on," the voice interrupted.

The buzzer sounded, allowing them to push open the inner door. As they moved toward apartment C, Donovan appeared in the corridor.

"Who the fuck are you two?" he asked belligerently. A big, bald man, he stood outside his apartment, dressed in baggy blue jeans and a blue sweater which called attention to his muscular frame. His nose looked like it had been disarranged in any number of brawls.

"Can we talk inside?" Jack asked.

Donovan gestured them into a bright three-room apartment attractively arranged with modern furniture. In this neighborhood and across Massachusetts Avenue all the way to Fenway Park, elderly widows lived isolated lives in dark, dingy apartments -- usually waiting to die, -- more often than not -- with a bevy of cats as their only living friends.

Jim Donovan walked to the small RCA television across the living room, shut it off and then sat on the couch adjacent to it.

"Sit down, sit down," he pointed to two newly upholstered chairs across from him. "So Leo sent you. So?"

"Mr. Donovan," Jack began, "Leo wants his money. You owe him $10,000 with no payments at all for a month."

Donovan stared at the two for a long moment. He had not offered any drink or food. Picking up his scotch and soda from the coffee table in front of him, he grinned at them.

"Look, you two fucking lackeys. Tell Leo what I told him last week. I'm not paying now. I got some problems. He knows I'm good for it. I've always been good for it. What the fuck is his problem anyway? Don't he hear good?"

Vin stood quickly, advancing toward Donovan. "Look, asshole, he hears fine. He wants his dough, and he wants it now."

Donovan barely flinched as Vin approached.

"Vin, Mr. Donovan says he has problems. Let's hear him out." Jack spoke calmly but in a commanding voice, never taking his gaze from Donovan.

Vin turned to Jack, recognizing his breach of their plan. Jack was to take the lead, and Vin had violated their agreement. He walked sullenly to the window, looking first to the bedroom and then to the kitchen, something he should have done in the first place, Jack thought.

"Mr. Donovan, what problems are causing you to miss these payments?" Jack asked, slowly, maintaining eye contact with Donovan.

Sensing some momentary advantage, Donovan stayed on his course. "Never mind my problems, errand boy. I deal with Leo, and I'll pay when I can."

Jack showed no reaction, instead continuing to stare at Donovan. "Mr. Donovan," he said, "I'm trying to be reasonable. I'm trying to be understanding."

"Fuck you and your understanding. Get the fuck out of here both of you. Just tell Leo the money's coming when I'm ready to provide it."

Jack leaned forward in his chair. "Mr. Donovan, let's try this one final time. You're right. The money's coming. It's coming tonight." Jack stood as Vin rotated toward the bedroom. Suddenly with Vin out of sight, Donovan reached under the pillow with his right hand.

40

Jack's right hand appeared from behind his back holding the .38 stashed behind his backbone. "Bring your hand out slowly, Mr. Donovan," he commanded. "We don't want you hopping around like Bugs Bunny on one stick."

"Fuck you, you haven't the balls, kid," rejoined Donovan, his hand still moving under the pillow.

Jack fired without hesitation, sending Donovan crumpling to the floor groaning in agony, grabbing his knee. "Oh, you did it. You son of a bitch!" he screamed. Jack reached under the pillow and pocketed the pistol.

Jack leaned over him, placing his hand under Donovan's chin. "Listen, you shit, and listen carefully. In about five minutes some cops are going to arrive here. So think fast. I either leave with a down payment, or you're dead. It makes no difference to me," he said, pointing the pistol aside Donovan's temple. "We write you off. Debt unpaid. Score settled. Chalk a tough guy like you up to experience. Think fast, asshole. You've got ten seconds."

"In the dresser," Donovan groaned, "second drawer under some underwear, there's money."

"How much?" Jack asked.

"There's $8,000 there," Donovan screamed in pain.

"Get it, Vin. Quick."

Vin moved swiftly, the sound of the drawer opening reaching them.

"It's here," he yelled.

"Go check the outside. I'll be right behind you," he directed Vin.

"Now listen to your da, Donovan. The rest of it better be delivered to Leo by Monday, fuckin' Monday, or I'll be back. Not here, but I'll find you. Nothing will prevent me from finding you. You listening?"

Twisting in agony on the floor, Donovan screamed, "I'll get it, for Christ's sake!"

Jack ran through the corridor, Vin signaling him forward from the stoop. Turning toward the Boston Arena, they separated, Jack crossing to the opposite side of the street. At the intersection of Massachusetts Avenue and St. Botolph, they each moved toward the car, mixing in with the crowd now leaving the Arena.

Vin inquired, "Hey, kid, who won?"

A squinty eyed boy about seventeen replied, "Tommy Collins."

"Christ, Jack, I thought you were going to kill him," Vin said, as they drove toward Copley Square.

"I should have, but this way we have the money, and there's no question in my mind we'll get the balance. It's Leo's call regarding the tough guy's future."

7

Tommy lay in bed, his hands clasped behind his head, thinking about his future. He was getting close; he could feel it. The hours of pounding the heavy bag, and the long hours of running from Lynn to Nahant on the causeway then back along Lynn Beach to Swampscott to Marblehead Neck and home -- ten miles in all -- were getting results.

The pain, the loneliness, the subjugation to an all-consuming goal were still worth it -- because he was going to reach that goal. He knew it. He lay there thinking of Robinson, pound for pound the best fighter in the world; of Bobo Olson, of on-coming Gene Fullmer from Chicago.

World class middleweights, all of them. Formidable foes, each with a long record of success. Yet he felt like he could eventually compete with them and fighters like them. He had never felt so confident, so determined. He was focused. He knew his strengths -- a determination to succeed, a strong jab, a powerful right hand, the ability to throw punches in combination, good defense. He needed just the experiences, the steps on the ladder upward.

Tony had urged patience. And because of his managerial skill and advice, Tommy had advanced rapidly through the amateurs -- winner of sixteen straight amateur bouts and most recently, the Lowell Golden Gloves middleweight championship. He was ready for the pros, and maybe in a few years ready to mix it with Sugar Ray or Giardello or any of the other top middles. Now was the time to advance, he thought. Tony could not keep him at this level forever. How many more amateurs did he need to defeat before Tony considered him professional material? They had argued about it in recent weeks. Tony wanted more time for him to learn the trade, then move to the nationals competing against amateurs from other regions, proving himself again and again.

But he knew he was ready. No one could hurt him the way life had hurt him. His mother's death had left his brothers and him to shift for themselves. A beautiful lady who cared for them all and asked nothing for herself, taken from them when they needed her most. And instead of caring for Jackie and Jerry and him, his father had turned to liquor, to an illusionary friend, to a deep cavern of a world of his own far removed from the boys, broken in spirit with no interest in them or their future.

He thought of Jackie and marveled at his ability to keep them together. His older brother worked full-time at Cushman's, cared for his two brothers, made sure they survived as a family and always had time to be there for Tommy's fights, for Jerry's academic awards. That had to end -- and soon. There was simply too much dependence on Jack, who himself was intelligent enough to go to college and not spend the rest of his life working in a bakery trying to hold the family together.

If Tony wouldn't agree to professional status, then he would find a way himself. In recent weeks overtures were coming from North End promoters, from Sam Silverman Promotions, from Rip Valenti, from the Boston Garden itself. Tony had told him of the approaches, saying at the same time that they were too early, he wasn't yet ready, maybe a year or two from now, etc. Maybe a year from now, he thought. My ass. I'm ready now. I'm ready.

From the next bedroom he heard a loud cry, a quick expression of pain. He moved across the dining room to his father's bedroom in anticipation of overhearing another conversation between his father and Luke. Yet the cry seemed different, submissive, not part of the normal conversation.

Tommy snapped on the light. On the bed lay the prostrate form of his father, arms askance, eyes protruding, a thin line of blood emitting from his mouth.

"Dad, Dad, what's the matter? Talk to me, Dad!" Tommy screamed. And then he quickly realized that their father had moved to join their mother in a far happier world than he had inhabited here.

8

The wake was held at their apartment. In the '40's, Jackie had been to a number of wakes in homes, but by the '50's the practice had faded. Yet his father had insisted that both their mother and he be waked at home. As friends and neighbors entered through the living room that first evening, they moved toward the sunroom, to the closed casket surrounded with flower sprays. A kneeling pad for prayer fronted the bier. Jack, his brothers, and their Aunt Alice and Uncle Bill greeted the mourners in the living room in a single file that led guests to the sunroom.

"I'm very sorry, Jackie," said Ed Madden, his father's long time friend and GE co-worker. "How are you holding up?"

Jack did not know what he felt -- he was simply numb. He knew he felt nothing like the pain of two years ago when his mother had left them. Then he had felt both numb and confused. On one hand he felt happy that she was no longer suffering, but he also felt a horrifying sadness, one devoid of tears. He could not cry.

He stood there, looking beyond Ed Madden, oblivious to him and to those gathering around them and thought back to the war years, to the days when he would race home to lunch from St. Joseph's grammar school to always find her there. Back then she had been slim, pretty and tall, her short auburn hair primly set in a permanent. He could never remember her being dressed in anything other than a linen or cotton dress concealed by a full apron. Invariably, he would find her in the kitchen preparing peanut butter sandwiches and hot soup for them all.

And at the end of each school day he would turn into Fayette Street and find her sitting in the sunroom, awaiting their return. He would sit with her and tell her of his day, of any problem he had encountered. He adored her laughing green eyes, like crescents shining on him as she listened.

He loved this anchor of his life, this magical lady who lived only for him and the family -- her gentle admonitions if one of them forgot his chores; her presence when he contacted any form of serious illness; her advocacy for her children, like the time she pleaded with Joe to take them to the Classical-Everett state championship football game at Manning Bowl because she knew what it meant to him, in particular.

When had his happy world come to an end? It had come on so suddenly. It had been during his first year of high school when everything changed. From out of nowhere, his mother became very sick. As her health deteriorated, she lost her energy, her vitality. She found it difficult to accomplish the simplest tasks. Neither his father nor Dr. Judge ever mentioned the cause of her illness, but he knew. It was just that nobody ever used the word.

Over the next two years it was left to him to hold the family together. He remembered his father sitting in silent despair each evening with his whiskey and water, alone in the sunroom, overwhelmed by events he did not understand. He would sit with his mother, attend to her needs, read to her and be sure she was comfortable as she listened to favorite radio programs like Jack Benny and Lux Radio Theater. He made sure his brothers completed their chores and saved the most difficult tasks for himself -- cooking, tending to the coal furnace, and carrying out the ashes scooped into the barrels.

As he attended to her, he noticed the physical changes. Her beauty had deserted her, the deep creases in her face making her at forty-one look more like fifty-one. There was a yellowish pallor to her skin, and her once magnificent figure was partially bent in pain.

And then, on a cold sunless January day his world came to an end. He remembered her slipping into a coma, and the ambulance taking her to the Lynn Hospital. A day later she left them. He would never forget that moment. The shock of it. The end of life. The failure of God to protect his loved ones. Why? He had felt the light leaving his life, and he knew his life had changed forever.

"Hey, Jackie, you all right?" Ed Madden asked again, pulling him back to the present, the question reminding him quickly of his promise to his mother. He would care for them all, he had said, and yet he hadn't been able to pull his father out of his war with the bottle.

"I'm fine, Mr. Madden," he finally replied as he walked toward the dining room.

For this night he had arranged rows of hardback chairs, most borrowed from neighbors. Women close to his parents' age sat in the dining room, weeping quietly into small white hankies while comforting one another. The small table in the center of the room held platters of ham and cheese sandwiches and tea, sweet buns and coffee, much of it also supplied by the neighbors.

In the kitchen, about ten men sat at the table with two whiskey bottles and an assortment of Narragansett beer bottles and glasses, acting in that curiously social way that always fascinated Jack. It was as if they were in another world, oblivious to the occasion, and their talk mesmerized him, it having so little to do with the event at hand or, for that matter, with their own parochial lives.

"I miss Pesky and Dropo, and those bums we traded them for stink," said Ed Madden.

"George Kell stinks?" Bill Murphy, their upstairs neighbor, asked incredulously.

"Look, you silly bastard, we finished sixth last year didn't we? That dope O'Neill must have been into the sauce. It's a wonder he could find the dugout, never mind manage that collection of crap we call a team," Charlie O'Brien muttered.

"Well, we'll do better this time round. I like that Piersall kid from Waterbury," Murphy said. "The Waterbury Whiz, they call him."

"Yeah, just what we need. A crazy bastard patrolling center field," Ed Madden countered, lifting his whiskey shot glass.

"But Lou Boudreau will be in charge this spring. He'll bring us back, provide some discipline, too. And I like that Sammy White as the catcher. We're going to be OK." Joey Cullen enthused.

"Milt Bolling couldn't hit a bull in the ass with a shovel," Jim Stacy snickered. "Christ, we've come a long way since 1950 -- a long way down. These guys ain't no Williams, Stephens, or Dropo. They drove in almost four hundred runs together that year," he added.

Bill Murphy said, "Look at the years Ted Williams is missing -- off fighting those Korean slanty-eyed assholes. Now what if he were still playing?"

"Well this is 1953 and he ain't," Paul Scanlon piped up.

"No shit! I know it's 1953, especially with that stuffed shirt Herter crunching my fuckin' wallet," Bill Murphy retaliated.

"Paul Dever, forever, I say," said Charlie O'Brien.

"Well, he didn't make it this year, never mind forever, did he Charlie? The jerk gave so many of his Democrat friends cushy jobs we now have a Republican governor," Ed Madden replied.

"At least young Jack Kennedy beat that other Republican iceberg for the Senate seat," Bill Murphy said.

As they talked, they passed two whiskey bottles around, most of them not using the Heald's Ginger ale on the table but moving to the pantry water tap for the chaser. Occasionally one of the weepy women would enter the kitchen, only to get a Narragansett, never to stay and sit with the men.

Paul Scanlon was just about to begin his story when Jack moved into the kitchen and stood among them.

"Jack, he was a good man. May he rest in peace," consoled Paul, passing the whiskey bottle to his right.

"He was something special, Jack," Bill Murphy said admiringly. "A real beautiful person, inside and out."

Jack simply nodded and walked back to the living room.

"Hey, there's Dan Golden going through the line," Charlie O'Brien said, looking toward the living room.

"He claims Irish blood from some relative," Bill Murphy stated.

"Golden has Irish blood? On his chauffeur's side, I say," Ed Madden said.

"And so," Paul Scanlon began his story, "I knew something was up when I went into the john. Mind you, I'm supposed to clean up the men's room on the night shift every night, right? So I'm just doing my job. Right? Anyway, I walk in and see four feet inside the second toilet stall. Now we've got a lot of jokers working at GE, but I don't know too many with four feet. So right away I'm suspicious."

"Well, what did you do?" asked Ed.

"Good evening, Father Dolan," stammered Bill Murphy quickly. Facing the pantry, he was the first to see the good reverend.

"And good evening -- and it's a sad evening is it not, men? Please continue your story, Paul." said Father.

"Father, it can wait," said Paul. "Would you care for a shot, Father?"

"No, thank you, Paul. I'm going to say the prayers now. Let's adjourn to the living room men."

Father led his small congregation through the rosary. As the priest moved his fingers over the holy beads, Jack noted his brothers' quiet, controlled demeanor. They, like Jack, were in an emotional no-man's land, simply withdrawn and uninvolved.

9

How many times had he, Tommy, and Jerry entered St. Joseph's for happy occasions? Not many, Jack thought, as they sat in the front row of the second floor of the church. Father Dolan solemnly moved through the steps of the Mass, assisted by the altar boys.

Jack had always been impressed by the majestic beauty of St. Joseph's. Located downtown on Union Street, the Gothic cathedral, like the school, convent, and rectory, was built of red brick. Its steeple seemed to almost reach the sky. Downstairs the first floor featured an ornate altar but everything was reduced in scope when compared to the sheer beauty of the second floor. Row after row of oak pews greeted parishioners who entered by way of one of the three stairwells. Brightly lit, the interior overwhelmed the mourners. Dozens of chandeliers hung down from the sloped ceiling. Luminous windows made of expensive stained glass ringed the two side aisles. Interspersed between windows were depictions of the Stations of the Cross. And at the center lay the sanctuary, and the massive white marble altar that dominated the entire upstairs. Above him, cathedral ceilings featured beckoning angels lifting young babies toward a new life.

Perhaps fifty people sat behind the brothers. He spotted Ray Horan and Leo Slattery behind them and to his left. Since Joe's incessant bouts with the bottle, he had lost many of his old friends. It was now more than two years since their mother's death, and in that time Joe had made it clear that visitors were not welcome in their home. This once handsome man, Jack thought, so conscious of his appearance, his dress, his toilet, had degenerated into a lonely, friendless, uncaring man, frequently in need of a bath and a shave. Perhaps the cerebral hemorrhage was a blessing.

Listening to Father Dolan's eulogy, he could only grimace. He knew his father did not deserve the flow of words that centered around themes like devotion, love, concern for family. Nothing, of course, would be said or should be said about the terrible burden he had placed on the brothers in recent years. Then he caught himself. He should be thinking of the good times. He thought instead of the father who had lifted him on his shoulders and strolled in the waters of Lynn Beach, of the father who had taken him to Manning Bowl to watch Harry Agganis and Lynn Classical defeat a strong Everett team, of the father who loved their mother above all others. There had been goodness in the man. Perhaps that should be what was remembered. On the ride across town to St. Joseph's Cemetery off Wyoma Square Tommy and Jerry, like him, seemed stoic, remembering probably as he did, only the good times.

10

Fisherman's Beach lies just beyond the Lynn-Swampscott line, the third jewel in the crown of beaches that come up fast after you turn north at the Nahant rotary. The first, Lynn Beach, stretches from a point a mile south of the rotary to a point a half-mile above it. As you head north, King's Beach quickly appears exactly a half mile above the rotary. Its main feature, Red Rock Park, lies in a semi-circular indentation of grass, walkway, and benches above the beach, at night a perfect walking spot for young lovers. A mile further along the coastline, just past Doane's ice cream stand, Fisherman's Beach, much smaller and more intimate, completes the string.

Families headed for Lynn Beach and its long, firmly packed sandy stretches, perfect for walking or running, for tossing a ball, for beach volleyball. Young boys and girls chose King's Beach, largely because they could play "outs" against its long seawall, which runs from Red Rock to Doane's. They threw a rubber or tennis ball against the wall, joyously chasing ground balls along the sand or fly balls into the onrushing waves, closing down an imaginary inning, with cries of "I'm Piersall!" or "I'm Chico Carrasquel!" punctuating the air.

But as those young boys and girls matured, they frequented Fisherman's Beach, the mecca for meeting the opposite sex. It was the least attractive place of the three to swim, but, at age fifteen and above, on any given summer's day, swimming was not the primary consideration.

"Jesus, look at the tits on that one," Jerry said, hoisting his elbows a little higher off the blanket, as he stared out toward the ocean.

"Jerry, didn't the nuns teach you anything? No swearing, huh?" Jack said spreading the Johnson's baby oil over his body.

"Swearing? That's not swearing, Jack. Tits is swearing?" Jerry said, his eyes not varying far from the statuesque brunette moving toward their blanket.

"Jesus is swearing, Jerry. Not tits. But tits isn't very good vocabulary for a guy getting ready for college either," Jack said.

"How come some of these broads are wearing shorts instead of bathing suits?" Tommy asked, standing near the blanket, scanning the water's edge.

"What am I running, a sex education seminar for you, guys? Use your imagination," Jack answered.

"What? What do you mean?" asked an injured Tommy.

"The ones in shorts have their period," Jack replied patiently, tossing the baby oil to Jerry.

"How the fuck do you know?" Tommy said indignantly.

"Trust me. You want to go ask two or three of them, Tom?"

Jerry paid no particular attention to this interchange, preferring to concentrate now on two girls heading toward their blanket after a swim in the ocean. "Christ, look at that!"

"Jerry, let me put this fixation of yours into a little broader perspective. If you can control your desire to plank anything that moves, maybe you can arrive at college this fall ready to make something of yourself. And maybe the dough I'm providing for a Harvard education will actually turn out to be a good investment," Jack said.

"Hey, I did get accepted, you know. They liked my perspective," Jerry laughed.

"I know that," Jack responded. "No one is prouder of you than me. And I'm proud of Mr. Muscle-bound here, too. Right, Tom? 37-0 as an amateur? Pretty soon you'll want to take on your older brother," he reached up and tapped Tom's stomach from his sitting position.

"I'm close to turning pro, Jack," said Tom.

"I know. Just don't let the assholes use you. It can be a dirty business," Jack said.

"You think that one in the red shorts has her period?" Jerry asked.

"Jesus," Jack sighed. "My tuition dollars."

"Jack, I'm feeling guilty about that. You're working too hard to just support the family. Where are you getting money for tuition? We can't afford it. I don't have to go to college. I can help by working," Jerry said.

"I'm going to tell you -- and you too, Tom -- for the last time. Let me worry about the money. I've got a good job. Dad had a little pension. I've won some money at the track. Tom's working part-time. We don't have any worries right now. How many times do I have to say it?

"You go to college, Jerry. You've got the grades. Number one in your class. Accepted to Harvard. One of us accepted to Harvard. Can you imagine that? Can you imagine how proud of you Ma would have been, Jerry? Think on that. And just make something come of it. You've got the chance. Make something of it."

"Yeah, but the girl in the red shorts..." Jerry teased.

"Jesus, I give up. I'm taking a walk," Jack said, rising.

He headed north, along the short, craggy beach, walking at the edge of the water, his eyes scanning the clear blue horizon, shifting occasionally toward the west, to the hills above Swampscott. But he concentrated largely on the ocean itself, as he felt the heat of the sun, the warmth of its rays on his skin. He loved Lynn in the summertime. To live next to the ocean, to experience its beauty, was something he had always treasured. He stopped at that point where the beach ended and stared at the horizon, watching the lobstermen setting their traps in the distance.

The ocean, like his city, provided him strength and energy. Whenever he felt the burden of his responsibilities, and needed to think things through, he would come to the sea. He was struck by both its equanimity and its undulating fury. It was an alive and inspiring work of nature that challenged him and allowed him to consider, to sort out a myriad of problems and

57

come to the right solutions for him and or those for whom he felt responsible.

Its vastness reminded him of his own aloneness, of the ever widening gulf between himself and others. Its emptiness always caused him to reflect on his loss. He would come often by himself, particularly in the winter, and fantasize that his mother was out there somewhere, watching over them all. He would never tell Tommy or Jerry, but he saw her there often on the horizon and he spoke silently to her of the events of his brothers' lives, and she, in turn, offered him counsel and smiled radiantly at the news of her sons' progress.

Today he was content to stare out happily, absorbed with the season, and with the activity around him. From the blankets the sounds of the Platters mixed with those of Elvis Presley and Little Richard. Occasionally a love song from Sinatra. He didn't share the change in taste. Music should be soothing, relaxing, not ear-shattering.

As he turned back toward the sandy beach, he noticed her for the first time. She moved gracefully toward the water, in his direction. He liked what he saw: her bronzed figure, her blond hair, high cheekbones and blue eyes. About 5'6", she exuded sexuality.

"Hello," she said as she passed him.

"Hi," Jack replied.

As she continued toward the water, Jack glanced at the three girls giggling on the blanket some twenty yards over her shoulder. She stopped at the water's edge, but just for a second, and then advanced, stopping again when she was at knee length.

Jack stood mesmerized for just a few seconds. He had to talk to her. He had to come to know her. He walked out toward her.

"Do I know you?" he asked.

"That's an original approach," she responded.

"You from around here?" he asked.

"I live in Swampscott, right around the bend on Puritan Road. And you?"

"Lynn. Fayette Street," Jack replied.

"I've seen you here before," she said warmly.

"Really? Probably. My brothers and I come here a lot. You go to Swampscott High?"

"No, I did. I graduated last year."

"So what are you doing now?"

"I work at Stanton Chevrolet on the Lynnway," she said. "I'm a bookkeeper."

"Hey, not bad. Pretty good job right out of high school."

"My father owns the place."

"My name's Jack Kelly."

"Marjorie Stanton," she replied, accepting his hand.

He picked up a rock and scaled it across the oncoming bluish-green waves, glancing back to his blanket to be sure Tommy and Jerry were occupied.

"So you come here often, huh?' he asked.

"Yes. My girl friends and I are regulars. We don't miss many summer days here. I work a split shift in the summers -- mornings and evenings."

"I work the graveyard shift at Cushman's," Jack retorted.

"Well, then," Marjorie said, "I hope we see each other again. See you." Without waiting for a response, she ran into the water, diving gracefully into the waves, then surfacing quickly, gliding in smooth strokes away from the beach.

Jack walked back up the beach, trying hard not to glance over his shoulder, thinking all the while that he had found her -- a woman who made him feel again. He hadn't been involved with anyone since his mother's sickness four years ago. One chance encounter and he felt this way, he asked himself. All he knew was he wanted to see her again.

11

"I need to see you this morning," said Leo as soon as Jack answered his phone.

"I'm free. Say when and where," Jack said.

"It's 9 now. I have to take care of some union business. Can you meet me in front of the Keith Memorial Theater on Washington Street at 10:30? And Jack, save some time for this. I'll need you at least until one o'clock. And dress up a bit."

"No problem, Leo. See you at 10:30."

At the Sunoco station around the corner from Fayette Street he gassed up the '52 green Chrysler he had bought in May and turned east toward the beaches and then south on the Lynnway, heading toward the Sumner Tunnel. It was a beautiful, cloudless June day, the temperature already climbing steadily toward the forecasted 90's. Exiting the Tunnel, he parked on the fringe of the North End and walked the mile to the Keith Memorial.

The '50's had not been kind to the movie industry, he thought, as he walked along Washington Street past the <u>Boston Globe</u> offices, the sun streaming down on the crowds moving toward Filene's or Jordan's or to work, or to one of the movie palaces lining the entire street. Television, the demise of the studio system, soaring costs and fewer productions had all conspired to lessen the crowds frequenting Loew's Orpheum, the Keith Memorial, the Metropolitan, the Paramount, the RKO and the other structures along Washington and Tremont Streets, where just five years ago, lines formed from 9 A.M. to 9 P.M. with standing room only crowds.

He spotted Leo resplendent in a light gray summer suit in front of the Keith. "What's up, Leo?" he asked as he extended his hand. Jack wore a baby blue sports jacket and dark blue pants. A red and blue tie and a white dress shirt added to his lanky frame. Leo had observed heads turning as the handsome young man walked toward him from lower Washington Street.

"Jimma wants to see you. He asked me to bring you to his house around 11. My car's parked over on Tremont Street. We'll drive out to the Jamaicaway."

Why would Jimma want to see me? Jack wondered. It had now been more than two years since he had joined them, and he had met Jimma only three or four times, or whenever the head called a meeting for the whole family. Such meetings usually occurred in Charlestown in a warehouse not far from the Bunker Hill Monument. If such meetings included everyone, as he believed they did, then the family numbered no more than a dozen key operatives.

At the sessions, Jimma usually reviewed a particular upcoming policy change, such as a new agreement he had recently struck with the Italians in Boston over jurisdictions or with Gennaro Biggio, the New England crime boss himself. Seldom would he mention specific actions to be taken against businesses or individuals. Such marching orders would come directly from Leo.

Flaherty operated a real estate business out of Boston, Jack had learned. His particular strength was in dealing with the police and courts, a consummate dealmaker, Leo had told him. Smart and effective, he seldom accompanied the group on any assignment. He distanced himself from the action, yet remained highly respected by Leo, Vin, Ray, the members Jack had come to know best.

They drove out Commonwealth Avenue past Fenway Park on Brookline Avenue, turning at the end onto the Jamaicaway. "Did you hear the news?" Leo asked.

"What news?"

"The Agganis kid," Leo replied. "He died this morning."

"Are you kidding me, Leo?" Jack stared in disbelief.

"The Red Sox had him in Sancta Maria due to pneumonia," Leo said.

"I knew that. But dead? What happened?"

"A pulmonary embolism -- a blood clot."

"God. He's only twenty-five or so. And hitting over .310 in his first full season. I can't believe it."

"You knew him in Lynn?"

"I didn't know him personally, but he was every kid's idol growing up in Lynn. An all-American high school and college football player, a major league first baseman. Jesus! The whole city will turn out for his funeral."

Leo tossed his cigarette out the window and pointed to a colonial structure on their left. "That's Mayor Curley's home. Now there was a character. A real fuckin' Robin Hood. Robbed from the rich and gave to the poor. We're stopping just a few houses up from here."

He moved across the painted divider line and eased into the driveway adjoining a large brick colonial looking as imposing as any in the select neighborhood. The two-story property was newly painted and well maintained. Close to the building a large bed of marigolds and peonies ran from one end of the house to the other.

Leo rang the bell, at the same time straightening his tie and smoothing back his hair. Jack stole a look across the road at Jamaica Pond, noting a number of strollers ringing the pond, some walking arm in arm, others pushing baby carriages slowly in deference to the onrushing heat.

The tall, well-groomed man opened the door and greeted Leo with affection. "Leo, Leo, come on in." With an angular face, and gentle smile, and dark hair crowning blue eyes, Jimma Flaherty was able to charm almost everyone who crossed his path.

Leo gestured toward Jack. "You've met Jack Kelly, Jimma."

As Flaherty extended his hand, Jack noticed the impeccable dress. The beautifully tailored dark blue suit must have cost $300, he thought. An immaculately white shirt, offset by a red and blue striped tie with stickpin, fitted perfectly. He guessed Flaherty to be in his early forties. A small scar ran under his right eye, but it was the eyes as blue as sky and the straight nose that caught your interest. He looked like what he was -- affluent, commanding, suave.

"Jack, welcome. Please come in," Jimma smiled.

"Mr. Flaherty," Jack said, nodding in respect.

"Jimma, call me Jimma. No need for formality," he said, leading them into a small foyer.

"Let's go into the library," he said, turning toward the first room on their right, sliding back the doors to reveal a massive oak desk in the center of the room. Each wall contained three levels of books and in front of the desk two comfortable red leather chairs blended with the wall to wall red carpet. To one side of the desk was a third chair and a matching red leather couch to which Jimma directed them.

"Sit down over here, fellas. What can I get you to drink?" he asked. As he moved toward the bar on the opposite side of the room, Jack noted the massive mirror behind it.

"Canadian Club and ginger ale for me, Jimma," Leo responded.

"I'll have the same," Jack said.

Mixing the drinks quickly, Jimma said, "Grab these, Leo, while I make myself a scotch and water."

Leo placed the drinks on top of rounded coasters to protect the glass topped table in front of the couch. Jimma sat in one of the leather chairs, facing them, but actually not relaxing, sitting on the edge, his feet in the position of a runner, poised on tiptoes, heels in the air. Despite the warm greeting and smile, he appeared agitated.

"Let me tell you why I asked you here, Jack," Jimma began with no further interest in social graces. "We have a problem. A big fuckin' problem. And Jack, if you're as good as this guy says you are, you can help me with it. Now Leo tells me that in the last year and a half you've handled collections in a first rate fashion. You've faced down some tough situations, some assholes, very successfully. He says you've got brains and balls. And for this job I need someone with both."

Jack sipped the CC and ginger, concentrating on Flaherty's words, occasionally stealing a look at Leo who sat impassively, with no thought of interrupting Jimma.

"Let me tell you about this business of ours which is growing by leaps and bounds. The numbers, the piece from the books, the waterfront kickbacks, prostitution are all going gangbusters. All good solid business lines. Collections are strong across the whole fuckin' Boston area. And that's for one reason only: fear. The welshers know we mean business. They pay, or they pay, if you know what I mean. We have strong shares of collections in parts of Boston, and in the bigger cities around us -- Cambridge, Arlington, Quincy, Lynn. Agreements have been struck and have held for years concerning the Mafia's share, our share, the Negroes' share."

Jimma walked to the library window sipping his scotch, as he continued in an evenly modulated tone. "So here we sit -- in good position in the city. The guys I speak to in Providence and Boston are happy with this branch of the family, all's well with the world, right?"

Leo agreed, "Things are good, Jimma. We're all doing good."

Jimma abruptly turned from the window, hurrying back toward his seat. "Well, things aren't going so good, Leo. That's the fuckin' problem," he said harshly. "About a week ago my wife was across the fuckin' street, walking around Jamaica Pond with my eight-year-old daughter. From out of nowhere this smoothie Negro bastard from Mattapan appears, heading toward them on the pathway. He stops them, saying he's got a message for me. He terrified them. Can you fuckin' believe the balls on this guy stopping my family, involving my only child, in our business? Unbelievable."

"What message?" Leo asked.

"Leo, can you stay with this a little longer?" Jimma replied angrily. "Never mind the fuckin' message. The point is George Jackson thinks he can involve my family in our business. The son of a bitch."

"George Jackson?" Leo said. "What's his problem? He has his piece of Roxbury..."

"Jack," Jimma ignored Leo, "let me explain. This George Jackson is a smooth article. He's the head man in Roxbury with about 20 percent of the action in the Negro neighborhoods. The Italians allow that. They control 60 percent and we've got the other 20. George is pushing hard at us to take some or all of our 20 percent. The guineas don't care, as long as we don't tamper with their percentage and pay them tribute from any scores out of the ordinary as well. But I care, and told him to back off. In the last two or three weeks we've had two number runners beaten up, some restaurant owners refusing to pay the protection, pimps saying they don't need to pay anymore.

"I called Jackson again on Monday and told him we needed to talk. He said there really wasn't much to talk about, business is growing and expansion was a normal thing. I let him know what I thought about his fuckin' expansion and slammed the phone in his ear.

"Then on Wednesday my wife and daughter are walking right the fuck across the street from my house -- my own house! And Jackson's key guy approaches them! A real pretty boy known as the Chocolate Drop, Jackson's number one lieutenant."

"How do you know it was him?" Jack asked.

"Mary says the guy was tall, very handsome, suave, with scars under his left eye. He used to box light heavyweight at the Mechanics Building and at the Arena. Now he's George's hit man. It was the Chocolate Drop all right. Can you believe a fuckin' hit man, a fuckin' killer, approaching my wife and daughter!"

"What did he say, Jimma?" Jack asked.

"Tell your husband to keep out of Roxbury or some bucks that look like me might visit you and the daughter some lonely night," Jimma said grimly.

"It's time to teach those animals a lesson. The Chocolate Drop is going down. If Jackson gets the message, fine. If not, then we'll send him some more messages after that, and there's where you come in, Jack.

"For better than a year now Leo here tells me that you are moving strongly ahead within our group. I heard how you handled that Donovan guy. You did the right thing. He would have been no good to us dead, and now he's scared shitless. Never misses a deadline, and we collect plenty from him.

"Jack, I don't know whether you feel ready for this assignment or not. The Chocolate Drop knows Leo and Vin, the two guys I would ordinarily use in a situation like this. He's going to be on guard. We're not talking about a dumbass here.

"It's time for you to make your bones. If you handle this guy for me, I'll be forever grateful. You're loyal to me, and I'm loyal back."

Jack knew it was important to listen carefully for nuances, for what went unsaid as well as what was voiced. There really was no choice. If he refused, there would be a limited future with Flaherty. If he agreed, he would move to Jimma's inner circle. He knew halfway through Flaherty's long presentation exactly how he would answer and, more particularly, why.

Jack set his empty glass on the table. "Mr. Flaherty..." he began.

"Call me Jimma, please."

"Jimma, you and Leo did something for my family and for me that I'll never forget. I want you to consider this problem solved. Put it behind you."

Jimma stared at him with new found respect in his eyes. Then he glanced at Leo, "Make sure the kid gets the support he needs to do the job." He stood, and as Jack and Leo followed, he embraced Jack. "I'll expect to hear from you soon."

12

"And where will you two be going tonight?" asked Grant Stanton.

Jack leaned forward in his seat, glancing at Marjorie sitting next to her father and mother on the lemon divan. The Stantons lived in an ostentatious white garrison with green shutters, just around the corner from the Ocean House hotel and restaurant on Puritan Road in Swampscott.

Stanton's hair was full and black, probably colored to hide the advancing gray. Portly in appearance, he had obviously enjoyed the good life for some time now. Paula Stanton was attractive, probably in her late forties or early fifties. She was of medium build with blondish hair that fell in bangs almost to the top of the pair of black-framed glasses. Green eyes glowed at him in anticipation of the answer to her husband's question.

"Wonderland Ballroom, sir," Jack answered.

"Dancing, huh? Isn't that place more for people older than you two?" he asked.

"Well, Marjorie's the one who knows about dancing and schedules, but I understand they devote two nights a week to some of the '40's music. As long as there's some Guy Lombardo slow stuff, I'll be okay. I'm not much into Bill Haley and the Comets." He remembered reading something Lombardo had said recently about providing music for lovers, not acrobats. Both Stantons looked relieved. It probably lessened their concern that Atilla the Hun or some 50's be-bopper was about to enthrall their daughter.

"Marjorie tells us you work at Cushman's, Jack," Paula Stanton said.

"Yes. Sundays through Thursdays. On those nights, like tonight, I have to be there by 11."

She smiled at his response, and he sensed, again, relief that Marjorie would not be playing Cinderella, but maybe the smile connoted something else -- a disdain that their daughter was dating a bakery worker.

"I understand you and your brothers live alone, Jack. You have quite a bit of responsibility for a young man. Do your brothers work too?" Stanton asked, with a slight glance toward his wife.

"Yes, sir. My brother Tom works at West Lynn Creamery loading the dairy products onto the trucks, and for the summer Jerry works the night shift at that small plant GE has on Allerton Street. He's been accepted at Harvard this fall," Jack added with considerable pride.

"At Harvard?" Stanton asked rhetorically. "Well, now. He must be quite a student."

"He's never had a grade below A all through Lynn English," Jack responded.

"Amazing," Stanton answered. "And how about you?" The real point of all the questions, Jack thought.

"Well, sir, I haven't had much time for it, frankly. Now that my brothers are older I plan to enroll in part-time courses in business administration this fall. Northeastern University runs a satellite campus at English in the evenings. I don't plan on staying at the bakery forever."

He could tell the answer and his manner were both very acceptable to Grant and Paula Stanton. "That's good thinking, Jack. Education is the key to success. I wouldn't have built up the dealership without it," Stanton replied piously.

Marjorie spoke for the first time. "Really, Dad, we have to get going. Jack has to be in work at 11, remember?" Both of the Stantons jumped to their feet and walked them toward the front door.

"Dancing begins at 7:30," Marjorie said for the benefit of her parents. Yeah, Jack thought to himself, the first dance at the Old Howard in Scollay Square. And on this, their fifth date, the burlesque show was exactly where she had asked him to take her.

13

The Chocolate Drop ran very much like a boxer, Jack thought. He leaned heavily forward, took short steps despite his lanky frame, and kept his hands higher than most runners. For the third straight day this week he left his apartment on Columbus Avenue at mid-morning, turned into Massachusetts Avenue, and ran by Loew's State Theater before crossing toward the Fenway Theater just before the intersection of Boylston Street. He then jogged over the Massachusetts Avenue bridge to Cambridge before taking a right onto Memorial Drive, following the walkway down to the MIT boathouse. There he would pause for a moment before reversing his course back toward Columbus Avenue, an overall distance of about four miles.

On this day, as well as on the previous two, Jack followed discretely in his Chrysler, alternately stopping to double park or to move ahead of the runner once he was reasonably sure of his probable course. A creature of habit, Jack thought. The exact same pattern each of the three days.

On that third night he had Leo paged at the Cafe Amalfi on Westland Avenue, just behind Symphony Hall "Leo, Jack. We're on for tomorrow. Can you pick me up at 9 A.M. at Goldfish Pond in Lynn? I'll walk the half mile from my house. And, Leo, don't use your own car."

"I'll be there, Jack. See you," he clicked the pay phone and returned to the lasagna and the wine, nodding to Jimma Flaherty and Vin Sullivan, who sat opposite him. "We're on."

That's an odd fuckin' combination, Leo thought, as he slowed the stolen '54 Chevy on his approach to the park benches fronting Goldfish Pond. Jack stood gazing out at the ducks ringing the small circular pond in the two feet of water. He wore dark brown dress pants, a gray sweatshirt, white sneakers with white socks, and carried a small duffel bag. He turned and entered the passenger side, and immediately Leo gunned the engine, climbing the small hill toward Route 1A, and the Sumner Tunnel to Boston.

"I heisted the car from a Stop and Shop lot in Arlington." Leo said. "And here's the weapon. We're guaranteed it can't be traced." Jack laid both the pistol and the bag he carried on the floor. Unbuckling the dress pants, he started to pull the sneakers off. He opened the duffel bag and took out a light brown sports shirt and a pair of brown shoes, and brown socks.

Leo grinned. "That's quite an outfit, Jack -- a sweatshirt, brown dress pants and white socks. What're you gonna do? Scare the Chocolate Drop to death?"

Jack pulled the dress pants down and over the white sweat socks, revealing blue cotton elasticized basketball shorts. He threw the dress pants into the back seat, along with the duffel bag. "When we clear the tunnel, go over to Nashua Street and drive by the Museum of Science so we can pick up Memorial Drive going west," Jack said, fidgeting with the baggy gray sweatshirt.

"What's the plan, Jack?"

"Stop opposite the MIT boathouse, and we wait. If I'm right, the Chocolate Drop's going to turn right after coming across the Mass Avenue bridge. I'm going to run toward him, just another runner like him out for the exercise. When you see the action happening, start up the car and pick me up. I'll cross the street toward you. When I get in, drive up to Mass Avenue and take a right."

Leo found a parking space directly across from the boathouse. At this hour traffic was relatively light, but almost all of the parking spaces were taken. "Jesus, Jack. You sure this

74

will work?" Leo said. "Why don't we wait until he's stationary somewhere?"

"He's not anticipating trouble when he's out running, Leo. Trust me. It's going to work," Jack said calmly, lacing his sneakers. "Here he comes now. See him? About a half-mile away. The guy in the white T-shirt and red shorts."

He opened the passenger door, adjusting the baggy sweatshirt over the blue shorts. He slipped the .38 into the holster between the shirt and shorts and, with a quick wave to Leo, crossed the street.

The sun slanted through the cloud cover, and off to his left sailboats dotted the dirty gray waters. At this time of day there were but a few of them, and even fewer pedestrians and runners on the sidewalk adjacent to the Charles River. As he looked ahead, he saw the white-shirted target moving at a normal runner's pace toward him. There were no other runners in front of him and a quick glance over his right shoulder confirmed that he was the lone runner heading west on the walkway. Just ahead of him, an elderly couple walked ever so slowly toward him, the man supporting his wife with his arm as she limped along, the two simply enjoying the outing, stopping every ten or twenty paces to admire the view across to Boston or simply to look at one another in that mutually supportive way that is the individual terrain of the aged in love.

Loping gracefully, he passed them, thinking for a moment of his track seasons at Lynn English, particularly his six hundred yard indoor race against the great Charlie Jenkins of Rindge of Cambridge, at the Boston Garden. He had lost, but only in the last few yards, to the state champion.

To his right a long series of benches, perhaps ten of them, were mostly unoccupied. He needed to approach the Chocolate Drop some distance from any observers. Once he passed the teen-age couple necking and totally absorbed in one another just twenty yards ahead of him, there was no activity in the closing distance between him and the target.

About sixty yards ahead, the Chocolate Drop paced himself, leaning forward, mostly studying his own feet, as many runners do, oblivious to his surroundings. He looked up for a moment, glancing ahead, noting the runner in the gray sweatshirt and blue shorts moving along with a confident stride, a lanky, black-haired athlete probably ten years younger than he. He prepared to give the runner's traditional wave of acknowledgment.

The Chocolate Drop glanced to his left at the immense MIT buildings and then, back again, to the runner closing on him, about fifteen yards in front of him now. He waved as they got ready to pass one another.

As Jack waved with his left hand, he simultaneously reached for the .38 with his right. As they passed, he said, "Jimma Flaherty and his family wish you a good life in the hereafter."

The Chocolate Drop turned toward the runner, and stopped in disbelief and shock. "What did you say?" he asked. But the runner had stopped and turned as well, and in his right hand The Drop observed the gun and in that instant knew his life was over.

Jack kneeled, raised the .38 and fired two shots, the first to the forehead, the second to the chest. Blood spurted through the white T-shirt, and the Chocolate Drop fell hard onto his back. Jack threw the weapon into the Charles, ran across Memorial Drive, toward Leo, who was exactly where he should have been.

Without looking around he entered the car, directing Leo to turn right on Massachusetts Avenue, as he simultaneously reached for the dress pants and light brown sports shirt in the back seat.

"Drive carefully, Leo. Stop at Central Square and let me out. I'll get back to Lynn on my own. You better ditch the car soon after dumping me. I'll call you later," Jack said. He took off the sneakers, pulled the dress pants over his shorts, the gray sweatshirt over his head, and then put on the light brown shirt and the brown shoes.

At Central Square, Jack got out as they stopped for the red light. Walking slowly, he headed for the subway station. He paused at the sub shop window just for a moment, ostensibly looking at the preparations for the noontime rush. He glanced back toward Massachusetts Avenue. The street bustled with activity, but he observed no signs of police activity, simply the normal sounds of summer and the fever pitch of urban life.

"It was done beautifully, Jimma," Leo emphasized, raising his glass toward Jack in respect. "You should have seen how smoothly it went down. No one around, and we're out of there in no time flat."

They sat once again in Jimma's library, the sun cascading through the windows on an atypically cool late July afternoon, four days after the hit. From somewhere in the house Jack heard the faint strains of Frank Sinatra singing "From Here to Eternity."

"Jack, I'm very grateful. And I'll never forget this. Great job. My source tells me that prick Jackson got the message. I don't expect any more trouble from him from now on," Jimma said.

"Could I ask why not?" Jack inquired.

"He knows he made a serious mistake. If he goes to war, he loses," Jimma answered, standing and moving toward the bar. "The guineas sanctioned the hit when I told Salvatore Cardoza about the approach to my own family. Family is sacred to them, as it should be. Jackson violated the pact that all of us together had agreed to. He'll get no sympathy from the Italians, even if he wanted to take us on. He'll back off -- be happy to keep his 20 percent and keep his nose over on Dudley Street."

He poured Johnny Walker Red into the glass and tossed some ice on top. "Jack, Leo here is changing your action. From now on, you get your $15,000 plus a percentage of our total take. How's that sound?"

Although he didn't know exactly what that meant, Jack knew enough to be appreciative. "Jimma, I don't know what to say. It's so generous. I'm just very grateful."

"You're grateful? I'm grateful!" Jimma enthused. "You've got a real future in this family, Jack. You have talent. A talent for planning, a talent for implementation, and together that's some lethal combination," Jimma said. "That was an imaginative plan, hitting that fuckin' ex-pug while he's out sweating his balls off, nobody around him to protect him."

"Leo," he changed course, "from now on use Jack on all the top flight stuff. He's inner circle now. He's to be in on all the major activities -- the planning and the action."

Leo smiled and stood to extend his hand to his protégé. At that moment the library door opened. A stunning woman sauntered toward them, swaying ever so slightly, the black hair flowing over her shoulders framing a full face. Jack noticed her full lips and fine white teeth as she flashed a smile in their direction. She wore a white blouse and a blue pleated skirt.

"Mary, hello. Something up?" Jimma asked.

"Aren't you going to introduce me, Jim?" she asked, moving toward Jack as he stood.

"You know Leo, dear. Meet Jack Kelly. Jack, my wife Mary."

Jack guessed she knew little about recent events and decided to say nothing unless she or Jimma introduced the subject. "It's very nice to meet you, Mrs. Flaherty," he said as she extended her hand.

"Mrs. Flaherty is it? Please call me Mary, Jack."

"Mary," he replied with a smile.

"Mary, you need something? Leo, Jack and I are going over a business deal here," Jimma said.

"No, dear. I just heard voices and wanted you to know Elizabeth and I are going to Filene's for a while," she replied. "I'll see you about 7 P.M. Okay?" From the hallway a pale little girl with long curls peered into the library, waving to her father.

Jimma walked to her and kissed her on the forehead, "Hi, Elizabeth. How's my girl?"

As Mary moved toward the door, she glanced back over her shoulder, "Jack, I hope to see you again. Welcome to our home." He sat slowly, reflecting on the importance of family, of belonging. Thanks to Jimma and Leo, he now belonged.

14

"Jack, Jerry. I want you to meet Petey Santangelo," Tommy said, a bit too eagerly. They stood in the European Restaurant on Hanover Street in the North End, waiting for their booth. Just as they shook hands, the maitre d' beckoned them forward.

When they were seated, Jack played with his gin and tonic, studying Santangelo while Tommy smiled at everyone. Around them waiters hustled from table to table filling lunch orders for the large crowd.

Santangelo lifted his beer toward a face battered by too many punches. His bulbous nose had been broken any number of times, and scar tissue ran from his left eyebrow to his cheekbone. He had the look of the world-weary, a man who had experienced a great deal, a man who had lost some enthusiasm for the game even if his words said otherwise. He had gone to fat, his stomach protruding against the table, his fleshy face indicating that he had long ago given up the battle to stay in shape.

"So how long you been a fight manager, Mr. Santangelo?" Jack asked.

"Call me Petey," he replied. "For the past ten years. Long enough to know it's a rough business and you've got to have heart to make a buck out of it."

"Mr. Santangelo," Jack smiled, "did you fight as a pro?"

"Seven years as a welterweight, three as a middle -- mostly out of New York's St. Nicholas Arena, a few bouts at the Garden. At one point I had a top ten rating. I know what it takes to get there."

"And Tommy can get there?" Jack asked.

"You bet your ass I can, Jack. I know I can. I'm ready despite what Tony says," Tommy said vehemently.

"And what do you think, Mr. Santangelo?" Jack continued to look only at Santangelo.

"I think he's a great prospect. He proved himself in the amateurs against all competitors. He's also a natural middleweight. He keeps himself within the 160 lb. limit, and he's dedicated, willing to work hard. He's focused, and he wants it. I think the sky's the limit if he stays on course," Santangelo said.

Jerry eagerly jumped in. "Jack, Tommy's ready. Never mind Tony's caution. He's dominated every one of his opponents to date."

Jack cast a sideways glance at Jerry, almost as soon as he began speaking. His look was both chilling and effective. Jerry sat back, now quiet in his seat.

"And tell me, Mr. Santangelo what downside do you see in Tommy's turning pro?" Jack asked, still fingering his gin and tonic.

"Not much. Technically he needs to improve certain skills."

"Like what?" Jack persisted.

Santangelo looked at Tommy, obviously uncomfortable with his deferral to his older brother, and decided to change direction. "Look, pal, I don't know what your concern is. The kid's an amateur. He's a successful one. It's time to move ahead -- shit or get off the pot as you Irish like to say. If you want him to turn pro, I say he's ready. I can teach him a better jab, proper footwork, pacing. Much of it is simply gaining experience and confidence. Now if he or you don't want professional status, I have other things to do." Santangelo said irritably.

"Hey, Petey, calm down. I want it. Jack, what's the problem?" Tommy asked.

"Jerry, you and Tom take a stroll outside for a minute, would you?" Jack said.

Tommy's body language showed he was about to object to this suggestion but Jack winked at him, and he slowed in his reactions. "Come on, Tom. Let's get some air just for a few minutes," Jerry said.

As they moved toward the street, the waiter approached the table. "Gentlemen, are you ready to order?"

Jack looked up. "You want another beer?" He asked. Petey nodded. "And I'll have another gin and tonic. And bring another round for our friends. They'll be right back," Jack directed.

"I gather you have a problem with me, Mr. Kelly?" Santangelo asked angrily.

"Mr. Santangelo, I've already asked about your know-how, and I'm satisfied. My problem is this: Tommy is my brother. I want him brought along carefully. As you say, it's a tough business. And I don't want self-serving management to make it tougher. I don't want him rushed. I don't want him put in too soon against guys he's not ready for."

Santangelo chugged the beer right from the bottle to gain some courage. "What are you, a fight expert? Who the hell are you to tell me how to bring a fighter along? That's my business. I say when he's ready. He fights when I say and who I say. Maybe I don't even want to take him on."

Jack laughed, saying nothing for the moment. He sipped the gin and tonic and set it down carefully. "Mr. Santangelo, Petey, or whatever the fuck you want to be called, let's not con each other. You want to manage him because you smell a winner. If you don't want to, say so now and we'll walk away because we can find three or five like you who will take him on in a second. If you do want to manage him, I only ask that you indulge a brother's concern. Bring him along carefully. Now, I ask you, is that expecting too much?"

Santangelo replied irritably, "I take care of all my fighters."

Jack leaned back in his seat, looking beyond Santangelo toward the bar and then toward the sunlit sidewalk where crowds of people strolled the North End. He spotted Tom and Jerry standing outside, animatedly gesturing to one another.

"Mr. Santangelo," he began, "of course you do. I just expect that you will take particular care of my brother." He leaned

81

forward in his seat, smiling, staring directly at Santangelo, his face within inches of the manager's. "In fact, I'm holding you personally responsible if anything happens to him. Anything out of the ordinary. Anything you should have controlled."

"Are you threatening me?"

"Mr. Santangelo, I only want to reach a mutually accommodating arrangement with you. You manage and train my brother for a good profit. Unknown to him, I'll supplement your cut by an additional ten percent, whatever the purse. In turn, I want your promise that you'll watch over him very carefully. If anything unusual comes up, I want to know about it. Our own personal social contract, Petey. You agree to perform your responsibilities, and I agree to provide greater rewards. What do you say?" He smiled.

Santangelo paused before answering. "I've got no problem with that."

Jack signaled the waiter. "Would you be good enough to ask those two men outside to rejoin us?"

"So what's up?" Tom inquired, as he and Jerry approached the booth.

"I believe we have a deal with Mr. Santangelo. A social contract not to be broken," Jack said, offering his hand across the table.

Tom and Jerry grinned at each other, holding their glasses up, then extending them to those offered by Jack and Santangelo. Petey tapped Jack's glass, staring across at those blue eyes, cold as stone.

For almost four months now Jack and Marjorie had been dating steadily -- movies at the Paramount and Warner, dinner at Anthony Athanas' original Hawthorne restaurant in Olympia Square, lunches of spaghetti and meat sauce at Sassone's walk-down restaurant behind the Warner, Red Sox games at Fenway, pizza at Monte's on Eastern Avenue, and long walks, both day and night, along the beach.

As they rounded the walkway leading to Red Rock, they paused and leaned on the railing, watching the high tide breakers smash against the sea walls, the early September afternoon warming them. From their elevated position above the beach they could look across to Swampscott, to Marblehead, out to sea and reminisce about the loss of the summer that had brought them each other.

He liked this buoyant young lady from a life of privilege. She was intelligent, perky, fun to be with. Each time she smiled, he fell in love all over again. On the second date he had gathered enough courage to kiss her and on the third to brush against her breasts in such a deceptive way that a month later she had laughingly inquired whether his actions had been deliberate. It was on the fourth or fifth date that she had moved his hand onto her breasts and allowed him to caress them through her blouse. In his car, or on their evening walks around the Red Rock promontory, or sitting on the benches in the dark at Goldfish Pond, she had gradually allowed him to explore the wonderland between her legs. But always, only with his hand. There was no way that she would entertain the idea of intercourse, and he had his own concerns about the possibility of getting her pregnant. Foreplay was end play, and that was that. Only with engagement or marriage would she or any self-respecting young woman consider penetration.

They walked along the pathway heading toward Red Rock, from where they could look south toward Lynn Beach, with Revere, Winthrop, and Boston far beyond, the John Hancock Building visible in the distance. Marjorie held his hand, and he occasionally slid his arm around her waist. She wore a white blouse and a black skirt, looking as if she were heading to work which, indeed, she would be within the hour.

"Jack, my father's going to ask you something next time you're at the house, and I hope you'll listen carefully. It's very important to me," she suddenly blurted out.

"And what's this all about, young lady?" he teased. He knew this conversation was coming, because he now knew her, and, more particularly, he had read her father and his body language during recent visits.

"He's going to ask you about joining his agency. Selling cars and learning about the business. He likes you, Jack. He admires your work habits, but he thinks you're wasting your time at the bakery," she said.

Seagulls circled over Red Rock in their perpetual search for food, and below them three boys walked across the huge bed of rocks, heading towards the highest point, an elevated crest from which they could dive outward to the ocean.

"What do you think about the idea, Marjorie?" he asked.

They sat on one of the benches ringing the promontory, watching the three youngsters scrambling back onto the rocks ready to jump again. The giddy laughter of teen-age girls observing the three young men reached their ears.

"It's not what I think, Jack. It's what you think. But I hope you'll consider the idea carefully. Dad knows people and he knows his business. He thinks you would be a natural," she replied.

He slid his hand into hers and moved closer to her. She excited him. Since the death of his mother, she was the first woman for whom he had any real feelings. He needed love in his life, and he knew she returned his adoration.

He also instinctively sensed opportunity. Jimma insisted they all be gainfully employed, always able to demonstrate a source of income, a regular job, thus the bakery had served its purpose. With Stanton's interest, he could move to white collar employment, and, because of the nature of a car dealership, be free to move about, to be more readily available for his real business.

Two female roller skaters raced along the semi-circular route of the promontory, and behind them girls in two piece bathing suits basked in the sun on blankets along the grass.

"If your father asks me, I'll accept, Marge. I started some business management courses part-time at Northeastern last week. I want to get away from the bakery."

She leaned over and kissed him on the side of his face. Just at that moment one of the teenage skaters whizzed by their bench. "I saw that!"

84

15

On a November night in 1955, over 13,000 fight fans poured into Tony DeMarco's back yard, the North End and the Boston Garden, to watch his can't-miss brawl with welterweight champion Carmen Basilio, the onion farmer from Canastota, New York. In June, Basilio had knocked out the Bostonian in twelve rounds, but only after a cruel, first rate fight delivered by two consummate professionals.

Following dinner at Polcari's on Atlantic Avenue, Jack and Jerry walked along Causeway Street, part of the large crowd buzzing in anticipation of the upcoming fight. A newshawk pushed copies of the <u>Traveler</u> and the <u>Record American</u> at the throng, simultaneously yelling "DeMarco fights to regain crown tonight!" But their interest would center on the first bout of the evening, a four-round preliminary, Tommy's pro debut. As they walked into the Garden ticket lobby, Jerry pointed to the placards on the walls, announcing the main fight and listing the participants on the undercard. "Christ, Jack, no mention of Tommy at all."

"Hey, how many fighters have an audience of 13,000 for their first one, Jerry? He won't see this type of crowd again for a while."

"Oh yes he will, Jack. This is only the beginning for him. You'll see him at Fenway Park or Yankee Stadium -- and soon."

They continued through the bowels of the Garden, meandering past popcorn vendors and hot dog stands, and stopped outside the dressing room where the bulging blue form of one of Boston's finest barred their way.

"Officer, we're related to Tommy Kelly, one of the fighters. He asked us to stop by," said Jerry.

"Who?" rejoined the red-faced sergeant.

"Tommy Kelly," said Jerry.

"Never heard of him. Hold here a minute," he said, opening the door. "Is there a Tommy Kelly in here?" he asked.

"Right here," came the familiar voice moving toward the door.

"You know these guys?" Bulging Blue asked.

"They're my brothers," Tommy winked at them.

"Okay, you're in," Blue stated, stepping aside and allowing them a view of a room no more than twenty by forty feet with six or seven lockers strewn against the back wall and an equal number of three-legged stools fronting them. No space, no rubbing table, a single shower head protruding from a built-in stall to their right. A pudgy trainer attired in blue slacks and a white T-shirt chewed an unlit cigar as he carefully wrapped one of the fighter's hands. The stink of sweat permeated the small room as three or four fighters occasionally stood to throw punches at imaginary opponents.

"Where's DeMarco?" Jerry asked excitedly.

"He's not dressing here, little brother, that's for sure," laughed Tommy. "Thanks for stopping by, you guys," he added.

"You ready?" Jack asked, eyeing the taped hands, the drops of perspiration falling from Tommy's forehead.

"I've been ready all my life, Jack. No problem," he said, playfully tapping a light punch toward Jack's chin.

Santangelo stuck his head into the room without even a hello. "Let's go, Tom. It's time. We're on first thing."

The brothers embraced, Jack amazed at the calmness with which Tommy was approaching his big night. If success can be measured by loving what you do, he was already a champion. Jack felt no tension whatsoever in Tom, and, as they broke from one another, Tommy turned and threw jabs at an imaginary opponent, total concentration having shifted to the task at hand.

As they searched for their seats in Section 30, a loge area directly behind the ringside seats, and slightly elevated above

86

them, Jack observed that perhaps 8,000 were already in their seats, even at this early hour. "Ladies and Gentlemen," intoned the long-boned announcer clad in a blue business suit and speaking from center ring through a microphone extended from the huge scoreboard above him, "welcome to Boston Garden and to world championship boxing."

As he spoke, Tommy climbed through the ring ropes, a white towel draped around his neck. No robe, thought Jack, mentally noting that he would correct that soon enough. "Ladies and gentlemen," the ring announcer continued, "the first bout of the evening--four rounds. In this corner from Detroit, Michigan, at 158 pounds, Bill Dunn." The well-built towhead who stood in the left corner had been hand picked by Santangelo. He had won four of his six pro fights but, according to Santangelo, was a light puncher and only a fair boxer.

"And in this corner, making his professional debut, from neighboring Lynn, the Massachusetts and national Golden Gloves champion, at 157 pounds, Tommy Kelly. Four rounds." The partisan crowd, loud and enthusiastic on championship night, gave Tommy a huge hand as he stood and waved confidently.

As the bell sounded, Tommy raced from his corner, firing a one-two combination to Dunn's face. Surprised, Dunn retreated a step, peppering a light jab at Tommy. He might as well have proffered lollipops, because Tommy advanced without hesitation, unleashing a vicious left hook to the side of Dunn's head. He followed with a right hand to the body, then backed up to survey the damage. Dunn continued to throw straight left jabs toward Tommy, who, in turn, moved ever forward, flashing combinations -- a left hook followed by a right cross, sometimes doubling up with the hook. The crowd roared in anticipation of a quick knockout, urging Tommy on, noting his aggressiveness, the power in his hands, the steadfast fixation on the goal. He was oblivious to all around him except for Dunn.

Dunn bicycled away, moving from left to right, waiting for the time when his onrushing opponent would leave him that momentary opening where he could follow his left jab with a short right hand. Tommy slid another strong left hook over the jab, and as they clinched, banged three hard rights to the kidney, causing Dunn to back away.

Tommy pursued him, feinting a left, quickly following with a right hand lead. Dunn staggered as if shot by an elephant gun, falling forward onto the canvas as the referee, not even bothering to count, stepped in, waving that the fight was over.

Tommy gleefully thrust his arms in the air, as the crowd stood in full appreciation of his strong effort and aggressive style. Jack and Jerry stood longer than any others, yelling, bouncing on their toes, whistling loudly, alternately letting all around them know, "That's our brother!"

"No shit! He's a killer! Going to be good," came a heavy voice from the crowd.

Jack scanned the platform at South Station once again as the conductor yelled out his last "All aboard" call. He checked his watch -- 8:00. Jerry had said he would be here by 7:30. On the last Saturday in November, snow was just beginning to fall, and the forecast for six to ten inches by afternoon did not bode well for their trip to New Haven. Suddenly, he spotted Jerry running down the platform toward him. "Drop in anytime," Jack said, as they climbed aboard about a minute before departure.

Despite the weather and the hour, the train was packed with revelers, almost all of them Jerry's age, talking loudly, poking at one another, slipping flasks to their friends from under heavy overcoats. About a quarter of them were young women, fresh faced and buoyant, dressed for the weather in long winter coats and crimson hats.

"Nice quiet people you hang around with, Jerry," Jack said, removing his blue topcoat before an overly zealous son of Harvard noticed its color.

"Come on, big brother, don't be a killjoy. You love football. I remember you zigzagging all over Laundry Hill -- all that action and you kept me on the sidelines," Jerry laughed.

Jack recalled the tackle football games the brothers and their friends had played above the railroad tracks back in the '40's.

Until he was ten, Jack refused to let Jerry do anything but referee or chase down and spot the ball. "We didn't like playing on a day like this, kid. I hope some of you Harvards brought snowplows to clear the field for that old-fashioned single wing shit you run," Jack said.

"Don't be so negative. Yale's light and fast this year, so maybe the snowfall will help us."

The snow thickened as they headed west, the slow New York-bound train chugging its way through Newton, Framingham, and Worcester. Strong northwest winds whipped the snowflakes against the window, making it nearly impossible to see outside. He turned to look at the handsome freshman sitting next to him. "So how's the first year going, Jerry?"

Jerry paused, giving Jack a few seconds to study close up the changes in his brother. If anything, he was even more handsome. At eighteen, his lanky frame resembled Jack's, in contrast to Tommy's smaller, more compact build. The matted black hair, parted on the left, the broad forehead with elongated black eyebrows above beautiful blue eyes, and the straight nose so characteristic of the Irish made him more beautiful than handsome. Whether at Fisherman's Beach or on this train, Jack had seen young women staring at him.

"How's Marjorie doing, Jack?"

"Fine. But I asked you about school," Jack insisted.

"I love it. The professors are absolutely first-rate. They challenge you to think, to be critical, to reflect before answering," Jerry enthused. "Some of the best minds in the world teach you to look at the big picture."

"How're you doing?"

"It's hard to know, Jack, but I think I'm holding my own. You know, Lynn English was great preparation for Harvard. I had good teachers who insisted we earn our grades. Yeah, I'm doing fine so far. I'll know more after first semester exams. But whatever happens, I owe it to you, Jack."

Jack tapped him on the arm. "You owe me nothing, kid. You've earned your way, all the way. I'm only helping the way

Ma would have expected me to. To take care of you, the way she took care of us. No problems, then?"

Jerry shook his head almost too quickly, Jack thought, and then, again, turned the conversation back to Jack.

"So now...what about Marjorie? What's going on between you two?"

Jack smiled, thinking of the past summer and of his growing closeness to Marjorie. Now that he was working for her father, he saw her constantly. They dated only each other, and he found himself always looking forward to the next time he would be with her. They were friends, confidants, eager young lovers totally absorbed in each other.

He grimaced, contemplating for the moment the lie he was living. In the evenings, about 9, he would use the excuse of homework for the two courses he was taking at Northeastern on Saturday mornings to drop her off. From Jimma's point of view, all was perfect. Jack now had a legitimate, less physical job, which left plenty of time for family activities in the evenings. Over lunch at Dini's on Tremont Street one recent day, Jimma had once again stressed the importance of legitimate enterprises for all family members and reiterated his insistence that the members live comfortably but never ostentatiously.

"It's important to live and look legit. Deal only in cash. No checks, no charge cards, nothing but cash. Charge cards are for suckers. And keep the cash out of the banks as much as you can. Stash it in some safe haven. Forsake the interest. Don't be piggish. If the cops ever ask where you got such an accumulation, then tell 'em the ponies at Suffolk or from those asshole dogs chasing the white rabbit at Wonderland. Whatever, be smart. Nothing in writing. Deal in cash, and be ready to show a pay stub for a good week's work."

The train lumbered along the track, moving more slowly than usual and usual meant moving with glacial speed. "She's doing fine. We're very serious about each other. She's kind, considerate -- she hasn't allowed her father's success to spoil her." He paused for a moment. "Jerry, I gave her a friendship ring last week."

Grabbing his hand, Jerry pumped it vigorously. "Well, big brother, you finally got smart. You don't deserve her. I'm happy for you." Although the words were sincerely stated, Jack couldn't help but notice the worried look in his eyes.

"Jerry, what's the problem?" Jack asked. "Something's bothering you."

"Aah, I guess I need to ask you for a loan, Jack. I need some cash," he stammered.

"Hey, little guy, that's okay. What? $25? $50? Will that do it?"

"Jack, I'm in some deep trouble. I need $5,000."

"$5,000!" Jack almost jumped from his seat. "You're shitting me!"

"Jack, I'm ashamed to even ask you. But I need your help. Do you have that kind of cash?" he asked anxiously.

Jack stared at his brother before answering. "Let's go back to square one. Why do you need that kind of money?"

Jerry fidgeted in the seat, looking at the window, the landscape now barely visible in the driving storm. "This fall I started betting on football games, using the expense money you sent with the tuition. Just little bets to begin -- $5.00, $10.00 -- no more. I had some early success so I doubled to $10.00 and $20.00 bets. Before I knew it, I was in the hole for $300."

"That's a long way from $5,000. What the hell happened?" Jack asked.

"This bookie I placed bets with -- Ferdie Gallipoli -- carried me for a while and then loaned me the money to pay the original debt. Later on, he surprised me. He says I owe him the vig on the debt, and the vig goes up each day I don't pay. I had no money to pay him, vig or no." Jerry's voice climbed an octave as he spoke.

"How much did you actually lose?" Jack asked.

"About $500," Jerry replied. "But there's something else, Jack. This guy Gallipoli means business."

"What do you mean?"

"Last Monday night I was walking near the campus on the way back from Harvard Stadium after watching the frosh practice. I was alone. Gallipoli and two of his heavyweights stopped me." He rolled back his sweater and revealed his left arm. A long knife slash extended from his wrist to his elbow, the cut skillfully sewn together with a number of stitches.

Jack stared at the wound, his lips thinning, his face grim. "Who did this to you? Which one?" he asked.

"Gallipoli slashed me. Said it was a warning. If I don't have the $5,000 by next Saturday, he says I won't be seeing many more Saturdays after that," Jerry replied nervously. "Can you help me, Jack? Jesus, I don't know how I can even ask you, but I don't know where else to turn."

Looking at the arm, Jack thought back to the time when Jerry had just been vaccinated. He must have been four or five years old when Jack had asked to take him on his tricycle to Goldfish Pond. "All right," their mother had agreed, "but be sure he doesn't get wet." Before Jack knew it, Jerry, pedaling down the steep embankment that led to the edge of the pond, had plunged into two feet of water. There had been no problem getting him out, but Jack would always remember his failure to protect Jerry and his mother's disappointment in him.

"New Haven, next stop," the conductor bellowed.

Jack carefully pulled the sweater down over Jerry's arm. "Jerry, you never worry about asking me for anything, you understand? I'm your brother, and your problems are my problems. Where can I find this guy Gallipoli?"

"Jack, if you can give me the money now, I'll pay you back, and soon. I can get a job as a waiter and..."

"Look, kid. There's going to be no waiting on tables. You just study and pay attention to those grades. I'll worry about finances, and you can repay me when you graduate. Deal?" he said extending his hand.

"Okay, Jack. I don't know what to say."

"Say nothing. I'll see him before next Saturday and take care of the debt. You keep away from him now and forever. You understand? Now where do I find him?"

The train slowed as they entered New Haven Station. Along with hundreds of others, they walked the mile and a half to Yale

Bowl, the storm intensifying by the minute. Blue clad Yalies yelled light insults at the Harvards as they drove by, half of them swerving just enough to toss slush from the tires in their direction.

At the Bowl, over 70,000 fans, undaunted by the weather, huddled in the cavernous old structure, fueled both by the excitement of the great rivalry and by the flasks they raised more than occasionally to their lips. For over three hours the teams battled, with the superior ground game of the Bulldogs leading them to a 21-7 victory, the only Harvard touchdown coming in the fading minutes of the contest on a five yard pass to Teddy Kennedy, a senior end from Hyannisport, Massachusetts.

16

"Jimma wants us to meet him at the warehouse over in Charlestown," Leo said. Jack eased the Chrysler out of Leo's driveway on Horadan Way and cut across Mission Hill, heading for Huntington Avenue. Young students, almost all of them obviously Irish-American, half ran and half walked in the direction of the Mission Church and the elementary school, their movement accelerated by the bitter cold that early December brought to the Hub.

"What's up?" Jack inquired.

"Not sure. He just said to be there," Leo said. "Right now, I'm glad to be anywhere except there," he gestured back toward the house. "The old lady's on the rag again, bitching to anything that moves, including her shadow. You aren't thinking of marrying that girl, are you, Jack? Well don't. Marriage is a great institution -- for the criminally insane."

Jack laughed, "Anything special causing the aggravation?" From Park Drive, he dipped down to Commonwealth Avenue and turned onto Marlborough Street, from where he could take a left to Massachusetts Avenue and cross the bridge to Cambridge.

"Yeah, the nun clipped Danny, our son, for mouthing off. He told her she looked like a penguin. So with a loudmouth son how's she to face the good sisters this Sunday, she says to me. And it's my fault for not clipping him enough and not being home enough. As my Aunt Helen would say, 'Jesus, Mary and Joseph!' I married her when she didn't have a pot to piss in or a window to throw it out of. You ask me, the whole lot of them -- her, the nun, the kid -- all ought to be clipped and with something stronger than a backhand."

From Memorial Drive Jack drove north across the Prison Point Bridge into Charlestown, heading uphill to Monument Square and Bunker Hill. They passed the fine Victorian houses around the square, once the province of the wealthy, now owned and well maintained by Irish blue-collar workers. Curiously Jack felt that Charlestown looked grim, an unkind neighborhood of warehouses and housing projects. But such an initial impression was false. In reality, the real Charlestown was about neighborliness, families bound together in common cause, Irish mothers rearing their young to better themselves. There was an essential goodness to those who lived and worked here that he admired. He cruised down to Medford Street and turned left toward the dilapidated warehouses in the 500 block, the majesty of the Monument now above and behind them. He stopped a block beyond 523 Medford Street and parked the car. They walked briskly back to the building, the fierce northeast wind biting through their clothing and whipping their reddened faces.

Leo tapped loudly on an old steel door with a pane of blackened glass in its center. The door was part of a larger roll-up, which allowed trucks to enter and exit. The door swung open, and Paulie Cronin stood there smiling at them. "Come on in," he gestured. Inside, the cavernous space was strewn with discarded boxes, used tires, car parts, and old kitchen appliances. Above, weakened pipes dripped incessantly, puddles forming all around the cement floor.

In the middle of the floor Jimma Flaherty presided, his attention riveted on an obviously frightened young man about Jack's age tied to a wooden chair, duct tape covering his mouth. Blood trickled from his broken nose and purple welts caused his eyes to swell and narrow. Behind Jimma stood Vin Sullivan and Freddie Quinlan, another Jimma soldier, who had accompanied Jack on some assignments.

"You son of a bitch!" Jimma railed, his coat off, shirt sleeves rolled to the elbow, the heat of this affair obviously surmounting any concerns about the heavy cold inside the warehouse. "You fuck! You think you could steal from me, and I wouldn't find out about it? You rip Jimma Flaherty off and think you're going to get away free? You fuckin' prick!" He threw his weight into a roundhouse right hand which clearly broke the jaw of the prisoner whose head shot back and then dropped to his chest.

Jack moved toward Freddie as Jimma continued the assault with a series of smashes to the face. "Freddie, what's this about?" he asked the gray-haired, middle-aged veteran.

"This guy and some others moved in on three of our bars in Southie, takin' the action, threatenin' the owners. They're fuckin' plumbers, for Christ's sake. Imagine movin' in on us? Jimma's teachin' this one that ain't the way to go."

It was vitally important that Jimma protect the chain of activities that comprised their empire -- bars and other businesses from which they extorted protection monies; pimps who kept the lucrative prostitution rings in Southie, Charlestown, Mission Hill and Cambridge flourishing; bookies and numbers runners throughout their share of the city and in the suburbs; loansharks who provided dollars at outrageous profit; and the downtown suits whose connection to the police and the courts guaranteed help if it were needed. To this point there had been little problem with either the police or the courts, and Jimma had remained strong through a combination of careful planning and a willingness to stay within the boundaries agreed to with the Italians and the Negroes.

Yet lately he seemed to be overreacting. Witness this scene, Jack thought. Jimma's strength had always been his coolness, his detachment, his ability to think before acting, traits Jack knew Jimma admired in him. Recently, however, Jimma seemed almost paranoid, overprotective of his interests, much less cautious. Normally, he avoided any involvement in direct action. What, then, was he doing here today? The family had plenty of enforcers who could handle such situations. Leo had warned him of Jimma's explosive temper, which surfaced infrequently and sometimes led to impulsive responses.

Blood spurted onto Jimma's white shirt, causing him to pause. "Vin, get over here and finish this fuck off," he directed. Jack stared, amazed that this offense would lead to death. The offender's face was now beyond recognition, his left eye closed, his lips swollen and gushing blood, his nose twisted to the side.

Vin placed the silencer on his .38 and then held the weapon next to the temple of the unconscious man. He discharged it, and the victim slouched forward, now forever alone.

Jimma looked at them, probably for the first time. "Jack, Leo, can you believe this fuck? Coming into my territory and rousting our people? Vin, when it's dark, dump this body right outside the asshole plumbers' union office as a warning to the others in case they or some other jokers still want to fuck with us," Jimma said.

"Walk with me to my car, you two," he gestured to Jack and Leo. He took the sports jacket and his trench coat from Freddie and started toward the door.

"Jesus, I'm losing patience with these intrusions -- first Jackson, now these fuckin' amateurs," he fumed. "But I called you here for something else."

"Leo, I want Jack and Ray to case the Zayre's department store on Route 128 in Woburn -- the one at the shopping center. Watch the comings and goings of the armored car service they're using. Case the situation carefully. I hear that on Fridays they're carrying payroll for some of the big firms on 128."

"Do we want to get involved with something that would bring real heat from the feds?" Jack asked.

Flurries whipped their faces in a frenzied dance as they walked toward Jimma's '54 Pontiac LeMans parked just beyond Jack's. "We'll see," Jimma responded. "Yeah, it's out of our line and maybe chancy. But I want it checked out. If we have a good chance of success, then we'll whack them. There's probably $2 million involved. How easy is it to whack it? Maybe it's worth the feds chasing our asses. See what's there."

They sat in Marjorie's darkened living room on the first Friday night in December, the wind pressing against the window, his erection pressing against his fly.

Jack fondled her breasts, the nipples coming alive in his hands, her lips opening, her pink tongue running along his teeth, darting between them to the back of his mouth. Gently, he eased her down on the couch, his hands kneading her nipples still, his mouth lowering to find her breast. He moved her blouse further aside, and flicked his tongue around the pinkness. She moaned, still very tense and aware, determined to go only so far.

She served as director. "Ready when you are, Mr. DeMille," Jack thought, his loins alive with passion, his brain signaling him that only engagement or marriage would allow him to go further. She opened her legs so that he could mount her and pound her through her uplifted skirt. His fingers moved her panties aside, and then probed, rubbing her clitoris. She groaned again, but she knew when to stop. She pushed his hand aside, yet still allowed him to push his pole against her, knowing that his layers of clothing protected her. In full frenzy, Jack drove it home, he, too, relieved they were safe and yet ashamed that he was coming in his underpants.

His concern was heightened by a voice in the distance. "Yoo, hoo, you people. Would you like me to cook some popcorn?" Marjorie's mother's tone indicated less of a concern for popcorn preparation than that the forces of darkness might be invading her daughter's vault.

They sat up straight, Marjorie quickly buttoning her blouse, for what purpose Jack thought, with her bra still undone, her breasts drooping toward the southern hemisphere. "No, Mother, we're fine," she answered quickly.

"Well let me know if you need anything," Mrs. Stanton said, retreating up the stairs.

Marjorie turned on the light, and he moved close again, his lips brushing hers, his embrace indicating that love followed sex wherever true love lived. "Jack, can we talk for a minute?" she asked, moving away from him to the adjoining chair.

"Sure," he replied.

"We've been going together for months now, and I've been out of high school almost two years," she began hesitantly. "I'm beginning to be embarrassed. Some of my girl friends are only nineteen and are getting married. They look at me and I know they're saying, 'What's wrong with her?' Jack, what's wrong with us?"

He took her hand, fingered her friendship ring, staring into her eyes. "Marjorie, there's nothing wrong with us. Nothing more than that I needed the time to establish myself. Thanks to your father, I'm learning the business. You know I needed the time to see both Tommy and Jerry on their way You've been patient, and I love you for that. I love you very much." He leaned over, touching her lips with his fingers, kissing her cheek, drawing her toward him. "Except for my mother, I've never loved any other woman. Not until you came along. I love you, Marge. Would you marry me this summer?"

She leaned into him, kissing him passionately. "Yes! Oh, Jack, I want to tell my mother," she gushed.

"Yeah, right. But not tonight. I don't think I'm as presentable as I might be tomorrow," he laughed. "By the way, I'm going to visit Jerry in Cambridge tomorrow. I'll call you as soon as I'm back. We'll tell them together, tomorrow night, Okay?"

What was that lyric from the Four Aces' song? he thought. A man chases a girl until she catches him?

17

Ferdie Gallipoli sat in his backroom office late Saturday morning counting the night's take, keenly anticipating the rush of action on this afternoon's games. He was a small man, with a top- heavy body and very short legs. He had a large, round head with filmy eyes that ran ever so slightly. He dabbed his white handkerchief about them as he thought once again of the easy take life had become. The saloon gave him his living, the students from the various Cambridge colleges flocking in for the beer and an occasional sandwich. But the gambling action would make him a rich man. Three or four more good years, and with the money he had already stashed away, he and Rita could head for Florida -- Miami Beach and the good life. That is if Rita could keep herself in shape till then. She was developing an ass like a Japanese soldier, but then again he could always dump her for one of those young Collins Avenue beach sexpots if she didn't turn herself around. Let her stay here in fuckin' freezing Boston and eat herself to death.

There was a loud knock on the door. "Come in," Ferdie said.

Kevin, his barkeep, cracked open the door and peered into the room. "Ferdie, there's a guy here wants to pay off the Kelly kid's debt."

"Give me two minutes to clear this shit and then tell him to come in," Ferdie said. Great, he thought, another $5,000 for the bank, a step closer to Florida.

After first knocking, a tall, well-dressed young man appeared in the doorway. He wore a navy blue suit with a white shirt and striped red and blue tie. "Mr. Gallipoli?" he inquired.

"That's right," Ferdie said from behind the desk. "Who are you?"

"Jack Kelly, Mr. Gallipoli. I'm Jerry's brother."

"Sit down over here, Jack Kelly. You go to Harvard, too?" he asked, pointing to the wooden chair in front of his desk.

"No, Mr. Gallipoli. I'm not a student. I'm here strictly to square Jerry's debt with you if I may."

Ferdie grinned broadly. "You sure as shit may, Kelly. You got the money he owes?"

"Of course," Jack said turning the wooden chair in front of the desk ever so slightly so that he could see the door as well.

Ferdie noted the movie star looks of the pleasant young man before him, particularly the clear blue eyes that seemed to fix on him. "Well, where is it?" Ferdie asked anxiously.

"Mr. Gallipoli, could I first ask you a question? Was it necessary to cut my brother?" Jack asked calmly.

"Hey, I'm sorry for that, truly sorry. But the kid owed a few hundred, and with the vig, the mark was growing by the day with no payments coming in. He wouldn't produce any dough. I had to show him we meant business. Sorry again. But it worked, didn't it? You're here," Ferdie laughed.

Jack laughed as well. "Yeah, I'm here, Mr. Gallipoli. Tell me, how much do you think would square the debt?"

Ferdie stared across at him. Was this guy stupid? "He should have told you -- $5,000, and it's due today. I hope that's what you have."

"No, Mr. Gallipoli, you misunderstand my question," Jack said as he stood. "How much do you think you owe my brother for the physical harm and emotional stress you've caused him? $10,000? $20,000? What would be the correct amount?"

Ferdie stared at him incredulously. "Are you fuckin' crazy, you Irish asshole?"

Jack pulled the .38 from behind his belt, leveling it at Gallipoli and, in a quick motion, gained the angle on both Gallipoli and the door simultaneously. Moving behind the desk, he pressed the gun against the left side of Gallipoli's head. "I need you to remain very quiet and I need to see some green very quickly, Mr. Gallipoli." Ferdie's hands shook as he slowly opened the drawer, revealing wads of dollars wrapped in elastics. A number of small money bags lay on the floor behind the desk.

"You haven't been to the bank yet, Ferdie, huh? Too bad. How much is there?" Jack asked, pressing the .38 hard against Gallipoli's head.

Ferdie stammered, "There's about $10,000 here."

"Put it all in one of those bags," Jack directed.

Ferdie scooped the money packets into the bag, working frantically, his eyes straight ahead, focusing on the task at hand. "Listen carefully, my limp-peckered friend," Jack said, "while I tell you a little story. You know when my brother Tom was about three he couldn't understand why he was being disciplined by our parents. If our mother slapped his ass, he would try to slap her back and he would say 'You hit me; I hit you.' Well, Ferdie, he wasn't far wrong. His actions sum up my philosophy of life -- you hit me, I hit you. The $10,000 makes us almost even."

Ferdie flinched, terrified. "Almost even? You're stealing my fucking money, and we're not even?"

Jack reached into the left pocket of his suitcoat. "You weren't listening, Ferdie." With a quick motion he raised the sling blade and slashed Ferdie below his left eye down to his mouth. Ferdie shrieked in agony, lifting his hand instinctively to the area. "You cut me, I cut you, you prick. Now we're even. You ever come near my brother or me again, and I'll kill you, your wife Rita, your fuckin' father, and the whore you've been seeing on the side. Do you understand me, Ferdie?" Sobbing, Ferdie nodded.

Jack picked up the bag and moved to the door. As he closed the door behind him and headed for the exit, Kevin asked from the bar, "What's all the noise about?"

"Ferdie cut himself shaving," Jack tossed over his shoulder.

When he was back in Lynn, he phoned Jerry at his dormitory. "Hi, Jerry. Everything going okay?"

"Jack, Jesus I'm glad you called. It's Saturday. What about Ferdie Gallipoli and the money?"

"That's why I called, Jerry. I met with him, and everything is fine. Would you believe he canceled the debt?" Jack said.

"He what?" Jerry practically shouted.

"We had a good talk. You keep away from him and his place, and he leaves you alone. No more betting with any books, Jerry. Do you and I have an agreement?"

"Jack, of course. I don't know how to thank you."

"Just learn from this. You want to gamble, bet with friends and bet small."

"You and he got along and settled all this?" Jerry asked. "That's hard to believe."

"Sure we did. He's a real cut up," Jack replied.

They walked west on Massachusetts Avenue heading toward the Symphony Deli directly across the street from Loew's State Theater, Jimma holding court with Jack and Ray. Two days after New Year's Day, 1956, pedestrians picked their way carefully through icy sidewalks, huddled against the punishing, unrelenting wind and cold, their heads down.

"Jesus Christ, we should have driven right to the front door, Ray. What are we, fucking penguins?" Jimma complained. "Look at the State Theater over there. Nobody going in. The movies are dead. That 3-D shit with lions in your lap don't cut it."

They sat in the back of the delicatessen facing toward the front so they could observe anyone entering. "Now tell me about the Zayre site. What've you learned so far?" Jimma asked, being careful to tuck a napkin beneath his collar so that his pastrami on rye with mustard did not drip onto his white shirt and blue tie.

Jack and Ray exchanged glances.

"I think it's too risky, Jimma. We don't need that kind of action. Armored car robbery means the feds could be all over us. We don't need the problem, not with everything going so well for us right now," Jack said.

Jimma bit into the pastrami, trying to decide whether it was more important to hear more of a detailed analysis or to demonstrate his will to Jack. He opted to listen a bit longer. "Tell me what you saw," he finally said.

"We watched the Brink's truck the last three Fridays," Jack began. "The drivers are always on time. They arrive between 4 - 4:15 P.M. There are three guards altogether, the driver and another riding shotgun, up front, and one with the money in the rear. When they stop, they park in the fire lane, and Shotgun comes around to open the back door. The driver waits a minute and then joins them at the rear of the truck. Then Shotgun enters the back. The third guy heads to the store for the pick-up. He's in there no more than five minutes. When he comes back, the driver starts up the motor, and Shotgun stands on alert outside while the other guard places the money in the vehicle. And off they go. Maximum time of stoppage: ten minutes.

"My guess is there's not much cash coming out of Zayre, but at that hour there's plenty in the truck itself. If we were to hit them, it has to be early, in my opinion. Hit them when they first arrive and are ready to enter the store."

"Why?" Jimma asked.

"The motor's off then, and the driver's out of the car. We can handle all three," Ray answered.

"Sounds like an easy score to me. And from what I'm told, a big payday," Jimma said.

"I don't think so, Jimma," Jack said.

Ray sipped his coffee slowly. The tension was rising. Jimma testing them, Jack, deferential and respectful, yet determined to have his analysis accepted.

Jack leaned across the table. "Look, Jimma. Let's suppose the best. We score, and no one's injured. We still have the feds and the locals all over us because the story's too big. If your sources are completely accurate, $1 million to $2 million is too big a score not to bring heat. Six years ago, Joe McGinnis and Mike Geagan and those guys pulled off the Brink's heist at the garage on Hull Street. And for the last six years they can't take a piss without being watched. Before the statue of limitations goes by on that one, someone's going to squeal. Someone probably already has. You don't need your family, this family, you yourself harassed for years so that we can't operate."

Jimma interjected, "Who says they know who did it?"

Jack sighed and changed course. "Jimma, for Christ's sake, look at what you've accomplished. You have your territories, and with them you control gambling, prostitution, loansharking, some of the unions. You get a piece of a lot of other action. The guineas are at peace with us, and the Negroes now leave you alone. We have no real problems with the police and courts. We're sailing along. We must be making a million a year now?

"Jimma, I know you'll consider this thoughtfully, carefully. Whatever you decide, I know it will be in the best interests of the family. We'll follow through for you as you direct."

Jimma relaxed noticeably, a slight grin crossing his face. Jack was probably right, but he needed to hear the words of respect, the deferential commentary, especially from Jack. Rising stars had to be kept in their place, appreciated but watched, and at the first signs of unwelcome ambition, discouraged.

He stirred his coffee as if pondering the matter very seriously. After a minute he looked up. "We'll forget it, at least for now," he said. "We're on track with our various businesses. We just need to evaluate good opportunities when they present themselves, and a couple of million bucks is worth serious consideration."

A gray-haired man entered the front door, ordered coffee and sat by himself near the front door. "Hey, that's Arthur Fiedler, the Pops conductor," Jimma said.

"Speaking of music, Jimma, Jack's facing the music in August," Ray said.

"No shit, Jack. That's good to hear. The girl from Swampscott, right? A young guy like you needs a good home, another kind of family," Jimma beamed. He extended his hand across the table, pumping Jack's hand, completely relaxed now.

<u>18</u>

Father Dolan married them on the hottest August 18th on
record. At St. Joseph's Church family and friends sweltered,
hoping for a quick ceremony so that they could leave for the air-
conditioned comfort of George Page's Colonial Restaurant in
Lynnfield.

It infuriated Jack that they had to be joined outside the rail.
Marjorie had undertaken course work -- indoctrination, she
laughingly called it -- during the past few weeks, promising to
bring their children up Catholic, among other considerations.
What difference did it all make? Making anyone feel morally
inferior was a serious error, particularly someone like Marge
who could teach more than a few Catholics something about
leading a good life. As they walked down the steps at St.
Joseph's, the air weighed on them like wet wool, yet it did not
dampen the enthusiasm of the 250 well-wishers who tossed rice,
groped for the newlyweds, and popped flashbulbs in their
direction.

The couple bolted toward the waiting car, escorted by
Tommy and Jerry, who cleared a path easily and helped
Marjorie with her long wedding gown as she stepped into the
rented Cadillac. "I love you," Jack whispered in her ear.
"Always and in all ways."

" And I love you, Jack." She moved into his arms. "I hope
it is always like this. I love you so very much."

The hilly road leading to the Colonial Restaurant allowed
members of the wedding and their guests to observe the golfers
on the surrounding course, little ants in the distance slowed
down considerably with the temperature at 98 degrees. At the

107

top of the drive wait staff led them to a special room for the obligatory photos. When Jack and Marjorie entered the reception room, the breezy hostess, acting as if her own children were being married, led the applause. Grant Stanton handed Jack a VO and ginger ale, as the women swept around Marjorie, virtually drowning her with giddy chat about everything and nothing.

"When do you two leave for New York, Jack?" Stanton asked.

"We're staying here tonight and taking the train tomorrow morning. We'll be there for a week."

"You've never been there?"

"No, sir. We're looking forward to seeing some shows, visiting the sights."

"Well, you two just have a great time and..."

Tommy jumped in brandishing his beer. "Hey, big brother. You two looked like something very special together at the church."

"You're the special one, kid," Jack retorted. "Mr. Stanton, Tommy's been fighting almost a year now, and he's 14-0. Soon we'll all be going to New York regularly to see this bum at Madison Square Garden."

"We need you now, Mr. Kelly," an effeminate photographer purred.

In the main reception room Jimma Flaherty, Leo Slattery, Ray Horan, and Vin Sullivan mingled with the many Stanton and Kelly guests. "Pretty fuckin' nice place," Vin offered.

"Watch your fuckin' language," Leo replied.

Waiters in short white jackets moved about the assembly providing glasses of champagne and hors d'oeuvres. Most of the men congregated around the two open bars while awaiting the wedding party, and with the drinks flowing, they did not particularly care about when the sit-down dinner began. "The father-in-law that Jack works for is coming our way," Leo whispered to Jimma as Stanton entered the main room.

As Stanton approached the bar with Jack, Jimma stepped forward. "Mr. Stanton, I'm a friend of Jack's -- James Flaherty."

Stanton offered his hand, "I'm pleased you could be with us today, Mr. Flaherty. What line of business are you in?" he asked.

Jack knew that this kind of situation always found Jimma at his best. He exuded charm and self-confidence, paid strict attention to the conversation, made the other person feel important, reining in the arrogance, the sarcasm, the temper for the occasion. "Real estate, Mr. Stanton. I sell in Boston and a few of the suburbs."

Jack introduced Ray as his longtime friend from Cushman's, Leo as his income tax advisor, and Vinnie, who was harder to explain -- he almost said my friend the legbreaker -- as his friend from the Lynn YMCA.

"It's good to meet you all," Stanton said. "Jack, working in the business, going to college part-time, dating Marjorie -- I don't know where you find the time for friends."

Jack laughed, looking across at Jimma. "There's always time for friends. They're like family to me, Mr. Stanton. Every one of them." He raised his glass, thrusting it forward and clinking it against each of theirs in turn.

"Jack, can I catch you alone for just a minute?" Jimma asked.

"Sure. Please excuse us, all. Let's walk outside, Jimma."

They stood outside, the sounds of "Love Is a Many Splendored Thing" reaching them through the walls. "Jack, I need a favor while you're in New York. Can you handle it for me?" Jimma swigged his drink and tossed the ice cubes across the grass.

"On our honeymoon?" Jack asked.

"It shouldn't take any more than an hour. When you can, call this number in New York and ask for Connie Ryan. He owns the White House Bar on the West Side. When you reach him, tell him you're my representative. He'll want to meet with you. Have you ever heard of him?"

"I don't think so," Jack said.

"He's Mr. West Side, the boss in an area of the city the Irish own. Nobody fucks with him there. Between Eighth and Twelfth Avenue, he's the big guy. He does me a favor every once in a while. I don't know what he wants, but there's something on his mind. He said it couldn't be handled on the phone."

As Jack nodded, Jimma pulled an envelope out of his pocket. "This is for you and Marjorie. Enjoy the big city and have a wonderful honeymoon. Start working on that family," he grinned, embracing Jack.

There would be a delay in starting a new family, Marjorie announced on the train halfway between Boston and New York. She had her period. Wonderful. An auspicious beginning.

They checked into the Hotel Peerless on Madison and 52nd, a moderately priced hotel recommended by Ray, and for the next four days enjoyed the city, even in the sweltering humidity. They visited the Empire State Building, took a ride on the Staten Island Ferry, rented bikes in Central Park, and held hands in the darkness of Radio City Music Hall. In the evenings they ate at Jack Dempsey's, at Lindy's, at the automat in Times Square, and at a small Czechoslovakian restaurant on Second Avenue.

Marjorie, especially, loved the theater. He bought tickets for two musicals, "My Fair Lady" and "The Most Happy Fella," and a play, "A Hatful of Rain," with an exciting new star, Anthony Franciosa.

When they tired of the pace, they sat for hours in the sun at the Battery Park Promenade, looking west to the Hudson and New York Harbor, talking of the magnificent gateway to a new life for immigrants who had come to America in the last half of the nineteenth century. Or they sat in Central Park, across from the Plaza Hotel, on the benches near the Fifth Avenue side, observing humanity passing by, planning their new life together, considering names for the three children they saw in their future.

"I want two boys and a girl," she announced firmly as they stood and walked toward the zoo. "The first born we'll name

Robert, agreed?" And without waiting for a response, "Do you like Susan for a girl's name? And the second boy -- how about Timothy?"

He grinned at her. "Robert, Susan, and Timothy, it will be," he responded, pausing to buy a chocolate-covered ice cream bar from a vendor surrounded by hand-waving little people. The sun slanted through the trees, bathing the pedestrians in flickering light. Small girls in light summer dresses and small boys in long pants and buttoned down shirts raced ahead of their parents. Elderly gentlemen on the benches ignored their activity, instead perusing books or papers in their daily pursuit of knowledge. Young women pushed baby carriages along at a leisurely pace, and young lovers like them walked along hand in hand, confident of the future simply because someone loved them. Marjorie's green eyes sparkled in the light, and, as he smiled at her, she lifted her face toward him kissing his cheek, squeezing his hand.

"Any chance we can get started on building this family this week?" he asked teasingly.

"Wiseass. I'm clean," she answered.

19

On the same Saturday and at the very same hour that Jack and Marjorie were married, Connie Ryan arrived at the Church of the Sacred Heart on West 51st Street between Ninth and Tenth Avenues. Many of Hell's Kitchen's best known families gathered in a festive mood, every one of the approximately three hundred guests enthusiastically greeting one another. After all, one of their own was to be married -- Crazy Johnny Ryan, Connie's brother.

At twenty-eight, with his slick black hair and handsome face, Connie Ryan was especially well liked by the neighborhood's elderly. He dressed in elegant five hundred dollar suits and for years now had bestowed favors on shopowners and saloon keepers along Ninth and Tenth Avenues. If a family were on welfare, he provided money. If he heard a neighbor was hospitalized, he had a fruit basket or flowers sent. At Thanksgiving and Christmas he assured that turkeys were on the tables of families in need. If a father was out of work, he provided for interviews with potential employers.

He had grown up at a time when Hell's Kitchen, like New York City itself, had changed. Following the war, the Ninth Avenue El train had met its demise, and to make way for the new Lincoln Tunnel the areas south of 39th Street had been devastated. Southerners, thousands of them unemployed, flocked to New York City, buoyed by the prospect of jobs. They were joined by a huge influx of Puerto Ricans, forced to work for virtually nothing in their homeland. Although neighborhoods all over the city experienced white flight, Hell's Kitchen was curiously slow to change. The Irish and the Italians

113

were firmly entrenched in the neighborhood's political and economic structures, and they stayed remarkably intact, despite the arrival of new populations.

The Port of New York boomed with post-war trade, enhancing opportunities for West Side racketeers. If longshoremen wanted to work, they kicked back as much as ten or twenty percent of their wages under the vicious shape up system. To make the pay-offs, workers turned to loansharks. In a world of shakedown artists, hijackers and gamblers, Connie Ryan shone. He also controlled the lucrative numbers game throughout the Port and was on intimate terms with the most powerful crime bosses of his day.

But on that brutally hot August day, Connie smoked his cigarette on the steps of Sacred Heart and reflected on the future. He was troubled. He could sense the relatively prosperous Fifties were swiftly coming to an end. The Port was in danger of losing business to the airlines, and if the waterfront suffered, so would he. For some years, Senator Kefauver and Governor Dewey had been pressuring for crime reform on the waterfront, landing hard on corrupt union officials, subpoenaing crime bosses across the city, and generally letting it be known they meant to be taken seriously. This, too, shall pass, he thought, nodding to guests as they entered the church. But to not anticipate change, in this case a certain diminution of revenues through the Port and through its companions -- gambling and loansharking -- would be a fatal mistake.

Without question, the future lay in drugs. Those who understood that fact would thrive; those who did not would be the losers. At meetings with the Mafia chieftains, the heads of the families, he could sense the upcoming dispute. The guineas will be at war over drugs, he suspected. Some families would favor it as a future business line; others would adhere to a strict Catholic abhorrence of its effects, particularly on the young.

But eventually, with its immense profits, it would become the main business line for all of them. He did not want to be left behind. And it would not affect his beloved neighborhood so much. The Irish would still gamble, plaster themselves with alcohol, live, he anticipated, a marginal life if they decided to stay in Hell's Kitchen. He and Johnny would sell to the dumb southern niggers and lazy spics moving into the West Side. Lots of profit in the '60's for sure, he thought.

"Hi, ya, Connie," an overweight, ruddy-faced stevedore named Tim Shea greeted him, decked out in a tuxedo for the occasion.

"Timmy, me lad," Connie extended his hand.

"Himself. Connie, Johnny is marrying a beautiful girl in Francine Nolan, a neighborhood girl of high quality. He's a lucky boyo."

"That he is, Tim. That he is. And I thank you for being with us on this lovely day."

He discarded the cigarette, stepped on it, and entered the church, moving to the extreme side aisle, waving to various guests, noticing that representatives of almost all of New York's families were in the assembly. Johnny was indeed lucky, he thought. Maybe the Nolan girl could help control his temper, curb his tendencies to act before he thought, settle him down. Only time would tell. On this gloriously beautiful day, anything was possible.

On the whole, the future looked bright. If his instincts were correct, they would strengthen their hold on the neighborhood. The guineas left him alone, and he respected their turf, providing them with a cut for allowing him to operate. There was still plenty of profit for everyone. And very few problems. He caught himself for a moment, just prior to entering the area behind the altar. There was the problem of Frankie O'Neill, that prick. But next week he would be meeting with the guy from Boston about shutting that engine down.

The stifling heat held the city hostage right into the following Friday but young lovers visiting the world's greatest city were not concerned. They reveled in its dizzy effects, the relentless energy of its population, the excitement and grandeur of its pulsating life. Above all, they enjoyed each other. On Wednesday they made love for the first time, searching and probing each other's body in the delight of full discovery, the long wait ended, the anticipation satisfied, the joy of fulfillment made richer by their having waited. On both Wednesday and Thursday they hardly ventured from the Peerless, alternating sleeping with making love, their bodies entwined. At rest, they talked of their future together, and Jack felt as relaxed as he had in years. After his mother had been taken, he had committed to family, but until Marjorie entered his life he had wondered whether he could commit to another woman. The thought of giving himself had been too painful. He had loved, and that love had been taken from him. To love again and to lose again would have broken his psyche. He wasn't sure it was possible -- until Marjorie.

Jack ran through the light rain shower on West 45th Street between Sixth and Seventh Avenue and stopped at Johnnie's Restaurant. He entered the brightly lit passage to the cashier's station, noting the signed photos of some of the world's great entertainers filling the stucco walls -- pictures with messages to Johnnie from Sinatra, Brando, Debbie Reynolds, probably a hundred of them in the lobby. He walked straight ahead and was greeted by the man in all the pictures -- Johnnie himself, a middle-aged, blocky man whose outstanding feature was a mane of snow white hair. Two chains complemented his open necked red silk shirt and tight fitting black trousers.

"I'm looking for Mr. Ryan -- Connie Ryan," Jack said wiping the raindrops from his suit.

The host smiled at him. "Welcome to Johnnie's. Let me show you to his table."

They walked through a main dining room with seven or eight round tables covered with checkered table cloths, to a smaller room on the right with three similar tables. Ryan sat facing the entryway, nursing a drink, reading the New York Herald Tribune sports section.

"Mr. Ryan, your guest," Johnnie announced and then walked away.

"Sit down, Jack. I'm Connie Ryan," he said, extending his hand. "I hear very good things about you from Jimma. How about a drink?"

"A pleasure meeting you, Mr. Ryan. Yeah, I'll have some Canadian Club with ginger ale."

Ryan gestured toward the waiter who moved quickly to their table. "Let me have another Manhattan and bring my friend a CC and ginger."

As the waiter stepped away, Ryan reflected on the tall, good looking young man perhaps seven or eight years younger than he. Jack wore a blue suit with a white shirt and maroon tie with a matching pocket handkerchief. He knew enough to dress well for this meeting -- a good sign. He also knew enough to address him as 'Mr. Ryan,' an obvious show of respect, and he knew enough to wait for him to take the lead.

"Jack, I appreciate your meeting with me, particularly when I understand from Jimma that you're on your honeymoon. You and the new bride enjoying New York?"

"It's the first time here for both of us. We're seeing the sights, taking in a few shows -- having a great time."

"Good," Ryan replied, a wide grin on his face. "Jimma tells me you were married last Saturday. It's a small world, Jack. My younger brother Johnny was married on the same day here in New York. They're off to Bermuda this week."

The waiter presented their drinks, taking the time to announce the luncheon specials as well.

"Bring us some antipasto to begin. What else would you like, Jack?" Ryan inquired.

"I'll have the spaghetti with the meat sauce."

"Make it two and bring us some good red wine with it -- your best.

"What did Jimma tell you about this meeting, Jack?" Ryan asked as the waiter left.

"Only that you had a problem and might need our help."

Ryan nodded. "Let me fill you in. Jimma and I go back a long way. We don't know each other well, but sometimes he needs assistance with a situation here in New York, and we've helped. Give you an example -- a good Boston Irish guy moving to New York needs a job. We put him to work on the waterfront. Same thing going the other way. We accommodate one another."

He lit a cigarette, offering the pack of Camels to Jack, who passed. "You have any brothers, Jack?" The change of direction caught Jack by surprise.

"Two. Both younger."

"What do they do?"

"My brother Tommy's a professional boxer on the way up. A middleweight. Undefeated. My brother Jerry's at Harvard. He wants to start his own business some day."

"You close to them?"

Jack studied Ryan for a moment. "Very."

"That's good. That's the way it should be. Life's all about family. How about your parents?"

"They died while we were still kids. I raised my brothers."

The waiter placed enough antipasto in front of them to feed six men. Ryan eyed Jack with admiration. "You did, huh? By yourself? That must not have been easy. Luigi, bring my friend another drink, please."

"I only have my brother Johnny. Our parents are still alive, and I've been able to see them retire to a nice home on Long Island. At East Islip."

Jack liked the relaxed manner in which Ryan approached the subject to be. Dressed elegantly in a powder blue sports coat with a blood red pocket handkerchief, a white shirt and tan trousers, Ryan wore only a Rolex watch for jewelry.

"Johnny is six years younger than me. I would like to think I wasn't as impetuous at that age," Ryan grinned. "I've met some hard-headed boyos, but my brother has to rate high up in that fucking league. His judgment is impaired. Either that, or he's a stupid fuck, which I would like to believe is not the case. I attribute his lack of good judgment to youth, to immaturity and hope the responsibilities associated with marriage will straighten him out. Do your brothers work with you at all?"

"They have no idea that I'm even involved in this life."

Ryan forked some antipasto, ate a bite, and brought the napkin to his lips before responding. "Maybe that's for the best," he finally said. "Jack, let me tell you directly what my problem is. Johnny is involved in our business. But as I said, he's young and less than thoughtful. About three weeks ago, he and a new member of our group, Frankie O'Neill, visited a numbers runner over on West 40th who we knew had been skimming. Probably stole $20,000 from us over the last few months. I don't know what you and Jimma do in Boston, but we don't allow that. We teach lessons when that occurs, and when the word travels around the West Side, then we worry less about its occurring again. You follow me, boyo?"

Jack nodded, knowing that Ryan expected him to listen carefully with few interruptions, to rivet on the story. The waiter delivered two large platters of spaghetti with meat sauce, provided parmesan cheese and quietly moved away.

"Well, Johnny and Frankie caught the prick in his studio apartment and -- the way I'm hearing it -- Johnny split the asshole's head like a watermelon with a baseball bat. Okay so far. The fuckin' thief got what he deserved. This Frankie O'Neill has been with us only a month or two. A Dublin immigrant with shit for brains. But shame on me for not understanding that. I was the one who paired him with Johnny. What I didn't expect was that the dummy was also a fuckin' spigot that never stops dripping. For the next two weeks or so, the scumbag hit the bars around Tenth and Eleventh Avenues describing how Johnny played tunes on the guy's head.

"With Kefauver and Dewey all over us down here the last few years, I need to act even faster than I would ordinarily. If the cops get to Mr. Loudmouth from Dublin, I'm screwed. So far we've been able to avoid their pressure, but I can't risk the exposure. Our sources tell me the feds are trying to locate O'Neill right now."

"Any idea where he is?" Jack asked.

"He skipped town when I sent for him. Someone had to tip him off, or he just panicked, probably guessing why he was sent for. But we located his pal who came over on the boat with him.

We put a blowtorch to his face, which helped his memory. Frankie's somewhere in Boston, he told us. Here's his picture."

"And you want us to find him?"

"Find him and eliminate him for me. As I said, right now with the heat on, I can't afford to involve my group. Tell Jimma I'll be forever grateful if this request is granted," Ryan said. "And, Jack, when I asked Jimma to send someone down here, he identified you as his key man. You understand this is my brother we're talking about? He's in Bermuda now, and I told him he's to fuckin' stay there until I tell him to come back. I want no connection back to him. What I'm saying is, find this asshole fast. I don't want to be supporting the longest honeymoon in Ripley's record book."

Jack proffered his hand across the table. "Mr. Ryan, I'll relate our conversation to Jimma back in Boston tomorrow. We'll get right on it. It'll get done."

Ryan returned Jack's smile. "I hope you'll be personally involved in its resolution, Jack. If you ever need a favor, you let me know." He paid the bill in cash and pulled two tickets from his wallet. "You and the new wife like baseball?"

"I do, but since I took her last year to watch the Sox in a sixteen inning game against the Indians I'm not sure she does."

"Here's two tickets to the Yankees game at the Stadium tonight. Don Larsen against Herb Score. It should be a great game."

Ryan stood to leave. "Those brothers of yours are very fortunate guys, Jack. Take good care of them and yourself as well." Jack watched him stride confidently toward the entry.

Johnny Ryan returned from Bermuda the following Wednesday. It had not been difficult to locate Frankie O'Neill. Jimma had readily agreed that they should honor Ryan's request. In doing so, they would be cementing a relationship with New York's key Irish crime leader. For the next three days, in teams of two, they toured the various bars in Southie, Charlestown, and Mission Hill with copies of the photo Ryan had provided. They asked questions discreetly of those they trusted until on Tuesday

120

the barkeep at Punter's Pub across the street from the Museum of Fine Arts on Huntington Avenue identified Frankie.

Swiping the rag across the bar, Eddie Collins nodded. "Yeah, he's a guy been in here alone every single night. Says he lives on Mission Street up near the Brigham Hospital. Comes in about 8:00."

Jack and Vin parked the stolen Ford Falcon at the corner of Huntington Avenue and Mission Street. From the top of the hill a lone walker descended the steep incline, hands in his pockets, a skullcap visible on his head, despite the August night. As he trudged downward, Jack stepped from the passenger side, moving up the hill so that he could intercept him about thirty yards from Huntington Avenue.

"Frankie O'Neill from Dublin, is it now?" he asked.

"Who the fork are you?" Frankie asked, stopping in his tracks.

"Connie Ryan says hello...and good-bye," Jack said, the revolver appearing from his side. He fired two bullets to the head, watched O'Neill fall backward, and turned quickly down the hill. Vin gunned the car away from the curb as soon as Jack stepped inside, staying within the speed limit, headed toward Kenmore Square.

<u>20</u>

Jack braced himself against the November cold as he left his Lynn Shore Drive garrison. Just after Thanksgiving the northeast winds announced themselves, informing the populace winter was fast coming in, and 1960 was to be no exception.

He crossed the street and descended to the walkway, planning his run toward Swampscott and Marblehead, round trip a distance of six to seven miles. He ran with the wind at his back, buffered by two sweat shirts and long woolen pants. To his right sea gulls swooped in from the east, their endless carping ever a part of their presence. A runner or two ran toward him along the walkway heading toward Lynn Beach, and in both directions walkers of all ages strode along briskly, many holding hands, already yearning for the return of autumn.

He loved to run. Ever since his high school days, he had always found the time for it. Along with the aerobic value of the exercise, he enjoyed the opportunity to think, or to forget. Whether he needed to deal with a particular problem or escape all problems for the moment, running provided him with the perfect outlet.

Today, with the start of a new year in sight, all seemed right in his world. There really were no particular worries. His family was both stable and growing, their future unlimited.

As he passed the high school football field in Swampscott on a steady course toward Marblehead, he began organizing his thoughts, check-listing his many involvements, categorizing their status. He did not find the running monotonous; he relished the opportunity to survey his world. The sun edged through the clouds, its rays warming him as he gathered speed, perspiration now beginning to run down the side of his face despite the cold.

He had never seen Marjorie happier. At work he had progressed to the position of assistant manager under her father. For each of the last four years, Stanton Chevrolet ranked number one in sales in Massachusetts. Between his salary and bonuses he was now making close to $20,000 a year, enough to move them from their first apartment on Maple Street to Lynn Shore Drive. And in five years she had presented him with two sons, Bobby and Timmy, now ages three and two respectively.

He had promised himself he would always be there for them. He would never disappoint them, never leave them rudderless as he had been left. Each would grow into a fine young man, get a college education, become a businessman or engineer or lawyer -- maybe even a United States senator or president.

Just two weeks ago he and Jerry had sat at Jerry's new home at Copeland Road, drinking Guinness and beaming with pride as the major networks proclaimed John F. Kennedy the 35th President of the United States. Anything was possible in this great country of ours, now that one of the boyos was going to be inaugurated in just a few weeks. Bobby and Timmy would lead respectable lives and, like the Kennedys, provide strong public service, particularly for those in need.

Jerry was now a Harvard alum, Class of 1959. With his dedication and diligence he had graduated magna cum laude, while also participating as a member of an outstanding Harvard crew. Jack smiled to himself. The little brother who was not allowed to participate in the Laundry Hill tackle games now stood over 6'2", a heavyweight with bulging muscles and a tapered waist. Upon graduation, he had been offered a position with the Atlantic and Pacific food chain and within the last year had been promoted to district manager. In his senior year he had married Sheila O'Brien, a Cliffie from Philadelphia, a beautiful girl who had borne him a first child, Marty.

For Tommy, 1961 would be the breakthrough year. He had been overly concerned about Santangelo, Jack thought. For five years the manager had brought him along well. The great middleweights of the '50's -- Robinson, Basilio, Fullmer -- all were showing signs of age. Tommy now ranked number three in Ring Magazine's monthly ratings and early in the new year should be in line to fight the number one contender, Sonny Man Hall.

In these five years Tommy had remained fiercely dedicated to his work. Along with the upcoming kid from Louisville, Cassius Clay, he was a favorite of the boxing world. Often compared to the young Robinson, he combined boxing prowess with some deadly artillery, particularly a strong right hand and a God-given ability to counter punch. Just two steps away from the world middleweight championship.

Running toward Deveraux Beach after crossing the Marblehead line, Jack sprinted down Ocean Avenue, racing hard toward the huge canopy that overlay the wooden benches fronting the beach. Thoughts of his brothers' achievements pushed him forward. He thought of their mother, the pride she would have taken in Tommy and Jerry, her work in setting them all right as young men, her insistence they develop values, her kindness and goodness in caring for them in those years before her sickness.

He rested on one of the benches for a few moments before the run back to Lynn. To his left a few walkers sauntered from Marblehead Neck on the causeway toward the beach. It was almost noon now, and the shafts of sunlight widened, cutting down on the cold. He stood and stretched, unable to shake the feeling that his mother would not be proud of him. He faced the sea, bending to touch his toes, reflecting that to guide and protect one family, he had joined another family, specialists in everything from extortion to murder. He, a young man who at one time had contemplated becoming a priest, was a murderer.

The word came vividly into his consciousness, but he didn't linger on it for long. It was history. What was, is. Decisions were made in the context of the time. A drunken father had not been concerned even about feeding his kids. He had deserted them, had left them without hope, young boys caring for a zombie living in his own world with make-believe friends. It had been a horrible time for him and his brothers, and Jack Kelly had chosen his course. He could not recall exactly when he had hardened, but knew he was a very different person at eighteen than he had been at fifteen. He was a man protecting his family, and in the process he had taken responsibility for a new family, come what may.

As he ran against the wind back toward Lynn, he began reflecting on that family as well. He owed much to Jimma Flaherty. For better than seven years now Jimma had provided the loyalty, the protection, the nurturing that his own father had neglected. And, in turn, Jack had become his most trusted associate, along with Leo.

During those years Jack had observed how carefully Jimma operated. All business lines -- loansharking, extortion, prostitution, gambling -- were confined to agreed upon geographical areas. Just as small operators within Jimma's territories brought tribute to him, so, too, did Jimma pay honor to Gennaro Biggio, Mafioso head for New England, in Providence, and to Salvatore "Salvy" Cardoza in Boston. As Jack perceived it, the peace between the Italians and Jimma had been well maintained out of mutual respect. Yet the relationship had always been and would remain tenuous. He had no doubt that Jimma had become wealthy, and those around him very well off through their various illicit activities. In each of the last five years, Jack had received more than two times his salary from Jimma. He had paid for Jerry's college, supported Tommy's early boxing career, bought the new home, provided Tommy with an apartment, put money in a savings account, and squirreled a great deal more in a special place in his bedroom closet. Of course, questions had arisen at home, initiated, he was positive, by Marjorie's father.

Were they living beyond their means? Where was Jack getting the cash to pay for a new home along the beach? Marjorie had inquired. He told her he gambled, which helped explain both his good fortune and his frequent absences from home. And he attributed their newfound prosperity to his clever investments in the stock market.

They could all go fuck themselves, he thought as he looped around Doane's ice cream stand between Fisherman's and King's Beach. They questioned, but they enjoyed the good life he was providing. Stanton himself ought to be jailed for some of the bullshit going down at his dealership. He knew outright thieves in Boston with higher values and morals than his father-in-law showed in his crooked deals.

Eventually, he knew, they would find out. This secret life could not go on indefinitely. But revelation had never been a major concern. He was their father, their protector. They would understand. And if they did not, it would make little difference. He loved them, but, curiously, he did not need their love in return. If they appreciated his efforts, he would be grateful. And, if they did not, then they simply did not understand the obligations of the paternal head of the family, the leader. He needed no one, he thought, as he watched the aggressive sea gulls swoop toward the beach out of the blue sky, descending near the shoreline.

He thought of the future with Jimma. He had been invited within the last few months to a meeting with Cardoza and Jimma, where he sensed serious problems on the horizon, despite the arrangements of the past. Back in 1957, at the famous mob meeting at Apalachin in New York, a ban on dealing in narcotics was voted, yet subsequently was never very effectively enforced. Strong rumors persisted that the vote was taken only to concentrate the immense profits in the hands of the bosses. At the meeting with Cardoza, various speakers argued about the coming of drugs as a line of business. Some anticipated a billion dollar annual industry in the '60's, pointing to the recent influx of Negroes and Puerto Ricans into the big cities and the burgeoning college student population expected throughout the decade. Still others expressed their deep concern about the ultimate consequences of widespread dealing in drugs. Policemen at all levels who might turn their heads at gambling or prostitution would have serious reservations about accommodating dealers. One or two others worried about the effects of marijuana, heroin, cocaine, and LSD, on their own people. We would be poisoning our own, some argued, but the prevailing opinion was that the dummies who became hooked were lost citizens anyway.

Gennaro Biggio, Cardoza reported, believed such a venture was inevitable. Biggio saw himself as a visionary, a leader able to look into the future and anticipate the tumultuous times ahead. He felt the extension of the Cold War into a new decade ensured widespread anxiety, almost guaranteeing that more and more people would turn to drugs for solace. Then, too, the new idealism symbolized by the rise of Kennedy to the presidency would lead to a separation ultimately between parents and children, the establishment and its young, the old and the new. Along with new counter-cultures, he envisioned surging new minorities, now creating turmoil in the South, moving about the country, discouraged with their economic status, turning to drugs and alcohol to right their days.

To Gennaro, the course was determined. Drug trade was an opportunity not to be missed, a boat on which to sail to new lands of opportunity. To his friend of long standing, like him the son of an immigrant from their beloved Sicily, the choice was clear as well. Drugs were evil, Cardoza had declared in Jack's presence at that meeting in Boston, but there really was no decision to be made. The profits ahead would be staggering. In no time at all, drugs would be their number one line of business.

Jimma had quickly declared his support of Biggio's and Cardoza's position to Jack and Leo. Drugs would bring real problems, Jack thought. He envisioned groups far beyond minorities and college kids engaged in their use, probably much of America, irrespective of social class status. In turn, the federal government, citizens groups, state attorneys general, politicians, judges -- many of the very groups both the Mafia and they depended upon for support -- would be, at best, conflicted and, in time, would have to desert them, and even turn against them.

Yet if any group -- Jimma's group or any other -- wished to distance themselves from this new involvement, then they would be overrun by any number of others. He also doubted whether the traditional agreements, the agreed upon boundaries, could ever hold with such profits to be made. In a very short time, he envisioned the birth of any number of splinter groups and the ultimate erosion of the stability they had known throughout the 50's.

Now fully exhausted, he stopped across the street from his house, sitting for a moment on a bench, small beads of perspiration dropping on the concrete before him. Only time would determine the actual outcomes. For the moment, he reflected on the '40's and the '50's. What would drugs mean for his personal world? How would Lynn be effected? He believed he knew the answer. A strong deterioration of the values he and countless numbers of others had been taught was bound to follow, and, very quickly thereafter, a gradual deterioration of his city and its people.

21

Sweat pooled on his eyebrow and descended in rivulets down his jawline, mixing with the blood. Gus Regan, his trainer, worked frantically to stem the cut on the edge of his brow. Santangelo moved up on the apron, imploring him to make an even greater effort. "You're blowing it, kid," he screamed. "We've got two rounds to go -- two rounds from a chance at the number one contender. I need your best effort, son."

Tommy looked out through the smoke toward the Boston Garden crowd, screaming in unison for the hometown hero to end their night. He gulped for air, breathing it in as Regan pulled on his tights, helping him inhale. Vito Astrangio was a worthy opponent but for seven rounds Tommy had dominated him. But in the eighth, the fight had turned. With a measure of resolve that all great athletes muster in difficult times, the middleweight champion of Italy had come alive, landing left hooks and right crosses in strong combinations. Although badly hurt himself, Astrangio had pinned Tommy against the ropes for the last minute of the round. Tommy had been pounded, culminating in his mouthpiece flying as Astrangio landed a solid right just as the bell sounded the end of the eighth round.

Gus placed a flat steel piece under his eye and pressed. With a Q-tip, he then put a coagulate on the streaming cut. "It's not deep, Tom. Just don't let this guy keep hitting on it," Gus ordered.

The buzzer sounded. "Tommy, listen to me," Santangelo barked. "Keep peppering him with your jab. You've got to keep him off you. He's going for broke now. When he comes at you with those wild swings, counter him. Short counters, got it?"

Tommy nodded, looking to ringside directly at Jack and Jerry. Jack motioned with a short forward thrust of his right hand and then pointed back with his thumb to his heart. Tommy smiled, traveling back in time to the early '40's and one cold December day on Laundry Hill. He must have been five years old or so, and a boy a year older had challenged him over some imagined slight. A fight broke out, the other boys forming a circle with their sleds. The older boy had knocked him down with a wild swing of his gloved hand, Tommy landing in the snow, a red trickle forming under his nose. Jack had helped him to his feet, scolding him in a whisper, "Don't you let this shit get the best of you, Tommy. Stick him," he had demonstrated with a thrust of his left hand. "Show some heart," and he had tapped his chest area. Tommy had attacked in a fury, hurling lefts and rights until the older boy fell over one of the sleds and stayed there, avoiding further damage.

As the bell for the ninth round rang, Italian-Americans in the huge crowd waved flags and urged Astrangio on, convinced of a turn in the flow of the battle. Storming out of his corner, Astrangio threw a strong left jab to Tommy's brow, hoping to open the cut quickly. Tommy answered with his own jab, popping it in -- one, two. Astrangio wrestled Tommy to the ropes, and once there, shot a damaging left hook to the eye before the referee separated them.

Tommy sensed the cut in his brow was open again, the blood flowing more profusely. As Astrangio closed toward him, flicking a light left jab, Tommy waited for the opening he knew would come. The Italian looped a right cross behind the left, but its arc was wide, much too wide, allowing Tommy the opportunity to counter in a straight line with a lead right.

Astrangio braked as if for a stop sign, his legs leaving him, forgetting to support him. He fell forward onto his knees, his sweat dripping steadily onto the canvas, his eyes glazed and unseeing. The referee joined the timekeeper in unison as they yelled out the count, "six...seven...eight." Astrangio willed himself off the canvas, staggering to an upright position, raising his gloves to defend himself. But suddenly, just as the referee signaled to Tommy to resume the action, Astrangio's hands drifted to his side. Moving in quickly, the referee threw protective arms around Astrangio, setting off a wild celebration in Tommy's corner.

Rushing into the ring, Santangelo joined the referee in raising Tommy's hand as the crowd applauded wildly in full appreciation of the effort expended by both fighters. "The winner by a technical knockout at one minute, twelve seconds of the ninth round -- Tommy Kelly," screamed the announcer into the overhead mike.

Jack and Jerry arrived at the dressing room just minutes after Tommy. Outside in the corridor reporters clamored for entry as two uniformed policemen guarded the door. With the special badges provided by Petey, the brothers were signaled ahead by the guards. While Santangelo cut away the tape from his hands, Tommy sat on a rubbing table as Gus and a Garden doctor administered to his cut.

"Great win, Tom. For a while there you had us worried," Jerry said.

"He had a lot of us worried," Santangelo retorted. "That Italian kid's got real guts coming back like that after the pounding he took in the early rounds."

"That eye hurt, Tom?" inquired Jack, moving between Gus and the physician. "You okay?"

Tommy snapped his thumb and forefinger together in a sign of dismissal. "The boxer hasn't been born yet who could hurt me."

"Yeah, sure. Famous last words, kid. He almost tore your head off with a couple of those combinations," Santangelo replied cynically.

Tommy grinned at him. "You worry too much, Petey. We're ready for a shot at the champ. Can you get us Fullmer?"

Jack watched Santangelo grimace. His concerns about Santangelo had proven ill-founded. Over a period of six years, Petey had fought off the quick deals, the attempts by the big cigars to move the young fighter into fights that would have overextended him.

"First let's make the match with Sonny Man Hall, Tom. He's the number one contender. One step at a time. We can have the fight in February or March at Madison Square Garden. The big guys want to match you two."

"How tough a fight for him, Petey?" Jack asked.

"Hall's a light hitter, made for Tommy. He is a great boxer though. A lefty. But he's aging, he's had one shot already at Fullmer and lost a close one. We can handle him."

Tommy laughed, "I love this 'we' shit, don't you Jack? 'We' don't get whacked in the eye co-equally, do we, Petey?"

"Can you come out for a drink with Sheila and me, Tom? She's outside waiting now." Jerry asked.

"Give me a half hour, Jerry. The press is waiting. You coming, Jack?"

"No. Marjorie's father asked me to meet him for a drink at the Kowloon at midnight. Some problem he wants to discuss. I'll catch you tomorrow, Tommy, Okay?"

"Okay, Jack."

"And, Tom," Jack said, starting toward the door, "Great finish. That guy had some guts, like Petey says, but you know what? My guy has great heart. See you, champ."

The A-frame of the Kowloon Restaurant hovered over Route 1 like a sentinel guarding the hill. The best Chinese food in Massachusetts, Jack thought, easing his 1961 Chevrolet into the parking lot. Too bad more restaurateurs did not appreciate the value of providing long time regular customers with a free first round of drinks, as the Wong family did.

He walked through the main entry extending greetings to the maitre d', declining a table and heading toward the circular bar at the rear. Grant Stanton sat by himself, nursing the last of a mai tai and looking like he had lost his best friend.

"Hello, Grant." Jack greeted his father-in-law, sliding into the seat next to him. "What's happening? Same as him, Sam," he addressed the bartender. "And another for my friend."

134

Stanton touched his lips with his napkin and sighed. "I had a visitor this afternoon, and he wasn't there to buy a car. Guy comes in about 5 P.M. and asks for me. Tells Stella he has a message for me and that it must be delivered personally. So she buzzes me, and I tell her to send him back to my office. This big white guy with a flat-top walks in. Tall, about 200 pounds, with a fairly pronounced scar above his upper lip. I told him to have a seat. Says his name is Richie Giarusso, and he's there representing Nick Rizzo of Revere. I say, 'Are you buying or selling? What can I do for you?' 'What you can do,' he says, 'is fork over five grand a month to Rizzo for protection, for insurance in case, say, the agency burned down.'

"Burned down? I say, after picking myself up off the floor. I told him he better leave before I called the police, and he said that would be a very serious mistake both for the agency and for me. Then he stood and walked to the door saying he would be back in a week for the first payment. 'Don't fuck up,' he says to me.

"Jesus, Jack. What do I do? I needed to talk to someone." Stanton gulped the second mai tai, glancing furtively around as soon as he set his glass down.

Jack stared at the assembly of tables, the buzz of the crowd and the three-piece band drowning out most private conversations at 12:30 A.M. "Do nothing, Grant. Just leave the matter to me. I'll get back to you."

"What can you do, Jack? Shouldn't we call the police?"

"I'll meet with this Giarusso. We'll see if we can reach a mutually accommodating resolution. I have some Revere friends who should be able to get me in contact with him."

He placed his hand on Stanton's arm. "Just go home and relax, Grant. You've done a lot for me. Go home and give me an opportunity to work this out for you before you involve the police or anyone else."

After Stanton left, he sat alone fuming over a second mai tai. From the Kowloon lobby he dialed the Revere number. He listened to the band playing "Lipstick on Your Collar" while the phone rang.

135

"Yeah?" a surly voice finally answered.

"Is Nick there?" Jack asked.

"Who wants to know?"

"Tell him Jack Kelly wants to see him tomorrow night -- just for a few minutes."

"Yeah, okay. We'll get back to you. He knows how to reach you?"

"He knows," Jack replied, then hung up the phone.

22

"That Dr. Kinsey says the niggers have bigger schlongs than white guys," Vinnie Sullivan reported.

"What the fuck does he know about it? What's he go around Harlem measuring their dogs?" Freddie Quinlan replied.

"They have ways to measure public opinion, ways to measure the replies of the people. It is a very precise scientific process," Leo Slattery said.

"Measure this," offered Freddie.

"Jesus, don't you guys ever read the papers. Stay up with what's going on in the world?" Leo sighed.

They sat at a rear table at the Powerhouse Tavern at Sumner and East 1st Streets in South Boston, a favorite hangout. There were no waitresses, attractive or otherwise. Inside the door stood a jukebox and a cigarette machine. The bar ran the full length of the area to the right of the entrance. An Irish flag adorned the wall behind the bar, with pictures of John Kennedy, Michael Collins, James Michael Curley above it. Two pool tables took up most of the left rear of the room. In the far corner, right rear, a singular men's room was fronted by swinging doors. There was no thought given to the possibility that a woman might ever need to use the rest room.

Regulars sat at the bar and at the tables in front of it. Regulars of all ages -- the old-timers, nursing their drinks alone, lost in memories; longshoremen ending their grueling day by hoisting beers, enjoying the camaraderie of their own, oblivious to the other patrons; and young Irish toughs, just barely of drinking age, strutting about seeking recognition, defying the others not to notice them.

"I fucking read, Leo," Vinnie protested. "I'm reading about those fuckin' smokies starting to move into our neighborhoods, more and more that's what I'm reading -- Dorchester, Jamaica Plain, Hyde Park. And I don't like it. The guineas belong in East Boston, the niggers in Roxbury and we belong in Southie, Charlestown, and on Mission Hill. That's been the agreement for years."

"You guys don't even live here. I do," said Freddie Quinlan. "Louise Day Hicks -- the lady from City Point? -- she tells it like it is. We're going to have war in this city if those liberal assholes don't back off. Fuckin' Kennedys are forgetting their own."

Jack sipped his highball, signaling Eddie Grogan, the bartender, for a refill.

"What do you think, Jack?" asked Leo.

"I agree with Freddie. Rough times are ahead. But in the end just as we gained rights to jobs, to respect, from the Yankees -- do any of you remember those 'No Irish need apply' signs? -- so won't the colored. They deserve a better life just like we did, and they are going to be much less patient about getting it."

Jack sensed the men's strong respect for him. When he spoke, they listened. In the past year they had been drawn strongly toward him. He had been concerned that Leo might be offended, but Leo had raised the topic himself one night when they were together. He was growing older, he said, and he knew his limitations. He bragged that he could handle the action as well as anyone, including Jimma or Jack, but he knew he didn't see the big picture as well as they did. He harbored no resentment, as life had treated him well. And he was particularly proud of his protégé's progress.

"Jack, a call for you," Eddie Grogan yelled from behind the bar.

Nick Rizzo waved to him as he moved through the tables at the Shawmut Grill on Boston Street in Lynn. About forty years old and chubby, Rizzo possessed the look of a man who harbored grudges. Beady eyes lost in a sea of fat stared out from skin burnished brown from frequent trips south. His black hair, containing but a few strands of gray, was slicked back, coated with heavy applications of grease.

"Sit down, Jack. What'll you have?"

"Nothing, Nick. This isn't exactly a social call. I thought we had a deal?"

"What are you talkin' about?"

"I'm talking about a visit to Stanton Chevrolet on the Lynnway made recently by Richie on your behalf, Nick. Seeking protection money from my fucking father-in-law."

"Jack, your father-in-law? I didn't know that, so help me," Nick replied, fidgeting in his chair.

"Let's talk about what you do know, Nick. You know division, don't you? You know where your territory supposedly begins and ends. Right, Nick?"

He didn't wait for an answer.

"Nick, keep the fuck out of Lynn. You have most of Revere, East Boston, and Jimma and I have respected those boundaries. Show us the same respect."

Rizzo smiled and nodded, extending his hand across the table. "Jack, so help me. Richie must have gotten overzealous. That dumb shit don't know one side of the General Edwards Bridge from the other. I'll correct this situation. Believe me, no offense intended."

Jack left his hand dangling across the table. "Nick, this is not the first time we've had this problem. It better be the last time."

"You threatening me, Jack?" Rizzo changed his tone.

"Take it any way you want, Nick. Just keep the fuck out of our areas."

He rose and strode toward the front door, Rizzo staring at his back. That Irish prick is asking for it, Rizzo thought. Some day he hoped his cousin's husband, Gennaro Biggio, would give him the signal to take both Flaherty and Kelly down. He would enjoy that day. In the meantime, he would have to speak to Giarusso. His dumb lieutenant couldn't do much right. He had asked him to be careful about their planned incursions into

Lynn. He might as well have talked to the fuckin' wall. Richie goes after the father-in-law of Jack Kelly. He ought to drop the asshole off the bridge separating Lynn from Revere.

True to the forecast, Boston was hit with a full-blown blizzard on Christmas Day, 1961. Big wind-driven flakes swirled about Copeland Road as Jack, Marjorie, Bobby and Timmy ran toward Jerry's front door. Before they pushed the bell, Sheila appeared, greeting them effusively, carrying little Marty in her arms and steering them into the warmth of the front hall.

From the living room above them Jerry yelled Christmas greetings, causing Bobby and Timmy to race up the carpeted stairs. Jerry scooped Timmy into his arms as Bobby wrapped his arms around his uncle's legs. "Merry Christmas, kids," Jerry said. "How about some cocoa or egg nog? What do you say to that, guys?"

"I'd like some cocoa," replied Bobby shyly.

"Well then, let's hit the kitchen, men. Let me take your coats. Sheila, can you get Jack's and Marjorie's coats and get them a drink?" He kissed her as he asked, admiring her full, shining brown hair, thick enough to bury yourself in, he thought. She was only a few inches shorter than he and he liked that.

Sheila walked into the living room, her brown eyes shimmering. "A highball, Jack? Right?"

"I'll have some of that egg nog you're selling, Sheila," Marjorie said.

In a far corner of the living room a tall hemlock almost touched the high ceiling. At its top a Christmas angel glowed, arms extended. Branch to branch, long strands of white tinsel wound around equally long strands of lights, and bulbs were freely sprinkled throughout its fullness. At its base lay piles of gaily wrapped packages. Jack stood in front of it, studying it, his mind elsewhere. After a time, he walked toward the kitchen.

"Do you remember when we were kids, Jerry? There would be one big present for each of us. Maybe supplemented by two or three lesser gifts like coloring books. Remember? You know, I think we appreciated Christmas more then than people do today."

Jerry bounced Bobby on one knee and Timmy on the other while he attempted to balance his scotch and water at the same time. "I can remember you receiving a Gene Autry gun and holster set when you were around six or seven," Jerry said. "You chased Tommy and me around the house until New Year's Day. When you caught us, you tied us up. Nice brother," he laughed.

"Well, you got to admit it beat the times when I dressed up like a nun, like Sister Superior, and you and Tommy were my pupils."

"Don't remind me. I still have the sores from the whacks you gave us."

The doorbell rang, and Sheila shouted, "I'll get it, hon."

Tommy lunged at Sheila from the doorway, lifting her, swirling her in a semi-circle. "Merry Christmas, sister," he said. From the kitchen Jack's boys ran down the stairs to embrace their uncle who set Sheila down to grab a boy in each arm, lifting them skyward. Standing slightly behind Tommy, a young woman smiled at them all, as he turned toward her.

"Sheila, this is Nancy Huff. Nancy, my sister-in-law Sheila," Tommy said.

"It's a pleasure meeting you, Sheila," Nancy said, extending her hand.

Nancy looked almost too good to be true -- creamy skin, pretty face, perky. She had the look of an angel, and a body like mortal sin, Sheila thought as she took Nancy's coat.

"So this is the young lady we finally get to meet," Jerry said from above them.

"You must be Jerry," Nancy said, climbing the stairs.

"He is that. And the other joker is my brother Jack," Tommy said as Jack appeared in the doorway.

"Please everyone. Come into the living room. What can I get you two to drink?" Jerry asked.

"Only a Coke for me. I'm in training," Tommy replied. "Scotch and water for Nancy."

For one reason or another, mostly tied to his travel schedule, Tommy had not yet introduced them to Nancy. They had met three months ago when both had been guests at the wedding of Nancy's cousin. And since then, they had been inseparable, spending any time he had free together.

"Where are you from, Nancy?" Jerry asked, handing her the drink.

"New York City, originally. But my family moved to Boston while I was in high school. After graduation, I attended Forsyth Dental School. I'm now a dental hygienist in Marblehead, and I rent an apartment there," she answered.

"All right, guys. Let's not give my lady the third degree. Besides which, I have great news for all of you." He paused, seeking their attention. "We signed the contract yesterday. The fight is on for February 6 at Madison Square Garden," he beamed. Loud whoops of excitement filled the room.

"How's that for a great Christmas present? One step from the middleweight championship," Tommy said. "If I beat Hall, then Gene Fullmer and I will fight for the title later this summer."

"What a match that will be," Jerry said. "Where will it be held? Yankee Stadium?"

"First things first, Jerry," Jack cautioned. "Sonny Man Hall's no picnic, and you'll be fighting him in his hometown, Tom."

Tommy leaned forward, desire burning in his eyes. "I know I can beat him, Jack. He's cagey, a real ring war-horse. But I've been waiting all my life for this chance, training days and nights, sacrificing. I'm not going to lose." He pounded one hand into the other to emphasize his point.

Jack grinned across the glass table, scanning the room, observing Tommy and Nancy; Jerry, Sheila, and little Marty; his own family. He remembered taking his two brothers to both Thanksgiving and Christmas dinner at Carroll's Diner on Union Street when they were teenagers. The three of them all alone on the holidays. Bitter Thanksgivings and bitter Christmases as well. And now, they were all together, surrounded by warmth and love and family.

23

In the week after New Year's Day snow fell intermittently, with northeast winds buffeting the coast, unrelenting in their intensity. Temperatures hovered near zero most of each day, causing most Bostonians to pray for an early spring. Jimma had asked to see him on the Tuesday following New Year's Day. He had called on Monday, ostensibly to wish Jack a happy new year but quickly mentioning the need for a get-together on Tuesday night, a matter of some importance, he had added.

They sat in the main dining room at Fantasia, just off Fresh Pond Circle in Cambridge, a favorite spot for dinner, just the two of them. "Thanks for coming out on such a horseshit night, Jack. I appreciate it. As I mentioned on the phone, a very important matter has to be addressed."

"What's up?" Jack asked.

"You remember Connie Ryan? New York?"

"How can I forget him. We did him a big favor."

"He called me last weekend. There's a big deal going down in New York." He paused, "It concerns your brother."

Alarm bells went off in Jack's head. "My brother?" Jack replied quizzically. "What business has Ryan with my brother? Who? Tom or Jerry?"

"It's Tom, Jack. Connie says the odds on the fight next month are 3-1 on Tommy to beat Sonny Man Hall." He spoke confidently, as if whatever the matter, he had it under total control.

"That's no surprise, Jimma. Tommy's going all the way, and Hall's slowing down. He had a crack at Fullmer before and lost."

"Jack, let me explain the situation to you. The Italian mob and Ryan work together in New York, same as we do here. Together, they control the fight racket in New York, and particularly at Madison Square Garden -- the fights, the labor force, the whole shebang."

"What are you telling me, Jimma?"

"I'm telling you the fix is on, Jack. That's what I'm telling you. Do I have to draw you a fuckin' diagram? At fight time the odds should be 4 to 1, maybe 5 to 1 for Tommy. Ryan's going for Hall to win. The kind of money they will lay down will give them millions in return. Tommy will be covered for a piece of the action, and in a year or so he'll receive a legitimate shot at the title.

"I need you to talk to Tommy. Explain the situation to him. He'll listen to you. He's always listened to you," Jimma spoke quickly. "He's to be knocked out, Jack. That price will be 6 or 7 to 1. Connie promises us -- you and me -- a serious piece of the action as well."

Jack had stopped eating as soon as Jimma had mentioned Tommy's name. He felt sick to his stomach, the bland scrod mixing with the bile rising in his throat to cause the sour taste in his mouth. "I'm going to tell my brother, who I've taught to give everything to whatever he undertakes, to fall down? I don't think so, Jimma."

Jimma sighed, the anger building in his voice. "Let me try this one more fuckin' time. You know Ryan's influence on the West Side. In the last five years he's become even stronger -- boxing, union growth, the docks. He's not to be trifled with.

"He called me directly, Jack. He knows Tommy's your brother. And that's why he's cutting us in for a big piece. Jack, they'll make five million down there -- Connie and his group -- and we'll be in for close to a half million for sure. We have no choice concerning cooperation. Ryan expects my commitment, and I expect yours. We're talking about mutually satisfying accommodations here. You following me?"

Jack's lips thinned, as he silently counted to ten. He knew it was very important to contain anger in particularly difficult situations. He thought carefully before speaking, trying to control himself, hoping that Flaherty could not read his body language -- the thinning lips, the cold eyes, the rising redness in his winter pale complexion.

"Jimma, I'll speak to Tommy," he finally answered.

"Good," replied Jimma, leaning back in the booth.

"But not until I first meet with Connie Ryan."

"What the fuck are you talking about? I'm giving you a direct order. I expect it to be honored."

He needed to relax Flaherty before they reached a point of no return. "Jimma," he began slowly, "you and I are friends. I would like to think, more than friends. I consider you like my father, my mentor. You should know I intend no disrespect. And after what we have been through together for almost ten years, I hope you can both understand and honor my request.

"You know Tommy knows nothing about my involvement in the life. Nothing. I'll approach him because I just told you I would. That by itself is going to change my relationship with my brother, a brother who sees me as I see you.

"But you and I did one big favor for Connie Ryan, a family favor that advantaged his brother. I want to see him again, to appeal to him directly to see if I can persuade him to forego this deal. It was a matter of family for Ryan, Jimma, and now it's a matter of family for me. I need to talk to Ryan."

Jimma scowled in his chair, irritated and annoyed by Jack's request. Jack was always careful with his words, as he knew Jimma could not tolerate challenges to his authority. Yet for now he needed Jack. If Jimma refused his request, he would cause an open breech. Jack guessed he would let him see Ryan. But pretty soon Jimma would find a reason to eliminate Jack Kelly altogether.

"Go see the fuckin' guy, Jack," Jimma finally said. "I'll call him and set it up. Then, whatever that outcome, we move on. Agreed?"

"Agreed, Jimma." He raised his glass, smiling, trying to demonstrate his gratitude.

"Happy New Year, Jack," Jimma said, lifting his glass, forcing a smile.

"And to you, Jimma," Jack touched his glass to Flaherty's. Were his lips full? Was the redness in his face receding? Had his eyes warmed as they spoke? He hoped so. Happy New Year, my ass, he thought. The beginning of 1962 would mark the beginning of the end of his relationship with Flaherty. His mutually satisfying accommodation for 1962 would be to assist Jimma in meeting his maker.

"What's it been, almost six years, Jack?" Connie Ryan asked as they sat in the lounge of the Red Coach Grill on Broadway at 51st Street. A short-skirted waitress dressed in the Howard Johnson-owned chain's traditional red uniform with meshed stockings served them a round, practically as soon as they ordered.

"Will that be all, Mr. Ryan?" she asked.

"For now, Dottie," Ryan smiled at her.

She reminded Jack of the circle of life. At fifty, she had obviously worked hard to appear twenty-five, the paint and powder heavily applied to hide the signs of advancing age. Forcing smiles at the customers, she looked tired, as if lifetime dreams had passed her by, and here she was playing out the string with so little to look forward to. We all age, he thought, and so few of us attain our early dreams. Across the room a second waitress, perhaps half Dottie's age, flirted with the wealthy customers from the nearby hotels. Her eyes were alive with life, her laugh contagious, her walk brisk and sexy. If he were to come back in twenty years, would she still be here? Her dreams shattered? Her ambitions gone? He thought of Tommy and the circle of life, and he suddenly felt cold.

"Jack, I wanted you to meet Johnny. That's why I asked him to join us. You did us a great favor for which we are both forever grateful. Right, Johnny?"

Johnny's attention was torn between watching Dottie's retreating ass and the waitress half her age across the room so he missed his cue. "Johnny?" Connie repeated harshly.

"Yeah. Right, Connie. I appreciated your taking down that fuckin' squealer, O'Neill, Jack. We heard you were the shooter," Johnny recovered.

"It was important for your brother and, therefore, it became important for Jimma and me," Jack replied.

"How are things going in Boston, Jack?" Connie asked.

Jack noted that the dashing good looks were still there. Ryan must be about thirty-five now, he calculated, and he cared for himself. He remained fit. The wavy black hair was cut shorter, in a '60's style wiffle, but that only accentuated the strong features -- the straight nose, blue eyes, the mirthful smile. In contrast, Johnny reminded him of Dottie and her colleague. Probably thirty years old, his face showed signs of the hard life he followed. He looked like the older brother. Touches of gray dotted his hair, and little crow's feet touched the sides of his eyes. His attention span was minus zero. Jack hypothesized that Connie had his hands full keeping his brother focused.

"We're doing well, Connie," Jack responded. "We're working well with Salvatore Cardoza. Jimma's done right by all of us."

"And I hear you're his number one guy now," Ryan said.

Jack shrugged.

"Drug traffic increasing there yet?" Ryan asked. The only traffic Johnny seemed interested in was that represented by virtually any female who appeared in the lounge area.

"Biggio sees narcotics increasing each year throughout the '60's."

"Biggio's right, Jack. It's our future. I'd prefer to stay with the unions, prostitution, the bookies -- the old traditional lines -- but they're not growth industries, like coke and heroin. The heavy money is going to be in drugs." He signaled to Dottie for another round.

"We going to Brian's later?" Johnny asked.

"Johnny, stay the fuck involved in this conversation, will you? You might learn something.

"Excuse me, Jack. But my brother has the attention span of a fuckin' ant. I have to constantly remind him that there's more

149

to life than chasing pussy or downing highballs. Some fuckin' day I'll be attending his funeral and the fuckin' headstone will read 'Dead for failure to pay attention to detail'."

Johnny stared at his brother.

"Jack, Jimma tells me you want to see me about the upcoming fight. Your brother Tommy has really progressed. Imagine, fighting for the right to take on the champion of the world. I remember you telling me about him when we first met."

"He's done very well, Connie. I..."

"Boyo, there will be another day for him," Connie deliberately interjected, a lilt in his voice. "But I interrupted you. Go ahead."

"Connie, I'm sure Jimma told you why I asked to see you. You're asking me to do a tough thing. For openers, Tommy doesn't even know I'm in the life. And you're asking me to get him to throw the fight he's been training for all his life."

"What are you, crazy?" Johnny stared at him, incredulous.

"Shut the fuck up, Johnny. I want to listen to my friend. Excuse my impetuous brother, Jack. If he ever is paying attention, he can't help ending conversations before he even knows what the fuckin' issues are.

"Jack, I know we're asking a great deal of you and of Tommy. As of this morning the odds are 4 to 1 against Sonny Man. They could shift prior to the night itself, upward to 5 to 1. Your brother's fought in New York before, and along with Clay is the most popular fighter around today. He's going to be a top heavy favorite. My partners on the West Side and I figure to make five million or more. I hope Jimma told you both you and your brother are going to be well covered."

"Connie," Jack interrupted, "I appreciate that. I do. But that's not the issue. I don't give a shit about the money. You once came to me asking for a favor, one very important to you, because it involved your brother. You told me then that if I ever needed a favor to come to you. There's still two weeks to go and most of the heavy bets won't do down until two or three days before the fight. I'm asking you to call this deal off, as a personal favor to me, a favor for which I would be very grateful."

Connie stared thoughtfully at Jack and then turned to look at Johnny, who concentrated now on the conversation yet hesitated to speak. When Connie spoke again, the lilt had left his voice, and a firmness and edginess had replaced it. He leaned across the table. "Listen carefully, Jack. I have a couple of boyo partners in this business deal, and our investments have been made and will continue to be made. I expect your cooperation and that of your brother in this matter. I'm sorry, but you're making a fuckin' mountain out of a molehill. My answer is no. This is business. Do you understand?"

"Are the Italians involved in this?" Jack asked.

"Only indirectly. It's my deal."

"Then I don't understand why it can't be changed. I don't like it."

Connie's eyebrows raised. "What does that mean?"

"Who gives a shit what you like?" Johnny said.

"It means just what I said. I don't like it, Connie. But, I told Jimma I'll talk to him."

"He'll listen to you?"

"Yeah, he'll listen. He'll listen to a brother he regards as a father telling him he has to lose a fight he knows he can win. Telling him all he has worked hard for until now isn't going to happen."

"He's still got a future."

"Has he, Connie? Doesn't that all depend on what fuckin' business deals there are in that future?" Jack asked sarcastically. Connie glared at him.

Jack threw a twenty on the table. "I thank you for the time, Connie. I'm catching the 10:00 o'clock shuttle." He nodded at Johnny, stood, and walked toward the door.

From inside, Connie studied him as he raised his arm to hail a cab. A man to be watched, he thought. The deal would happen. After all, he had Flaherty's assurance. But he had long ago learned that men of conviction were the most dangerous. He

151

admired Kelly, and if he were Flaherty, he would watch his back.

"Can we go over to Brian's place now, Connie?" Johnny broke into his thoughts.

"Shut the fuck up, Johnny."

24

Tommy pummeled the heavy bag, ripping left hooks and right crosses into the hanging leather, actually denting it with the ferocity of his attack. As Gus Regan gripped the bag from behind, Santangelo nodded approvingly at his boxer's pace, relentless energy and dedication.

Although most boxers preferred Valenti's Gym near the Boston Garden for training, Santangelo favored the dingy rear area of the Boston Arena. Tommy preferred readying himself in Boston, where he enjoyed the camaraderie of the other local boxers -- Paul Pender, Tom McNeeley, and any number of up and coming bangers trying to make their marks. He also loved to run through the streets of Boston, over to Cambridge or South Boston and back to the North End, merchants and pedestrians alike recognizing him and urging him on as he jogged. With obvious pride in the local boy making good, they would yell to him as he passed.

"You look great, Tom."

"Best of luck against Sonny Man, Tommy."

"One step more, champ!"

Only two more weeks, he thought as he banged away, imagining that Sonny Man's stomach, and not the bag, was taking his blows. He would leave for New York City tomorrow and finish his work at Stillman's Gym in Manhattan.

Hall would be tough and dangerous. A crafty left-hander, he knew all the tricks and was a superior boxer. A few months ago Gene Fullmer, the champion, had outpointed him in a close fight, so now Hall had something to prove. He had to win. If Tommy beat him decisively, he would be through as a top contender. And though aging, Sonny Man Hall still possessed the heart of a lion.

To ready his boy, Santangelo had imported a group of left-handed middleweights and heavyweights, but Tommy drove through all of them. Santangelo was a teacher, and Tommy an apt pupil. "Circle to the left against a southpaw. Bend. Don't allow him to jab. Bend and move in. Drive those shots to his body early and often. Loosen him up. Later, when he's slowed down, we'll bang at his head.

"Time, Tommy," Santangelo announced. "That's it for today. Take a shower."

Not wishing to interrupt, Jack had stood in the back of the Arena Annex. As he walked toward them, he wondered if Petey knew anything about Ryan and the fix. Probably not. The West Side guys were depending on Flaherty and him to deliver Tommy.

"How you doing, Jack?" Santangelo asked.

"Fine, Petey. That cut eye holding up?"

"So far there's no problem, but I worry."

"You always worry, Petey. Hey, big brother, how's it going?" Tommy asked, as Regan dropped a robe over his shoulders.

"Tom, I need just a little time after you shower. Can we sit for a minute in the Arena?"

"Sure, Jack. Be right with you." Tommy replied, turning toward the locker rooms.

"I'll be in the grandstand."

The Northeastern University hockey team raced up and down the ice, as the coach yelled out instructions. "Stop! Skate! Stop! Skate!" And young men in red and black obeyed the commands, probably wondering what this excruciating activity had to do with winning hockey games. Jack watched them without thinking much about hockey, however. He thought only about how to introduce this difficult subject, just as he had thought about little else for the last two weeks.

Tommy eased into the end seat. "What's happening?"

154

"Hey, you're looking pretty good there, boyo. But the heavy bag doesn't punch back."

"I'm ready, Jack. I can beat him. I'm stronger than him, and stronger than Fullmer. I can taste it, Jack. We're almost there."

Jack shifted almost imperceptibly in his seat. "Tom, I need to talk with you."

"So talk, I'm listening, big brother."

"Tom, it's about me."

"Now there's a twist. Do you realize how infrequently I have heard you talk about you?"

"Tommy, listen to me carefully. I need to tell you a few things." He paused for a moment. "You know things aren't always what they appear to be."

"What's that supposed to mean?"

"You know I work for Marjorie's father on the Lynnway. But what you don't know is that I'm involved in some other..."

"I know you work with Jimma Flaherty."

Stunned, Jack sat upright in his seat. "How do you know that?"

"Jack, I've been fighting for almost six years now. If there is any other business closer to the rackets than this shit, I don't know what it is. In the last two or three years one wise guy or another around the gym says to me 'Your brother Jack's with Jimma,' or 'Flaherty and your brother have a piece of the bookies.'

"I've known for at least two years, Jack. But even when I was starting out, don't you think I wondered where the cash you gave me was coming from? It didn't make sense that a job in a bakery and betting on dogs and nags could provide for all of us and send Jerry to college."

Jack looked straight ahead. "I should have told you and Jerry a long time ago. But how do you tell the people you love that you aren't what they think? And how do you tell them you're involved in the rackets?"

Tommy tapped his chin lightly. "I don't care *what* you are, because I know *who* you are. Do you think guys in this fucking

155

racket of mine are pure white? There's a lot of stuff I'm not so proud of that I just don't talk about."

Below them the Northeastern wingers peppered the goal with shot after shot. "Cut down on the angle when the shots are coming from the wing!" the coach roared at the goalie.

"Jerry or anyone else know anything about me?" Jack asked.

"Not from me. I don't think so."

Jack mulled his response, as he focused on the practice session below. He was stunned for the moment, having never anticipated that Tommy would know of his other life. Did others know or suspect? Probably not, he thought. Yet he should have recognized the connection to Tommy's world.

But it was the next part of their conversation that most concerned him. For the last two weeks he had thought of the way he would introduce Ryan's and Flaherty's scheme to his brother. Ultimately, he had decided to tell him directly and then describe the plan he had developed.

When he did not respond right away, Tommy took it as a sign that Jack was despondent about the revelation. "Hey, I told you it doesn't matter to me. You're my brother."

"Tommy, I appreciate that so much, so very, very much," Jack said as he leaned forward in his seat. "But there's another piece to all of this. Have you ever heard of a guy named Connie Ryan, from New York?"

"I know who he is. He's big time in New York as far as the fights are concerned. You don't fight in New York without his say so, according to Petey."

"You don't do a lot of things in New York without his say so," Jack said. "He's also into union kickbacks, gambling, prostitution, extortion, on the West Side."

"Do you know him?"

"Yes, I do. Flaherty and he are connected buddies. I've met him once or twice through Jimma."

"So what's he got to do with you or me?"

"Ryan wants you to take a dive against Sonny Man Hall, Tom. Ryan and some of his Irish friends down there figure you'll go off a 4-1 favorite. Maybe even 6-1 that Hall won't

156

knock you out. They figure to make a big killing, five million minimum."

For a moment, Tommy just sat staring straight ahead at the Arena ice. "Jesus, Mary, and Joseph," he finally replied. "Jack, are you telling me to deliberately throw this fight? Because if you are..." His voice level rose with each word.

"Tommy, hold on. Flaherty and Ryan asked that I reach you, talk to you. That's all I told them I would do."

"You know I can't do that, Jack, and I won't do it. Not after all I had to sacrifice..."

He gripped Tommy's forearm. "Did I ask you to do anything? We're not going to throw anything, Tom. But we're going to have to be smarter than those two. They play rough, and they're not fools. You win, there could be repercussions. You need to know what we're dealing with, that's what I'm telling you today.

"I'll handle those two. You just concentrate on Sonny Man. If I ever tip them off ahead of the fight that you're not going in the tank, they'll cancel the fight. Ryan will concoct some story, like Hall cutting himself training or straining an elbow. They'll cut you right out of the fight. You beat him, then there'll be public pressure for the Fullmer fight."

Tommy nodded, reacting very slowly. "We don't deserve this deal, Jack. You can't get Ryan to back off?"

"I tried, Tom. I visited him in New York. No go. They laid down too much money already. But even if they hadn't, they don't give a shit about us, that's clear."

"I'm going to take him, Jack."

"Just go for it, Tom. You do your job, and I'll take care of the rest."

"Something new, huh?" Tommy managed a smile.

"Where are you staying in New York?" Jack asked as he stood.

"The Mayflower. Central Park West right off Columbus Circle. I can run in the Park across the street."

"I'll see you down there a few days before the fight, champ. We'll be all right," he said as he started to climb the stairs of the old Arena.

Ryan loved to play cards at Tommy Murphy's Social Club, a first floor walk-up at 722 10th Avenue. Today, like all days, he had a dozen or more runners out collecting the three digit numbers and the money to go with them. Suckers, he thought. With an anticipated payoff of 500 to 1, the numbers attracted non-gamblers as much as the pros. He had to split the profits, and the profits from all his other enterprises with La Cosa Nostra, the "Five Families." He accepted that fact, and he held his guard high at the same time. He didn't trust the guineas, and he was sure they didn't trust him. But together they thrived, working the docks, and the unions in particular, and they had scored big time with the building of the New York Coliseum in 1956.

He pondered his call to Flaherty that very afternoon. He had been assured that Tommy Kelly had been reached and that the fix was on. Yes, of course, Jack had spoken to his brother, Jimma had reported. And put Jimma himself in for $200,000 of that price on Hall, Flaherty had added. With only a week to the fight, something gnawed at him. Something just didn't feel right. He glanced at the full house in his hands and flicked ash from his cigarette onto the floor. Maybe he worried too much. But in this game, he had long ago learned, you could never worry enough. He'd better talk again to the kid's brother.

25

Crazy Johnny Ryan sat alone at the far end of the bar at the White House at 10th Avenue and 45th Street. His left hand was swelling badly, but the bucket of ice water Joey had provided alleviated the pain.

That fuckin' Little Eddie Sheehan, he fumed. He and his crowd obviously thought Connie an antique. On the West Side there would always be challenges from the young guys who lived to replace the Ryan brothers. For years, despite the brutal way in which they dealt with challengers, someone would always come forward, someone like them, fresh from a life of poverty vying for position. But in Little Eddie's case ambition was enhanced by a thirst for revenge. Some years ago Connie had Eddie's father eliminated for skimming big time on them, and now that Sheehan had just returned from a short term at Sing Sing, word had reached them that he intended to move against them.

Earlier that evening, Johnny had taken care of the problem as Connie had directed. He had walked down Tenth Avenue and let himself into one of the buildings with a jimmy bar. Moving to the top floor, he identified the roof stairs and pushed at the door leading to the outside. He then walked across the roof to the edge. As the buildings were closely connected, he simply stepped over the separation to Sheehan's building. He lowered himself down the fire escape, but in doing so smashed his hand against the railing in the dark. He almost screamed out in agony but gritted his teeth and knelt for a few minutes to gain his bearings, his head spinning and causing him to lose focus. Once he had composed himself, he moved quickly down the flight of stairs one floor and leaned against the wall, peering through the open lone window. Open in the fuckin' middle of January, he thought. Either you froze to death in these fuckin' apartments or you were overcome with heat. Never any in-between.

He listened for sounds and heard only a low snoring coming from the bedroom before him. Taking the pistol out of his waistband, he attached the silencer and eased himself cautiously through the window, the sound of Little Eddie's snoring the only sound in the room.

Johnny crossed to the bed, his left hand now throbbing. "Eddie," he whispered to the form lying face down. "Eddie."

"Huh? Who's there?" Sheehan awoke with a start.

"Eddie, you fuckin' midget, it's Johnny Ryan. Go back to sleep," he whispered and shot Sheehan twice in the head.

He had then retraced his steps to the White House Bar as Connie had instructed. If anyone along the bar wondered about his hand and the bucket of ice, they did not ask. He reflected on the West Side code of silence and knew no one with brains would ask. If anyone did, he would rap him in the head with his jimmy bar and then dump the bucket of ice over the fuckin' guy's bleeding head.

A half hour after Johnny arrived, Connie walked past the long bar to effusive greetings from the regulars. He noted that no one sat anywhere near his brother, who was known for his short fuse and reputation for causing fights without provocation. He hated the nickname "Crazy Johnny" and knew that it was never used in either his or his brother's presence. He loved his brother and saw him as a first class enforcer who only needed to be carefully directed.

"What happened?" Connie asked, sliding into the seat next to his brother, pointing to the injured hand.

"No problem, no problem at all. We do have one less ambitious Irishman. Little Eddie is sleeping tonight with the angels."

Connie embraced him, laughing. "Your sense of direction may be a bit off."

The Atlantic and Pacific people had no problem with Jerry's taking the four days off. After all, how many times did a brother have an important fight in Madison Square Garden? And his group of stores, stretching throughout Essex County, was outperforming the balance of the chain. He sensed their high regard for the results and knew that a vice presidency was in the offing.

On Tuesday he packed his suitcase while Sheila and little Marty sat on the edge of the bed. "I wish we could come with you," Sheila said.

He zipped the lining and turned toward them. "It's only a few days, Sheila. I'll call you every night."

He leaned forward and kissed her, and she rose to embrace him. And then together they gathered little Marty in their arms, holding him between them until Jerry finally elevated him to his shoulder tops and trotted him around the bedroom as the two-year-old screamed in glee.

"You're driving alone?"

"Yes. I'll meet them at the Mayflower. I left the number on the kitchen table for you. I'm stopping at one of our vendors in New Haven on the way," he said, picking up the suitcase.

"Call me tonight then when you arrive. And tell Tommy we'll all be watching on television Friday night. I have everyone on Copeland Road coming over here." She raised her face to him and kissed him on the lips.

"I love you, Sheila. Always and in all ways," using one of his older brother's favorite expressions.

Connie Ryan decided to talk to the head man instead. From a public phone along the Battery Park promenade he looked toward the great width of the Hudson River, noting the boats of all shapes and sizes sailing into New York Harbor. He loved the salt air and even on a cold day such as this he came down from the West Side to walk and to reflect, and to watch the tourists pointing outward to Ellis Island and the Statue of Liberty

"I need to speak to Jimma Flaherty. Tell him a friend from New York is calling," he told the deep-throated woman who answered.

"Yeah. Jimma Flaherty here."

"Jimma, Connie. Two days to go. Do I have anything to worry about?"

"I'm assured and you are assured all is in place."

"Tell our mutual friend I'm holding him and his brother personally responsible for this action."

Connie hung up quickly. Flaherty stared at the phone for a moment before dialing Jack's number at Stanton Chevrolet.

"Our friend from New York called, making a last minute check on things. Any problems?"

"I told you I talked to him," Jack replied.

"Fair enough. Have a good trip. I'll see you when you get back from New York."

<u>26</u>

As they drove through Connecticut, Jack reflected on the situation. He had asked Leo and Ray to be his guests for the fight, and Jimma had no problem with the idea, since he had other plans himself on Friday night. Flaherty had assured him that only the two of them were aware of the fix. He considered that possibility very carefully and concluded that it fit. Above all else, Jimma was a selfish man, so it did not figure that he would make Leo or anyone else aware of the fix. Why include Leo in any large payoff when he could come away with more profit for himself?

Yet Jack had learned long ago to take nothing for granted. It was possible that Jimma had included Leo and instructed him to watch Jack throughout the trip. He could not be sure.

How, then, to react? He had finally decided to trust his instinct. There was no way Jimma Flaherty would include Leo in this scheme. Beyond that, he had confidence that Leo was as much his friend as Jimma's. He weighed the possibilities and decided to make the request. He had asked Leo to sit in back with him during the trip. He needed to face him, to judge his response to the request.

"Tommy ready for this guy, Jack?" Leo asked somewhere along the long road between Hartford and New Haven. "Can he handle him?"

"You bet on the fight, Leo?" Jack asked.

"$25,000 on your brother with only a small payoff if he wins."

"I'd say your money is pretty safe, Leo. You place any dough, Ray?"

"$15,000 on Tom -- to knock him out. Bigger payout that way, Leo."

"Leo, can you do me a very special favor after the fight?" Jack turned to observe Leo.

"What's that?"

"Stay close to Tommy. Be sure to keep all the crazies off him. I already cleared with Petey so that you will be admitted to the dressing room right after the fight. You keep the car in case you need it. But stay with him."

"Something the matter, Jack? Where will you be?"

He doesn't know, Jack surmised by the way he asked the question.

"I asked Ray to get a rental and drive me back right after the fight. Marjorie's planning a big breakfast for her father's birthday at the agency early tomorrow, and I promised I'd be there."

"No problem, Jack. I'll stick with him like glue."

"Thanks, Leo," he answered. Later, when everything was in order, he would have to face Leo, but one step at a time. He was confident his mentor would understand and that their deep friendship would survive.

They crossed Columbus Circle heading toward Eighth Avenue. It was only a short ten block walk to 8th and 50th and Madison Square Garden, and Tommy wanted to taste the fresh air and stretch his legs prior to the fight. The sixth of February had dawned clear and cool, and the early evening remained calm with temperatures hovering near twenty degrees. Frigid air blew up the canyon as they walked briskly along, Tommy and Petey following behind Jack and Jerry. They were all dressed in topcoats except Tommy, who wore a long green parka topped by a soft gray fedora. No one said much, all respecting Tommy's desire to concentrate on the night ahead.

"Jerry, I'm going back to Boston directly after the fight," Jack said. "I have to drive back -- it's too late for a plane -- to be there in time for an important early morning meeting. Can you stay with him until I get back tomorrow afternoon?"

"Sure. But he's planning to fly back tomorrow afternoon anyway. I was going to leave sometime in the afternoon by car. Why come back?" Jerry replied.

"I'll be back by noon, just to be with you guys. I'll call you in the morning to see what's developing. I'm sure they'll be requests for interviews, television appearances, whatever. You won't be getting out early."

As they crossed West 51st Street, fans from the milling crowds recognized Tommy and yelled out their support.

"You can beat him, Kelly."

"Go get him, Tommy."

"For Boston, Kelly!"

They all paused on the street corner for a moment, looking across to the front of the Garden on 8th Avenue, Tommy in particular taking in the brightly lit arched marquee which announced: "Boxing Tonight: Sonny Man Hall vs. Tommy Kelly; Tuesday: College Basketball Holy Cross vs. Notre Dame; Boxing March 24: Emile Griffith vs. Benny (Kid) Paret - Welterweight Championship."

"We're going over to the side exit," Petey said. "We'll see you two after the fight, right?"

The brothers embraced. "You take him, Tommy," Jack whispered in his ear. "I'll take care of the others."

Jack and Jerry crossed the avenue and moved into the Garden lobby where over 18,000 fans pushed and shoved their way toward stadium seats and the staircases leading to the balconies. Tommy had arranged ringside seats right behind his corner for them. Not five yards away from them came the melodious voice of boxing airing the Friday Night Fights. "Good evening, everyone. This is Don Dunphy, your ringside commentator. Tonight New York's own Sonny Man Hall, the number one contender, takes on hard hitting Tommy Kelly in what for both shapes up as the most important fight of their respective careers. Stay tuned, America, for what promises to be an outstanding middleweight battle."

In the dressing room Santangelo paced the room while Gus taped Tommy's hands in the presence of Hall's handlers. "Five minutes to go," announced a Garden representative with a loud bang on the door. As soon as they finished the taping, Tommy knelt on the floor, alone with his thoughts for a brief moment. Then he stood. "Let's go," he said.

Dressed in green shorts and a green robe with a huge four leaf clover covering his back, Tommy followed the Garden security team down the aisle, the crowd applauding and cheering as he bounced on his toes, flicking imaginary punches while half walking, half running toward the crowded ring.

To Jack he appeared grim and determined, as he always did prior to a fight. He climbed through the ropes and moved to his corner. He winked at his brothers and waved to the tens of fans hoisting the Irish flag in the balcony. Walking across to Hall's corner, he tapped his adversary's gloves, and then turned along the ropes, acknowledging members of the press.

Johnny Addie approached the lowered microphone to introduce each fighter. "Ladies and gentlemen, welcome to Madison Square Garden and the main event of the evening. In this corner, in the green trunks, from Lynn, Massachusetts, the number two contender for the middleweight championship, with a record of 37 wins, 0 losses, 1 draw, at 158 pounds, let's give a Madison Square Garden welcome to Tommy Kelly." Considering the fact the fight was being held in New York, the applause for Tom was strong and enthusiastic.

"And in this corner, the number one contender, in the white trunks, from Harlem, at 159-1/4 pounds, with an outstanding record of 53 wins, 2 losses, 3 draws -- New York's own, Sonny Man Hall." Applause swept the Garden as Hall stood in recognition, tall for a middleweight, lanky, a good looking veteran whose boxing prowess had kept his features strongly intact after more than a decade of fighting.

Tommy stood by his stool, listening to Santangelo as Gus Regan pushed his mouthpiece in and applied grease to his forehead, an extra gob to his scarred brow. "Tom, watch his jab. It's his best weapon. Remember we can't outbox this guy. Hammer away at his ribs, and protect your eyes. Slow him down. Press him."

The bell for round one clanged, and the crowd became noticeably subdued as they watched the fighters scout one another for most of the first three minutes. Hall flashed his right jab as he bounced in and out, and Tommy cautiously waited for opportunities to counter or to land body shots without being punished by the jab. Jack looked around the vast arena and saw no signs of Connie or Johnny Ryan, but he was sure one or both would be here.

Halfway through a similarly slow round two, the fight turned. As the combatants came together in center ring, they accidentally butted heads, and as they separated, Tommy sensed the flow of red and quickly touched his eye with a glove to assess the damage. Hall pressed forward aggressively, peppering Tommy with that piston-like jab that had bothered opponents for years. For the balance of the round, Tom retreated, not seriously hurt but anxious for the bell so he could judge the extent of his injury.

"That's two rounds for him, Tom," Santangelo chided as he sat down. "When are you going to get off?"

"What's with the cut?" Tom asked as Gus pressed hard with a Q-tip and then applied a coagulant and a smooth covering of grease to the area.

"It's in the brow, Tom. Exact same place as the last fight. We'll work on it between rounds. Can you see OK?" Gus asked.

"I'm OK so far."

"Tommy, listen to me. You're fighting at his tempo. You have to press him harder and slow him down," Santangelo directed.

But in round three Hall continued to dictate the pace, the left hander turning to his right to shorten the distance to his new target, Tommy's left brow. Tommy landed a few solid body shots that kept Hall away but the jab bothered him. It landed constantly -- sometimes one, two, three in a row. Suddenly, near the end of the round, as he blinked back the blood flow, Sonny Man followed a right lead with a quick left hook Tommy simply did not see coming. Blood spurted from his brow as he fell against the ropes on one knee as the referee started his count.

Touching his gloves to the canvas, he rose at the count of six and weathered the round by tying up Hall along the ropes.

Between rounds Gus worked frantically on the cut and on the swelling that had developed around the eye. The white haired doctor representing the New York State Commission ascended the steps, pushing Gus aside. "Let me look at that."

"He's all right, Doc," Santangelo insisted.

"It looks ugly to me. Too much more damage, and I may have to stop it," the doctor said.

Tommy sat erect, pushing the bucket Gus proffered away. "Don't stop this fight, Doc. I can see fine."

Across the ring Hall's handlers led him through deep breathing exercises. Unmarked in the facial area, he nonetheless had been bothered by the thumping body shots Tommy had landed. "Crowd him, Tommy. He's feeling those body shots. You can't let him shoot those jabs," Santangelo instructed.

It was as the bell sounded for the fourth round that Jack saw the pattern developing that he had witnessed with Tommy from that very first fight on Laundry Hill. When hurt, he focused even more, and from the depths of a fighting heart came an also superhuman response to any crisis. He bent lower and stalked his opponent, reminding Jack of a poem that the nuns had taught him in the 1940's -- "Tiger, Tiger burning bright, in the forest of the night," it had begun.

In the ring his brother moved through the jab, now paying it scant attention, smashing left hooks to Hall's body, crowding him against the ropes, cutting down all angles so that Sonny Man could not fire out the jab. He ripped a right hand under Hall's heart, yet Sonny Man dug a right himself to the head and, once again, blood flowed into Tommy's eye.

But now he was a man possessed. He hammered a left hook to the jaw and a right uppercut delivered with such force that Sonny Man was lifted off the canvas for a second. "One minute to go," Petey yelled, and Tommy increased the pressure, looping a strong left hand over Sonny Man's guard. He staggered and slipped to his knees, as Tommy backed off.

"Three...four...five...six," the referee yelled out.

At the count of six, Sonny Man stood, but the old aggressiveness was gone. He slid forward on shaky legs to meet Tommy, now turned loose by the referee to continue the action. Tommy faked another shot to the body and, again, came over the top of Sonny Man's gloves with a solid left hook quickly followed by a short, crisp right hand, both landing to the head. Crimson ran down Hall's face, his nose twisted under the barrage of blows. He threw a weak right jab, and, in return, Tommy shot a hard right to the body and a vicious left hook. The accumulation of punches delivered in rapid succession caused Sonny Man to collapse backward, the back of his head bouncing on the canvas.

The referee did not bother to count. He waved Hall's handlers into the ring to administer to him while Tommy's team surrounded him, hoisting him on their shoulders as the crowd stood on its seats, applauding wildly.

On the apron, uniformed security guards wrestled with exuberant fans attempting to join the celebration. Both television and radio announcers shoved their microphones at Tommy and the entourage surrounding him. As the center microphone dropped from above, Johnny Addie pushed through the crowd toward the center of the ring. "Ladies and gentlemen...in 2 minutes, 41 seconds of the fourth round, the winner by a knockout, and still undefeated...Tommy Kelly," he boomed. Once more, the crowd erupted.

Jerry pummeled Jack on the back and tossed both their hats into the air. Waving to the crowd, Tommy now walked around the edges of the square. He grinned down at Jack and Jerry as Regan followed him, trying to press a towel against his damaged eye. Crossing toward Sonny Man Hall, Tommy threw his arm around the beaten fighter's neck as they shook hands.

Jack turned to his left and signaled Leo, sitting about eight rows behind them. Nodding in recognition, Leo stood and headed toward the exit. Jack wanted him at the dressing room and close to Tommy from this time on.

"Jerry, I'll see you tomorrow," Jack shouted in his ear above the bedlam. "You and Petey stay with Tom. He's going to the hospital for sure with that cut. I'll call you early tomorrow morning."

"You're leaving right now?" Jerry asked, surprised.

"Yeah. I'll see you tomorrow," he replied, forcing a grin.

As Don Dunphy began his interview with Tommy, Jack joined the raucous crowd moving toward the Garden lobby. Cautiously he studied the mass of faces, not really expecting to see Connie Ryan but still conscious of the possibility. As he exited on Eighth Avenue, Ray gestured him toward the waiting car double parked in front of the Garden. He glanced at his watch. "Let's get out of here," Jack ordered. "We need to be in Boston by 3 A.M., Ray, so let's move it."

"Son of a bitch," fumed Crazy Johnny Ryan as he stared at the television set behind the bar at the White House. "Son of a bitch!" Those Boston fuckers had double crossed them. Connie had never felt completely at ease about the whole deal. But then again, Johnny had also never felt anyone would dare cross his brother on a deal of this magnitude -- five million dollars.

Johnny downed the shot glass and the beer, and banged on the bar for a repeat, his eyes never leaving the celebration taking place in the ring just five blocks away. Where had the papers said the fighter was staying? The Mayflower, he finally remembered. He glanced at his watch. He had plenty of time. He would be at Central Park West long before the fighter returned from his celebration.

"Joey, another shot and beer," he bellowed at the barkeep. "And turn that fuckin' TV up so I can hear what they're saying."

27

Jimma Flaherty rolled off Claire just before the final round started. He had wanted to watch the whole fight, but she had been demanding this night, insisting that he satisfy her. Jesus, what was the world coming to? Used to be you could time these things. Now with all those expert '60's sex therapists writing about sexual satisfaction, the importance of proper foreplay, the need to understand a woman's sexual feelings, they all wanted to take a fuckin' hour and a half to finish the act. Christ, he yearned for the days when you just jumped on and rode them. Five minutes was time enough for any of them.

She finally stood and strolled, naked, toward the bathroom. He liked to watch her rounded ass, but here was his chance to switch on the television and catch most of the fight with any luck. As the black and white slowly came into focus, he saw Hall jabbing at Tommy, blood cascading down Kelly's brow. Kid is making it look good, he thought. As he adjusted the sound, Don Dunphy was commenting on a turning of the tide. Good, he thought. Connie would want a real fight. He didn't need a Commission investigation like that dumbass Jake LaMotta had caused with the Billy Fox fight back in '47.

Claire walked in front of the television, fondling her own breasts, turning to display her ass. "Claire, let me just see what's happening here, for Christ's sake. This is Jack's fuckin' brother fighting."

"You would rather watch a lousy fight?"

Jesus H. Christ. Hurt feelings. "No, dear. Just for a few minutes, that's all."

Claire huffed off into the motel bathroom, probably to admire her own ass some more, the narcissistic bitch, Jimma thought. He trotted to the front of the bed to adjust the volume and, in that moment, saw Hall fall for the first time. He stood stunned as Hall rose, obviously in serious trouble. The referee waved Tommy forward, and in the next few seconds he relentlessly smashed combinations to the head and body, sending Sonny Man to the canvas for a second and final time.

He tried to concentrate. Was he dreaming? Had he fallen asleep after satisfying Miss I Love Me? This could not be happening. Had Tommy gone completely crazy? Jack had assured him Tommy was delivered. And he had just knocked out Sonny Man in four rounds? He sat stark naked on the edge of the bed, staring at the screen, trying to focus.

As he filtered his thoughts, he could come to only one conclusion. Connie would call him tomorrow. Ryan would want to know if he had any part in this double cross. Once Jimma reassured him, he would insist that Jimma take Jack Kelly out. And it would have to be arranged. There was no choice. They had both been double crossed. A kid he had trusted, a young man who had become his number one lieutenant had now embarrassed him in the eyes of Connie Ryan. He would have to assure Ryan he would handle it here. And maybe not so bad a move after all, Jimma thought. Change in any organization is sometimes necessary. He sensed the high regard the other family members had for Jack. He commanded respect and loyalty, and his presence in crisis situations had endeared him to the entire family. Frequently Jimma had felt twinges of jealousy, yet he never had sufficient cause to move against him. Now he had that reason.

He picked up his watch from the bedroom table -- 11:15 P.M. They had a few more hours. As usual, Mary would expect him home in the early morning hours, by 4 A.M. at the latest. As long as he did not stay out all night, he had her fooled. She understood that Friday was his boys' night out.

Flicking off the television, he peered into the bathroom. Claire applied lipstick in careful motions, as if she were going somewhere butt naked, he thought. He slipped his arms around her waist, turning her, rubbing her breasts against his chest. She responded willingly, reaching down to stimulate him. He also wanted to sleep for an hour or so. Maybe this time it could be an old-fashioned fuck, like in the good old days.

Connie Ryan signaled to his driver as he exited Madison Square Garden. Six million dollars to be gained, and instead he and his partners had lost over a million. A fucking million dollars! He tried to calm his anger, to concentrate.

He would wait until tomorrow and call Flaherty. He could not believe Flaherty would double cross him. Their relationship had been friendly enough over the last decade. Jimma was content with his own businesses and had himself placed a heavy wager on Hall. No, it had to be Kelly. Yet the action did not fit Connie's impression of the handsome young Irishman. He seemed a natural leader, a thoughtful man, one who understood business. And this was strictly business. He had appeared to accept that fact, despite his protestations and his expressed dislike of the deal. Could it be the younger brother had simply lost control? It really didn't matter. Jack was responsible. He was a dead man.

Jerry flashed the pass Santangelo had given him. The guard stationed in front of Tommy's dressing room nodded in recognition and opened the door for Jerry and Leo to enter a scene of ordered chaos. Reporters and photographers bumped against each other in the crowded quarters as they circled the long table where Tommy sat answering a seemingly endless succession of questions while Gus Regan cut away the tape from his hands. In the corner Petey stood with the New York State Commission doctor as Jerry and Leo approached.

"Let's get him over to Bellevue now," insisted the doctor. "That eye needs to be tended to. No one can work on it in this madhouse. The ambulance should be here by now."

"Ambulance? How bad off is he?" a startled Jerry asked.

"The ambulance is just a precaution, but that eye doesn't look good. I'm less worried about the cut than I am the eye itself. He took a lot of punishment tonight, and for him there's been a lot of tonights," the doctor responded. "I've asked Dr. Peterson -- he's top notch -- to meet us there and do the stitching."

Jerry found the doctor's analysis difficult to believe. There was Tommy, joking with the reporters, recounting key moments in the fight in response to their questions. His right hand now hung in the ice bucket while he held an icebag against his left brow.

"Take that bag away, Tom, so we can get a good shot," a photographer yelled.

"Not until I'm looking a whole lot better," Tommy laughed.

"When will the fight with Fullmer occur?"

"New York or Boston, Tommy?"

"Can you handle a tough boxer who can hit like Gene, Tom?"

Petey stepped into the firestorm. "Okay, guys, that's it. Everyone out. We need to get him to a doctor and have some stitching done." With the help of two guards, he slowly ushered the group toward the door of the steaming room.

"Make it a quick shower, will you Tom?" Santangelo yelled over his shoulder. "We need to get you over to Bellevue."

Johnny Ryan stepped into the alley next to the White House Bar and spun the cylinder of his .38 to be sure it was fully loaded. Jesus, it seemed cold, even for this time of year, he thought. Exiting carefully, he turned uptown on Tenth to walk the fifteen blocks to Columbus Circle. When he reached 57th Street, he headed east toward Seventh Avenue. He stopped at that corner and turned to observe the tan sphere of the Mayflower on Central Park West, just a block across Columbus Circle.

It was 12:30, and if the television reporter was accurate, Kelly was probably now at a local hospital, if not celebrating somewhere. It would be at least another hour or two before he returned to the hotel, Crazy Johnny calculated. Plenty of time for a cup of coffee to keep warm. He entered a small all-night shop at the Circle and sat facing the front door. He blew on the black coffee the sad-eyed lone waitress had delivered and looked around. Nobody in here except those two kids across the room staring at him trying to look tough. Keep it up, you two rat fucks, and I'll put a couple of holes in each of you, too. But what was it Connie always stressed? Focus on the task at hand. Right. Maybe after he took care of the boxer and his brother he would come back and air condition these two dirtbags.

He moved quickly and expertly, his dexterous fingers working in unison. He stepped back to observe his work, turning Tommy's head from side to side. "Ten stitches to close the cut," Dr. Peterson reported to Tommy as he sat on the table in an examining room off the main emergency room at Bellevue. "How do you feel, son?"

"Like I've been in a fight, Doc," Tommy deadpanned, "but you should see the other guy."

"It's this swelling that worries me. Other than the flow of blood tonight around the brow, have you been experiencing any trouble with your eyes lately?" the doctor asked.

Tommy hesitated for a moment. "After the last fight, the Astrangio fight, once or twice in training, I thought I saw a flash of light and, one or two other times maybe a little loss in peripheral vision, but no pain and no swelling."

Peterson frowned. "Well, there's nothing more we can do tonight." He turned to Jerry, Petey, and Leo. "When this swelling subsides, he should see an eye specialist, an ophthalmologist."

"You think something's wrong, Doc?" asked Jerry.

"I didn't say that. He's a boxer, and he's been absorbing punishment for how many years now? He should have a careful examination back in Boston. I can recommend someone at Mass Eye and Ear if you want."

Tommy stepped down from the table. "Thanks, Doc. I'd like that." He extended his hand. "I appreciate your help tonight, Doc. I'll call you when we're back in Boston."

"Are you up for a celebratory drink, Tom?"

"Let's just go back to the hotel, Jerry. I'm tired, and I'm hurting. Tomorrow night back in Boston, I'll feel more like celebrating."

"Come on, I have Jack's car," Leo said. "I'll drive you back."

<u>28</u>

Ray pushed the rental so that they reached the intersection of Routes 128 and 1 approximately three and a half hours after leaving New York. Flying time, Jack thought. It was now 2:30 and on a cold winter evening there had not been much traffic the entire way.

They proceeded south on Route 1 into Saugus, passing Frank Guiffrida's Hilltop Steak House a mile up the divided highway. "Cross over Route 1 after the next overpass," Jack ordered.

Ray passed under the Main Street overpass, took a sharp right and crossed over Route 1, reversing his direction, now heading north. "It's right across the street from the Hilltop. Move over into the right lane and slow down. Wait a second. There it is," Jack pointed to the blinking neon sign announcing the Skylark Motel.

Ray cut his lights as soon as he entered the paved driveway. He passed to the side of the small motel, avoiding the main office in front, and backed into the parking area so they could observe each of the ten units across from them. A slanted roof ran the length of the building. Only four or five cars were aligned outside the doors.

"That's Jimma's car. He's still here," Jack said. "He's like clockwork with these Friday night trysts."

They sat for fifteen minutes in the dark before Claire emerged from the third unit on the left, one almost directly across from them. She smoothed her hair and buttoned her coat before entering the white '61 Ford Galaxie, never once looking toward them. Without hesitation, she started the engine, backed out, and turned toward Route 1 North.

"You stay here. When you see me talking to him, start the engine and come across to me. Keep the lights out," Jack instructed. "You okay with this?"

"You sure you don't want me to handle it, Jack?"

Jack touched Ray's hand on the wheel with his own left hand. Ray would always be with him. Before he had explained his plan to him, he knew what Ray's reaction would be. "No. Thanks, Ray. I have to take care of this myself."

He stepped from the car and crossed toward the fifth unit, moving under the slanted roof and positioning himself about ten yards away from where Claire had exited. He attached the silencer to the .38. Within five minutes Jimma appeared in the doorway, hurriedly closing it behind him.

"Hey, Jimma," Jack whispered from the darkness.

"Jesus Christ! Jack? That you? You scared the shit out of me."

Walking toward Jimma, Jack kept his hand at his side. "You fucked with my family, Jimma. You supported Ryan against one of your own. Against my own brother. You shouldn't have done that."

"Jack, what are you talking about?" He turned his head as he heard a car engine starting in front of him. "I'm going to tell fucking Connie Ryan I can't cooperate with him?"

"Family transcends business for me, Jimma. And it should have for you," Jack replied, raising the .38 from his side.

"You're going to kill me, Jack? The guy who brought you to where you fuckin' are today?"

"Jimma," Jack spoke calmly, "we both know that as of tonight I'm a dead man in your eyes and in Ryan's. It's you or me, Jimma. There's no other way to see it."

As Ray wheeled the car across the courtyard, Jack lifted the .38 and fired one shot to the head and one to the chest. Jimma stumbled backward onto the asphalt, his head striking hard against the doorstep. Jack leaned over Flaherty's body and fired a third shot to the head. As Ray opened the passenger door for

Jack, he ordered, "Let's go. Keep those lights out until we're on the highway." He looked around as they left the courtyard. Not a sign of movement anywhere.

For the past hour Johnny Ryan had stood huddled in the doorway of the Gulf and Western Building, observing the traffic circling the rotary. The Kellys should be here almost any time now, he figured. It was better than three hours since the fight had concluded. It was time he changed positions so that he could better watch traffic approaching the hotel in both directions. He would be more exposed to the elements, but they could not stay out much longer, he reasoned.

He crossed Central Park West and positioned himself on a park bench directly opposite the Gulf and Western Building. Even at 2:30 in the morning, in this bitter cold, lovers and lone strollers moved by every few minutes, paying only scant attention to a well-dressed young man who seemed absorbed in his own thoughts. Occasionally, a taxicab rounded Columbus Circle and stopped in front of the Mayflower to leave off noisy revelers returning from a night on the town. If they walked toward the hotel, he had them. If they arrived by taxi, that would make it more difficult, but not impossible. He had the element of surprise on his side.

He turned to his right to observe four males walking toward him on the opposite side of the street. It was the Kellys, he was sure. Four, though. Who were the others? He didn't care. Their tough luck to be at the wrong place at the wrong time. They must have parked at one of the garages on West 63rd St. and were now walking east back to the hotel.

He reached for the holster and placed the gun against his right side. Rising from the bench, he walked diagonally across the street, planning to intercept them outside the Grisline's grocery store on the corner of West 61st. He lowered his head, seemingly as a stop against the slight wind, but actually to avoid any possible suspicion until he was on them. He quickened his pace as would any pedestrian on this freezing night.

Suddenly one of the four was yelling something he could not understand, some kind of warning to the others. As the yeller reached into his coat, Johnny stopped in the street about ten to fifteen yards from them and fired four shots in rapid succession, hitting at least two of the group. One of them, the guy doing the yelling, toppled backward. With the light change back at Columbus Circle, a fleet of cars raced toward him hell bent to move through as many cross street lights before the next change occurred on Central Park West.

He turned and ran toward the Park. Vaulting the stone wall behind the benches, he worked his way quickly through the brush toward Central Park South. Before he descended to the walkway, he smashed the gun against the stone wall. No one could trace it, he was sure, but he still felt better now that it was in three pieces. He deposited each piece in a separate grating along the roadway that circled the park. He exited onto Central Park South thinking he should have anticipated that some of them would be armed, too. Jesus, he thought, Connie will be proud of me. I think I hit at least two of them. Was one of them Jack or Tom Kelly? He wasn't sure.

"You did what?" Connie screamed as they sat at the far end of the White House Bar. Johnny stammered as he once again began to trace his actions.

"What are you, a fuckin' kamikaze pilot?" He knew Connie didn't expect an answer to the question.

"Connie, we can't let them get away with..."

"Listen to me, Mr. Shit-for-Brains. You don't fuckin' move, you don't take a shit without first checking with me! Do you understand? Jesus Christ." He shook his head from side to side. "God bless us all."

Reaching for the boilermaker in front of him, he downed the shot rapidly. "You know, Johnny, there's such a thing as planning. I'm going to see Jack Kelly dead if it's the last thing I do. But be smart. In time, Johnny. In time. We have to think out the steps. And step one is for Flaherty to take care of this, not you. It's his fuckin' problem, or he's my fuckin' problem. You following any of this?"

Brushing a small tear from his eye, Johnny nodded. Connie looked at him and suddenly threw an arm around his neck. "Hey, brother, come here. No one fucks with us, right? Not here on the West Side." Johnny beamed at Connie's sudden civility toward him.

"You think you hit a couple, huh?"

"I think I hit at least two of them."

"Maybe you saved Flaherty the trouble. But I don't need the fuckin' Boxing Commission or the police on my ass, that's for sure."

All soldiers were to be present at the warehouse in Charlestown at 9:00 A.M. It was Ray's job to make the calls, make sure they all appeared. He had Ray drop him off at Lynn Shore Drive where he quietly entered his home so as not to disturb Marjorie and the children. He removed his shoes in the hallway and tiptoed into the kitchen. Flipping on the small light under the oven cover, he made himself a cup of tea. At 4:00 he sat alone in the dark at the kitchen table, sipping the hot tea. He could not sleep, nor did he intend to. He needed to consider the events of the last twelve hours, define his own options, as well as Ryan's, and prepare for the meeting at Charlestown.

So far, so good. He felt confident that Ryan would not dare attack Tommy. Anything that called public attention to the fight game would not be good business, Ryan would think. But he will seek vengeance against me, and quickly, Jack thought. He guessed that Ryan would demand Jimma eliminate him, thus teaching Tommy a lesson as well. He had needed to strike first and he had. Jimma's ticket had been canceled. Ryan would initially be shocked to learn of Jimma's death. He had bought time to both anticipate and counter Ryan's next move.

Immediately ahead, two key matters had to be addressed. First, he needed to meet with all the family members. He sensed their respect for him, their high regard for his work, their friendship. On the other hand, they individually and collectively

181

belonged to Jimma. He had recruited them, advanced many of them and he had been an effective leader. He had commanded loyalty because of his competence. Could he sway them? They would consider it a sign of weakness that Jimma had acceded to another Irish crime boss, whatever Ryan's reputation. He had not supported his most trusted lieutenant in a matter concerning family. Then, too, he thought, they wanted stability in their lives, a continuation of their world, its rewards. Who to provide those if not Jack? Especially if he had the support of Leo. He was also positive that Ray would speak for him.

And very quickly he would need to meet with Salvatore Cardoza. He would have to explain the entire situation to Cardoza's satisfaction. He was banking on the fact that the Mafia would wish to maintain stability. They would want his assurance that current agreements would be respected, and he would guarantee that fact. In the end he felt they would dismiss the coup as strictly minor league Irish stupidity. Let them kill each other, they would feel. With the newly found gold mine of drug profits fast coming upon them, it would be in the Mafia's interest to continue with him.

Suddenly the harsh ringing of the phone broke his concentration. He pulled it from its cradle quickly before it rang again and woke the entire household.

"Hello," he whispered.

"Jack, it's Tommy."

"Tommy. What's wrong?"

"It's Jerry and Leo. Ryan's brother caught us near the hotel. Leo's dead, Jack. Jerry got winged in the arm, but he's all right."

Jack sank down into the kitchen chair. "Leo's dead?" he repeated, stunned. "Tell me what happened."

Tommy explained that Leo had driven them all back to the hotel following the trip to Bellevue. They had parked in a garage on West 63rd Street and walked to Central Park West. As they neared the hotel, a lone man appeared in the street, crossing from the Park. As he closed the distance, Leo yelled out a warning and reached for his own gun. The gunman shot

Leo in the chest and fired two or three other rounds, one of which hit Jerry in the arm before he fled.

"Jerry's all right? You sure?"

"He was lucky, Jack. The bullet passed right through his arm. It's just a flesh wound. Gus looked at it."

"Jesus Christ, Leo's dead," Jack repeated to himself. He thought for a minute. "You sure it was Ryan's brother?"

"Yes. It was the guy in the picture you showed me. The younger one."

"Son of a bitch. They moved faster than I thought they would. What happened with the police?"

"I hid Leo's gun. Right now they believe it was an attempted mugging gone wrong. There were no other witnesses around. But that could change," Tommy answered.

"And, Jack..."

"Yeah?"

"You're going to have to explain things to Jerry. You can't leave him exposed like this. There could be other..."

"I know that, Tommy. Let's first get you all home safely. I'll have some people there early in the morning. In the meantime, stay put."

"See you soon, Jack."

Jack stood and walked slowly around the kitchen in the dark. Leo dead. His mentor dead. And his youngest brother, who had absolutely nothing to do with this, lucky to be alive. Ryan had surprised him. He had to think.

"Let me be direct, Dan. Is it possible to bury the matter?" Ryan asked as they sat in the rear of the White House Bar early Saturday morning scanning the newspapers, sipping coffee. He looked across at the balding policeman dressed in a regular business suit. He had just heard the report of the shooting provided by Captain Dan Hines of the Midtown North Precinct, in whose jurisdiction the killing had occurred.

"It can be taken care of, Mr. Ryan," Hines replied, pursing his lips. "I'll need to grease some palms here and there, but it can be handled. Right now it's listed as an attempted mugging gone wrong. The shooter panicked and ran. I can keep that story flowing."

"How about the press?" Ryan asked, pointing to the newspapers spread open on the round table.

"That's a real problem where the fighter is concerned, he being well-known and all that. With the proper release of information, we can keep it a one-day story, I think."

"What can you tell me about the dead guy?"

"Individual's name is -- was Leo Slattery, a bookkeeper from Boston, a friend of the boxer, they say."

"No criminal record?"

"No."

"See if you can lead the press off in the direction of a mugging then. Under this asshole liberal mayor, they've become a daily occurrence anyway. Steer it away from any connection to the fight and its outcome, Dan."

"I'm sure we can do that, Mr. Ryan. I'll keep you informed."

"I very much appreciate your efforts here, Dan. I won't forget." Ryan spoke sincerely, handing him an envelope.

"I'll get back to you, Mr. Ryan," Hines said, rising from the table and pocketing the envelope.

As soon as Hines left, Connie continued his perusal of the newspapers. He read, but yet he did not read, his mind focused instead on the events of the previous evening, his thoughts absorbed in what he would say to Jimma Flaherty.

"You want some more coffee, Connie?" the daytime barkeep asked.

"Not now, Joey. Thanks anyway."

The wall phone at the edge of the bar rang, and Joey stepped from behind the bar. "White House Bar."

"It's for you, Connie."

Connie stood and walked the short distance to the phone. "Yeah?" he said.

"Connie? Richard Howard, from Midtown North. I thought you might like to know we just received word that Jimma Flaherty of Boston was murdered last night."

Connie could not believe what he was hearing. "Are you sure?"

"Positive. He was shot at a motel a few miles north of Boston."

"Thanks for the information. I won't forget it."

He placed the phone back on its hook. Son of a bitch, he thought. Could Jack Kelly be involved in Flaherty's death? He guessed yes, but in the next few days word would drift back to him and he would know for certain. In the meantime, he was in no hurry to take care of Jack Kelly. He judged it best to let some time go by, particularly with the events of last night still under investigation. He would bide his time and then clip the bastard, for sure.

29

Jack rang the bell at 34 Copeland Road at exactly 7:00 A.M. Lights blazed throughout the garrison and through the picture window he saw Sheila crossing the living room in response to his ringing.

"Jack, oh, God," she sobbed as she opened the door.

He drew her into his arms and rested her head on his shoulder. "Jerry call you?"

"Yes. What happened down there, Jack? Is he really all right? Should I go down there?" She blurted out the questions one after another between sobs.

"Let's sit down for a minute, Sheila. Over here." He guided her up the stairs toward the living room. Handing her his handkerchief, he sat with her on the couch, shedding his topcoat and tossing it on the chair opposite them.

"First of all, I hope you heard that Jerry is fine. Just a flesh wound. That's the most important thing. He's fine, and he'll be here today about noon. I sent some friends to drive Jerry and Tommy home."

Sheila wiped her eyes with his handkerchief, her hands shaking. "Jack, what happened?"

He placed his hand in hers and drew her closer. "Sheila, I don't know right now, but I'm going to find out."

She looked at him for a long second, her eyes brimming with tears. "I didn't even ask how you are. Leo was your friend. You must be devastated."

He flashed a soft smile at her. "I'm fine, Sheila. You just relax until Jerry arrives. If you need anything, call me.

Understand? Right now I have to visit Leo's wife, and I have some other business to take care of. You going to be all right?"

She smiled at him. "I'm all right. You know, Jack..."

"What?"

"I don't know what we would do without you. I just don't know."

He stood, leaned down, and kissed her.

"I'll call Jerry later today, Sheila. Just sit there. I'll let myself out."

As he drove toward Charlestown across the Mystic River Bridge, the report of the shooting death of real estate businessman James A. Flaherty of Jamaica Plain at a Saugus motel led the morning news. People had to wonder what such a prominent Boston businessman was doing at a sleazy Route 1 motel, Jack thought. Most of them would come to the same conclusion over time, he surmised. Most would think a jealous husband had exacted vengeance, particularly when the motel owner was questioned and revealed that Jimma was a perennial, every Friday night. Only the woman changed.

Those in the know would either be convinced or suspect a gangland killing had occurred, for example the police on Jimma's payroll, as well as some of the honest ones. Yet there would still be doubts. An investigation would follow, but with some luck the idea of a womanizer caught in the act might prevail. For many years, Jimma had been able to avoid press coverage. He had no criminal record and had even played a small role in supporting charities in the city. If today's papers and the radio news were indicative, then the story would center on the killing of a respected businessman caught in a sleazy circumstance.

He parked in front of the warehouse on Medford Street and then tapped twice on the glass door. From within, someone rolled up the front door, and, as he entered, a scowling Vin Sullivan pressed a button to bring the door down.

Every key family member stood around inside, talking in small groups, clapping their gloved hands together. When he walked toward them, the talk ceased. He sat on a crate, beckoning them to do the same. Together, they formed a semi-circle, staring in anticipation at him.

He made eye contact with each of them before he began to talk. With Vin Sullivan, who was the most dangerous of the group, and the most fiercely loyal to Jimma. With Ray Horan, now and probably always his most trusted friend and associate. With Freddie Quinlan, a solid soldier who could easily transfer loyalty. With Chris Kiley, one of the best of the team leaders whose influence on the waterfront was critical. With Joey Dunn, baby-faced Joey who organized the various numbers runners within their boundaries. With Stevie Guptill, relied on by the group to control the pimps and prostitutes. All were there with the exception of Paulie Cronin, who along with Vinnie, served as a key enforcer for their extortion enterprise.

The events of the long twenty-four hour period were now beginning to wear on him. He needed sleep, some opportunity to rest and yet was pleased that he had planned this long day well. Tommy had emerged the victor in the most important fight of his life, and Jimma Flaherty lay dead. As with most situations in life, there had been surprises. He had not planned on the Ryans' quick retaliation, but now he could use their killing of Leo as an emotional weapon in his presentation today. And Tommy and Jerry were safe. Next he would take care of the Ryans.

With the men it was important that he explain the circumstances simply and clearly. He took them through the key events, emphasizing Jimma's collusion with the Ryans regarding the fight; his failed attempt to turn Connie Ryan; the attempt on his brothers' lives in New York; the death of their respected friend Leo at the hands of Johnny Ryan. Should they have bowed to the orders of a New York-based family -- Irishmen, like themselves? Bullshit. Jimma had betrayed him and his family, and, indirectly, their entire family. Jimma's actions had led to Leo's death. There was still unfinished work, he reminded them. He would see Sally Cardoza this very noon. And then there was the matter of the Ryans, which he would take care of himself, he told them, his voice strong and confident. He covered all the bases both logically and emotionally. He was logical when the issue required it, but in the main, appealed to their emotions, which, as most leaders understand, is the key to commanding power.

When he had finished, they reacted as he had anticipated. All of them. His comments about the importance of stability in their operation in the time ahead were well received. They agreed Jimma had failed both him and them, and they sought vengeance for the death of a friend they all loved. In the end they encouraged his visit to Cardoza and awaited his orders regarding the Ryans.

Only Vin Sullivan remained both quiet and uninvolved. He glared at Jack as pledges of allegiance were proffered from each lieutenant in turn. He twitched in his seat on top of an orange crate. And Jack studied his every movement, half listening to the show of support being rendered by each of the others in turn.

"And you, Vinnie, your own feelings truly? I would appreciate your own thoughts."

"You want me to be honest, Jack?" retorted Vinnie, squinting in Jack's direction.

I'd like you to be dead, Jack thought. But this was not the time. He never did like the enforcer's manner or methods and wondered if he could ever fully trust him in the time ahead.

"Of course, Vin. We all know of your high regard for Jimma, which we all shared. What do you think?"

"You shouldn't have killed Jimma, Jack. Whatever. He was good to you, to me, to everyone here." He raised his hand, panning the room. "I would have liked to hear his version of all this."

Jack nodded his head, in acknowledgment. "I understand, Vinnie. He was good to me and meant a lot to me. I don't want any of you to think that I'm unappreciative of Jimma. Let's talk about that for a minute. Vinnie here says I should not have killed Jimma. I want you all to understand I took this action -- an action I believe was necessary -- reluctantly. I balanced his goodness toward you and me, and his leadership of our family

190

against this weakness, this caving in to New York groups that, frankly, care nothing for us, for our family, or for you, Vin. And, of course, I take this betrayal personally. It's my brother Tommy we're talking about. My brother should step aside for a New York Westie who dictates to us? Are we supposed to stand still when Leo is killed -- Leo, who we all admired -- and when my other brother is a target, as well? I don't think so, Vin. But, I understand your feelings. If this morning you want to walk away from us, I understand. And I promise you, no repercussions. I respect your feelings and only ask, as I ask of all those present today, for your loyalty and friendship, should you decide to give it to me and stay with me."

He had isolated the fuck, he thought. Whatever Vin decided was immaterial to him. If he left, good riddance to bad rubbish. He would just have to make sure he stayed out and caused no harm. If he stayed, he would never again trust Sullivan. He would try to work with him but would protect his back at all times.

Vin searched the crowd, seeking support for his point of view. Seeing none, he reacted as Jack has anticipated. "Jack, I'm satisfied. It's just hard for me to see Jimma Flaherty as you describe him. But he's gone, and I harbor no ill feelings, except toward those New York bastards who caused all this."

Jack nodded in agreement. "Thanks for your confidence, Vinnie. And I appreciate your support, and the support of each of you here today. For now, I ask that you each continue to function as you have. First thing I am going to do is even things up with our New York friends."

They looked at each other, pleased. He knew and they knew a soldier could be sent, but if that individual failed, it would reflect on him. No, at this stage, their own leader would be the one to seek vengeance. And in his fulfillment of that quest, he would truly become their leader. None of them could picture Jimma taking such a risky step himself.

They each stood in turn, walking toward him, extending their hands in recognition of new leadership, embracing him one by one in a sign of support. Pledges of loyalty. The ritual of friendship. All to be kept in proper perspective, he thought as he received them.

Salvatore "Salvy" or "Sally" Cardoza walked into Jimmy's Harborside Restaurant on Northern Avenue as if he owned the popular eating place. From his vantage point at the bar, his back to Boston Harbor, Jack looked across at the Mafia leader. Now in his early fifties, of medium height, Sally walked like a patrician, a man of proud bearing. His slicked back, brilliantined black hair parted almost in the middle made him appear other-worldly in contrast to the short haircuts preferred by most men in 1962. As he removed his Chesterfield, Jack waved from the bar, signaling him over.

Muttering a grudging hello, Cardoza sat beside him. His skin, almost brownish-yellow, called immediate attention to his badly damaged yellow teeth, stained by the constant Havana cigars he favored. His eyes showed no emotion and divulged no signs to be read of his intent.

"So we now have the trouble, Jack?" he inquired, not bothering with any social amenities. "What the hell happened?"

Jack related the series of events succinctly, ending with his meeting with the family in Charlestown. He took care to report with the same mix of logic and emotion he used with the family members, but he related the information more slowly and carefully. As he spoke, Cardoza toyed with his drink, his eyes straight ahead, studying the luncheon customers who entered across from them.

He weighed the story carefully, sipping his club soda, occasionally nodding at Jack, never once interrupting him. When Jack finished, he pointed to the tables. "Let's get something to eat. A piece of fish. They have the best here."

They sat in the bar area at one of the small tables with a perfect view of the Harbor. Fishing boats approached the tall windows, their heavily clothed occupants waving to the restaurant patrons. In the far distance a cargo ship weaved through the cold, gray waters on its way to the Atlantic.

"Jimma respected all boundaries, Jack. You prepared to do likewise?" Cardoza asked, finally speaking to the central issue.

"Sally, I intend to operate as before. There should be no problems with our arrangements. I'll honor all commitments."

Cardoza nodded. "I'll report to Gennaro with my opinion that this change was necessary, and also with my strongest recommendation that we proceed with our arrangements."

"I appreciate your confidence, Sally."

"Don't take it as such, Jack. To me it's not a matter of confidence or lack of confidence in you. Only time and events to come will determine whether you earn our confidence. To me, it's a matter of expediency. A need for stability for now. You follow politics, Jack?"

"I do," he answered.

"Then what do you see ahead for this country of ours?" Cardoza asked, his eyes dead cold like those of a fish out in the harbor, Jack thought.

"Under Kennedy?"

"Yes. Under the bleeding heart liberals. What do you see?"

"A continuation of the Cold War in the years ahead. Possible entanglements like with Korea in the '50's, a war in another country, probably a limited non-nuclear war."

"And the cities?" Cardoza asked.

"The population is going to continue to change and racial tensions will increase. A very difficult time ahead for a city like Boston."

"And what about our business?"

"Richer profits than ever before but more trouble than ever before as well. We'll see the formation of splinter groups, offshoots. Among my own people, we'll see Irish gang wars. The established groups like ours, the Winter Hill gang in Somerville, McLaughlin in Charlestown, we're all going to face challenges from the upstarts."

Cardoza once again simply nodded. "Very good. You don't know Gennaro Biggio well, do you, Jack?"

"Hardly at all."

"He said much the same two years ago prior to Kennedy's election, when most were anticipating a continuation of the quietly conservative '50's. He's a great man, Jack. He also speaks of erosion of authority. The loss of respect for the church, the breakdown of discipline in schools, parents so money crazy they both work, no one responsible for the children, and that fucking crazy music they play. We're heading down like the Romans.

"Winston Churchill once said that the best way to predict the future is to study the past. He was right, but I would add to that. We learn from the past, but we never return to it. Once down this road, there is no turning back. So you see, unfortunately, drugs are our future. I regret it, and I had hopes it would not be so, that our traditional lines would hold, but Gennaro is right. What do you think?"

"Like you, Sally, I regret the direction. But we'll be left behind if we're not involved. Although our national leaders forbid drug dealing, they're already involved with a piece from the dealers and eventually will be in even deeper."

Sally puffed on his cigar and nodded. "Jack, I appreciate your asking for this meeting so quickly. I'll speak with Gennaro and assure him we can work together. In turn, we ask for your respect."

Jack extended his hand. "You will always have that, Salvatore."

"And what of the Ryans?"

Jack knew Gennaro Biggio and Salvatore Cardoza could care less if groups of crazy Irish-American gangsters wanted to clip each other. Let the stupid Micks murder each other, they would think, as long as it didn't affect their business.

"That is my problem to solve, Sally, and I will solve it."

30

Jerry's wound was clearly superficial, but the hurt look in his eyes as Jack related his story revealed deeper wounds that would last forever. The three brothers sat alone in the living room at Copeland Road that Saturday evening. The trip home from New York had proven uneventful, with Paulie Cronin, by far the family's best wheel man, having taken all precautions, including a second car driven by one of the soldiers following directly behind them.

Serving as bartender, Tommy moved to the kitchen to refill the whiskey glasses with VO and ginger ale. He had spent part of Saturday morning giving further interviews to the New York media on his victory and the attempted mugging, and in late afternoon had met in Boston with the local media. In the early evening, scores of neighbors from East Lynn had stopped by Fayette Street to offer congratulations and express their civic pride in a Lynner who would now fight for the middleweight championship of the world. It was a relief in some ways to be sitting in Jerry's living room, away from the crowds, the questions, the traumatic event of Leo's death. Yet, as he searched for and wondered about Jerry's reaction to Jack's long story, he was not sure how much relief existed here.

"You had Jimma Flaherty killed, Jack?" Jerry asked incredulously. "Am I hearing this right?"

"No. I killed him myself."

"Jesus, Mary, and Joseph."

"Jerry, listen to me." He paused for a long moment. "It had to be done, or he would have had me killed. I offer no excuses or apologies for my actions or for my life. Maybe I should have told you something about it years ago, but to what purpose? You have your own life, you made something of yourself, and you now have a new family."

"You still should have told me, Jack. I'm your fuckin' brother."

Jack ignored the comment and continued. "Jerry, I need you to understand something else. In no way do you or Sheila need to worry about your safety. What happened in New York was a case of mistaken identity, and that's all. You were not the target. It is an unwritten law of my world and theirs that uninvolved family are never targets. I tell you..."

"So now I know why my gambling debts back at college were erased, huh, Jack?"

Jack shrugged. "Let me finish.

"You and Sheila and little Marty can continue to lead your life your way. I know I disappoint and hurt you, but I am what I am, Jerry. And nothing can change that now. I..."

"What you are is our brother, Jack." Tommy interrupted. "You don't need to make apologies to him or to me or to anyone. If it wasn't for you, I'd be nowhere. And so wouldn't you, Jerry."

"Don't you think I know that, Tom?" Jerry frowned. "I don't need the reminder. I just need some time to understand all this, that's all."

"Look, it's late. I haven't slept for over thirty hours. I need some rest," Jack said, standing.

Jerry stood with him, his eyes watering. Quickly he embraced Jack, fighting back the sobs. "Nothing is going to change with me, Jack. You know I'll always be with you."

Tommy smiled, stood, and moved into their circle. "Hey, you two need a referee to separate you? No clinching."

Little Eddie Sheehan's brother Patrick tried to restrain himself when he heard the date being made. He looked deep into his drink, trying to hide from the others around him what he hoped was not his expressed glee. For weeks he had feigned friendship with the Ryans, accepting their condolences at

Eddie's wake, their expression of sorrow, such as the food baskets they had sent to his grieving mother in her apartment at West 49th Street. The bastards had clipped his older brother. They must think him a turnip just off the truck from the old country, a fuckin' stupid Dubliner who did not know his ass from his elbow.

Rumors abounded that Connie Ryan had authorized the hit and that Crazy Johnny had executed his brother. Eddie had warned him to beware of the treachery of the Ryans. They were unforgiving, fearful of reprisals, devious in their plotting. If anything were to happen to him, he had said, then look no further than around the corner to the White House Bar for his murderers.

For some years all male members of the Sheehan clan had frequented the White House so his presence there was both expected and accepted. It was difficult for him to face almost nightly the murderous bastards, but time was something he had plenty of. He would await his moment.

It was even more difficult for him to sit near Crazy Johnny at the end of the bar, but he buried his pride, and extended his hand, and said all the correct things. When the crazy bastard spun one of his bullshit stories about his conquest of some woman or his pummeling of some poor defenseless civilian, he laughed with the rest, hoping against hope that some information of importance would fall into his hands. He was smart enough to realize he could not handle the enforcer by himself, not one-on- one. Yet perhaps he could catch him with his defenses down, or come upon a situation where someone else could service him. And that is exactly what happened.

On the two nights following the Kelly-Hall fight, Johnny would drink too many boilermakers and speak, among the small group at the end of the bar, of his animosity toward the Kellys. He and Connie had been double-crossed with some high stakes in play. Although Patrick Sheehan could not discern exactly who did what to whom, it became obvious that Jack Kelly of Lynn was an enemy, along with the fighter himself. A serious enemy to be eliminated in the very near future, and you could take Crazy Johnny's word for that. The fuckin' Lynn car dealer would pay and pay soon.

On the Monday following the fight, Patrick Sheehan struck gold. One of Johnny's many lady friends called the White House Bar and above the din Patrick heard the words that triggered his idea. "I'll meet you on Friday night at 10 for a nice quiet late dinner at the Red Coach Grill on Broadway. OK? Love you, babe."

Patrick Sheehan looked up from his drink, now sure that his grin had, indeed, been suppressed. He could almost guess what Johnny would say next. A long story about how he planned to seduce the married woman to whom he had just spoken, that is if he had not already succeeded in doing so.

On Tuesday morning, Patrick Sheehan placed the long distance call to Lynn, Massachusetts. "Stanton Chevrolet," the sweet voice on the other end answered.

"I need to speak with Jack Kelly."

"One moment, sir," Miss Sweety Voice said.

"Hello, this is Jack Kelly. What can I do for you?"

"You watching your ass, boyo?" Sheehan began.

"Who's this?"

"It bears no matter, boyo. What matters is what I'm going to tell you as a fellow enemy of those fuckin' Ryan brothers. You with me boyo?"

"You have the wrong number, mick."

"No, I don't Mr. Kelly. But there's no need for you to reply, no need at all. Just listen and act if you want to. Your first reaction is to suspect a trap, and that it is not, boyo. But you will check out that possibility, as you should."

"Mister, this is a car agency. I don't know what you're talking about."

"Johnny Ryan will be at the Red Coach Grill on Broadway on Friday night at 10 P.M., alone with his married woman of the week. Take him out for both of us, boyo. I'm telling you he will be alone with her."

At the hum of the disconnection, Jack stared at the desk and then walked out of his office to the main receptionist's desk. "Rita, hold all calls for the next hour. I need some time alone."

31

On Thursday Jack drove to New York City by himself. He registered at the City Squire Inn on Broadway under an assumed name, confining himself to the hotel for the balance of the day and night. He would have loved to catch the double feature at the New Amsterdam Theater on 42nd Street, or walk over to the Stage Deli on Broadway, but he took the safe course, unsure about the call he had received.

There was more than a distinct possibility that the Ryans were setting a trap for him. Still, there was something in the caller's voice that told him otherwise. The voice had been urgent, hateful, and Jack's instincts told him this was an opportunity not to be missed.

On Friday morning he rose early, shaved, ready to follow the plan he had outlined in his mind. He left the tiny lobby and turned left to West 51st Street and passed by the Red Coach Grill. At 7 A.M. scores of pedestrians hurled their bodies against the force of the strong, biting winds, determined to get where they were going quickly. He peered into the window of the Red Coach, noting that the dining room was adjacent to the bar and lounge where he had previously met the Ryans.

Crossing the avenue, he walked the two blocks between 50th and 52nd Streets, occasionally stopping to look across at the restaurant. He needed to identify at least two locations from where he could observe the comings and goings that evening. He would arrive around 9, an hour before Johnny Ryan was due to appear. He would watch for telltale signs of a trap -- Johnny arriving with other men; a team of men scouting the area themselves; bodyguards following the couple when they finished dinner; a suspicious loner entering the dining room.

He settled on the small coffee shop fronting the avenue at 51st Street for one location. Enjoying a breakfast of orange juice, coffee, and a plain doughnut, he looked directly across the street at the Red Coach. It was an excellent location from where he could also view any approaches threatening his safety. For the second location he chose the steps of the Americana Hotel just up the street. At night he could easily mix with the crowds climbing the steps toward its lobby and those descending and hailing cabs for a night on the town.

He was set. For the balance of the day he would occupy himself with reading, watching television, and, around 2 he would go to sleep until close to 9. It would be another long night, for once he had disposed of Crazy Johnny Ryan he planned to drive out of the combination hotel/motor lodge directly to Boston.

When he entered the City Squire, he walked to the reception desk and informed the assistant manager that he would be leaving around midnight, but, of course, would be willing to pay for the two nights. The prissy young man beamed his approval, and was all too willing to accept Jack's request that his bag be placed in his car around 9 P.M.

Back in his room, he flipped channels and found one that was playing an old John Wayne movie, one that he had seen more than once, but "Red River" was also one of Wayne's best. He couldn't concentrate on the film, his mind wandering to the man he would murder in a few hours, a man who had killed one of his best friends and nearly killed his brother. He also thought long and hard of Marjorie, recognizing that it was only a matter of time now when he would have to tell her of his involvement. He needed to prepare for that meeting, and he anticipated a most difficult confrontation.

He must have fallen asleep early and slept soundly, for at 8:30 P.M. he was startled by the incessant ringing of the telephone.

"Hello."

"It's 8:30, Mister Cummings," the breezy voice related. "Thanks so much."

He threw cold water on his face and then dressed in the white shirt and blue tie he had laid on the chair. He studied his appearance in the long mirror behind the bathroom door as he put on the blue suit coat. He picked up his bag and his topcoat and took the elevator to the lobby, where the bellhop readily relieved him of the luggage, promising to place it in the car.

He ordered coffee in the shop at 51st Street, and for the next hour carefully observed the foot traffic around the Red Coach Grill. He saw nothing unusual throughout the hour, nothing to concern him. Then around five minutes to ten, a young blond woman got out of a yellow cab and proceeded to the dining room entrance. He scanned the area, looking toward Times Square in particular. He could see back to 49th Street clearly and from that direction he saw something that started his juices flowing. Crazy Johnny Ryan walked briskly across 50th Street, heading toward the restaurant. He was alone and paid little attention to the crowds around him, instead walking, hatless, with his head down. He turned into the restaurant without looking around at all.

Jack sat attentively for the next fifteen minutes, looking north and south for any signs of activity, any sign of collusion. Again, he observed nothing out of the ordinary. He sat for another half hour, then paid his bill and walked north toward the Americana. He calculated that they would leave the restaurant around 11:30, but he never let his eyes wander from the front door. Occasionally, he stepped into the Americana lobby to warm himself. With all the movement of people, no one paid particular attention to him. What if Ryan left the restaurant with her by taxi? If that happened, then he would have to wait for another time. On a matter concerning family, he could wait forever.

At 11:25 they came out of the restaurant, Johnny Ryan trying to hail a cab as the blond held his arm. Jack descended the hotel steps and crossed the avenue, walking south toward the couple. As he closed the distance, he saw Ryan bend to kiss her and assist her into the taxi. He waved as the taxi pulled away, then turned right toward Times Square.

Trailing now from a distance, Jack observed Ryan turn west at 48th Street toward Eighth Avenue heading straight into the neighborhood. Johnny moved along at a normal pace, again paying little attention to the crowds of pedestrians.

Jack quickened his pace as they approached Eighth Avenue. The more they moved west, the more the crowds dissipated. The theatrical district quickly turned into scores of tenements rising above them in the blackness. Hit him now, Jack, he told himself, before he's any deeper into the neighborhood. He felt behind his spine for the short-barreled Smith and Wesson .38. All the while he continued to look around him. He had long ago dropped his concern about a trap, but now it was important he act when no one was near them.

Almost halfway between Eighth and Ninth Avenues, Jack closed to within fifteen yards. He concentrated on the sidewalks both before and behind him for any sign of activity. Now there were no other pedestrians within half a block of them. Hearing the quick steps, Ryan turned and stopped.

"Remember me, Johnny?"

Without hesitation, Jack raised the .38 and shot him in the stomach. Ryan staggered for a brief moment and then fell backward into the gutter. Quickly Jack stood above him. "That was for Leo Slattery, Johnny, and the next one is for fucking with my family." He shot Ryan in the head and then turned quickly back toward Eighth Avenue.

As he neared the corner of Eighth and 48th Street, he tossed the weapon into a sewer opening. He turned left toward 50th Street, losing himself in the crowd, and proceeded rapidly toward the City Squire Inn. Within ten minutes he would be on the road home.

Connie Ryan received the news of his younger brother's death at the White House Bar. Dead on arrival at St. Clare's Hospital. Dead. Connie sat stunned, not really hearing the rest of Denny Coogan's words. Denny had been tipped by a Midtown North homicide detective, he was saying.

Standing, Connie walked to the men's room and locked both the outer door and the stall door, sliding the bolt firmly shut. He vomited repeatedly into the toilet, standing there for the longest time, letting his stomach turn over and then settle. Who could have killed Johnny? It was not an easy question to answer. Despite the respect and the fear they engendered in the neighborhood, they had many enemies among the up and coming, among those they had moved against -- including any number of West Side Irishmen with an insatiable thirst for revenge. He paused. Or those Irish pricks from Boston. The answer might lie there. Whether they were involved or not, he was determined that Jack Kelly was going to die. Johnny had killed one of the Kelly group. That same day Flaherty is murdered before Ryan could even talk with him. And now, a week later, Johnny is dead. Maybe someone else -- one of impulsive Johnny's many sworn enemies -- had retaliated. Maybe. He would have his men fan the neighborhood for any information concerning Johnny's murder. But Kelly was going to die regardless.

And then he thought of his mother. How was he to explain this to her, he wondered. Her youngest boy assassinated in the street by some unknown assailant. And how to explain to Johnny's wife, now a widow after just a few short years of marriage.

He regained control of himself, unlatched the bolt, and stepped to the sink. He splashed cold water on his face and wiped the last of the bad taste from his mouth. Only when he was completely composed, did he step out toward the bar. He could hear increasing commotion in the bar area as loyalists, having heard the news, came in from the streets. "I need a ride to my mother's home on the Island," he announced to no one in particular.

"I'll take you. My car's right out front," said Denny.

As they exited the Queens Tunnel, he sat silently, thinking of the words he would use to convey their loss to his mother, to ease her pain. He thought of Johnny as a youth, of his roaming the streets outside their flat on West 44th Street, his teen age crush on Molly Kiely, his stint in reform school, his rise in stature within the West Side family because of the fearlessness with which he faced difficult situations. If only Johnny had been less impulsive, more careful, Connie thought. He was like a train going down the track, one directional and ever-increasing its speed. A collision had been inevitable. With the back of his hand, Connie wiped a tear from his eye. His loyal, faithful younger brother, so dependent on him, was dead. Now he searched for words he knew their mother would only partially hear.

Two weeks after the fight, Tommy sat in the ophthalmologist's office on the second floor at Massachusetts Eye and Ear, listening carefully to Dr. Ralph Curtin. The retina, the tall bespectacled doctor explained, is a delicate layer of light-sensitive cells that lines the rear three-fourths of the eyeball. Beneath the retina is a layer of blood vessels called the choroid, which provides the outer retina with oxygen and nutrients. Sometimes, he went on, the retina lifts away from the choroid. A hole in the retina causes this detachment. The hole usually forms due to degeneration of the retina. "What you have, Tom, is a detached retina."

"How long will it take to heal, Doctor?" Tommy interrupted.

"Tom, these flashes of light you've been experiencing, the loss of peripheral vision, the blurring you've been having lately, tell me you need an operation. What I am saying is your central vision has been impaired."

Tommy hesitated to ask the question both of them knew was coming. "After the operation, when can I resume fighting?"

Dr. Curtin moved from behind his desk and adjusted the blinds so that more sunlight entered the office. He came around to the front of the desk and sat on the corner in front of Tommy.

"Tommy, let me try to answer that question," he said gently. "Central to your condition is the fact that detachment has already occurred. When we operate -- and we ought to arrange the operation soon -- we may find that your full field of vision is restored, but your central vision, most probably, will be blurred to some extent."

Tommy stared ahead. "What you're telling me, Doctor, is that even with the operation I can't ever fight again. Right?"

The doctor paused, obviously attempting to choose his words both carefully and sensitively. "I'm afraid that's it, Tom. I hate to give you this kind of news, but it's not all bad. You can lead a normal life, with the blurring, but you won't be able to fight. No legitimate boxing commission would ever allow that. If you fight, then you risk becoming permanently blind. We're going to have to watch the other eye as well," he added. "Once you experience detachment in one eye, there's always the possibility of a similar condition in the other one."

Tommy sat stunned, riveted to the chair. "All of my life I've been a boxer, Doctor. I just don't know what else I can do. I..." His voice trailed off.

Dr. Curtin placed a hand on his shoulder. "Tom, with your ability, your youth, your contacts, there are bound to be any number of opportunities for you to consider. For now, we must move aggressively and schedule the procedure as soon as possible. Are we agreed, or would you prefer a second opinion?"

Tommy stood and extended his hand to the doctor. "I'm not sure, Doc. Let me think a bit about the whole situation. I'm getting hit with a lot of shots to the body all at one time."

32

The heads of New York City's Five Families were not happy. For decades they had proudly outstripped the Irish and every other ethnic group in almost every facet of their various businesses. That fool J. Edgar Hoover was so infatuated with chasing Communists that he had even denied the existence of the Mafia, thus allowing them to build a network of national proportions, centrally controlled by the Five Families from New York.

But now New York City was changing, almost too rapidly. Across the metropolis neighborhoods were deteriorating and in areas like the Bronx great ghettos sprouted. The physical changes were symbolic of old alliances that were also fast breaking down. In the recent past the ward enforcers, the neighborhood leaders could provide stability for their business interests. But now there was too much in-fighting, too much selfish behavior not conducive to assuring maximum profits. In particular, the dumb Irish seemed to involve themselves in more vendettas than existed even in their beloved Sicily.

"We need strong generals. As with any military operation, we require leadership, daring, the ability to maintain discipline within the ranks, and we have this with Connie Ryan on the West Side. He has respected our covenants and has even strengthened our interests in Manhattan in a highly effective manner. We must support him in this current dispute and allow him to move against his enemy in Boston," concluded Mario Gianelli, head of the Manhattan family.

On this late wintry February day they gathered in an oval library on the estate of Don Michael Forelli in East Islip, Long

Island. The heads of the families sat quite comfortably around the large conference table while, behind them, their various representatives stood on call, providing, on a whim, a drink, a cigar, a match, a whispered conversation. To each, it was important that these interruptions be rather constant in order to demonstrate their relative power, their position within the Families. Outside the library topcoated soldiers encircled the estate, vigilant to provide both security and fair warning in the event of intrusion by outside forces, thoughts of Apalachin still strongly infused in their bosses' memories.

"With all due respect to my colleague, I must suggest an alternative," offered Don Anthony Zicardi, head of the Staten Island family. "We cannot afford to alienate friends of ours in New England, in particular Don Gennaro Biggio in Providence and Salvatore Cardoza in Boston.

"I must remind my colleague that we are a national organization, indeed an international enterprise. I'm offended that we sit here today, with all of our problems that concern such an enterprise in these trying times worried about avoidable Irish warfare between factions in New York and in Boston, two of our major areas of involvement.

"I say to you all here today..." he paused, beckoning forward his representative to fill his wine glass. "I say to you all here today," he began again, "that our best approach is to send our representative to insist that this vendetta end."

"I agree with my friend," interjected Vincent Giardello, head of the Queens family. "Like Don Zicardi, I want stability. We are a fuckin' international business. It is, then, less so a matter of supporting our friend on the West Side and much more a matter of asking him and our New England colleagues to reach a mutual accommodation, an understanding of the minds, an end to this ugly business that threatens all of our interests. I recommend that we insist, through our representative, that this fuckin' problem end. To make sure this happens, I suggest that Don Zicardi be asked to handle this pimple on the face of progress. I suggest he be authorized to meet with both these assholes to end the distraction, and insist of these people that they cooperate or all be replaced."

As presiding officer, and as the don of dons, Don Forelli listened to all viewpoints, knowing that when he chose to speak his word would be final. It would be final for two reasons: the respect shown him for his ability to coalesce the Family these past three years, and the wisdom of his decision-making in the eyes of all participants.

As Don Giardello concluded his remarks, Don Forelli surveyed the conference table, awaiting any further commentary from the assembly. He considered Giardello crude and coarse, but his comments made sense. Pausing for an appropriate period, he waited while the various representatives serviced their dons. He knew that this period of silence would result in a focus on the chair, and he played to the moment.

Finally, he spoke. "My colleagues, on this particular matter, I respect all the points of view brought forward this afternoon. It is important that we present various alternatives for consideration and in a spirit of civility, proceed in this matter, as in all matters, with what is in the best interests of all our families. I agree with those friends of mine who suggest our interests transcend any loyalty to one faction; therefore, I respectfully ask Don Zicardi to serve as our emissary and deliver our wishes to our friends. I now ask that we proceed to the next matter for our deliberation."

A thin, wiry man, he sat erect, his hawkish face bearing the definitive mark of the statesman, his piercing eyes searching the room for any signs of dissent. His hair was longish and steel gray, his dress impeccable, the gray pinstripe suit fitting him well. In a brief period of time he had built the strongest record of achievement on behalf of La Cosa Nostra of any leader of the recent past. He smiled to himself at their concurrence. "Then on to more important matters," he said firmly.

"You're leaving? You're not serious?" Jack asked incredulously. He stood in the doorway of their bedroom as

Marjorie slammed the overnight cases and set them on the bedroom floor.

"I'm not serious? You bring a life of crime to our bedroom door. You tell me my husband is not what he appeared to be. Instead, he is a gang leader, a family head as you present it. There's blood on your hands, Jack, for all I know."

"Marge, I assured you that is not the case. Our business is illegitimate, yes. We offer our clients protection, the same as an insurance agency does or opportunities to borrow money like a bank does, to gamble like at the track, or to engage in sex -- opportunities that lessen the daily pressures in most people's lives."

"You really believe your own bullshit, don't you, Jack? Like you're some kind of legitimate businessman, some kind of father figure to a family."

"That's right, Marge. In the same way your father is some kind of legitimate businessman. He steals every day from every customer under the guise of legitimacy. I don't see big differences between us."

"You bastard!" she screamed. "You dare compare your activities with my father's?"

He did not answer her, deciding instead to change course. "I had hoped you would understand, that we could talk this out more," he said gently.

"I'm leaving, Jack. I'm taking the boys and going back with my father and mother. Right now I need the separation and the time to think. To be very frank, I don't think I can handle this. I know right now I can't."

The day before he had held her hand in the kitchen and traced the story for her, with the hope that her love for him and their full life together would transcend the shock and allow her to understand. She had listened attentively, in obvious confusion, as he described his early involvement, his ascension, and recent events involving Flaherty and the Ryans. He avoided references to his own part in the killings, as he knew she could never handle it. In a large sense he continued to live a lie with

212

her then, but in his judgment there was only so much she could be told.

She had asked very few questions in response. But what else should he have expected? Although she was a strong woman, he sensed that the revelations were simply too awful, too shocking for her to accept. At this point she did need to know, however. All members of the family needed to be aware, on guard, although he seriously doubted that Connie Ryan would order hits against uninvolved family members. He still felt that Jerry had just happened to be present in New York. For the immediate future, he had assigned bodyguards to stay close to his brothers and to Marjorie, when he was not near.

Curiously her lack of understanding and support did not surprise him. He loved her, and yet he did not. He realized that made no sense and that he was the major problem, not Marjorie. Since the loss of the most important woman in his life, he felt emotionally uninvolved. It was as if once God had taken his most precious love, he had steeled himself against further hurt. He could never be hurt again. And yet, as with his brothers, he was devoted and fiercely loyal to Marjorie, but in a different way. He still felt a deeper responsibility to them cemented by a male bonding that would always hold. They were his brothers, and they were his children.

He felt something different for Marjorie. For sure there was a strong sexual attraction. He admired her devotion to their sons but not her black or white no shades of gray way of looking at the world. Like her father, she was too absorbed in self, incapable of adjusting. Her world was contained within this house, her father's home in Swampscott, and within a very limited, narrow perspective. And now he had shattered that world.

She turned to look at him, awaiting some answer to her comments. Let her leave, he thought. Her loyalty would always be wafer thin, totally dependent on her own personal comforts. Sexual attraction had been what brought them together, and now six years after, that was not enough to sustain a threatened relationship.

He answered her in a cold tone, his voice hard and harsh. "Fine, Marge. You leave and we'll separate. We can even divorce, if that's what you want ultimately. But let me be clear about one very important matter. Bobby and Timmy are my boys too, my family as well as yours. Don't ever think -- not even for a minute -- that you can isolate me from them."

She picked up the suitcases without answering and stormed down the stairway. He followed her halfway down. "I need an answer, Marjorie."

She moved to the coat rack in the hallway. "They're your children too, Jack. You can see them whenever you want. I'm asking you to help me explain our new situation to them. Maybe in time we can work things out," she said coldly.

As she stepped into the frigid February day, he knew they had passed that point. In his way he loved her, and in her way, she loved him and yet she could not be loyal to him. So close the door and keep it closed, he reflected.

33

"Thank you both for honoring my request," Don Anthony Zicardi began. "I'm deeply appreciative that both of you could accept my invitation on such short notice."

They sat in Anthony Zicardi's living room on the first floor of a modest three decker on Stone Street on Staten Island. Across from him Connie Ryan stared belligerently at Jack, only occasionally turning his gaze toward Don Zicardi.

"Anna, thank you so much for the cappuccino. Would you leave us alone now for a few minutes, dear?" the Don asked gently.

"Of course, Anthony," answered the middle aged, overweight wife of one of the most deadly crime lords in the country. She slid shut the doors separating the living and dining rooms.

Jack noted that with his gray creased trousers, checkered woolen shirt, and gray cardigan buttoned almost to the top, Zicardi looked the part of everyman's uncle. And about him, the furnishings mirrored the man, modest, neat, clean.

"I won't take much of your time, as I don't plan to review the serious matters which brought you to my home today. I believe I've been made fully aware of your cases against one another, and the denials of responsibility that each of you evince concerning the death of your friend and the wounding of your brother, Mr. Kelly, and the death of your brother, Mr. Ryan. To begin, I express to each of you my personal condolences for your losses."

He sipped his cappuccino, shifting his gaze from Jack to Ryan, warm, gray eyes that exuded friendship in sharp contrast to the words he carefully enunciated. "Our Five Families have asked me to indicate to you our regret concerning these events, but, above all, our insistence that there now be an ending to this unacceptable situation. My message to you is a succinct one. This vendetta, it is to end, and end today.

"Now I must relate to you both," he continued, "there are those who believe you should both be neutralized. 'Who needs this trouble,' they argue, 'trouble which endangers our interests here and in Boston?' On the other hand, Gennaro Biggio and Salvatore Cardoza speak well of you, Mr. Kelly, and here in New York we know full well of Mr. Ryan's effectiveness. A strong majority of our leadership is willing to continue our relationship, provided you two can set aside this recent difficulty."

He paused, allowing time for his full meaning to register with them. He sipped his cappuccino and eased back in his chair.

Jack knew it was important that he speak next for a number of reasons. Zicardi would note that fact later when he reviewed the matter with the other heads. Then, too, he wanted to be first to show his respect for the Don and first to demonstrate his willingness to cooperate, to accept the judgment of the many fathers when there was really no choice anyway.

"Don Zicardi," he began, "I thank you for calling us together, particularly here in your own home. I'm grateful for your intervention in this extremely difficult situation. As you suggest, I have felt a deep personal loss with the death of my good friend Leo Slattery, and most particularly, with the attempted murder of my own brother, a completely uninvolved civilian. And at the same time, my other brother's future is in serious doubt. He is now awaiting final word on whether he can ever again return to the ring."

Across from him, Ryan, nattily attired in a powder blue suit with a red and blue striped tie, sat expressionless listening intently to Jack's words.

"I have absolutely no knowledge of the death of Johnny Ryan," Jack lied, "yet I extend my deepest sympathy to Connie

216

for this terrible loss. It is a devastating tragedy, and I am aware that no words of mine can diminish the pain Connie must feel.

"From my view, enough is enough. Today, like you, Don Zicardi, I want peace, and an agreement to end all hostilities. In Boston we're having enough trouble among the various Irish factions, and with drug dealing becoming more prevalent I expect even more trouble to surface. I have enough to do to consolidate our position and remain vigilant concerning these cowboys threatening my interests.

"Don Zicardi," he concluded, insuring the proper tone of respect in his comment, "I do accept the recommendation of the Five Families and swear my acceptance of the conditions you require."

Zicardi nodded, the slight suggestion of a smile on his lips.

Jack knew what Ryan would say before he even began. He would believe none of what he heard.

"Don Zicardi, you asked us to be brief here today, so I will honor your request. I thank you for your hospitality, and I, too, accept the judgment of the Five Families that peace must be made here today. My brother lies dead, and his mother mourns him daily, even today not understanding this loss, unable to cope with her baby's death. Mr. Kelly says he did not commit, nor did he direct, my brother's death. I'll accept him at his word.

"I regret the death of Jack's friend and the wounding of his brother. For the record, I insist that these actions were never ordered by me and I have no knowledge of the perpetrator. I bear no further malice despite the fact that the Kellys broke my business deal with them."

Jack wanted to reply, but knew it was important he not interrupt. He had made his statement.

"Don Zicardi," Connie concluded, "I accept the peace made here today and, again, am grateful for your intervention."

"It is I, on behalf of the Families, who thank each of you for your willingness to forgive and forget and to move forward. I will report to my associates that this matter is concluded." Don Zicardi shook each of their hands as they all stood together. Jack offered his hand to Connie, who accepted it.

They exited the apartment together and, without saying anything more, parted, each moving toward a parked car along the street. As he walked toward Ray, who opened the passenger door for him, Jack knew, and he sensed Ryan would feel similarly, that the matter was far from concluded. The Italians could not understand there were no such words as "forgive" or "forget" in the Irish mind, only in their vocabulary. It was possible that he might never see Connie Ryan again. But it was more probable that he would. Because whatever Connie Ryan felt, he was responsible for Leo's death and Jerry's shooting. He was a dead man, sometime in the future.

34

Jack knocked on the front door of the apartment at 140 Horadan Way on Mission Hill. A young pre-teen with a cowlick over his eye peeked across the chain at him. "Ma, it's Mr. Kelly," he yelled toward the rear.

"Well, let him in, Danny," Catherine Slattery called out in frustration.

Danny Slattery slid the chain and opened the door. "How are you Mr. Kelly?"

"I'm fine, Danny. Just fine. Are you doing OK?"

The pimple-faced young man shyly flipped his cowlick back before answering. "I'm watching out for Ma like you said I should."

Jack tousled his hair just as Catherine Slattery entered the front room.

"It's good to see you, Jack. Can I get you some tea or coffee?"

"Tea would be perfect with a little milk."

"Just like mother made for you, I'll bet."

"And how would you know that, Catherine, my dear?"

"Because the Irish never change their diet. Anything aside from meat, potatoes, and tea is beyond their comprehension. Come on into the kitchen, Jack. Danny, can you hang the wash in the backyard for me?"

"Sure, Ma."

"You like the house, Catherine?" Jack asked as soon as Danny disappeared.

"Of course, Jack. Who wouldn't? A beautiful home in West Roxbury. I just don't know how to thank you."

"When will you be moving?"

"In a month. As soon as Danny finishes the school year."

"Do you need any money?" he asked as she set the cup of tea on the kitchen table and beckoned him to a seat.

"Jack, it's now been three months since Leo's death and every week a man comes by and presents me with an envelope with $2,000 in it. 'That's from Jack Kelly' he always says, and I say back to him 'God bless Jack Kelly.' I hope you get these messages."

"Did Leo leave you much, Catherine?"

"Over $400,000 in life insurance alone. I've invested it with someone he trusted. I also have $200,000 in cash in safe places. We're going to be fine."

She looked tired and worried, the creases around her face deeper than those of most women not yet forty. Her eyes were joyless, her face too pale. He reached into his suitcoat and pulled out a small brown envelope. He pressed it into her hand as she lowered her teacup into its saucer.

"And what's this?"

"It's $10,000, Catherine. I want you to take it and invest it in bonds or certificates of deposit. It's for Danny's college education."

"Jack, I..."

"Shhh," he said gently. "Please accept it. For me. He meant so much to me, Catherine. And if something had happened to me instead of him, he would be sitting in my home doing the same thing right now."

She lowered her head and wiped her eyes with the napkin on the table.

"You ever need anything you call me, right?" he asked, coming around the table to lift her face.

"Bless you, Jack."

"Catherine, in time I hope you will find someone. It would be good for you, and for Danny as well."

She stood to embrace him. "Perhaps in time, Jack. We'll see."

He kissed her on the forehead and stepped back.

"I have to leave now, Catherine."

"You take good care of you, Jack."

"That I will, Catherine."

"Remember," she said, "there never was a horse that couldn't be rode or never a cowboy that couldn't be throwed."

"Now that's solid advice, but definitely not an Irish saying," he smiled.

"John Wayne, 1960," she laughed in return.

35

Tommy finally decided to seek even another opinion, but he did so without enthusiasm. He had known the answer before the ophthalmologist at John Hopkins in Baltimore sat with him in the fall of 1962. His career was over, his opportunity to move to the top of his profession cut off. He listened to the hum-drum presentation of one of the world's premier experts on detached retinas without displaying much emotion. Looking backward over the last few months, he tried to remember when he first knew.

For the balance of the winter he had rested the eye, staying completely away from the gymnasium. He still had hope that the original diagnosis had been incorrect, or at least too conservative, but two other doctors had agreed with Dr. Curtin. With the media he remained upbeat, indicating he planned to return to the ring late in 1962. He would be cautious, he told them, and would probably schedule a tune-up bout in the fall, rather than face Fullmer right away. Outwardly, he exuded confidence when he and Santangelo presented themselves to the media on the day of his first workout, exactly three months after the Hall fight. Inwardly, he had never felt so depressed in his life. At home, when he stood and threw jabs at imaginary opponents, he could sense that his initial optimism had been misplaced. His peripheral vision just wasn't right.

Yet he had continued to work hard all through the spring and into the summer, running in the streets, dutifully performing jumping jacks and push-ups at the Lynn Y, keeping his weight down. He fought depression by believing that the problem would clear up any day now.

It was early September when he finally faced the mountain he had to climb. He had asked Petey to arrange a private three-round bout against a tough unranked middleweight from Houston named Lonny Salinas, a journeyman willing to meet him at the Boston Arena Annex. During the summer he had banged the light and heavy bags about, but had avoided live competition, hoping the additional rest would be of benefit. He even regained hope during the late summer, as he had experienced no problems with his eyesight in working the bags.

For most of the three rounds, with only Petey and Gus present in the rear of the old Arena, he had jabbed away at Salinas, his shots to the Mexican's body as damaging as they had ever been. But when Salinas moved from side to side, particularly to his own right, Tommy could not see a number of the right hand bombs coming. Toward the end of the third round, Salinas glided away from him, tossing out a straight left followed by a vicious right hook he simply never saw coming. He fell backward, dazed and bewildered. In the distance he could vaguely hear Petey calling an end to the match. Someone helped him to his corner -- Gus? -- and then the world came into focus again, but it was not the world he had hoped it would be.

Now here in late September, he listened to Dr. Cameron Stevenson at Johns Hopkins telling him officially that his condition had worsened, that he must have the operation, and that he must never fight again. He really had no questions to ask so he thanked the doctor and left quickly.

On the Eastern Airlines flight home, he tried to concentrate on the future, as both Jack and Jerry had urged, but he preferred to think of the chance that had slipped away. He had been one step away from the middleweight championship of the world. He would call a press conference in the next day or two and announce his retirement.

When he came out of Terminal A at Logan, Jerry beeped at him from the parking lot across the street, waving from the open window. He crossed the walkway and entered the red and white Mercury Comet without saying a word.

"So how did it go, Tom?"

Tommy shrugged. "Just the way I told you it would. No way I can fight again. There's even been further deterioration."

"I don't know what to say, Tom. It's such a tough break."

"Say nothing, brother. In fact, I'm getting tired of both talking and thinking about it myself. I need to start thinking of doing something else."

They drove around Bell Circle in Revere and took Route 1A toward Lynn. On a beautiful September day, Tommy noticed the few yellow leaves on the otherwise green trees as they sped toward the city.

"Tommy, I can get you a position at A&P like I said," Jerry said, rushing the words.

"Jerry, I don't ever want you to think I'm ungrateful, but for a lot of reasons it's not right for me. I have little education, and, frankly, I'm not very interested in going back to school. School and I never did get along very well. Secondly, I need some action, some excitement. The problem with boxing is that everyone's all over you, you feel like someone, you're king of the hill. You know what I mean? You're on a perpetual high -- people slapping you on the back, everybody recognizing you. After the last seven years, I can't give that up. Somehow, I have to hear the roar of the crowd."

"You're going with Jack, aren't you?" It was as much a declaration as a question.

"Yeah, Jerry, I am, but it's my call all the way. He hasn't been encouraging."

"I didn't think he would be, Tom."

"He even tried to talk me out of it, but it's more me than some job where I'd be sitting on my ass all day."

Jerry nodded. "You need any money now?"

"Money?" Tommy laughed. "No. I saved plenty from the fights. The question should be reversed."

"I'm doing okay, Tom. A&P treats me first class. I keep getting offers from the other chains, and they keep me satisfied so I'll stay."

Tommy smiled. "Now there's a smart company."

It was exactly a week after the assassination of President Kennedy that the call came from Marjorie. Since the separation they had kept in frequent communication, talking cordially by telephone on average once a week as they planned for his visits or for a myriad of family social events.

On Friday, November 29 he sat in his office at Stanton Chevrolet studying the weekly sales report when the receptionist buzzed him.

"Mrs. Kelly on line two."

"Yes, Marjorie."

"Jack, I can't talk right now, but I'm with Dad at the Lynn Hospital. He's had a massive heart attack and I..." She began to cry.

"I'll be there in ten minutes."

By the time he arrived, Grant Stanton had succumbed. When he entered the intensive care area, Marjorie sat with the doctor on a long wooden bench in the corridor. Just six months ago, she had lost her mother to breast cancer and now this. She dabbed at her eyes as he approached.

The doctor stood and shook hands with Jack. "I'm very sorry, Jack," he said. "I'll leave you two alone now. Call me if you need anything."

"Marjorie, I'm so sorry," Jack said, sitting next to her.

"Oh, Jack," she cried, leaning her face into his shoulder. "Thank you for being here. I..."

"Don't say anything, Marge. Just let me hold you, please."

She buried her face in his shoulder and began to sob uncontrollably. He stroked her hair and just sat there with her for the longest of times, wanting simply to help her in any way he could. He stayed at her side throughout the wake and funeral, taking care of all the arrangements for her. She valued his kindness and his consideration, his strong effort to guide her through the difficult period. In the weeks that followed she asked him to manage the dealership for her. Whatever else might happen, she knew he would always protect her financially, as he had since their separation. Sometimes ex-lovers make the best friends.

"Jack? Bill Blaney here. Tommy's here. And..." He paused.

"And what, Billy?"

"He's had too much to drink, Jack. Before he even got here. He's not causing any problem, but he's alone and down in the dumps. He shouldn't drive home."

"Thanks, Billy. I'll be there in fifteen minutes. Keep an eye on him."

He nodded to the bartender as he walked into Monte's from the bar entrance. "Thanks, Billy," he said, as he slid into the seat next to Tommy's. Overhead, the Boston and Maine train shook the small restaurant as it rattled over the bridge above them on its route to Gloucester.

"Want somethin' to drink, Jack?"

"VO and ginger, Billy. Get some black coffee for him."

"Sure."

Tommy raised his head, for the first time, acknowledging his brother's presence for a moment before lowering his head back onto his elbows.

"Here, drink this," Jack said as he pushed the coffee cup toward Tommy.

Tommy lifted his head and stared at the cup. "I need something stronger than that stuff."

"No, you don't. You've had enough. Drink the coffee."

"I know when I've had enough, and I say I need a shot," Tommy shouted.

"Shut the fuck up and drink the coffee."

"Jesus, aren't we uppity tonight."

"You know, you keep this shit up you'll be seeing guys like the old man used to. Fuckin' Luke will be coming back from the dead so you and he can climb walls together."

Tommy shook his head. "No way that's going to happen to me, brother."

Jack stared him down. "Is that right, Tommy? Look at you. You're like the old man come back to life. Drinking almost

227

every day and night. Denying the problem. Do you remember how the old man was always in denial?"

"I don't need to hear this shit. I'm going home."

"And you're not like the old man, huh, Tom? Come on, I'm taking you. You're in no condition to drive."

Sliding off the stool, Tommy staggered against the bar as he attempted his first step. "On second thought," he slurred, "I'll wait and go home later."

"You'll go home now," Jack said standing to support his brother. He placed a twenty dollar bill on the counter. "You covered, Billy?"

"Thanks, Jack."

He drove the short distance to Goldfish Pond without saying anything more. He would wait until morning when what he had to say might be better heard. He would stay overnight and cook breakfast for both of them.

"So did you meet with the McLaughlin guys and the Winter Hill guys yesterday?" Jack asked as he spooned out the fried eggs and bacon onto two separate plates.

From the kitchen they could look directly across Goldfish Pond up to Laundry Hill and Fayette Street. In the background the radio announcer droned on about the upcoming election, emphasizing the uphill battle Barry Goldwater faced in unseating President Johnson. Jack flipped the dial to the all-music station and lowered the volume as the sounds of "I Want to Hold Your Hand" filled the room.

"We met for coffee yesterday morning over in Southie," Tommy responded. He was alert, clean shaven, and engaged, in direct contrast to the night before.

"Who showed?"

"McLaughlin sent Matt Duggan and Joey Galvin, and Jimmy Bulger and the Rifleman -- Flemmi -- represented the Somerville guys. Like you asked, I brought Vin with me."

"How'd it go?"

Tommy nodded affirmatively. "I think we reached some understandings for you guys to bless, and I made the points we agreed on."

"Take me through the scene."

They sat at the oval oak table sipping the hot coffee while they ate slowly. Jack shut the radio off, waiting for Tommy to begin.

"I explained you and Cardoza were very concerned with the ongoing gang fights between the two of them. Fuckin' Charlestown versus Somerville, as if we don't have enough troubles. Over twenty hits in the last year alone, and maybe more. I told them it was unacceptable to you and to Salvatore and to our friends in Providence."

"How'd they react?"

"My opinion? Fine. Thanks mostly to the Winter Hill guys. They're smarter than the Charlestown guys. Particularly Bulger -- the white-haired young guy? He's someone to watch in the future. He helped push the conversation along. He said his boss wants peace as well. He suggested along with Vin and me that they move to a truce. Calm down before we and the Italians have to clip a couple of them, I told them."

"You mention that our family would serve as mediator on any disputes that remain?"

"Yeah. Both of them will relay our messages to their heads. I think we're home free. But you were right. There was no way they could settle the beefs themselves. I'll be surprised if they don't accept our advice and our offer to step in. They don't need trouble with us and the Mafia."

Jack paused before answering. "Let's hope so. There's way too much attention being called to all of us with bodies being found every other day all over the Goddamn city."

He cleared the dishes and placed them in the sink. "Hey, I'll take care of those later," Tommy said.

"You want more coffee?" Jack asked.

"I'm set."

Sitting down slowly Jack asked, "You enjoying this life, Tom?"

"What do you mean?"

"I mean you've been with us now more than a year. Are you enjoying what you're doing? Because I can't believe you are. Not with your drinking like a fuckin' lush, which is likely what you'll become you keep it up."

Tommy frowned. "I'm watching myself, Jack."

"No, you're not, Tom. What you're doing for me now isn't too far removed from boxing. You have to stay sharp, alert, focused. Just like you did in the ring, kid. Right now you're undisciplined, unfocused, careless. Guys like the ones you met with yesterday look for weaknesses like booze, broads, gambling. Then they have you. They exploit that weakness. They'll eat you up."

"I'm handling it."

"And I say you're not, champ. Did you hear anything I said last night?"

"About what?"

Jack let out a long sigh. "Well, that answers my question for sure."

Tommy rolled his eyes toward the ceiling and studied some spot on the ceiling.

"What now? You looking for bugs like the old man used to? You don't have a problem, huh, Tom? Two months ago we took the boys to the Sox game to see Tony Conigliaro, the kid from St. Mary's play? You remember that? You're half in the bag before we get there, and then in the first inning you go for a beer, so you say, and I never see you again. Not for the whole fuckin' afternoon. There I am with three screaming kids as much interested in Tony Conigliaro as they are in Marilyn Monroe or Mamie Van Doren, or whoever the actress is he's dating. So after a couple of hours of no Tommy, and three kids asking me fifty times or so 'Where's Uncle Tommy?' I corral them all in the seventh inning and head to the phones and dial here. And guess what, Tommy? A sluggish voice slowly answered. 'Hello.' You remember who answered the phone, Tommy? And you don't have a problem?"

"I told you at the time I met a guy. We had a few beers. Then I headed home."

"You listening to yourself?"

"You asked me if I like the life, Jack. Definitely. I need the action. I miss boxing and all the excitement around it. The life is a great replacement for what I lost."

"Then act like you respect the life the way you did boxing. You have a responsibility to Vinnie and the others you're paired with to be as sharp for them and for the opponents you now face.

"You remember years ago you told me there wasn't a fighter born that could hurt you, that you couldn't beat? Then show me you can get this problem under fucking control, Tommy. I don't believe in alcohol counseling or AA and some asshole standing up telling the world he's a fuck up. What I do believe is that my brother has the balls to admit he has a problem and to give it that same attention, that same discipline that he gave to becoming an undefeated fighter, a champion. Stop feeling sorry for yourself and get on top of this situation."

Tommy sat in his chair, not saying a word. Jack stood and leaned against the refrigerator. "One more thing, Tom. In our lifetime together, have I ever asked anything of you? How many times have I asked something of you? I'm asking you to beat this thing for me."

Tommy stood and walked toward his brother. "What I told you is true. There's never been a fighter born that could hurt or defeat me. You'll see."

"I know I will, Tom. I know I will."

36

Jack drove slowly down Union Street, the blight of urban decay all around him. The huge department stores of his youth had closed, victims of the white flight to suburbia. The few three-story tenements lining the route looked unkempt or dilapidated, and empty lots now stood where once-thriving small businesses had prospered. Jack turned down the volume as Helen Reddy reminded her audience "That Ain't No Way to Treat a Lady." Feminism on the rise, he thought. He passed St. Joseph's Church, still erect, still majestic in the sea of disinterest Union Street had become during the 1970's.

The Paramount Theater, the Warner, in fact all nine of the city's movie houses were now gone, and in their place lay parking lots, undeveloped parcels, or small businesses doomed to fail.

Despite his ever growing personal prosperity, he had never considered leaving this city of his youth. He was as loyal to Lynn as he was to his family. To him, it was family, and yet he sorrowed at its diminution. Failure by the city's leaders to anticipate middle class movement to the suburbs and to build the necessary transportation systems to compensate for that attrition had led to the decay. Not so in neighboring Peabody, where leaders with foresight had connected that city to new major routes such as 128 and 114, where shopping malls now abounded and businesses, large and small, flourished. Federal policy didn't make sense to him. On one hand, Uncle Sam passed out millions of dollars so cities could eradicate blighted neighborhoods. On the other, he provided a similar fortune to build highways leading out of the cities, heightening the move to suburbia.

He headed toward the ocean. Once out of the center of the city, he always felt rejuvenated. His city had changed dramatically, but his ocean was everlastingly the same. On this particularly lovely July day he decided to park his Chevrolet Impala and walk along Lynn Shore Drive near Red Rock for a while. The sun had dropped down a bit, painting the area with soft colors of orange and purple.

At high tide, bathers dove from Red Rock into the disdainful ocean, and he paused briefly to watch the young males demonstrate their prowess to gleeful young females tittering on the rocks. As he looked seaward, he was carried back to a time when he, Tommy and Jerry would also seek attention both here and at Forty Steps in Nahant.

He circled the pathway, now moving briskly, mindful of the stares from women walking toward him from Swampscott. Now close to forty, he had aged well. Obsessed with his exercise program, he had, for years now alternated his running with weight lifting, keeping himself at 175 pounds. He wore his coal-black hair long, parted on the right, the sideburns running below his ear lobes. Only tiny signs of crow's feet detracted from the blue eyes that caught most people's attention on first contact.

For better than twelve years now he had held together his "Irish Mafia" family. Just as Boston had prospered under Mayor John Collins' leadership throughout the sixties through his ability to build new coalitions with businesses and, particularly, with new Irish Catholic leaders, so too had he effectively established and nurtured his alliances. In town, the old rivalries between Catholics and Protestants had been largely forgotten, and Boston enjoyed an urban renewal as strong as any. During the same period he had cemented relationships with Gennaro Biggio and Salvy Cardoza. Always respectful of their position and of the declared boundaries, Jack ensured that tribute was theirs. If he approved any free-lance activity in his territories, then its beneficiaries were similarly expected to forward a fair share to the Italians.

He controlled activities in the traditional Irish enclaves of Charlestown and South Boston, along with parts of Cambridge and Somerville as well as Lynn. In turn, he respected the boundaries that allowed Black leaders to work their home territories of Roxbury, the South End, and Dorchester. George Jackson had been retired for almost five years now, but to date no one leader had stepped forward, creating a potential problem down the road for both him and the Italians. Too many cowboys operating there, he thought. Sooner or later a crisis would occur, a crisis triggered by sociological developments in the city.

The gains fashioned by Collins and his successor Kevin White in making Boston a world-class city had also led to a deep-seated unrest in the minority community. Much as the Irish had been made to feel unwelcome in the early part of the century, now, particularly since the death of Martin Luther King, Jr., the Black community felt that same lack of empowerment. For the first time highly credible Black candidates sought public office just as the Irish had sought a voice late in the nineteenth century. Just last week, Judge Arthur Garrity had ruled that the Boston schools had intentionally run a dual system of education. The call of Black leaders for greater involvement in decisions affecting their lives was not being greeted well in the city. Tensions, particularly between the Irish and the Blacks, were escalating. And that could, and he guessed would, trickle down to his businesses. He empathized with the Black point of view. Deja vu, he thought. When people -- Yankee, Irish, Black or whatever -- feel alienated, unwelcome, cut off from an opportunity to prosper, to work -- then they fought back hard.

He crossed Lynn Shore Drive and climbed the steps of the garrison, glancing at Bobby's Mustang parked in the driveway.

"Hi, Dad," Bobby yelled from the kitchen as he opened the front door. "I'm making a ham and cheese on rye. Want something?"

"No thanks, Bob," replied Jack, tossing his sport coat over the coat rack as he walked through the entry toward the kitchen. At seventeen, the handsome young man before him strongly favored his mother, Jack thought. Tall, erect, with excellent bearing, his features were soft and effeminate. Light blond hair flowed over his ears almost to shoulder length. The sun had tanned his skin and left some dark streaks in his hair. His eyes -- like his mother's -- were deep green. The nose was long and narrow, the lips full and sensuous.

"So you survived another year of Open Campus at Swampscott High?" Jack teased, generating the reaction expected.

Bobby laughed. "Dad, you have it all wrong. The whole town is our laboratory for learning. We move about all day long, meet people, interact with businessmen, the selectmen, social agencies."

"Yeah sure. Sister Constanza used to let us wander around, too. One step out of your seat and your ass was hers."

"Times change, Dad. We're learning by experiencing."

"Not with the curriculum you're taking. No English, right? Instead of a year of English, you guys take a quarter of literature of the unknown, a quarter of Jack London, and two quarters of God knows what. That's learning? I don't think so, but we'll see. This trend too shall pass," he smiled.

Bobby smiled at him. "I hope not."

"How's your mother, son?"

Since 1962 the boys had continued living with Marjorie in Swampscott. To her credit she had never interfered with his right to see them, not that he would have allowed such a step. She never spoke of filing for divorce and never spoke of remarrying. They had remained separated yet had come together civilly for numerous family occasions and special events. The tension was always there between them, the inability to move beyond his revelations of a dozen years ago. He recognized she could never forgive him or approve even tacitly of his business. He had made no further attempt to influence her viewpoint himself. She was gone. He afforded her the respect she was due as the mother of his children, and made sure he protected her ownership of the dealership.

"She's fine, Dad. She's been keeping busy with her volunteer work and her painting."

"And Tim? How's his summer so far?"

"That job you got him on the waterfront is keeping him busy this summer. We don't see so much of him," Bob replied, sitting down at the kitchen table with his sandwich.

As different as night and day, Jack thought. This fall, Bob would enroll at Emerson College, much to his mother's delight. A solid student, his love of the arts, of all things cultural, had endeared him to her. Jack understood and appreciated his interests and recognized Marjorie's strong influence on their oldest son. In this case his desires and Marjorie's coincided. He wanted no part of his life for either of his sons, and so he approved of Bob's choice of Emerson.

But Tim was another story. Straight college-bound curriculum or open campus made no difference to him. He struggled either way, and both Jack and Marjorie realized early that their second son was no student. He had jumped at his father's offer to work as a summer intern on the waterfront, at the opportunity to flex his muscles. He reminded Jack so much of Tommy. Athletic, fearless, but not yet as focused on a goal as his uncle had been at a similar age. At sixteen he was taller and physically more mature than Bobby. He played offensive line and linebacker at Swampscott High under the tutelage of legendary coach Stan Bondelevitch, who regarded Tim, about to enter his senior year, as one of the best athletes he had ever coached.

Long ago Jack had made the decision to tell his sons of the kind of life he led when they were old enough to understand. He had informed them of his involvement two years ago, carefully relating his role, sparing them the heavy details, describing the life in the most favorable light, but still helping them recognize their father lived on the edge. They accepted it partially, he knew, because their mother provided stability and also must have hinted about his involvements over the years, and partially because they loved him, were comfortable with a father who had always been there for them. In Tim's case he sensed acceptance and excitement as well.

"Any calls while you've been here, Bob?"

237

"Yeah. I almost forgot. Courtney called about a half hour ago. She wants you to call her as soon as you can."

Courtney Stahl. A reason for being. On a particularly warm early July evening in 1972 he had met her at the celebration and dedication of Jerry's new building just off Route 128 in Wakefield. He had arrived a bit late from Lynn, and entering at lobby level, had taken the elevator to the mezzanine. As the door opened, he joined hundreds of celebrants roaming the atrium, admiring the view overlooking Lake Quannapowitt, lifting wine glasses from the trays proffered by the wait staff.

He had spotted Jerry in the crowd and was in the process of congratulating him on the opening when, from across the room, a tall brunette, brown hair glistening and falling to her shoulders, approached them. "Congratulations, Jerry," she offered, extending her hand, a glowing smile on an angel's face.

Jerry embraced her. "Hey Courtney, thanks for being here. And, above all, thank you for all your work in getting us in here."

Jack stared at her, aware that he was doing just that. She was both tall and vaguely awkward with beautiful legs and long hands that seemed forever in search of a resting place. She wore a white blouse and a black skirt that fell midway across her thighs. Brown eyes sparkled in youthful gaiety, as she looked from Jerry to him. She stared directly at him, the long hair falling to her shoulders, framing her oval face. He guessed her to be ten to fifteen years younger than he.

"Courtney Stahl, meet my brother Jack. Courtney's my real estate attorney. She pulled all this together for me."

"Pleased to meet you, Jack. But if he's your brother then you know who has made the deals that have allowed Kelly Food Enterprises to actually require all this space."

Suddenly someone whisked Jerry away, and he was alone with her, completely absorbed in their conversation, hoping for no interruptions so that he could learn as much as possible about her. They walked toward a small round table in the corner, and sat alone for an hour before they later further isolated themselves by strolling around the lake, she talking about her background.

Courtney Stahl was twenty-seven years old, born in San Francisco, educated at Boston University and at Northeastern University Law School. Somewhere along the way she married her BU college classmate, but, she explained, that ended in divorce due to conflicting aspirations -- she anxious to climb the corporate ladder, a typical baby boomer who wanted the most she could have of the good life, and he content with living out the suburban dream, pleased to teach junior high school and raise kids. She had wanted no part of a sedentary life, so they had agreed to go their separate ways. Working for a small group, she had moved steadily ahead as a real estate attorney and, with Jerry's huge success, had been recruited as the lead attorney for his firm.

Jack found himself talking of the car dealership on the Lynnway, of his children, of Tommy, and of his pride in Jerry. He surprised himself with his willingness to speak openly of his family with someone he had just met.

As they ran through a gentle rain back to the building, he asked her to dinner the following evening. She accepted, and within the week they slept together at her home in Saugus, and now, two years later, he still felt that he could not wait until the next time they would be together.

"Well, Dad?" Bob forced his thoughts back to the present.

"I'll call her. How long you going to be able to stay?"

"Leaving right now. I'm meeting some friends at Nahant Beach."

"Say hello to your mother and Tim. I'll see you this weekend, right?" Jack wrapped his arms around his oldest son, embraced him warmly, and in turn, felt the affection offered in response.

He dialed the Saugus number as soon as the front door had closed.

"Hello."

"Courtney? Jack."

"Get your body over here tonight. I need you."

That evening, as he finished dressing, Tommy called. "We have two situations, Jack. I need to see you."

"How soon?" Jack asked, careful not to inquire any further about the matter.

"Tomorrow morning at the latest," Tommy replied edgily.

"I'll meet you for coffee." No need for elaboration. No business ever would be conducted over the telephone, especially with the accelerated pace with which the feds now watched all suspected crime figures. No matter how urgent the matter, they disciplined themselves to use short code words. Tommy knew where to meet him the next morning and who else to invite.

37

He drove his new blue Toyota Cressida toward Saugus, laughing aloud when he recalled Vinnie Sullivan's reactions to the purchase just three weeks ago. "How do you like the Toyota, Vin?" he had inquired as they ate Harold's Delicatessen famous "sandwich and a half" in Central Square, Lynn.

Vin peered out the window at the parked vehicle, wiping the mustard from his ham and cheese on rye off his chin. "You bought a fuckin' Toyota and you're a Chevy dealer?"

"It's a well-made car, Vin," Ray offered. "The fuckin' American cars can't hold a candle to them."

Vin raised his voice an octave. "It's a fuckin' Jap car, that's what it is. You bought that after what those guys did to our boys in World War II?"

One thing about Vinnie. He never forgot. Jack constantly reminded himself of that fact, although to be fair, Vinnie seemed to have adjusted well to his leadership.

The heat had broken and big white clouds nestled against an azure blue sky. He shut off the Cressida in front of the chocolate brown split level on Elizabeth Court, a quiet dead end street containing only three homes. He used his key to let himself in and walked up the five stairs. On his left lay the living room and to his right a long corridor led to the bedroom, a bathroom, and a reading room. Directly ahead at the top of the stairs Courtney stood in the kitchen arranging a tray of colby cheese and crackers.

"Hi, handsome. Can you make the drinks?"

"After I get my just desserts," he said, moving to her, stroking her bottom as she faced the window. She wore a long thin rose-colored robe which he lifted waist high, revealing nothing but her bare, tanned olive skin.

He turned her toward him, pulling her close, and they held each other and kissed for a long moment. Her tongue flicked in and out of his mouth, arousing him. Without a word she led him to her bedroom and dropped the robe on the floor. She pressed against him, and they kissed again as she moved her hands up his shirt, opening each button slowly, pressing her naked body against his skin as each button came open.

They made love with the same intensity they had for the past two years. Each time for him was like that first time. She sat down on the edge of the bed, spreading her legs for him. He knelt and flicked his tongue along her thighs, steady and gentle, teasing her, sensing her shudders as she both urged him to find her spot and then backed off a bit.

He lifted her legs, pushing her back on the bed and gently inserted his tongue as she rocked with glee, moaning as his feather-like tongue darted ever so slowly in and out. Suddenly, she pulled him toward her, into her, lying on her back as he thrust rhythmically until she screamed in delight, signaling his moment as well. He rolled off her, extending his hand to his head. "Jesus, Mary, and Joseph, as my Irish aunt would say."

"Don't you like the way I love you?"

"You'll be the death of me yet," he replied.

Later, they sat in the kitchen on high backed wooden chairs around her circular table. Jack sliced pieces from the colby cheese wedge, relaxing on the stool as Courtney flipped the pages of her new Redbook, occasionally sipping the scotch and water before her.

"What?" she looked up, catching him admiring her.

He bit her nose, and she delightedly yelled "Ow!"

"How's work going with you?" he asked.

"Just fine. Your brother's winning some big contracts. Just last week we clinched with two of the large universities in Boston, and last month a couple of the new engineering firms on

Route 128 signed with us. He had a great idea, Jack. Most businesses, particularly institutions, don't want to manage their own cafeterias. He steps in and even brings in other franchises with him."

"He's building an empire, huh?" Jack said. "The kid's really something. All his life he's worked hard. Top of his class in high school and college. Key performer for A & P. And now his own company booming."

"He's as proud of you, you know."

"I'm not so sure of that," Jack said, stirring his VO and ginger ale.

"Jack, he's long ago forgotten New York and what you had to reveal. He's as loyal to you today as he was before then."

"I know that Courtney. I know that. But I'm also sure he doesn't approve of the life."

"It's not a matter of approval or disapproval. He chose a particular route, and you chose yours. He would never second guess those choices out of love for you, out of respect for his older brother. He worries about you all the time. That's what you're sensing."

Jack pointed to his empty glass. "My doctor says I need nine of these every night."

"He must be a pisser of a doctor."

They laughed together, touching each other constantly, completely relaxed in one another's company, lovers at peace.

"He also said I need to have intercourse three times a night," Jack quipped.

"Does he guarantee a long life under those conditions?" she laughed. "How's Tommy doing?"

"OK, I guess. I'm not sure he's ever really recovered from the events back then. For instance, I don't think he's ever accepted that eye injury. One step away, he constantly says. One step away from the championship. It's like Marlon Brando in 'On the Waterfront.' Remember? 'I could have been someone.' That's Tommy."

"But, Jack, you took care of him. He's with you."

"That he is, but he's not relaxed. I wish there was someone else in his life that could help lift his spirits."

"What happened with that girl he had?"

"Nancy? Nancy Huff? They just drifted apart. I think she loved him. But he blew it. Always on his mind was that championship. Always. We're talking about a completely focused guy whose dream blew up. Even now he doesn't think of too much else, Court. I worry about him, Court. I do. He needs a diversion. At least he's stopped his heavy drinking. That's what cost him Nancy."

She stroked his hair, leaning her body into his. "Speaking of which, you know what you said about your doctor?"

"Yeah?"

"Mine says I need to be laid three times a day, too."

"What kind of a doctor is he?" Jack laughed. "He must be a pisser." And they embraced.

38

"Fuckin' niggers belong in Roxbury, Dorchester, Mattapan, not all over the city," Vinnie Sullivan snapped.

"You ever hear of Affirmative Action, Vinnie?" Ray Horan teased.

"Up your ass, Ray."

"Thank you, Vinnie. You fuck."

"Shut the fuck up, all of you," Paulie Cronin said. "I don't give one shit about the marmalukes. They don't count for nothing. The dumb fucks are killing each other every day, anyway."

"When's Jack coming in?" Ray asked.

"When he gets here," Tommy replied. "In the meantime, why don't all of you shut the fuck up."

"That judge has his head up his ass. He has no understanding of neighborhood loyalties. Blacks coming into Southie and Charlestown, right into the fuckin' white men's schools," Vinnie continued.

"Hey. At least its keeping the locals and the state police busy enforcing the court order," Ray said.

"Yeah, between Garrity, the streakers running naked all over town, and the broads cavorting in string bikinis at Carson Beach, there's no time left in their day to fight real crime," Chris Kiley laughed.

They sat on crates at the warehouse on Medford Street in Charlestown. In the office area to the right of the entrance, coffee percolated and they took turns serving themselves.

"Mayor Black is what I call Mayor White," Vinnie said.

"Black is best, Black is beautiful," quipped Chris Kiley.

"Speaking of which, I can't wait for fall to see George Foreman destroy that pretty boy Ali in Africa," Vinnie said.

"He's got no chance at all against that Big George. He's unbeatable," Paulie interjected. "Right, Tom?"

"It looks like the end of the trail for Ali, for sure. But that Ali has heart. I wouldn't count him out, ever."

Jack knocked on the blackened glass window that was part of the roll-up door. Ray raised the door enough for Jack to move under.

"Hey, Jack. How's the boyo?" Paulie said.

"On a beautiful day like this, I couldn't be feeling any better. So what's up, Tom?"

"Two things, Jack. One kinda immediate. We have two boys in town from the olde sod, wanting to buy guns. IRA, they say. Vinnie met them in Southie the night before last."

"Vin?" Jack turned to him.

"They seem legitimate to me. Two dumb fuckers from Dublin. Fuckin' zealots. Say they want to buy machine pistols, automatics, silencers, .357 Magnums, grenades. They have the cash here in town, they claim. They want $400,000 worth, they say."

Jack raised an eyebrow. "$400,000?"

"Yeah."

"Our guys in New Hampshire have what they want, Tommy?" Jack asked.

"For sure. It will take a week to put it all together, though."

"These dumb fuckers, as you call them, tell me more about them, Vin," Jack said.

"The first one -- tall, thin-lipped -- says his name is Matt Folan -- does most of the talking. He seems legit. He spoke a bit in Gaelic. 'Baile Athe Cliath -- that's Dublin in Gaelic -- is where he lives. He talked about O'Connell Street, about the Dublin Garda. Ladbake Street is where he lives, he says. Near the Bay, a working man's district, he says. He's a plumber by trade."

Jack listened intently. He and Courtney had visited Dublin last spring, the third time he had been there. "What about the second one?"

"A little fat shit, quieter. Says he's a student at Dublin City University. Lives on Goff Street in the city. Name of Billy Quinn. They're legitimate. Claim they have the money from IRA sympathizers from Boston. Some of those rich Irishers in Weston and Newton."

"How're they getting the goods back to Ireland?" Jack asked.

"By boat."

Tommy walked in a semi-circle around the perimeter of the crates. "Sounds awfully good, Jack. They want only to deal with you and me, though. They want a meet ASAP to clinch the deal."

Jack smiled. "They must be good businessmen. No one should ever deal in this gun shit without knowing who they're dealing with."

"They're assholes with hard-ons to attack the Limeys," Vinnie said. "They want to see the people they're doing business with is all. Be sure all details are covered at the meet by the people who make the decisions."

Jack thought for a long time. The 1970's had brought a period of unprecedented progress in the fight against crime. Now the FBI was armed with the new RICO racketeering laws and new court-authorized surveillance ability, and the Bureau, long in the dark in the fight, now coordinated its work well with various local and state strike forces, causing lots of problems for everyone. For years, infatuated with communists, the Bureau had limited numbers to throw into the fight. But they were off and running now, causing havoc with impressive arrest records, infiltrating families with imaginative strategies.

"Tell them Tom and I will meet them. Just don't tell them when and where until an hour before the meet. Put them on stand-by, Vin," Jack said.

"What if they won't buy it?" Tom asked.

"Then tell them to find guns somewhere else. Tell them we'll be in touch, Vin. In a few days. They'll accept it. Now, what's the other problem, Tommy?"

"The Black guys. You know there's been no leadership since George Jackson. There's all kinds of factions developing. With these times, you know? We're getting new guys bouncing into our operations. Like the other day, right in Southie, you know that bar on East Third and K? A zoot-suited guy walks in in the daytime demanding a weekly share of the profits and pistol whips Eddie O'Brien's barkeep when he gave him some lip. Same thing in Somerville at Barkley's near Dilboy Field. Another kid, stoned, with hair like fuckin' Veronica Lake -- only black -- you know peek-a-boo style? -- claims he's with some splinter group from Annunciation Road and demands a piece of the drug dealing action. Like I said, this shit is escalating. We have to do something, Jack."

Jack nodded in agreement. "See if we can set up a meeting with Lonnie Woods. Supposedly he's in control since George. Ask that he bring three or four of the other leaders to that meeting. And, Tommy, make it the week after next. Anything else? No? Then let's split in twos. Leave at intervals."

On the drive back to Lynn, he voiced his concerns to Tommy. They crossed the old Mystic River Bridge, now newly named for deceased former governor, Maurice J. Tobin. Tommy sat in the front passenger seat, quiet, observing the boats below moving under the hot sun into Boston Harbor. Over to their left the Boston Edison plant across the river belched hot steam.

"Tommy, tell Vin to set that meet with the two boyos from Dublin for Monday afternoon at 5 for you and me. You OK for that?"

"I can make it."

"We'll meet them in a public place. Have Vin tell them the International House of Pancakes on Route 1 South in Saugus. When we're talking with them, follow my lead, and be very careful what you say. They could be wired."

"You hear about Connie Ryan?" Tommy asked, changing the subject.

248

"I'm always watching for him, Tom. He got elevated, again, huh? You know he moved out of the West Side just at the right time. All kinds of young toughs have been splintering the leadership in Hell's Kitchen. Guy named Jimmy Coonan is the big man there right now.

"One of the guinea heads of the Five Families is Ryan's sponsor," he continued. "Don Mario Gianelli of Manhattan. He's moved him right along over the last few years so that the rumor mills now say he's there in Gianelli's inner circle. Right up there with the top fish."

Tommy shook his head. "An Irisher in their top group? Hard to believe The son of a bitch can't be trusted, Jack. He's going to come after us sooner or later. We should take him out now."

The sun ran behind broken clouds and the smell of rain reached them.

"No, Tommy. Not now. He's under the same chains we are. Biggio and Cardoza are our protectors, and Gianelli needs Ryan in these times. We just watch and wait. We'll have our right moment."

"Well, I don't like it, Jack."

"Tommy, I told you before -- there'll be our time and our place," Jack said gently. "Look, back in '62 you asked me to move you into the life. You've taken to it to the point where I depend on you more than anyone else -- you and Ray. I don't need you going off half cocked, Tommy. We're in a business -- a business that's flourishing. We have enough problems without creating more. And, in the end, Tom, we'll take care of Ryan."

Tommy stared out the window as they stopped to pay the toll. "You know, Jack, that talk back there about Ali and Foreman. I was one step away. One step from being champion of the world. Then this fuckin' eye trouble. One more fight to have earned the respect of people all over the world. Now look at Ali today, and look at me."

"Tommy, people around here today remember you in the same way they think of DeMarco, Pender, Collins. They don't forget the thrills you provided them. Tom, you never lost a fight. The fans love you. You should be happy."

"Happy? I'm happy enough. What's happy anyway?"

"Happy means I need you in the right mental state, little brother. I don't need you taking unnecessary chances, or letting your emotions guide your action. Think, Tommy. Like you did in the ring. Think. Wind down a bit, will you?"

"What do you mean unnecessary chances?"

""Just what I said. Ray tells me the other night he had to pull you off the guy over in Southie who owes us the $10,000."

"He paid, didn't he?"

"Tommy, listen to me. We don't need the fuckin' guy dead. I would like him to continue to borrow. Charlie Cowan's been good for us for ten years now. In the end, he always pays with a big vig attached. You kill him, you kill a regular. He's not a guy that has to be shown the way. What you did is what I call a fuckin' dumb move."

Tommy glared at his brother. If any other man talked to him this way, he would take him apart.

"You listening to me, you thick shit?" Jack half laughed now. "Calm your pee water down."

Through a lifetime of ups and downs, triumphs and tragedies, they could always communicate. Tommy smiled back at him, poked him with a light jab on the chin. "I'm trying, Jackie. I'm trying."

39

On Monday night they sat in the rear of the International House of Pancakes restaurant, facing Route 1 and the entrance itself. To their left, midway between them and the entrance, Ray Horan sipped coffee in another booth, facing Jack and Tommy. Only a few elderly couples looking for the early Monday night specials sat scattered around the brightly lit place.

At exactly 5 o'clock two young men walked in, surveying the area. The thin one led the way to the rear of the restaurant, the dumpy one trailing behind.

"Are you Jack Kelly?" asked the first man, stopping at their table. "Matt Folan," he introduced himself with a smile. "And this is Billy Quinn." Folan was actually not tall, probably less than six feet, but he carried himself like a tall man. His skin was pale, his short-cropped hair rising above a slender nose.

"Sit down. My brother Tom," Jack gestured. "Sit down won't you boys? Coffee? Tea?" He signaled the waitress who moved toward them.

"Something to eat, fellas?" she asked through puffy eyelids.

"Just the tea for both of us, thank you," said Matt Folan.

"And how are things in the old country?" Jack asked.

He remembered last April. Sunlight had streamed yellow through new leaves on old trees as he and Courtney strolled across the green of the walled campus of Trinity College, where at one time had sat George Bernard Shaw, James Joyce, and William Butler Yeats. Students had passed in raucous groups while professors in turtleneck sweaters and corduroy jackets walked heavily laden with briefcases, caught up like professors everywhere in their own self-importance. He and Courtney had gradually made their way all over town, across the River Liffey footbridge from Trinity College, up O'Connell Street, over to the mall on Grafton Street. Finally they had paused on a bench at St. Stephen Green watching freckle-faced teens holding hands as they strolled toward the water to sit on checkered blankets. There were no people like the Irish, he thought.

"And things are fine in Dublin," answered Matt Folan, the lilt of the old country firm in his voice. Despite the hot day and warm evening he was dressed in a light blue sweatshirt and dark blue slacks. "But not so in London, and that is why we are pleased to make your acquaintance."

Jack avoided Folan's rather direct move toward a business discussion. "Where are you from, Mr. Folan? What part of Dublin?"

"Just outside Dublin in a bit of a rundown area in Dun Laoghaire. Ladbake Street. We don't have much, the wife and I. You even been to Ireland?"

"It is indeed a beautiful country, is it not?" Jack added. He remembered that first view on the Atlantic horizon. The great landfall itself, the country of his grandparents. Line after line of surging waves smashed against the coastal walls and, at their tops, there was green everywhere. There is nothing like that first view of Ireland. "No, but someday I hope to visit.

"And you, Mr. Quinn. Vinnie tells me that you are a student at Dublin City University. What are you studying there?"

Billy Quinn was dressed similar to Folan, but his paunchy stomach hung over his belt. He was bald, except for a gray monkish fringe, and he wheezed noticeably when he answered. "The law, Mr. Kelly."

"The law, indeed. Just what we do not need in America -- more lawyers. Maybe that's not the case in Ireland."

"I understand you sell cars here in America, Mr. Kelly?" Folan said.

"Yes. For some twenty years now, and a delicate, difficult business, it is. Our mutual friend Vinnie Sullivan tells me you wish to do business with my brother and me?"

Folan beamed. "And, indeed that is a fact. How many could you provide?"

"How many do you need?"

"As many as $400,000 can obtain for us. That is what we are here to negotiate."

"I don't understand, Mr. Folan. You say you need $400,000 worth of cars?" Jack asked, feigning astonishment.

"Guns, Mr. Kelly. We need guns for our IRA soldiers, the good lads fighting against those fuckin' Brits."

"Mr. Folan, there must be some mistake. I know nothing of guns. I sell cars. If someone has informed you otherwise, that person is in error. Now if you wish to buy a number of new Chevrolets, I would be willing..."

"You're telling us you can't provide fuckin' guns," Billy Quinn almost leaped from his seat.

Jack raised his hand. "Mr. Quinn, please stay calm. Now my brother and I are legitimate Boston businessmen. I'm not a criminal. In America it is against the law to sell guns without a license to do so. I am proud of my Irish heritage and indeed proud to have met two gentlemen from the land of my grandparents, but now I believe it's time for my brother and I to leave you and wish you well in your endeavors. We appear to have a misunderstanding here."

Matt Folan and Billy Quinn sat dumbfounded as Jack and Tommy stood. Jack winked at Ray as they walked toward the front entrance.

"What the hell was that about?" Tommy asked as soon as they were in the car.

"They're federal agents, Tommy. Probably FBI."

"How the hell do you know that?"

"I don't, for sure, but I'll bet I'm right. I'll tell you one thing -- they don't live in Dublin. For one thing, Ladbake Street is in Dun Loaghaire, all right. But the area is elegant. About an hour outside Dublin. Baroque homes, houses with ivy-covered stone Georgian doorways. Rich man's land. Like Dover or Weston. No way a plumber lives on Ladbake street. As for Mr. Quinn, there's no law curriculum at Dublin City University. It's a cooperative education university like Northeastern University in Boston. Students work their way through college, alternating work with study."

"How do you know?"

"I had Vinnie ask them about their backgrounds, then I checked their answers out. And I've been to Ladbake Street, for another thing."

"They were wired then?"

"No question in my mind."

"Jesus Christ. What do we do about those two?"

"We do absolutely nothing about them. We know we're being watched so that means we take extreme care concerning wiring. You still having that guy -- Joe Glenn -- check our office, our homes, the warehouse, the social club in Southie, regularly?"

Tommy nodded. "Every week. He's a genius that guy. So far he hasn't found any bugs."

"It also means we need to be careful about new people we meet, new people we bring into the life -- very, very careful. And one other very important point. We keep our eyes and ears open for a possible infiltration from within. They may also try to turn someone against us. It's a new day, Tommy. The cops are not playing like the good guys anymore."

"It's been ten years, Catherine and I still miss him."

They walked along LaGrange Street in West Roxbury. The day had the clear bleached look of sunshine on a cold morning. Along the way, the grass, no longer growing, was tight to the ground. As they spoke, mist gathered between them.

"Me, too," she responded.

"You've adjusted well," Jack said.

And she had. Her coal-black hair was perfectly styled, her makeup fresh, the sparkle back in her eye. She was tall but possessed none of Courtney's grace and feline physical agility. Yet he found her curiously attractive in her black thigh-length leather coat.

"It's never easy," she said.

254

"You need anything?"

She gripped his arm and turned to him, her eyes meeting his. "You've done too much already. Money's not a problem."

"How's Danny doing?"

"You're invited to his college graduation next June, you know. He wants you to be there with us."

"Wouldn't miss it. Is he sure he wants to be a cop?"

"Absolutely. He's already talked to the FBI recruiters at Northeastern. They like his strong record in accounting. I think they'll hire him."

"Leo must be turning over..."

"Don't say it."

"I can hear him now. A fuckin' copper?"

The street shone with last night's rain, but the place was quiet except for the grumble of mid-morning traffic. They turned toward her home, dead leaves swirling from the trees. She had fallen in love with the streets around her the first time she saw them: the red brick exteriors cleanly kept, the brightly painted window frames, and, in the summer the flowers spilling from the pots placed on virtually every front door step.

"Any guy yet?" Jack asked, as they neared her front door.

"A girl has to have a guy, is that it?" Answer a question with a question, she thought.

Jack stopped short. "I didn't mean to pry, I just care about you and Danny, Catherine."

Doe-brown eyes washed almost green by contact lenses focused on him. "I know that, Jack." She turned almost too quickly as he sought eye contact with her.

"Oh, I've dated. You know that. But there's nobody special."

"You should fine someone, Catherine. You deserve someone special."

"I have that, Jack. I have you, as my very special friend." She reached for his hand and squeezed it, almost too hard, she later felt.

The house appeared small as they climbed the front steps, but she found it more than comfortable enough for two. At the top step, Jack leaned to her, pecking her cheek. She found it hard to restrain herself from reaching out and kissing his perfect lips.

"I'm giving Danny the tuition money for his Master's degree in Criminal Justice when we go to the Patriots' game Sunday," he said.

"Jack! You don't have to..."

He touched his forefinger to her mouth. "I don't have to, but I want to. He's like my son too, Catherine."

She nodded and said good-bye. She gathered herself quickly opening the front door so that he could not read her eyes.

<u>40</u>

A thin veil of gray embraced the westernmost thirty blocks of San Francisco, partially blotting out the Golden Gate Bridge. On the horizon the green acreage of the Presidio provided a lush background to the gigantic stanchions of the Golden Gate. They sat on a hill above it all, lovers absorbed in one another, and in love with The City.

For three days now they had walked from the Fairmont on Nob Hill to all points of The City, concentrating particularly along the waterfront, typical tourists taking boat trips around the Bay, over to Alcatraz, to Sausilito. They toured Taylor Street, where Courtney had been born, across the street from Joe DiMaggio's childhood home at number 2047. At twilight they welcomed evening together from the Top of the Mark at the Mark Hopkins Hotel, overcome by the view of the City from on high. They ate dinner two different evenings at Ernie's on Montgomery Street, and on other nights visited the Chinese restaurants on Grant Avenue or the Italian eateries at North Beach.

On their last day he had rented a car from Hertz on Mason Street, and they had crossed the Golden Gate to the Muir Woods, where they walked for hours among the cathedral-like redwoods, veiled from the public and at peace with nature.

And now in the early afternoon, they looked down from the hillside of Mount Tamalpias, enthralled by the majesty of the great Pacific below them.

"Isn't it amazing how different it is just a few miles outside the city?" she said. "It must to 80 degrees here vs. 60 degrees in

San Francisco itself. But for a June day, it's even a bit chilly up here."

Courtney pecked his cheek when he placed his sportcoat across her shoulders.

"Well, my little Jewish American princess, have you enjoyed the visit home?"

"Except for that noise last night," she replied with a straight face.

He laughed, and she laughed. Last night as they lay in each other's arms, he had drifted asleep when she suddenly woke him in a panic. "Jack, listen. Do you hear that noise next door?"

He had cleared his head, sorting out the sounds of low moaning and excited frenzy, muffled grunts, a bedboard banging ever so slightly against the wall.

"I think someone is being assaulted in there. Shouldn't you call the front desk?"

He had listened a while longer, then broke out in wild laughter. "She's being screwed, Courtney. She's animated, letting herself go. Nothing wrong with that. You should try it yourself sometime."

"You Irish prick," she had screamed, throwing a pillow at him. "I would if I could find someone to excite me."

"A good fuck would kill you."

"I wouldn't know," she answered.

On their first night they had visited her parents in neighboring Sausilito. A successful banker in town, her father obviously adored his only daughter, as did her mother, a housewife content to make her daughter's return home memorable based on the delicacies she provided. They had doted on Jack as they did Courtney, loving parents anxious to learn more about the man their daughter had brought home.

Her mother had awkwardly asked the question they knew was coming while they drank coffee after dinner. "So will you two be getting married soon?"

"Mom!"

Jack grinned at Mrs. Stahl. Jake Stahl looked slightly embarrassed but still, now that the question was out in the open, came to attention for an answer.

"Mom, we have a wonderful relationship right now with no plans to marry," Courtney finally answered. Especially to a Catholic still legally married she could have added, Jack thought. But overall, the visit had gone well and on one other afternoon he had insisted Courtney spend time alone with her parents while he went out to Candlestick Park to watch the Giants play the New York Mets.

Below them now, tiny sailboats bobbed and weaved through the windy, blue waters of the Pacific. As other ships of all sizes passed beneath them, Jack thought of the thousands of men who had passed under the Golden Gate to cross the Pacific during World War II.

"So how did you like my city?" she asked, breaking into his reverie.

"The best, Courtney. It reminds me so much of Boston."

Up the trail behind them roared a red pick-up truck, probably heading toward the top of the mountain. It screeched to a halt, as if its occupants had suddenly decided to observe the view from the hills instead. A young man and woman exited the vehicle, the man garbed in an open leather vest which exposed his chest and matching leather pants. The scrawny blond with him wore only tight blue shorts and sandals, her tiny breasts fully exposed for all to admire. No wonder they had not proceeded to the main entrance above.

"I don't know whether I'm ready for the hippie scene, though. We don't have too many Catholics running around nude in Beantown," Jack said, pointing to the couple.

"You and your Catholic guilt."

"You hate me, don't you."

"Don't you love the way I hate you?"

He could agree with that.

Tommy toyed with the little brass elephant on Jerry's desk, waiting for his brother. He stood, strolled to the window and in the distance watched the runners and the strollers circle Lake Quannapowitt. Directly below him a fleet of white ducks walked along the edge of the water in single file, oblivious to the crowds, and off to his left, about thirty yards off shore, young boys jumped in obvious glee from a raft into the warm waters.

Behind him the door opened and Jerry quickly closed the distance between them, embracing his older brother. "Tommy, sorry to keep you waiting. I got caught in some long meeting with some possible new clients."

"No problem, Jerry. You know Jack's still in San Francisco, right?"

"I saw him last week just before he and Courtney left. I thought they were coming back yesterday. That's why I asked if you could both meet me today. But the agency called, and it's later today that they return, I now know. Sit over here on the couch with me, Tommy. Want something to drink?"

"I'm fine, Jerry."

"Well, thanks for coming. I need to talk to you and Jack about Marty and Timmy."

"A problem?"

"Tommy, let me try to say this right." He paused, carefully organizing his thoughts. "Look around you. I'm building the largest food services business in New England. We're everywhere. We're even beginning to provide a number of the airlines at Logan. That's why I was late today. I've a good chance of picking up the concessions both there and in Hartford as well.

"Sheila and I have hopes that someday Marty will take this over, take the company even further. I love that kid, Tommy. But I can't seem to reach him, to interest him in college or the business. Instead, he would rather work on the waterfront, and he can't wait to graduate from English and work there regularly," he said, with barely concealed disdain.

"Jerry, he's just a kid, a high school kid, for Christ's sake. There's lots of good guys, good family men, on the waterfront. They're not going to corrupt him."

"Yeah, and lots of guys to show him the way to trouble, too. You seen Marty or Timmy anytime this week, Tommy?"

"No. Why?"

"Three or four days ago some guy -- a big guy -- shoved Timmy in some argument over nothing. Something about whose job it was to unload cargo. Timmy beat the shit out of him. They had to pull him off the guy.

"After work the guy and two of his friends are waiting in the parking lot for Timmy. Our two teenage assassins send two of them to the hospital. According to the police, Marty put one guy's head through a car windshield."

"Sound like chips off the old block to me."

"I'm serious, Tom. If it wasn't for the longshoremen's relationship with you and Jack, the two of them would be in the clink right now. Instead, they look like shit and could just as easily have been killed. I don't want him back there. I never should have allowed him to work down there in the first place. His mother's going to have a heart attack before much longer."

"Jerry, the cousins are good kids. Jesus, they remind me so much of us when we were younger. They even look more like twins than cousins." He stood, walking toward the window.

"Be careful how you handle him, Jerry. Timmy's his father's son all the way. He idolizes Jack. Wants nothing more than to be like him. And your Marty and Timmy are like the fuckin' Corsican Brothers. They're inseparable."

"Tommy, I don't want my only son to..."

"To become a criminal, Jerry?"

Jerry stood up. "Don't be offended, Tommy. You know I'm forever grateful to you and Jack. I wouldn't be here today, talking about servicing national airports if it weren't for you two. I would do anything for you or Jack. Sheila and I just want something different for our son."

Tommy walked to him, again embracing him. "I know that, Jerry. I know that. You want my advice? Talk to him, but don't alienate him. Don't drive him away. Marty's loaded with the same kind of Kelly determination and stubbornness you have."

Jerry nodded. "I'll do that, Tommy, but I don't want him anywhere near the life."

"Here they come," Tommy announced from his position at the front window.

The white Cadillac slowed as the driver scanned for the right Lynn Shore Drive address. They parked opposite Jack's house and sat at the curb for a very long minute, surveying the area.

"Jesus, they move with glacial speed, don't they?" Tommy said.

Finally four Black men started across the street, led by a fat man dressed in a light blue sleeveless jersey and black pants, a soft gray fedora gracing his head.

"Lonnie's out of the car," Tommy said.

Jack moved to the front door, opened it, and waved through the screen to the advancing group. "You found it all right, huh, Lonnie?"

"No problem, Jack," he replied warmly.

As they entered, Lonnie stepped aside for each of the men who followed him. "Jack, you know Henry Hollins." A short, bulky man extended his hand. "And Virgil Johnson," nodding to a sour looking, slender older man. "And this young fellow here is Bobby Latimer." Staring back at him coldly was a light skinned, handsome young man not more than nineteen or twenty years old, almost pretty in his handsomeness with delicate features offset by dead eyes.

Jack smiled at them all. "Come in, come in You know my brother Tommy, Lonnie."

"Sure, Champ. How you doing?"

"And Ray Horan, my associate?" Ray shook hands with each in turn.

As a gesture of good will, Jack had invited them to his home, an invitation that he seldom extended to business partners, but he wanted them to relax, to feel comfortable in the setting so that they could conduct their affairs, or more particularly his agenda, under the best of conditions.

"There's a buffet spread in the dining room -- cold cuts, salad. Help yourself. Soft drinks, beer, too. If you want something harder, Ray's manning the bar in the kitchen. Grab what you want, and come on out to the patio. We have some hamburgers and hot dogs on the grill out there. We can sit around in the backyard and talk a bit."

"This is fine living indeed, Jack," Lonnie Woods said, looking out the front window toward the beach. "Lots of bikinis walking up and down the boardwalk, huh? But I don't see too many of our people around."

Jack laughed. "They're coming in strong, Lonnie. Lynn's changing. Used to be all European -- Irish, Greek, French, Italian. Now people are coming in from Boston, New York, the South."

"And what you honkies think of that?" Bobby Latimer asked belligerently.

Jack ignored the question. "Let's go eat," he said.

Just off the patio they arranged themselves around the long wooden table, the conversation light as they socialized before they got down to business. Jack stood at the grill with Ray, passing the food on plates down the line.

"Some people of color now joining the Red Sox are goin' to make a big difference next year," Virgil Johnson said. "Watch my man Jim Rice in 1975, Cecil Cooper, too. The Red Sox are finally seeing the light, I mean the dark." He laughed at his own pun.

"I like Evans in right field. Kid's got a howitzer for an arm," Ray said.

"Those fuckin' Orioles are tough, though," Lonnie Woods said. "Friggin' Palmer's the best, and Weaver knows how to play for those big innings."

"Coffee, anyone?" Tommy offered.

"Maybe next year will be the year," Henry Hollins said. "El Tiante, Spaceman Lee, both good pitchers, with those hitters like Freddy Lynn coming in. Just maybe."

"Lonnie, you probably know I didn't ask you guys here for just an afternoon of sociability," Jack began, sitting down at the head of the table.

Lonnie laughed out loud. "No shit, Jack. I thought you Irish guys made it a regular habit to integrate your neighborhoods."

"In fact, Lon, that's what I wanted to talk about -- your integrating my neighborhoods."

Bobby Latimer gave him a look that said fuck you, but said nothing. In fact, Jack noted, he hadn't said a word since they moved outside.

"Our integrating your neighborhoods? What the fuck you talking about, Jack?" Lonnie asked.

"I'm talking about what is rapidly becoming an out-of-control situation, Lonnie. You and I, Henry and Virgil here we've always had agreements -- agreements based on trust and respect. Lately, those agreements show some pretty strong signs of erosion."

"What the fuck that mean?" Bobby Latimer sneered.

"Shut the fuck up and listen, kid. Maybe you'll learn something," Tommy glared.

"Fuck you, pug. Nothing you can teach me."

"If we can stop the 'fuck yous' for a minute, I would like to continue," Jack said, using his home field advantage to take control.

Lonnie nodded in agreement. "Go on."

"Those signs of erosion are occurring in my territories, Lonnie. Cowboys attempting a piece of the weekly action in areas like Somerville, Southie, right here in Lynn. Extortion and drug dealing inroads in particular. Nothing too serious yet, although the guy pistol whipped in Somerville a couple of weeks ago might not agree. You got your guys under control, Lonnie?" he asked, with barely veiled sarcasm.

"Mr. Kelly, Lonnie here is one of my oldest friends, but he don't speak for me," Virgil Johnson stated emphatically. "It's a new time in our community. The old system under people you knew, like George Jackson, is no longer operational. Lonnie here is respected as our elder, as a man who paid his dues. But

264

we have many leaders now. The times call for new strategies, many views from different quarters."

A critical moment now, Jack thought. Keep your tone even. "Virgil, I can respect your viewpoint. With the tension in Boston now, the Black community needs the involvement of many of your people to better their lives. I agree with that; I'm all for that. But, Virgil, I'm not a social scientist. I'm a businessman. And I don't know of any business that can flourish without controls, without discipline. Haven't the Italians long ago proven that point? All I am asking is that you all bring some order out of growing disorder."

"I don't give a fuck about no order or disorder. On Mission Main I do my thing," Bobby Latimer chimed in. "If my guys fall into some good deal outside our area, then it be no business of Lonnie or Virgil or Henry or you. Whitey be stealin' from us for years anyhow. I don't see signs up about no territories, and if I did, I don't be givin' a piss about them."

"Hey, cool it, man," Henry Hollins said gently. "Jack, from my end we intend to work with you as we always have, but you need to give us a little time."

Jack nodded. "I can wait, Henry. I can wait a reasonable amount of time. But understand something. In the end I'm not going to sit still while out-of-control quick shooters move against my family or my interests," he said firmly.

"I believe this meeting has been fruitful, Jack. Let's keep in touch," Lonnie Woods said. "Next time you come over to Bob the Chef's for some soul food. Might even see some other white folk there."

"Sounds good to me, Lon." Jack stood, extending his hand to each of them as they rose along with him. As they walked toward the front door, Jack paused with Lonnie Woods at the doorway. "Have a second, Lonnie?"

"Wait for me in the car. I'll be right along," Lonnie directed the others.

"What's with Billy the Kid, Lonnie?"

"Bobby Latimer? Wild kid of the streets, the main man on Mission Main. He's looked up to by the young men. Mean as a

265

snake, but fearless. No mother, no father. Lives in one of those urban renewal failures on Annunciation Road."

"He has a real attitude problem, Lonnie."

"He don't like white folk much, Jack. Especially Irishers. You might remember his father, the Chocolate Drop, ex-fighter worked No. 1 behind George Jackson? The kid's heard all sorts of rumors about some white Irish gangsters being responsible for his death."

Jack tried to hide the surprise that he knew must now be registering on his face. But he didn't forget to register the news himself.

<u>41</u>

Matt Folan and Billy Quinn both stared across the conference table at Lieutenant Peter Halloran of the Boston Police Department. They sat silently on a cloudless November day, the chill of winter already upon them long before Thanksgiving Day. As Halloran scanned the paper work, they could hear the sounds of people scurrying back and forth in the corridors of Police Headquarters at 40 Berkeley Street. Below them, on the first floor, some angry hippie defended his right to piss wherever he pleased.

Folan dropped his cigarette stub on the tile and ground it into the floor. Quinn sipped his coffee, studying the veteran cop while he read. Halloran was narrow of head and hips with sandstone hair gone to gray.

"So shit's what you got, right?" Halloran summarized.

"The guy's no dummy, Lieutenant. It's going to take time. But eventually we'll get him. And the Mafiosos, too -- Biggio, Cardoza, their whole crews."

"There's nothing here that shows any progress in that direction, Mr. Folan. Kelly spotted that gun sale scam right away," Halloran said, tapping the papers with his hand.

"What's your take on the guy, Lieutenant? Forget all the fuckin' reports for the moment," Folan asked.

"You want my honest opinion?"

"Yeah."

Halloran took a long drag on his cigarette before beginning. "Jack Kelly is the smartest of them all. Let's look at some of the factors. Your office is surveilling Biggio and Cardoza, as well, right? Big mistake they're making is their withdrawing more and more from contact with the lower-level soldiers, the street guys. Maybe that cuts down on the stress the big guys feel, but in separating themselves from the stink of the streets they're beginning to lose control. Rising young stars like Nick Rizzo over in Revere are the beneficiaries. Distant leadership doesn't cut it, not in the '70's.

"Now you take Kelly. Never stops being a hands-on boss. He commands loyalty the way the Italian guys think they do. They delude themselves into thinking they have graduated to the status of an upright citizen's life. They stop working, they stay home, try to run the life from the home, enclose themselves in mansions, bang some broads when the old lady goes shopping. Delusional. On the other hand, Kelly remains one of the guys. He goes to work every day. Pays his taxes, federal and state, on time. You got nothing there according to this report. You can't even surveil his home. He fronts the beach and that's no accident. He can spot anyone looking at him a mile away.

"He doesn't talk on telephones. Never. The guineas tell you the last time they took a shit on the phone. They're emotional. This guy's detached. If he talks business it occurs on the streets, one on one, or at some safe house somewhere with a group.

"He lives the life of an ordinary businessman. Member of the Lynn Chamber of Commerce. Rotary Club. YMCA guy. No big expenditures. No living in any way different from what you would expect from the head of a car dealership.

"What's he do with his money? Huh? You guys know? Of course not. It's laundered someplace. He probably has accounts in some fuckin' Swiss bank."

Quinn interrupted angrily. "Jesus, you act like this guy's a fuckin' brilliant rocket scientist."

"Hey, they all make mistakes in time. You asked me about him, and I'm telling you. You got nada so far, and he's smart. He's a challenge, is all I'm saying," Halloran responded.

Folan lit a cigarette and blew smoke toward the ceiling. "What about the personal side? What about that?"

Halloran sighed. "Bits and pieces picked up over the years which add to a picture at least to me. First of all, he's a natural

268

born leader. Idolized by those close to him and the key captains in his family. Second, and this is only my theory, understand? Maybe there's no validity to it. He reeks of loyalty to his immediate family, to the six or seven captains around him, to the top guineas. Nothing unusual there, right? It's the other side of the coin that makes him so different, hard to figure, fascinating to think about."

"What's that?"

"Like I said, this guy's detached. He's emotionless. Undemanding in personal relationships. It's almost like he expects to be disappointed. He can walk away because he really has no friends. A guy who can walk away is doubly dangerous. You know what I mean?"

"Your theory is as useless as a nun's cunt, Halloran," Quinn snorted.

"No, no it helps to hear your view, Pete," Folan said. "Tell me about the key people around him. What's the word on the street?"

"Most of Jack's key people are what the IRA would call 'sleepers', members without police records. His brother Tommy you know about. Much more emotional, lives alone. He never fully recovered from the bad break. Used to be in his cups a lot, but lately he's controlling it. The action is his juice. The other brother, Jerry, is straight as an arrow, married. He has nothing to do with the life.

"Ray Horan's been with him since the '50's. He's like a brother to Jack. Word has it Horan introduced him to the life. Horan's smart, quiet, the exact opposite of Vinnie Sullivan, but the two of them would kill you in a second at Jack's command.

"Vinnie Sullivan's been there since the '50's, too. A real physical intimidator. Cut your balls off as soon as look at you. Flaherty's guy to begin with. When Flaherty went down, it crushed him, but he stayed with Jack. The number one enforcer, we hear.

"Then there's Stevie Gargan. He oversees the whores. Runs with half the whores himself. It's a wonder his dick still works.

"Paulie Cronin..."

"I guess what I'm really asking, Pete, is can any of these guys be turned? Could we get one to testify for us?" Folan interrupted.

"Anything's possible. For a long while I thought omerta was a fabric never to be broken. That was before Joe Valachi," Halloran said. "Sure, it's possible, but highly unlikely.

"You ever hear of an Irishman squealing on his own in this country? Remember that movie with Victor MacLaglan, 'The Informer'? Remember what happened to the stool pigeon? Same thing happens here."

"And why's that?" Quinn inquired.

"Because at least with the guineas there is a respect and an understanding of the importance of business. They like to consider themselves as stable, business-minded criminals. You might live if you hurt them because, after all, business is business.

"Whether here, New York, or the olde sod, the Irish are crazy. You double cross them, and they learn about it, you are fuckin' dead. Business or no business. Someone will find you with a hood over your head and a bullet in your brain. If they have to reach you from the grave, they will. If you squeal on them, the action not only will be avenged but dishonor is heaped on your family forever. The Irish would rather suffer murders than be called squealers."

"What are you saying -- we just pack it in? Let the bastards run wild?" Quinn asked.

"I think you need to be patient is what I think," Halloran responded. "The Irish Code of Silence is stronger than omerta. You need to wait for a cultural metamorphosis, or wait until the fuckers shoot each other or someone else shoots them for you or..."

"Or what?" Matt Folan asked.

"Entrap one of them so deeply he has no choice but to cooperate with you. That's the way I would go."

"Sit down," Jack ordered the two young men standing before his desk. Outside the dealership a light snow fell, whipped about by the bitter wind pummeling the Lynnway. On the Wednesday before Washington's Birthday, scores of customers trudged about the lot seeking the right buy. Every so often an overly polite salesman would whisk a customer inside seemingly showing genuine concern for his comfort, at least until the deal was consummated.

"You want some coffee or a soft drink?" Jack asked as they sat in the twin straight back chairs in front of his desk.

Knowing that they were not here for a social visit, both Timmy and Marty declined. They were both dressed in white turtlenecks and black pants, their hair cascading over their ears, their sideburns running the length of their jawlines. Jesus, they must check with each other before they face the world in the morning, Jack thought.

"So you two continue to act stupid, huh?" he began.

"What do you mean, Dad?"

Jack studied his son and his nephew, then looked again at the picture on his desk taken in high school of Tommy, Jerry and himself on a bench at Goldfish Pond. The resemblance to the two in front of him -- the black hair, the low foreheads, the heavy black eyebrows and the straight noses leading to thin pursed lips -- was uncanny.

He ignored his son's question. "You remember last summer your father being worried about you, Marty? When you and King Kong here beat the shit out of those waterfront guys? This, by the way, after, out of the goodness of my heart, I find you both jobs on the docks for the summer. Then, your Uncle Tommy and I get attacked by your father. Now I hear from my wife that you both don't want to go on to college next fall so she's on the warpath as well. What's going on?" he asked, standing and carrying his coffee to the window.

"Uncle Jack, I've explained myself to my father and mother," Marty said. "I don't want college full-time. I want to work."

"You're a better than average student, Marty."

"I've told my mother and father that I'll continue, Uncle Jack. I want to attend North Shore Community College and study business administration part-time in the evenings, and maybe later get my bachelor's degree. For now, I've had enough of full-time school. Maybe a year or two from now I'll feel differently."

"What are you going to do for work then?"

"We want to work with you, Dad," Timmy chimed in. "We want to work with you and Uncle Tom and learn this business."

Jack surmised that by "this business" Timmy meant more than the car business. As Bobby was his mother's son, Timmy was clearly his. He had mixed feelings about Timmy's potential involvement in the life. On one hand, he was proud that his son idolized him, and wished to follow him; on the other hand, he wanted his son to lead a respectable life, not an existence on the edge.

He sat down once again. "Boys, listen to me. I've told you both repeatedly, you don't want any part of the life. You want to work the lots here with Tom and me, we'll teach you, bottom to top. We can make that deal. But we make that deal with one strong condition. You both continue your education full-time, not part-time and you can work here nights, weekends, summers.

"Timmy, your mother wants you in college. This way, we compromise. She insists that you further your education, and I agree with her."

He knew they would accept his proposal, and he also knew there would be a struggle in keeping them away from the life. If they were to drift into such activities, he would rather have them under his province, he thought, but he would do his utmost, particularly with Marty, to keep them away.

"Think about what I'm saying. If you accept the terms, I'll talk to your mother, Timmy. I'll talk to your mother and father as well, Marty."

The boys nodded at him, almost in unison. Jesus Christ, he thought, what was it Tommy had called them? The Corsican Brothers, he remembered. Douglas Fairbanks, Jr. come back to life.

"The only way to handle this is for Vinnie and me to whack one of the leaders with a baseball bat. That way, they'll know we mean business," Tommy grumbled.

They sat in the bar lounge at the Fantasia Restaurant at Fresh Pond Circle in Cambridge. Across from Tommy, Vinnie Sullivan nodded vigorously in agreement with Tommy's analysis. At 4:00 in the afternoon the lounge was quiet, the lone cocktail waitress moving between the three small parties seated in different sections of the lounge.

"Absolutely not," Jack replied. "Think about it. Is splintered leadership so bad? I don't think Lonnie, Henry, or Virgil can speak for anybody but their own small crews. There's no real Black leader in Boston. Not anymore. Did you two ever stop to think there is some advantage to us in that as well?"

"What's it been since we had them at the house?" he asked rhetorically. "A few months? From what you're telling me, there's been no real escalation of intrusions into our affairs. Let's just keep watching the situation."

"Jack, you're too fuckin' soft with these niggers," Vinnie Sullivan bellowed. "They hit one of our operations, we need to hit back right away."

"Who's hit us recently and where, Vinnie? An odd hit from some lone ranger once every month on average? Is that what we're talking about?"

Vinnie sighed in frustration. "Jack, you know whatever you decide is fine with me. I'm only asking that you weigh this carefully," Vinnie said. "And, after you weigh it, let me straighten out one of the motherfuckin' leaders. Cause if you don't, this is not going to get any better."

"I said no. I want to continue to coast for a while. Right now, if anyone moves on us, we counter by identifying the guy and we find out who he's with. So far, it's working, isn't it? There's been no connection back to any of the group we met with. The jokers have all been mavericks operating on their own. We don't need to help unify the Blacks when they can't get that done themselves."

"Jack..."

"End of subject, Vin."

42

In the spring of 1977, Jerry half walked and half ran down the steep slope of Joy Street and stopped at the corner, waiting for the traffic to clear. He crossed Beacon Street and descended the stairs onto Boston Common. He chose the path toward Park Street Station, heading for the benches close to Tremont Street.

The noise of the cars on Tremont Street was interrupted by the scampering of the many squirrels leaping from limb to limb in the budding trees that surrounded him. Old men sat alone on benches along the path reading newspapers or lost in their reveries, seemingly at peace with the world, occasionally glancing up at passers-by. Young lovers dressed in business suits huddled together sharing sandwiches, talking of office politics or of marriages gone wrong. Long-legged women in pants suits laughed as they walked along together, loaded with shopping bags.

He spotted Jack sitting alone on a park bench facing Tremont Street, about fifty yards back from the thoroughfare. He appeared to be studying the people bustling back and forth, and, like everyone else, enjoying the spring weather after another terribly long New England winter.

"Hi, Jack," Jerry greeted his brother, sitting next to him. "Thanks for making the time."

"How's my entrepreneurial brother?"

"Business couldn't be any better, Jack. We're picking up new contracts virtually everyday. Courtney keeps grinding out favorable language that gives us every edge with terms. How's everything between you two anyway?"

"Perfect," Jack smiled. "You know, Jerry, I don't think I've ever been happier. She's made me feel alive again. Every time I see her is like the first time, every time we touch it's like I'm touching her for the first time."

"The Lord knows you deserve some happiness. You've helped enough other people." Jerry paused for a long moment. "And I feel guilty that I need your help once again, Jack."

Two hippies, one male and one female, unwashed and half naked, walked past them, their eyes glazed, the female starring into space at some unseen object. They carried small cardboard signs around their necks which read: "Pardon Vietnam Draft Evaders in 1977."

Jack stared at his brother. "A problem with Sheila? Marty?"

"Marty. I don't know where we've gone wrong with him, Jack. I just don't know. Through high school we always saw signs of trouble -- some drinking, a good mind going to waste not concentrating on his studies, an above normal aggressive nature, -- but at least he graduated. When he was younger, I thought he would go to school, take to the business, but he's never shown any interest.

"If it weren't for you, he wouldn't have gone to the community college. He certainly wouldn't listen to Sheila or me. You remember I didn't like your idea of his working the car business, but at least the compromise kept him in school. You've known I didn't want him anywhere even close to the life, Jack."

"We recently moved him into sales. He may work out very well as a salesman, Jerry. He can be a real charmer when he wants to be. Both he and Timmy are doing well so far. I'm sorry he just coasted through the two year college, but he wouldn't have done even that, or my guy either, if you and I didn't insist they finish."

"Well, now there's a new problem, Jack, and Sheila and I are frantic with worry. Marty's in serious trouble with the Lynn police. He punched out some guy in a fight in one of the bars on the Lynnway two nights ago. A fight over nothing, from everything I know. According to the police, Marty smashed this

Marblehead guy's head against the bar. The guy suffered a concussion along with cuts across his face. He hurt the guy bad, Jack. I bailed Marty out, but he's due for a hearing tomorrow, and the guy's family is furious, pushing the police hard. There could be a lot of publicity, and..."

"What's the guy's name?"

"Palmer Caldwell from Marblehead. The father's name is Walter," Jerry replied, fumbling for his cigarettes.

He stood, his hand shaking as he lit the cigarette. "Jack, that's not the only reason I needed to see you. You know, it's not the first time I've been aware of Marty's drift, and it's not the first time he's been in serious trouble. I've been able to bury other bar fights, some larceny charges, car theft charges. I don't know how to say this. I..."

"Jerry, you know you can say anything to me you want. What is it?"

"If we can get him out of this mess, I want you to take him into the life."

Jack paused before answering, trying to choose his words carefully. "Jerry, you've asked me repeatedly, and Sheila's asked me, to keep him out of it."

"I know we did, but if he continues down this pathway, we're going to lose him, Jack. Jesus, I found a gun in his room the other day. I don't know what the hell's he's into. We want you and Tommy to take him under your wing and watch over him.

"He worships the two of you. He'll listen to you, and you'll protect him, Jack. You'll make sure he doesn't end up in Walpole, which is where he's heading otherwise. You will at least make sure he settles down, gets some order in his life."

"Jesus, Jerry, I don't know. No one can guarantee his safety."

"I realize that, Jack. But he's going to be better off with you than he will be running on his own. We know what we're asking. We've thought about it long and hard. Will you do it?"

Jack touched his brother's arm. "Let's first clean up this immediate mess. Let me talk to my connections with the police and to Caldwell directly. We'll spread around whatever money we need to, Jerry. Tell Sheila to relax. Give me a day to work it out." Jack stood and extended his hand. He then crossed Tremont, as Jerry turned back toward Beacon Street.

As he walked along, Jack calculated it would cost close to $100,000 to reach the mutually convenient resolution he would seek for Marty. Whatever it cost, he would get it done. If Marty came into the life, then Timmy would follow. Jerry was right, and what applied to Marty applied co-equally to Timmy. They were usually together in activities that eventually would lead both of them to prison. He judged their pushing the envelope was, in part, a direct plea to be invited. He would bring them in. After all, Timmy was his son, much more so than Marjorie's. She would not be pleased but would find solace in Bobby. He would try to explain why he felt their entry was for the best, but whether she accepted it or not, he would go ahead. He would swell with pride that both his son and his nephew were now with him.

43

In the fall of 1978, Connie Ryan performed the service that eventually elevated him to the position of key counsel to Don Mario Gianelli.

Married with two grown daughters, Mario Gianelli was esteemed by his consignores and capos for his honesty and loyalty in dealing with all of them. That same loyalty, of course, he gave to his immediate family, who perceived him as did everyone in his circle as a good man who emphasized the importance of fidelity to them all. At age sixty-one, he, unlike so many of the family heads, had seldom indulged himself in extramarital involvements. Only once in his early thirties had he strayed, much to his own consternation. He felt, then, and for years afterward that he had violated all he held dear -- his family, his church, his values. He had lived with the guilt for nearly thirty years, managing to eventually confine it to the deeper recesses of his memory.

Then, one night early in October of 1978, he sat alone in the bar lounge of the Grand Hyatt near Grand Central Station, nursing his favorite drink, a manhattan, bemoaning the fact that his beloved Mary had left earlier in the day to visit her sister in New Jersey for the weekend. He had absolutely no premonition that his life was about to change.

At first, he hardly noticed the young Black girl, no more than seventeen or eighteen, beside him, so absorbed was he was in watching his Yankees, fresh from their one game playoff triumph over the Red Sox, in the last inning of the first game of the World Series against the Los Angeles Dodgers. Trailing 11-5 with one out to go, they hardly stood a chance, and the impending defeat of his favorite team only added to his melancholy mood. How many manhattans had he ordered already? Well, one more would do no harm. Lately, he more often felt his advancing age, and the liquor helped chase away his fixation on the subject. He studied his profile in the bar mirror. He looked like an aging professor. His cheeks held a deceptive healthy glow from too much liquor, and his stomach hung over his belt. He dreaded the thought of the long, lonely weekend ahead.

Her name was Polly Fuller she volunteered, shortly after asking him who won the game. That one question led to another, and although he recognized her almost immediately as a prostitute, the light conversation did not bother him. As a matter of fact, he welcomed the opportunity for human companionship. Her light complexion, high cheekbones, and almond eyes reminded him so much of a young Lena Horne and, above all, of the wonders of youth. What was that line from the Frank Sinatra song? Something about love, like youth, being wasted on the young.

He ordered her another rum and coke and himself another manhattan. As the evening progressed, they spoke of New York, of his family, of her move from Jersey City to New York before finishing high school just a year ago. And when the inevitable question was asked, he surprised himself with his response. Yes, he did have a place nearby, and yes, he would like to spend some time with her.

To Mario Gianelli, the price was irrelevant. He enjoyed her company, her attention to his long stories as he drove across town to Eighth Avenue and up Central Park West to the apartment he maintained in the city on West 83rd Street. Once inside the second floor apartment, they drank some more. He now felt relaxed, pleasured by the attention from his friendly, buoyant companion.

She sat beside him on the couch, watching the Jack Paar show, occasionally brushing the inside of his leg, his loins coming alive at her touch. Suddenly she stood, and unzipped her blue skirt, letting it fall around her ankles to the floor. She stood there in white panties, curlicues of dark black hair fringing their edges. She turned from him, unbuttoning her white blouse and tossing it on the chair next to the couch. Still facing away from him, she undid her bra and then lowered her panties, showing her perfectly formed buttocks.

His penis bulged in his pants as she turned to face him, pausing for the moment, allowing him to observe her tiny firm breasts which she kneaded with her thumbs. She knelt before him and unbuckled his pants, slowly pulling them down around his ankles. And then it happened.

As she worked her hands and then her mouth over his penis, he could feel himself losing his hard. And the more he tried to relax, and the more she tried to help him, the more embarrassed he became. The flaccid thing hung down at half mast, his flag of failure.

"Well, I don't perform miracles," she concluded, looking worn out from her ministerial efforts.

Fuck you, he thought. But then he remembered he couldn't. "Don't worry about it. You'll get your pay."

"Hey, don't get uppity with me, old man. You can't light up any scoreboards, ain't my fault," she retaliated, zipping up her skirt.

Much later, he would ask himself how the situation could have escalated as it did. "You got a big mouth, lady. If I were you, I'd learn to control it. Get the fuck out."

"Fuck you, limp dick. I don't need advice from some old fat guy. I want my money now."

By now, he had decided there would be no money, not with this exchange.

"Get out. You want money? Go out on the street and earn some," he said, standing up, moving to escort her out.

Suddenly, she leaped at him, clawing his face with her nails. "You fat prick! I want my money."

He slapped her hard across the face, the force of the blow causing her to lose her balance. She stumbled backward and fell hard against the side of the coffee table. She lay still, not moving at all, a trickle of blood running from her mouth. Jesus

Christ, he thought. She's dead. He felt for a pulse that was not there.

Panicking, he paced around the room, finally moving toward the window, expecting to see a fleet of police cars advancing down Central Park West. How loud had they been? Was the sound of her fall buffeted by the thick red carpet? He eased himself behind the bar and poured himself a straight VO, trying to get his thoughts together. He, Mario Gianelli, head of the Manhattan Cosa Nostra, and a family man, involved with a young Black prostitute, guilty of murdering her in his own apartment. What of his wife and daughters? What would his fellow dons think of him? His associates?

If he were to call his trusted associates now, they would be aware of his terrible lack of discretion, of his weakness, of his poor judgment. Never again would he hold their confidence. To whom could he turn? And then he remembered. He could turn to Connie Ryan.

Ryan had elevated himself out of the West Side just before the outbreak of wild and crazy violence perpetrated by the ruthless yet disorganized gangs now known as the Westies. His experience in working with the unions on the piers had proven valuable to La Cosa Nostra, and they had been pleased with his work in managing their growing interest in boxing. He sat in Don Gianelli's planning council occasionally, giving advice whenever called upon. He yearned for a stronger role in family matters, but as a non-Italian was severely limited in his advancement. He would never become a made man. The Don had always respected him, yet had been most careful not to irritate his fellow paisans by placing Ryan in any position of prominence. He could never, for example, direct any of the Don's capos.

Yes, he could turn to Ryan, he thought. He sensed Ryan burned from ambition. He could satisfy that thirst, and in turn expect his complete loyalty now and in the future. Better to share this horrible problem with a non-Italian. That, in fact, was his only choice. In the end, if he ever felt pressure from Ryan, then he could be sacrificed. What Mafioso would believe a mick's story against his version?

He dialed the number for O'Neal's Restaurant on the corner of Sixth Avenue and 57th Street, Ryan's favorite hangout the past two years now. He asked for Patrick, the bartender.

"Patrick, this is Mario Gianelli. Is Connie Ryan there?"

"Yes, Mr. Gianelli. Just a moment, please."

Above the din, the happy laughter of men and women from both the business and theatrical worlds intermingling, he heard Patrick's beckoning call. While he waited, he stared at the prostitute's body, her eyes bulging from her head, seemingly looking right at him.

"Yes, Mario."

"Connie, I need a great favor from you. Could you come over to my apartment -- the one I keep uptown -- right away? I need your help with an important matter," the Don said, as calmly as he could.

"I'll be right there."

Within fifteen minutes Connie parked his car in the Kinney garage on West 80th and walked the three blocks toward the apartment. A full moon hung over the city, shrouded behind a transparent section of cloud. He wondered what could be of such immediate importance for the Don to seek him out. In the twenty years of their association, he had very seldom received a call directly from Gianelli.

He entered the vestibule and pressed the intercom for number 2A. Once buzzed inside, he decided to use the steps to the second floor. There were three apartments on this wing of the floor, and Gianelli's was the one just to the left of the stairwell. As he approached the door, Gianelli slid the bolts open and beckoned him inside.

Stunned at the scene he encountered, Connie quickly assumed full control of events at a time when he knew the Don needed his best thinking. After listening to the Don's story, he reacted swiftly, first familiarizing himself with the apartment and then wrapping the body in sheets torn from the bed. He then left the apartment, anxious to acquaint himself with the Don's

'78 Lincoln parked in the restricted area directly in front of the building. He raised the trunk to assure himself that the body could fit. Returning to the apartment, he walked straight through to the bedroom and gathered the largest of the two throw rugs. He then placed the corpse on top of the rug and rolled it. He lifted the carpet to test whether he could carry it the required distance. No problem, he could handle it.

"Stay here, Mario. I don't want anyone seeing you this evening. How about when you came in tonight? Anybody see you and her?"

"No one. It was after eleven o'clock when we arrived. No neighbors around at all," Gianelli replied nervously.

"Good. Now just stay in the apartment. I'll take just a few seconds to open the trunk. In the dark it will look like I'm carrying out carpet. I'll return the car in an hour, and I'll leave the keys under the seat. You okay?"

"I'll be fine, Connie," he said uncertainly. "We'll talk tomorrow. Call me."

As Ryan lifted the carpet, he asked the Don to scan the small corridor. At his signal, Ryan moved quickly down the stairs, the body hoisted on his shoulder. He lifted the trunk and deposited the body, all in less than two minutes. To his knowledge, no one saw him leave.

On the following day they strolled through Central Park, walking in from West 72nd Street, circling toward East 72nd, reviewing the events of the entire evening. On that day they forged a bond built on shared confidences and mutual interest that could only advantage them both in the years ahead. Assuring the Don of his fidelity and of his complete confidentiality, Ryan had, in turn, his future assured. "I cannot elevate you above all others officially, but that is where you will be, at my right hand. Connie, you will also become a rich man, more respected than ever before."

As they walked toward the Waldman Rink, heading back toward Central Park South, Connie raised the issue uppermost on his mind throughout the last sixteen years.

"My Don, could I ask you a question which I hope will not offend you?"

"Of course."

"Will there come the time in the future when I am allowed to avenge the murder of my brother Johnny?"

From the time he had dialed for Ryan at O'Neal's, Don Gianelli knew this question would eventually be raised. He was ready with the answer.

"Connie, as you have pledged your loyalty to me, as you have served my interests in confidence, I promise you vengeance will be yours. Just allow me the time to influence Don Forelli and Don Biggio in the matter.

"We must be respectful of their position, of their view of the importance of Mr. Kelly to Biggio's interests, but I'll work on Don Forelli in the time ahead. If you allow me this time, you will be pleased with the end result."

Connie Ryan smiled. He had already waited sixteen years. For an Irishman seeking revenge, that was not a long time. His ancestors had waited hundreds of years. He could wait. He would eventually piss on Jack Kelly's grave. He pictured himself in Lynn doing just that in the not too distant future.

44

In that same fall of 1978 Jack Kelly looked forward to visiting his older son in New York City. Just after Thanksgiving, Bobby had called him, inviting his father to visit. Following graduation from Emerson, he had moved to New York, his interest in show business now heightened, his desire to latch on as a production assistant or bit actor or both, driving him forward. Although Marjorie was not thrilled with the idea of their older son leaving home, his choice of New York appealed to her and already she had visited him three or four times, enthralled that his interests were her interests.

He had landed a position as a very junior production assistant with "Ain't Misbehavin'" and a very small walk-on bit in the movie "An Unmarried Woman" now filming in New York. Elated, he wanted to show his father his city, and Jack was just as eager to see him. They agreed to meet about a week before Christmas.

For two days Jack toured Bobby's Greenwich Village haunts with him. They strolled by benches in Washington Square, watching old men playing chess and young men selling drugs. With time no particular factor, they sat in coffee houses sipping expressos, talking about everything and nothing. They visited the cinema revival house on Houston Street and at night, the disco joints. Bobby beaming with the magic of discovery, sharing the spirit of the world's greatest city with his father.

He took his father backstage to meet some of the cast of "Ain't Misbehavin'" and with considerable pride over beers in his West 4th Street apartment, announced that his aspirations were now focused. He wanted to become a movie star, a DeNiro, a Pacino, a man of the city.

Just three days before Christmas, they sat in the Coronet Theater at Third Avenue and 59th Street, awaiting the early afternoon showing of "The Deer Hunter." They listened to the Warner Brothers audio score filling the theater prior to the start of the movie. With obvious delight, Jack listened to the themes from "Casablanca," "Passage to Marseilles," "The Big Sleep," Treasure of the Sierra Madre," and other Max Steiner arrangements played by the New York Philharmonic. He was completely relaxed and was not ready for the emotional trauma of "The Deer Hunter," although both he and Bobby were fascinated by DeNiro, by John Savage's ability to project sheer terror and by Christopher Walken's superior acting.

"I need a drink or seven after that," Jack said, as they left the Coronet into a blinding sun.

They crossed Fifth Avenue at 57th Street and walked crosstown toward Broadway. At the corner of Sixth and 57th, they paused in front of O'Neal's Restaurant. They peered through the window, noted the bar, and walked in the front door on Sixth Avenue.

To the right an elongated bar led to an eating area up three or four steps in the rear. Across from the bar, the large restaurant portion was almost empty. But the bar was abuzz with activity, with only a few seats available for new arrivals. Aspiring actors and actresses, playing the temporary roles of waiters and waitresses, smiled at customers as they moved through the bar area to the tables.

Close to the entrance they found the only two available seats at the bar, and very quickly one of the handsome young bartenders asked for their order. Content, happy to be with his son, enjoying New York, Jack sat back on his stool, downing the VO and ginger, welcoming the opportunity to unwind following Michael Cimino's interpretation of the Vietnam War and its effect on middle-class America.

So he was not ready for the tap on his shoulder.

From the tables at the rear, Connie Ryan, sitting alone, had observed Jack's entry with the young man. For a moment he studied the figure facing him close to the entrance. Was he mistaken? It couldn't be. Yes, it was Kelly. Handsome, self-confident, poised. Ryan noted various women, from twenty to forty, eyeing both Kelly and the young man. For a half hour he just sat and watched, as the bar began to run two and three deep behind those sitting.

"Jack? Jack Kelly?" a familiar voice accompanied the tap on the shoulder.

Jack turned in his seat, shocked to see the elegantly dressed man standing above him. It has been sixteen years and yet Ryan had not changed much at all. Streaks of gray in his black hair only added to the picture of the suave, well-groomed, gentleman he presented.

"Connie Ryan." Jack tried to act not too surprised.

"What brings you to New York?"

"I'm in town to take in some shows, see the sights."

Jack noticed Ryan looking at the young man, waiting for an introduction. He decided not to identify Bobby. Suddenly, offering his hand, Bobby blurted out, "Bob Kelly. Pleased to make your acquaintance."

"My older son, Connie," Jack volunteered, hoping to end that part of their conversation. But again Bobby spoke.

"I'm showing my father the sights. I live here. Down in the Village," Bobby enthused. Jack bit his lip.

"Is that so? Well, I hope you two enjoy the town together. Business going well back in Boston, Jack?"

"Terrific. And how are things for you, Connie?"

"Going very well, Jack, very well. Well, look I have to get moving. But first...Wes," he yelled to the bartender, "a round for my...friends." He deliberately paused before the word "friends," making sure Jack caught the hesitation.

"Nice to have met you, Bob. Maybe we'll see each other again soon around the city." He stared at Jack as he spoke to Bobby.

"Who's that guy?" Bobby inquired as soon as Ryan had departed.

"You remember I told you about your Uncle Tommy and the trouble we had back in '62 with the New York people? Connie Ryan is the New York people I was talking about. A very dangerous man. A good person to steer clear of."

"Jesus, Dad. I just met him. I wasn't planning on a lifetime friendship."

"He won't bother you, Bob. You're not part of the life," Jack assured him. Now all he had to do was assure himself that he was right.

45

The Mystic River Bridge links Boston with communities to the north. Opened to traffic in 1950, it was acquired by the Massachusetts Port Authority in 1959. A part of U.S. Route 1, it extends across the Mystic River from the Charlestown section of Boston to Chelsea and connects Boston's Central Artery and the Northeast Expressway. The high level, steel truss, double-decked structure runs about 135 feet above water and, with a length of more than two miles, is one of the largest bridges in New England.

In 1979 over 24 million cars a year crossed the Bridge, their drivers feeding 50 cents into the automatic coin collectors or exchanging dollars for change at one of the seven toll booths manned by staff. While the remnant of the Monday morning commuters wrestled their way over icy highways from Chelsea toward the booths at the apex of the bridge, Timmy and Marty Kelly sat in the rear of Paulie Cronin's stolen Ford Mustang on Chelsea Street, just off Rutherford Avenue in Charlestown.

"What time is it, Paulie?" Timmy asked.

"10:00 o'clock."

"Just right," Marty remarked. "Up at the tolls they have the last three days' receipts. If my information is right, there should be close to $100,000 there after the morning commute. Traffic's light enough here that we should be able to get away easily and fast.

"Paulie, drive down Chelsea Street right into the Port Authority's parking lot below the bridge. Keep the motor humming. Five minutes from the time we enter, pull over close to the entrance and be ready to move. You got it?"

"I'm always ready to fly, Marty. Don't worry. I'll be there."

"Let's go."

Paulie drove into the Bridge employees' parking lot. Access to the Bridge itself, 135 feet above them, was either by elevator or by the stairwells. The elevator led to four levels of floors, with the administration offices housed on the second floor, the technical services unit on the third, and the tolls themselves on the fourth. At that level a see-through one-way window allowed the supervisor to observe the various transactions at the tolls.

Dressed in navy blue peacoats, each carrying an empty gym bag, Marty and Timmy entered the elevator foyer at 10:10, assuring first that no one else was in the area. If anyone were to approach the foyer, Paulie would signal them by hand. They waited in the lobby for what seemed an interminable period. Suddenly the flashing light indicated the elevator was moving from the third floor. Within ten seconds they placed stocking masks over their faces and waited for the card-accessed elevator to descend. As the doors opened at the lobby level, both men pulled the snub-nosed .38's from their pockets.

The elderly electrician almost dropped his toolbox at the sight of two stocking capped men waving him back inside. "Get out that fuckin' access card and take us to the second floor," Marty said.

"Who the fuck..."

"I'm going to tell you just one more time, asshole. Get that card out," Marty said.

Quickly, the electrician inserted the card and the elevator began its ascent.

"Remember, one armed security guard will be on the floor," Marty said.

As the door opened, the electrician, prodded by Marty, exited first. Timmy immediately positioned the heavy cigarette butt container against the open elevator door to prevent its use. Briskly they covered the twenty yards along the short corridor to the administration offices on their left. As they walked in, the young receptionist looked up and emitted a shrill, short scream.

"Shut the fuck up and get over against the wall with him. Get the other two," Marty ordered.

From the twin offices directly behind the reception area an older man, the director of bridge operations, and his associate suddenly appeared, alarmed by the receptionist's cry.

"What's going on here?" the director demanded. Marty dug his .38 hard under the man's ribs, causing him to stagger forward searching for air.

"Find that fuckin' security guard before he finds us," he commanded Timmy.

Timmy moved back to the short corridor. If he were on the floor, the only possible place he could be was the men's room just beyond the administration offices. He slowly turned the knob and observed the guard at the urinal.

"What the hell is this?" the guard asked meekly.

"Keep your hands on your dick, fat boy, until I tell you to do something else." He advanced toward the security guard and took his piece from his holster. Quickly he threw it into the receptacle beside the window.

Back in the office Marty grabbed the young associate by his arm. "Which of you can open that safe in the corner for me?"

The two administrators looked at each other, trying to buy time. "Neither one of us can open it," the older man finally replied.

Timmy marched the guard into the office area and pushed him toward the four others against the wall.

"Is that right?" Marty responded, then suddenly smashed his gun across the younger man's face.

"Mister," he addressed the older man, "you have exactly ten seconds to open that safe or one of your four friends here isn't going to be inhaling air much longer."

"Please, please. Don't hurt anyone. I'll open it," he stammered. He walked to the corner where the small safe sat in the open on a huge wooden slab. He quickly spun the dials and opened the door.

"Watch them," Marty ordered, dropping to his haunches to pull out the bags of dollars. He threw two bags into each of the gym bags, leaving the coins.

"I'm all set," he yelled to Timmy.

"All five of you now, down on your knees, facing the wall. Hands behind your back," Timmy directed. Together they slipped handcuffs from their jackets on each of the employees.

Marty lifted both the gym bags over his shoulder as they moved toward the elevator. "Everyone remain exactly where they are. Don't try to be a hero. This isn't your money."

They entered the elevator, and Timmy inserted the electrician's access card and pushed the lobby button. As they descended, Marty kept his .38 down at his side. Timmy positioned himself to leave the elevator first, his right hand inside the pocket of his peacoat, at the ready.

At this time of day, they had reasoned, there would be little activity on the first floor, as the Bridge employees were at their stations. As they exited the elevator, they pulled off the ski masks, stuffing them into their pockets, once they were assured no one waited in the foyer. The entire operation had taken eight minutes.

Paulie Cronin raced the motor as the cousins jumped into the back seat of the waiting car. Paulie drove the stolen car carefully back down Chelsea Street, taking a right onto Rutherford Avenue.

"A tit!" Marty yelled. "One private security guard, no alarm systems. I told you it would be a breeze, Tim. They're more worried about some blue collar fuck not paying his 50 cents than getting robbed themselves."

"It's no fuckin' breeze getting away from here," Paulie complained. "Only way out is Chelsea Street. If something had gone wrong, Marty..."

"You worry too much, Paulie. It went just like I told you it would. Let's ditch this car over in Everett by the football stadium. Then let's go celebrate, right Tim?" He slapped the back of his cousin and best friend.

"You fuckin' did what?" Tommy couldn't believe his ears.

"Jesus, Tommy. Don't have a fuckin' heart attack. The two of them pulled it off smooth as silk. None of us could have done any better." Paulie beamed with pride.

"Can you believe this dumb mick, Jack?" Tommy fumed. "Is he a turnip off the truck or what?"

Jack, Tommy, Vinnie Sullivan, Ray Horan, and Chris Kiley sat on the crates at the Charlestown warehouse on Medford Street, not more than a mile from the Bridge. Jack tried to remain calm.

"Paulie, tell me what happened."

"Jack, you know the last year or two we've been slowly introducing the two boys to things, right? They're two naturals. I'll tell you that. You should have seen how calm your son..."

"Paulie, skip the accolades and just tell me what happened, please."

"Okay. Okay," Paulie stammered. He sensed it was critical that he describe the events accurately.

"Like I said, the last year the boys have been with us on some loanshark stuff. Ray and I also took them to collect from some of the pimps, the taverns, you know. You said to introduce them slowly to different parts of our work. You asked Ray and me to do that, right, Jack?" He looked for signs of approval from his boss, but none were forthcoming. Ray sighed and looked to the ceiling.

"Well, they've been coming along real well, you know? Ray and I always have them in our sights, right, Ray?" No response from that quarter.

"Last night -- Sunday, right? Marty called me and asked me to pick him up in Everett near the football stadium Monday morning. Says Timmy will be with him. So I figured it's just a ride he wants for some job you designated, or he's just being sociable. Anyway, I didn't think anything of it."

"You didn't think to tell Ray or me?" Tommy interjected. "That's because you didn't think period."

"Like I just said, how am I supposed to know what he's doing? I'm now a fuckin' mind reader?"

"Yeah, that's you, Paulie," Vinnie snickered.

"Fuck you, Vinnie," Paulie shot back.

"Paulie, let me ask you a question," Jack said. "Say again, when did you know they were going to heist the Bridge?"

"Jack, I picked them up in the stolen car..."

"Wait a minute, Paulie. You just finished telling me you thought they might just be being sociable. Why the stolen car?"

"Didn't I mention that? Marty asked me to swipe one, not use my own."

"And you didn't think that was unusual?"

"No, Jack. Honestly. I...I guess I didn't think about it much, you know? We do it all the time. Anyway, I picked them up, and that's when they told me the plan."

"Paulie, this is very important. So think before you answer me. Right then, when they tell you they are going to heist a fuckin' state facility with all the heat that entails -- robbing a fuckin' bridge -- armed robbery -- what do you say to them?"

"Jack, you think I'm a dumb shit or something? Well, I'm not. I says to them, 'Does Jack know about his hit?'" Paulie paused to let them feel the full effect of his statement.

"And?" Jack said.

"And Marty says, 'Don't worry about it' so I figure I wouldn't."

"You meathead, Paulie," Vinnie said contemptuously.

"It's all right, Vin. Leave him alone," Jack said, standing and walking toward Paulie. He sat on the crate next to Paulie and roughed his hair playfully. Paulie sighed, as the tension left his body. He started sobbing uncontrollably, his head in his hands. Jack placed an arm around him.

"Paulie, listen to me. I know you would never deliberately hurt me. Don't you think I know that?"

"I don't know, Jack. I'm scared. Your son and your nephew, for Christ's sake. I don't know what I was thinking. I..."

"Paulie, are you listening to me? It's not your fault." Jack looked at Vinnie, who stared back in disbelief at his reaction.

"Paulie, just learn from this, will you? For old times sake? Have you ever heard me talk of a hit that public? Huh? Of course not. Any of you guys ever do time? No. Because we're smart enough to realize there's no percentage in armed robbery. Half of Charlestown is involved in attempted armed robbery on armored cars and banks. It's like a rite of passage for any Irish kid who wants a life of crime. And it's a dumb business."

Jack knew that in his condition Paulie was not taking in much of anything he said. "Ray, take Paulie home, will you? Tommy, tell Jesse James and Billy the Kid I want to see them at my house in two hours. Whatever else they're doing, drop it. You and I need to see them at noon."

46

The January snow fell in wispy circles whipped by the heavy winds off the Atlantic. Light, fluffy snow that would not accumulate served mainly to slow cross-town traffic. Marty cursed the long line ahead of him, weaving its way like a giant snake along the Lynnway. "We're going to be late, Tim. Nothing moving very fast in this stuff."

They listened to WXKS Medford. The DJ played "I Will Survive," "The Pina Colada Song," and "YMCA." All music, no talk. Just what they wanted.

"What do you think he wants?" Marty asked.

"I don't know. Tommy just said to be there at noon."

The wind out of the northeast pelted the wet snow against Jack's window. Standing at the edge of the window, Tommy suddenly turned toward his older brother. "How you planning to handle this, Jack?"

"Let's see what they tell us after the first few questions."

Without knocking, the cousins appeared in the front hall.

"In here," Jack yelled at the noise. He put his feet up on the glass-top coffee table, leaning back in the white chair. Tommy sat on the couch, and from there beckoned the cousins toward him.

"Sit down over here," Tommy ordered.

"What's up, Dad?"

Jack stared at him. "I don't know, Timmy. You tell me what's up. Like maybe starting with what was up yesterday?"

"Yesterday? What do you mean?" Timmy looked from his father to his uncle.

"This isn't 'Twenty Questions', Timmy. And I don't have all fuckin day to play games with you two. So cut the bullshit fast, and let's all get on the same wave length."

"Paulie's been talking to you, right, Uncle Jack?" Marty said. "I ought to have known that fuckin' rabbit couldn't keep quiet. We were going to tell you, you know?"

"You know, Marty, some people close to us think you have a real talent for leadership. You know that? Shows you how dumb people can be," Jack said.

Marty looked down at the floor, averting his uncle's stare.

"You're stupid, you know that, Marty? Real stupid. You took advantage of poor Paulie."

"Dad, Paulie didn't know anything in advance. We just wanted the best wheel man to be with us. We wouldn't do anything to hurt Paulie in your eyes."

"You know, Timmy, I never thought I would say this. You disappoint me, son. Really disappoint me."

Timmy recoiled on the couch. A slap across his face could not have brought more pain. He would have preferred the slap to the words he was hearing.

"Uncle Jack..."

"Marty, just shut the fuck up and listen," Jack broke in. "When I want your opinion, I'll ask for it."

"What was the purpose of this hit?" Tommy asked.

"You've both told us we have been doing well. We love the action, Dad. The flow, the rush. We just knew we could pull the heist off. We were ready for it."

"Uncle Jack, with all due respect the plan went off without a hitch. We were in and out in eight minutes. No one hurt," Marty said.

"Did you read the papers today, Marty?" Jack asked. "Look at that headline." He picked up the <u>Boston Globe</u> from the coffee table. "Bridge Heist Nets $100,000," he read aloud.

"You know I really blame myself for not educating you two more carefully. We don't need this kind of publicity. Now, every state cop's on the alert looking to catch the two cowboys involved. I made a big mistake. I didn't realize you two were still playing amateur night in Dixie. Let me make something very clear. We're not armed robbers. We run an organization, a professional business where everybody follows the rules. No free lancing. No independent scores." Jack tried to keep his voice even.

"You want to go independent? Go. Get the fuck out now. I don't have time to baby sit two boyos off the boat from the old country." He paused to make sure his words were registering.

"Well?" Jack raised his voice.

It was Marty who answered, as he knew it would be. Jack had observed it developing for some months now, and he was sure Tommy also saw it. The men flowed toward Marty. Older men spoke of his ability to think, to strategize, to consider all angles, to cover the bases. The younger men admired his courage under fire. But about him there was still an annoying arrogance, a cockiness. He had not yet developed the concern that every leader must adopt -- a caring attitude for the larger family, for those who depended on him.

"Uncle Jack, we made a mistake." The right response, Jack thought. "I wasn't thinking right. It was there; it seemed so easy. We just knew we could do it. I apologize for creating this problem for you, for Uncle Tom, and the family. Is there anything we can do to make good on it?"

"Where's the $100,000, Marty?"

"We have it stashed, Dad," Timmy answered.

"Anyone else know anything about the score?" Tommy asked.

"No one. Just us two. Then Paulie at the last minute," Marty replied.

"The $100,000 belongs to the family. You two receive no part of it. What did you give Paulie?" Jack asked.

"Ten grand," Marty said.

"Get it back from him and fast."

"Not one word to anyone about this score. You two understand?" Tommy asked.

"One more slip-up, and that's it for the both of you," Jack said. "Now I would appreciate your leaving us alone."

The two cousins stood without saying anything else and left quietly. As the front door closed, Tommy moved to the window. The snow had now been replaced by a wet drizzle. "Aren't they fuckin' something else? More balls than brains for sure."

"We're fortunate one of them didn't get killed or kill someone else. I would like to see a little less balls and much more brains from the two of them. They're twenty years old, for Christ sake."

"You want me to keep them with Ray and Paulie?"

"No. Keep Ray involved if you want. Can you step in more directly with them? Spend more time with them?"

"Of course. If you want me to, Jack."

"You know someday, Tommy, I may not be here. It's you and them that will be running things. We need to help them understand something about thinking and planning and taking responsibility for people beyond themselves."

Tommy smiled at him. "My own special project, huh?"

"You got it."

He stopped there and did not say what he felt. He hoped the assignment would also stoke the fires that used to burn in Tommy's belly once again. Could the teacher become rejuvenated through contact with his students? The cousins needed more attention and guidance, and their new mentor needed some purpose, some spark to make him care once again.

They walked away from the White House and turned toward Fifteenth Street, Danny leading the way. At the corner a vendor proudly lifted a copy of the <u>Washington Post</u> high in the air, its masthead featuring a colorful small American flag aside the headline proclaiming the USA hockey team's victory over the world champion Russians.

"You realize you're with an old guy, Danny?" Jack said as he guided Catherine across the wide street. "Slow down a bit."

"Come on, Uncle Jack, don't give me that crap. A big marathoner like you can't take this pace?"

Since early morning the three of them had been touring Washington. They had started at the FBI Building itself, where

Danny gave them a tour reserved for important dignitaries and from there they climbed to the Washington Monument looking down to the Mall where vendors of all types worked from tents and trucks selling everything from T-shirts to hot dogs. Then they paraded through the Mall, stopping at the old Smithsonian, its dark red edifice standing in such contrast to the new buildings spanning the area. Then on to the White House.

Now at 4:30 they entered the Old Ebbitt Grill and headed directly to the bar. Animals of all types -- turtles, frogs, bears and boars -- were mounted above the elegant bar, and around them waiters in starched vests bustled around the main dining room depositing silver and napkins at each of the green velvet booths.

"She said she'd be here around 4:30," Danny said glancing around the restaurant. He flicked his light blond hair off his forehead and felt for the part in his hairline, assuring himself that he was presentable. In fact, he had grown into a very presentable young man, Jack thought. He possessed Leo's wiry frame and height, and his mother's soft, delicate features.

"Calm down, Danny. You'll have a lifetime to wait for her. Don't let her keep you on edge in the first few months," Jack said, a mirthful grin crossing his mouth.

"Now leave him alone, Jack. Try to remember when you were young -- if you can."

"Catherine, there's no need to be nasty," Jack replied. "I'm only trying to give good advice to the lad so that he doesn't make mistakes along the road to romance."

"If he listens to you and does the exact opposite of what you advise, he'll be a whole lot better off I say," Catherine said, focusing sparkling eyes on Jack.

"Mother, Jack. Please. She could be here...any... Here she comes!"

From the doorway she walked toward them. The room, large and square, seemed to make her look smaller, for she was indeed small and lean with fine, subdued features, with thick black hair and with burnished Mediterranean skin. As he turned, Jack first noticed her eyes, her most prominent feature. They burned under heavy Grecian eyebrows, staring down those directly in front of her.

Danny almost stumbled off the barstool as he stood to greet her. He waved her toward their stools and embraced her as she approached them.

"Christine, let me introduce my mother Catherine and my very good friend, Jack Kelly, the most important people in the world to me," he said.

Jack stood and shook her hand while Catherine offered her a seat next to her.

"We're so pleased to meet you, Christine," Catherine said. "Danny has told us so much about you."

For the next hour they sat in relaxed fashion, inhabiting that world of mutual admiration known to lovers and friends, unwinding in full acceptance that those about them loved them or, at minimum, bore them no malice.

An FBI agent and a female Washington D.C. detective. Jesus, Jack thought. The day before he had flown with Catherine into National from Boston so pleased that Danny had asked him to meet the woman he intended to marry. He had to admit that she was a catch. Her warmth and compassion shone through good humor and her obvious devotion to Danny impressed him.

Catherine's poke to his arm brought him back to their gaiety and laughter. "We're so happy for the two of you, aren't we, Jack?"

Christine smiled fondly in his direction. "He tells me you've always been there for him. Well, I'm there for him, too, now," she said, squeezing Danny's arm.

Danny looked at his watch. "I need to drive Christine over to Alexandria so she can change. And you two should rest for a while. We'll meet you at Paul Young's on Connecticut Avenue at eight. Okay, Jack?"

"We'll find it. You two get along now," he replied.

When they had gone, Jack asked if she wanted another drink.

"I'm content, but let's stay a little longer," Catherine replied.

"Well, what did you think?" Jack asked.

"She's everything he said she was. I like her very much."

Jack deliberately forced a frown. "Two coppers in the family. I might as well pull in my tent and go honest."

"God forbid," she replied, raising an eyebrow in that sassy way he liked.

He laughed easily and put his hand on hers, lifting it so that he could brush it with his lips.

"You're priceless. You know that, Catherine?"

"Please, don't do that, Jack," she said, withdrawing her hand.

"I meant no harm, Catherine."

She had overreacted, she knew. "I'm just a bit touchy what with meeting her and all." She tried to smile.

He knew there was more to it than that. For some time now he had sensed her affection for him. And although he found her attractive, she was his friend, and he would never take advantage of her, and he never had. Not with his love for Courtney, not with his respect for Catherine.

"Maybe we should head back to the hotel," she said. "I could use a little rest before dinner."

He noticed the tears welling in her eyes and looked away at the check. He had fucked that up real good, he thought.

47

Jack and Courtney jogged through the Breakheart Reservation in Saugus, turning in tandem with its winding road. Bright orange leaves crunched under their feet, and above them only a few leaves remained on the trees that arched above the roadway, partially hiding the sun.

The light touch of perfume she sprayed on her throat every day lingered in the air as they moved deeper into the park. He enjoyed her scent.

"What time do you have to meet him?"

"Cardoza? For dinner at Jeveli's at nine o'clock," Jack replied, breathing in and out easily.

"I'll miss you. Can you come over afterwards?"

Jack shook his head. "Not tonight. It must be important. Probably take some time. He doesn't ask to see me that often."

"In that case we'll have to make up for lost time this afternoon."

"You'll be the death of me yet."

"I doubt it," she said. "I plan on keeping you, old man."

They looped the Reservation, running along the lakefront, moving uphill back toward the Lynn Fells Parkway, and down Main Street, Saugus to Vine Street and then to her home. Once there, they showered together, the hot steamy water cascading down their bodies, rivulets of cold sweat replaced by the invigorating spray. She stood closest to the shower head, and from behind her he admired her body, occasionally brushing her wet hair with his hand. She sensed his admiration, giggled and turned to face him. She threw her arms around him, drawing his lips down to hers.

"I love that body of yours," he said.

"It's for you," she said.

Later, they lay on the bed, naked under the covers. Relaxing. Without talking. He had long ago realized that lovers did not need to talk. Like old friends, there was not the need to perform for one another, to demonstrate one's wit, or simply to chatter away. It was enough just to be together.

As soon as Jack entered Jeveli's in East Boston, he knew there was trouble in the air. Why else would Nick Rizzo be with Cardoza?

"Jack, thanks for coming. You know Nicky Rizzo, of course," Cardoza said. They had been standing in the lobby of the restaurant awaiting his arrival.

"Yeah. How are things, Nick?" Jack asked, as if he could care less.

The maitre d' immediately signaled them to a booth and presented them with menus. Cardoza waved to one of the elderly waiters standing together near the back of the room. Immediately he walked toward their booth. "Louie, some drink orders, please. Jack? Nick?"

"VO and ginger for me," Jack replied.

"Dewar's," responded Nick.

"And bring me some wine, Louie. And start us off with some antipasto, and then some slices of pizza. You know the little ones that I like."

"How goes business, Salvy?" Jack asked.

"Miserable. The FBI is finally waking up. They're all over the place, since they realized the fucking communists aren't going to invade New England tomorrow. Gennaro is very nervous, very concerned. But, we have our small successes as well. We still run ahead of the feds.

"It's a very different story in New York. The feds have developed a pretty good number of informants among some of the families, for instance the Gambinos. Some are buying their way out of prison terms or ratting for revenge. Not a good situation at all.

"Remember your old friend Connie Ryan? He's now chief counsel, unofficially of course, to Mario Gianelli. He's moved right up the ladder. And his old neighborhood is something else. Your Irish friends who replaced Ryan there are out of control. They're fuckin' crazy. More homicides than ever there now even with the new developments being built. But one thing I give the Irish credit for. They don't rat on each other."

Louie arrived with the drinks, the antipasto, and the pizza all at once. Cardoza then ordered the main course, acting as if he were choosing the Nobel Peace Prize recipient, his attention riveted on the menu. "Fettuccine Alfredo for everyone," he finally said. Rizzo sat perfectly content, like the cat who had swallowed the canary. Not a good sign, Jack thought.

"And you've been doing very well, Jack?" Cardoza asked a question to which he already knew the answer.

"Fine, Salvy. Gambling, loans, prostitution, drugs, all more profitable than ever. In this age of instant gratification the poor, the middle class, the wealthy -- whoever -- they're all gluttonous. They all want what they want when they want it."

"Like those fuckin' baseball players out on strike ruining the '81 baseball season," Rizzo interjected.

"A perfect example," Jack said.

"How's your brother Tommy?" Cardoza inquired.

Jack wondered why all the social chatter. Cardoza would know perfectly well how Tommy was doing.

"He still dwells too much on that lost opportunity, Salvy. But other than that, he's doing well, thank you."

"And your son and nephew, Jack? How are they coming along?" Cardoza asked.

"How about that Mystic River Bridge job two years ago, Jack? You ever going to tell us who pulled that off?" Rizzo smiled at him.

Jack glared at Rizzo. "How should I know? No one we know, for sure. My guess is some pros from out of town. The cops haven't any suspects."

Cardoza gave Rizzo a disapproving glance and moved rapidly away from such a delicate subject into the new waters he

309

really wanted to navigate. "I'm pleased things are going well for you. Your tributes to Gennaro and me demonstrate your skill in keeping the fuckin' enterprise thriving in both the good and the difficult times. We value your work, and most especially, your loyalty to us."

For sure, Jack thought, the bad news is coming. "It's been a mutually beneficial accommodation with my good friends of these many years, Salvatore," he replied.

Cardoza smiled and sipped his wine slowly. "Jack, I have to ask a great favor of you based on our long and profitable association. I speak for both Gennaro and myself in this matter. As I mentioned, these increased pressures we're facing are beginning to hurt our profit margins. Not overwhelmingly mind you, but still they hurt. Our being watched so carefully forces us to defer action on pressing matters, and tends to promote a certain lack of initiative that's becoming more troublesome."

Jack rolled the whiskey around over the ice cubes in his glass. The bite of the whiskey always helped him focus, and he wanted to catch Cardoza's every word. Outside, the first leisurely raindrops fell against the window. A portent of the words yet to come? Jack wondered.

"We ask you to consider an alteration of our long-standing arrangements," Cardoza continued. "We're in need of supplementing the profit lines for our colleague." He gestured toward Rizzo. "Those areas of Lynn, Revere, Chelsea, Cambridge, Charlestown, Somerville, South Boston where you have served us need to be re-aligned. We want Nick here to assume a stronger share of what we all see as a very profitable pie."

Jack knew there was little if anything to be considered. He was receiving an order. He began to think of a response while he listened to Cardoza.

"We ask that our family, through our representative and mutual friend here, be provided with the oversight of 12-1/2 percent more of the various businesses."

Rizzo concentrated on Jack, neglecting both his food and drink. His eyes danced with the pleasure that comes from being in the driver's seat, and he pursed his lips so as to suppress his great desire to smile in front of Cardoza. They all knew such an arrangement was outrageous. Already the Mafia controlled 75 percent of the areas under discussion. In effect, they were halving Kelly's operations. Jack decided to ask some questions first, partly to hide his anger and partly to give himself more time to think.

"Salvy, is business so bad that you must make this request?" he began.

"I'm afraid so. We're losing market share. To make up for our losses, or rather our lack of growth, we need to gain more of a percentage of the take from the satellite operations."

"Is there unhappiness then with what we have provided you?" Jack knew that was not the case, but the question had to be asked.

"Not at all, my friend," Cardoza responded, touching Jack on his forearm.

"Then why not simply ask for a greater percentage?" Jack asked calmly. He knew the answer to his question, but asked it anyway.

Cardoza forked a small amount of fettuccine into his mouth. "In our mind, with the situation the way it is, it's critical that our own people be given the opportunity to supervise the operations. It's a matter of family, as well. It's not to be interpreted as any lack of confidence in you, Jack." The real issue. Guineas taking care of guineas, Jack thought.

Jack knew what his answer had to be tonight. But he also knew the answer he gave tonight might not be his final one.

"Salvatore, I would be less than honest if I didn't let you know of my disappointment with these new arrangements. With all due respect to Nick, he hasn't performed for Gennaro and you as I have. Is it fair for excellent performance to be rewarded this way? I don't believe so. But because of my high regard for Don Biggio and for you, and in full appreciation of our history together, I accept these new terms and wish Nick well.

"I ask only one thing in return, Salvatore. I ask that you consider my request that should the future change for the better economically for Don Biggio and for you, we can, together, restructure these terms."

Salvatore Cardoza had always admired the handsome Irishman. He even talked like a Mafioso during the course of negotiations. But, more impressively, he knew how to conduct himself, showing no indications of hurt, no expression to demonstrate displeasure, presenting arguments that looked to the future, taking a global approach to difficult situations. The piece of shit to his left couldn't think beyond tonight. But he was a paisan, and a favorite of Gennaro's, the nephew of Gennaro's wife. He couldn't carry Kelly's water, Salvy thought.

Jack waited for Cardoza's reply, cognizant that it would be veiled, polite, accommodating when, in reality, the terms would never change. For the moment it was only important that Cardoza felt comfortable with his answers.

Cardoza smiled at him. "My friend of long standing, of course. Accept my assurance that once we free ourselves from these difficult present circumstances, once our economic base is again solid, and the fuckin' FBI is off our asses, we can again reconsider our arrangements. You have my word, and I speak for both Gennaro and myself."

Jack extended his hand across the table. "Thank you, my good friend."

"Now the hour grows late, and I'm afraid such good food and wine only leads to more tiredness for those of us more advanced in age," Cardoza smiled. "I must then excuse myself, in order to go home and digest the eight or ten pills that my doctor insists will prolong life, that is, if I don't become a drug addict in the meantime.

"Jack, Nick, get together soon to discuss the necessary details of our new arrangement. I hope to see each of you again soon." He stood, and, in respect, both Jack and Nick rose.

"We will walk with you to your car, my Don," Rizzo said.

Once on the sidewalk, they waited only a few seconds in the light rain before a black Cadillac moved toward the canopied entrance. As the Don entered the car, Jack turned abruptly toward Rizzo. He did not need any further conversation with this asshole, he thought.

"I need to run, Nicky. I'll call you to set up a meet."

"Call me soon, Jack. I'm anxious to get things settled," Rizzo commanded.

Jack drove along Route 1A, heading from East Boston through Revere to Lynn. The radio blared the new James Bond theme "For Your Eyes Only", and at its conclusion the news anchor previewed the upcoming world news for 11:00. The lead headline related the plight of Bobby Sands and the twenty-one alleged IRA supporters on hunger strike at Belfast Prison. The announcement made him think of his heritage.

First there had been the old Yanks and their "No Irish Need Apply" job policy in early twentieth century Boston, he thought, as he drove toward Revere Beach, as always enjoying the coast and the water, whatever the time of year. He looked out to the black waters, to the Atlantic through the night, and envisioned as he had so frequently during his lifetime, the hardships that his forefathers had endured in order to reach this land of promise. And, once here, decades more were to pass before basic fairness would win out, before influence in politics and in the courts led to a middle class standard of life for his people.

And, now, in 1981, some Neapolitan gang lords were dictating to him. Or at least they thought they were. Fucking guineas. Their mistake was they always assumed they were smarter than everyone else. A big mistake, he thought. They were heading downward, both Biggio and Cardoza, caught up in their own importance, oblivious to the forces of the '80's, despite their protestations. They were not taking the proper precautions in this new technological age of wiretapping, of law enforcement's ability to infiltrate an organization, undermining a family from its base. Their arrogance would eventually bring them down.

For now, he would appear to be cooperative and wait for the proper moment. In his estimation, both Biggio and Cardoza would spend a good part of the new decade on the defensive, in courts, the victims of their own excesses, their bloat, their inability to truly understand how to operate in a new age. But he needed to formulate a plan of his own as well. He couldn't simply depend on circumstance or fate to assist him. He never had, and he never would.

He guided his 1981 Chevrolet Impala over the General Edwards Bridge and decided to turn toward Central Square, rather than toward the beach area and home. He wanted to absorb the sounds and sights of Lynn, to touch its pulse, to become one with it. For some reason, whenever he had problems, coming home strengthened him. Like him, the city had experienced its share of problems during the '70's and early '80's, no question, yet its resiliency impressed him. It had bounced back, its new populations fighting for social justice as had his ancestors. And always, there was the sea to the east in its majesty, symbolizing promise and opportunity to be realized, to them as it had to him.

From Union Street, he gunned the car toward the beach, content in the knowledge that he could outthink both Cardoza and Rizzo. They thought like fat cats, and he was forever lean and hungry.

48

Bobby Latimer pushed the frightened white man up the stairwell of the burned out seven story brick building on Annunciation Road. He prodded him with the military knife as they neared the top floor. At 2:00 A.M. no one else was about in this long forsaken firetrap, but below he could see lights in about one-half of the other tenements that comprised the project at the corner of Ruggles Street and Annunciation Road.

The tape Bobby had wound around the man's mouth completely muffled his cries for help, but now his eyes bulged in his face, registering the abject fear he could not convey with words. Bobby shoved him ahead.

From the top step of the small landing leading to the roof, Bobby Latimer slammed his shoulder into the door, causing it to fly open. Light rain fell, obscuring the massive twin towers of the Prudential Center just a mile away.

He yanked the man onto the rooftop using the rope wrapped around his bound hands to lift him over the final step. Once on the roof, Bobby inhaled the fresh air. The smell of urine had been everywhere throughout the seven-story climb.

He smiled as he observed the fear in the man's eyes. Earlier this evening, Bobby had visited his favorite gay bar on Dudley Street. Occasionally, suburban honkies like this guy cruised in, looking to meet Black men for sex. Bobby loved that set-up. He was bisexual, and he enjoyed the sex, but the thrill came from having some white guy go down on him and then afterward, beating the shit out of a guy who could not report such incidents to the police.

Tonight things had not gone as expected. The guy had turned ugly, changed his mind right in the middle of their foreplay at Bobby's apartment over at Mission Main. He had even taken a swing at him. Bobby had to cut him with the knife to settle him down. Then he had tied him up and moved him across three streets in the rain. He had kept to the shadows and to the edges of buildings.

Bobby guided the man to the edge of the roof. Even with his hands tied behind him, the man began to struggle, as he anticipated the worse. Bobby plunged the long knife into his back, causing the man to stagger and turn toward him. Again Bobby thrust the knife into him, this time into his stomach. The man lurched forward, trying to fall. Bobby held him upright, pleased to cause him as much pain as possible before the end. He slashed the knife across the man's face, then turned him to the edge of the roof. Holding him around the neck, Bobby shoved hard and watched the body topple to the asphalt below.

Quickly, he raced down the seven flights. Enough of a rush for tonight, he thought. What was it the white woman in "Gone With the Wind" had said? Oh, yeah, "Tomorrow is another day."

<u>49</u>

Vinnie Sullivan now owed the book over $150,000, and he had no intention of paying it. He had known the old guinea from Framingham for years, in fact he had met him through Jimma back in the '50's. He had been careful not to gamble with any of the books in the Irish neighborhoods or in any of the areas where the family collected for Jack. Jack would not be happy to learn of his insatiable habit. Like Jimma, he had insisted they stay clear of any vice that could call attention to the family.

In the twenty years of his association with Jack Kelly, he had become a wealthy man. He now earned close to $40,000 a year on the waterfront, and he had consistently worked and paid taxes on those wages as both Jimma and Jack had insisted. In addition, he guesstimated his earnings from the life approximated a quarter million a year, tax free. But what did he have to show for it? Not much. The house in Charlestown. He had had to sell the boat last year to pay Ray Faucetti. He had $30,000 or so in the bank, but almost everything else was gone.

Faucetti had carried him for almost three years now, but the vig was a killer and now he owed the book $150,000. Lately, Faucetti had been complaining about his slowness in meeting the payments. He couldn't afford to pay him, and so he had begun to think of his options, of which there was only one. He had to eliminate Faucetti. And it would work. Faucetti was a loner, operating out of Framingham, right out of his home on Grove Street, just off Route 9.

Vinnie had called Faucetti earlier, letting him know that he now had the money. Could he bring it by tonight? Of course he could. The greedy bastard would stay up all night for $150,000.

317

Vinnie could picture him waiting right now, playing with his paper records in the swivel chair before his rolltop desk. All he needed was a fuckin' eyeshade.

At twilight Vinnie had his wife drop him at Lechmere's in Cambridge, near the Museum of Science just off the McGrath Highway. He walked into the store, turned, and stood in the lobby watching the parking lot for a few minutes. To his right an elderly couple stepped out of a blue Ford Fairlaine about three rows over. As they slowly approached the front entrance, he followed them with his eyes. They leaned on one another, and appeared in no particular hurry. Once they had entered the store, he fell in behind them for a few minutes, ensuring they were absorbed in their shopping.

He left through the front door and headed for the Ford. They had parked in a crowded row, so he could use the other cars as blockers. It would take him less than a minute to gain entry. He looked around. No one in the immediate area at the moment. Pick the lock. Pop the ignition. Thirty seconds and he was ready to roll.

By the time he reached Grove Street, it was pitch dark. He stopped outside Faucetti's ranch house and pulled the .38 from his shoulder holster, slipping the silencer from his sportscoat pocket and positioning it on the barrel. A nice quiet suburban neighborhood, he thought. Just perfect for what he had in mind. One car, then another, passed by and behind him yet another stopped to park, about seventy-five yards back. He placed the .38 in the briefcase and stepped out of the car.

He walked up the three steps to the front porch and rang the bell. Through the parted curtain, an eye peered out at him a second before the door slowly opened.

Ray Faucetti was probably sixty-five years old, but he looked more like eighty-five. A lifetime bachelor, he was thin and gaunt, his face a series of deep and deeper fissures, his hair balding, his body half bent from arthritis.

He smiled at Vinnie and opened the door wider. "Come in, Vin. Come in. I'm so pleased to hear your good news. Come, sit down."

They walked into the living room where three angora cats sat on various pieces of furniture around the room. Jesus, does this place stink, Vinnie thought.

"A drink, Vinnie? To celebrate our new found fortune?"

"I don't have the time, Ray. Can you dig out my IOU's? I'm due back in Boston in a hour."

"Sure, Vin. That briefcase contain my money?" he asked as he turned toward the rolltop desk and an adjoining file cabinet.

"You got it right."

Faucetti pulled open the four draw file and searched the manila folders for a moment. "Here we are, Vin," he said, turning toward him.

Vin snapped the locks on the briefcase and withdrew the .38.

Faucetti blanched. "Hey Vin. Whoa. What's this all about?"

Without responding, Vinnie shot him twice through the heart. Faucetti fell backward, his head striking the side of the desk as he slumped.

Vinnie picked up the file folder and studied its contents for a moment. It contained a complete listing of their transactions over the years along with the IOU's. He now needed to search the desk and the file cabinet to be sure there were no other references to him.

They decided to take him on the front porch, just as he exited the house. From the shadows Folan signaled to Quinn on the other side of the door. They waited in silence, staring beyond the broad expanse of well-tended green grass, toward the line of trees across the street.

After what seemed an interminable wait, they heard the rustling sound of movement closing toward the front door. Folan raised his .38 high above his head, while opposite him, Quinn stayed low in the shadows, now down on bended knee.

Vinnie Sullivan opened the door and turned almost immediately to ensure that he had locked it. In that instant he heard Folan's command. "Freeze! Right there, Vinnie. Turn around slowly with your hands over your head. Do it! NOW!"

"Who the fuck are you?" Vinnie demanded, following the commands.

"Now very slowly, Vinnie," came a second voice to his left. "Lean into the wall and spread your feet. We wouldn't give a shit if we had to drop you right here and now. Put down the briefcase."

Folan patted him down meticulously, lifting the .38 from the shoulder holster. He smelled the barrel and ingested the clear signs of recent firing.

"Been hunting recently, Vinnie? This thing's still hot," Folan commented sarcastically. "Put the cuffs on him, Billy."

"Let's go inside, Vinnie. You can introduce us to your bookie friend," Quinn said.

As he snapped on the hall light, Vinnie recognized them for the first time. "Fuck you, both. So you guys are fuckin' cops. IRA, my ass."

"Federal Bureau of Investigation, Vinnie, Boston," Folan responded.

"Let's see some I.D."

"Sure. Let's go inside. You can I.D. us, and we'll I.D. the guy you just iced," Quinn said.

"You guys can kiss my Irish ass. You have no jurisdiction here. No reason to enter these premises."

Folan laughed. "Vinnie, cut the bullshit and save us all time, Okay? We've been following you for weeks, so we know who the guy inside is -- or was. Which is it, Vinnie? Let's go see."

In the living room Faucetti's body lay stretched out on the floor, his eyes wide open, as if he were totally surprised that such an ending could come his way. The three cats strolled around his body, occasionally brushing against him, probably in hope that, like Lazarus, he would rise again.

"Well, what do you know?" Quinn said. "You were right, Matt. He saw you through the porch window, Vinnie. Two fuckin' eye witnesses to murder! You're going down, Sullivan."

"Let's go, Vinnie," Folan ordered. "The stolen car stays here. That old couple will be happy to learn the police operate

320

so efficiently that they have their car back the same night. Get in the back seat with him, Billy."

They drove out to Route 9 and headed east toward Boston. "You hungry, Vinnie?" Folan suddenly inquired. "It's eight o'clock, and I could use some food. My treat, and we could talk a bit."

"Why not?" Vinnie replied.

Folan entered the left lane and, at the light, reversed direction, heading west for half a mile before turning in at Duca's Restaurant. He parked and killed the lights. "Uncuff him, Billy. Let me explain something, Vin. In case you missed it back there." He turned in his seat, facing Vinnie and Quinn.

"We can enjoy a leisurely dinner, have a drink or two, talk for a while. In fact, you might find what I have to say interesting. On the other hand, you could have some crazy idea about bolting. In that case Billy here or I would have to shoot you in the back without flinching. You follow?"

"I hear you, cop."

A maitre d' with a pencil thin mustache greeted them in the ornate lobby. Statues reminding customers of Rome, Florence, and Venice adorned the lobby, and on the walls reproductions of Italian masters added to the ambiance. To their left was a large circular bar, and to the right the main dining room.

"We'll need a table for three in a quiet area if that's at all possible," Folan said, flashing his identification.

"We can arrange that," the maitre d' responded, leading them toward a small elevated area with just three tables in the rear of the room.

As soon as the waitress served their drinks, Folan set the stage. "Vinnie, you're going down for life on this one. Cut and dried. Two FBI agents willing to testify they saw you murder Mr. Faucetti. A file folder indicating the reasons for the killing. The murder weapon in your possession most certainly containing your prints. Now you or Kelly can find the best criminal lawyer in Boston, Vinnie, but you're going to spend your fuckin' remaining years in Walpole."

Vinnie downed his scotch and soda in one gulp and flashed his eyes at Folan. "What is this? Fuckin' happy hour? I don't need the aggravation, Folan."

Folan paused. "There's another option, Vinnie."

"And what would that be, cop?"

"We want your bosses, Vinnie. The Kellys, Jack and Tom."

"And you expect my help?"

Undaunted, Folan plowed ahead. "Yeah, we do, Vinnie. You think about it, and think carefully. And listen some more. You want another drink?"

Vinnie nodded. "I don't know anything about the activities of the fuckin' Kellys."

"We think you do, Vinnie. We know you're a part of the family. But if you don't, c'est la vie. We deposit your ass in Boston tonight on the murder one. But if you can help us, then you can walk. No charges, Faucetti was done in by some unknown assailant. You walk, Vinnie. Free and clear." He stirred his drink, pausing to let Vinnie absorb the offer.

"I walk on a murder one charge? Just what kind of help are you talking about?"

The waitress appeared with orders of scrod and pasta for the agents and a huge slab of roast beef for Vinnie. They paused for the moment.

"For now, Billy here and I keep this evidence between us and our supervisors. We see just how cooperative you can be, Vinnie. Sort of a test case. If the information forthcoming from you is valuable to us, we see that as a sign of good faith. Our supervisors will know you're helping us. If that level of cooperation brings us the Kellys, then we recommend you walk, right into a witness protection program eventually."

Vinnie speared a big piece of the roast beef on his fork and swallowed it practically whole. He glanced around the restaurant, considering his situation. "Tell me what I would have to do."

"There are three acts to the play, Vinnie. One, you tell us all you can about the Kellys. Two, we will ask you to wear a wire..."

"Hold it," Vinnie interrupted. "I ain't wearing any wire around Jack and Tommy. If they ever found me wired, I'm dead. Right there on the fuckin' spot."

"Suit yourself, Vinnie," Quinn interjected. "No wire, no deal. We want them on tape talking about their business. You're in the inner circle, big shot. Remember, we're talking about you ducking a fuckin' murder one rap. Hey, you take risks crossing the fuckin' street, right?"

"What's the third piece?" Vinnie asked.

"In the end, Vin, when we're ready to roll, we'll ask you to appear as a witness for the government. That's when you speak publicly of your knowledge of the activities of the brothers. From there, we enter you into the witness protection program..."

A frightened look spread across Vin's face. "You realize what you're asking me? To be a fuckin' informer?"

Folan took a deep drag from his cigarette and stared straight ahead. "No, Vinnie. We're giving you a chance at a whole new life, and for your dodging a murder one rap, we expect your cooperation. All of this is contingent on your full cooperation. Take your time before answering us. We still have coffee coming. Yes or no. Sit and think for a change."

Vinnie asked for another scotch and soda, not coffee, and Folan acceded. Vinnie played with the stirrer, grateful for the silence which allowed him to concentrate. He thought of Jack Kelly and their first meeting at Wonderland, of Jimma Flaherty his mentor, of his wife and family and their bleak future. He felt trapped, and he was trapped. He found his mind racing toward rationalization. Flaherty had been like a father to him, and Jack was responsible for his death. That was almost twenty years ago, and he had never really forgotten Jimma. What did he owe Jack anyway? He couldn't do a life sentence, and they had him dead to right.

Folan set aside the pie dish and lit another cigarette. "Well, Vinnie? What's it to be?"

Vinnie nodded affirmatively. "I'm in."

Folan tensed and leaned forward in his chair. "That's good to hear, Vinnie. It's the right decision."

"What now?"

"We'll drive you home tonight, Vinnie. You sleep in your own bed. And realize what a treat that is. Sunday morning at 10 meet us at this address -- 60 Orange Street, Chelsea, Apartment 4A. Memorize it. It's a residence. We'll begin to talk then."

Vinnie started to rise.

"Hold it," Folan commanded. "Just for tonight, Vinnie, to show us a little good faith, how about a sign from you? Tell us something to perk our interest, something to demonstrate your sincerity, something to cement our new found budding friendship."

Vinnie thought for a moment as he looked out toward the Route 9 traffic. "You remember the Mystic River Bridge robbery two or three years ago?"

"Yeah?" Quinn nodded.

"The $100,000 heist, if I remember," Folan said. "So? That's not Kelly's m.o."

"His son Timmy and his nephew Marty pulled it off."

"No shit," Falon said. "Jack approve that?"

"He knew nothing about it. Cowboy action by the two John Waynes. They've straightened out the last two years. They're comers. Taking to the life like fish to water."

"Let's go," Folan stood. "I think we're off to a good start."

<u>50</u>

Salvy Cardoza loved the walk from his apartment near the Government Center to Prince Street in the North End. On this Saturday morning, as always, he was dressed impeccably, his soft hat pushed forward over his brow, his cashmere wool blend topcoat wrapped snugly around him to ward off the cold spring air. Occasionally, he raised a gloved hand to return a greeting.

He paused near the pushcarts just outside the Callahan Tunnel, inhaling the pungent smells of fruits and vegetables, of meat and cheese. He loved to watch the crowds of suburbanites strolling the area, looking for bargains, arguing with the pushcart vendors up and down the area leading to Haymarket Square. For decades, he had observed this scene yet never grew tired of the old traditions, the smells and feel of his old neighborhood. As he crossed to Prince Street, he stopped to observe the pulse of the street before him.

Women, young and old, held the hands of their children or grandchildren, while examining produce outside the various markets or prices pasted on their windows. Occasionally hawkish vendors took to the sidewalks to promote their wares, acting as if they were ready to lasso the potential buyers right off the street. Outside a number of the small restaurants, old men congregated, discussing politics or the Celtics or the embryonic Red Sox season, and further along the young men sat on tenement stoops, trying hard to look important, rushing the spring season in their light sports coats and spring jackets.

He stopped at the Prince Street Social Club with its "members only" sign stenciled on the glass in the front door. He entered and nodded to a young man polishing the brass rail of the small, immaculate bar to his left. On his right about ten small circular tables were scattered over the black and white tiled floor. In the rear of the club three pool tables stood unattended, in the early morning hours.

He walked toward the rear, toward the elderly man who sat sipping his black coffee in the lone booth adjacent to the pool tables.

"Gennaro, my friend," Cardoza greeted him, a warm grin creasing his lips.

With the help of a cane, the most dominant crime figure in New England stood slowly. The full head of white hair was his most prominent feature, its color lustrous in contrast to most men's dullish gray heads in their early seventies. In his youth, Cardoza thought, Gennaro had been a young man with a big, strong body and a wonderful face -- a real man's face with clean lines. Even today, with the prominent cheekbones and heavy brows under a high forehead, he was handsome. That once strong body was now tired and slightly bent from the arthritis that plagued him.

"Salvy, it's so good to see you, as always," Gennaro Biggio spoke sincerely. "Please sit."

"How's everything in Providence?" Salvy inquired, signaling to the young man.

"Mixed. Business continues mixed all over New England. The new sex disease scare continues to hurt both the prostitution and drug businesses, particularly among the middle class. Profits are going to fall during the time ahead as the young people move away from the fucking we saw in the '70's. But, still, there're many fools out there still purchasing drugs, and gambling their week's pay away.

"You know, Salvatore, we've made the right decision some years back. Diversification is so very important. We have to offer many lines of service to many different groups to hold and enhance our position. There will always be times when one business goes well and another does not." He paused for a moment before changing course. "You agree I was correct years ago?" Biggio always loved to remind him of his foresight in

326

anticipating the huge profits from drugs, despite the admonitions of the leaders at Apalachin.

Cardoza smiled. "You were right, Gennaro."

The young man placed a coffee cup in front of Salvy and filled it slowly. He then refilled Don Biggio's cup, never once speaking. After leaving the pot on the table, he retreated to the bar and continued to polish the brass.

"How is your wife?" Cardoza inquired.

"Fine. Unfortunately for my wallet, she loves Boston. She's off now shopping at Nieman Marcus in all probability. And why did you want to meet, Salvatore? It costs me money every time I come here."

"Two matters of business, my oldest friend," Cardoza responded deferentially.

"Please, go ahead."

"On the first matter, I seek your permission to eliminate the Pizzotti brothers over in Medford. They've been skimming on us. Caught red-handed."

Biggio lit his cigarette slowly, understanding immediately why Cardoza sought his guidance on a local matter. "Carmen and Salvatore Pizzotti," he finally said. "How much we talking about?"

"I estimate $25,000 a month for the last year."

His wife's second cousins, caught stealing from the very people who had employed them. Two years ago he had prevailed on Salvatore to take these two young men, both small-time petty thieves, into his organization, to provide them with a piece of the numbers rackets north of Boston.

Now they had embarrassed him. Wife or no wife, they had to now pay the consequences.

"You have my permission to proceed," Don Biggio stated firmly. "And Salvatore, my friend, be sure they suffer. I want them to suffer."

"Yes, Gennaro. I'll see to it."

"And the other matter?"

"The Kellys, Gennaro."

"The Irishers? Haven't they accepted our new arrangements?" Biggio asked, pouring his third cup of black coffee and offering the pot to Salvy.

"No more, thank you. Oh, they've accepted it, and they've seemingly working with Nick to implement the new splits."

"Seemingly?" Biggio raised a brow.

"On the surface, yes. You know of my high regard for Jack Kelly. For two decades now he has served our interests while running his territories, his own business very well."

"Then what's the problem?"

"The problem is that he is smart. He will anticipate that 12-1/2 percent will soon become half of that again. In my estimation he knows our intention. We'll have trouble with him--and soon. We should eliminate him now."

Biggio shook his head vigorously. "Salvatore, I thought we have already discussed this strategy. We need time for Rizzo to solidify the first transfers. How's my nephew doing by the way?"

Cardoza bit his lip. "All right so far," he answered. "He's no ball of fire, Gennaro."

"All the more reason we go slowly, Salvatore. It's my wish that, through Nick, we control the entire operation within the year we have agreed upon. I see no reason to change the schedule."

"Gennaro, I respect Kelly, and I know his character. He will not sit still. We are heading for open warfare with him and his people. We should strike first."

"I don't believe it, Salvatore, with all due respect. We will eliminate Mr. Kelly soon, but it is to our advantage to assure a smooth transition to Nick. We need Kelly for now. Is there anything else today? If not, I must join my wife before all of last week's profits are in the hands of the fashion merchants."

He stood, his white mane glistening under the lights, his tobacco stained teeth flashing as he extended his hand to his lifelong friend.

"You want a ride?" Cardoza asked.

"No, No. My driver should be outside," Biggio answered.

They walked together toward the sunlight, exiting into the old world neighborhood. Biggio beamed as he observed the crowds gaily strolling the sidewalks. "That old fool and his busing policies haven't destroyed this neighborhood, hey, Salvatore? Bon Giorno."

51

On Easter Sunday, 1982, Jack stared into the hall mirror, putting the final touches to his wardrobe. He knotted the light blue tie and placed a light blue handkerchief into the pocket of his traditional cashmere sport jacket. He stepped back assuring that the dark brown pants complemented the balance of his dress. He carried his coffee to the living room window and looked out on the cloudless spring day. Across the street he watched the strollers basking in the warm sun, celebrating the rebirth of a new season of hope. He decided to join them, to walk toward Fisherman's Beach to Marjorie's home on Puritan Road.

Below the walkway, on the beach itself at low tide, little children ran away from their parents and dogs of all sizes scampered to catch frisbees in mid-air or raced to capture sea birds before they took flight from the water's edge.

He sensed he appreciated the holidays far more than most people, and not one ever went by without his thinking of past Thanksgivings, Christmases, and Easters when he would take Tommy and Jerry to Carroll's Diner on Union Street for dinner with money taken from his father's wallet. They had sat with lonely single people and derelicts, but at least they had a holiday dinner. Since that time he had vowed to spend each holiday with family, and despite his separation from Marjorie, they had always come together for these very special days.

He quickened his step in anticipation of seeing Bobby once again. In a brief four years, he had firmly established himself. He now moved between Hollywood and New York. A featured role in a soap opera called "The Golden Dawn" had led, just last year, to both a small part in a major film and a recent opportunity in a new off-Broadway play. Jack beamed with pride at the accomplishments of his oldest son, only twenty-five.

And Timmy would be there. So different from his older brother. Hard, where Bobby was soft. Disinterested in anything pertaining to education, where Bobby loved to discuss the arts, politics, current events. Yet, Timmy was gaining an inner strength as he matured. Now mentally tough, Timmy seemed to be absorbing his uncle's teaching.

Jack credited Marjorie with assuring the brothers remained close. If she favored Bobby, she was also careful to show her love for Timmy. He knew she depended on him to protect Timmy, and perhaps the knowledge that he was vulnerable allowed her to demonstrate her love to Timmy so openly. Concern for their boys actually had brought Marjorie and him together in a common mission that had made two friends of former lovers.

As he approached the large brick edifice, he heard the shouting and laughter in the back yard. He rounded the side of the house to the long stretch of green grass behind. Tommy and Jerry were deriding their opponents even before the game had begun. They spotted Jack and virtually in unison yelled, "Hey, here's our third man now."

At the other end of the yard, Marty, Timmy, and Bobby slapped each other on the back, pointing toward the older team, threatening bodily harm to their seniors. To their right, assorted jackets and ties lay on the barbecue table. Marjorie waved to Jack from the kitchen window as he joined Tommy and Jerry.

For thirty minutes the two teams scrambled through the game of tag football. Laundry Hill, deja vu, Jack thought. He quarterbacked, while Tommy blocked and Jerry ran the pass routes. They occasionally alternated to fool their opponents, but their roles had not changed so much, he thought, in over thirty-five years. With Marty at quarterback, Timmy leading his way, and Bobby occasionally cutting free for a pass, Jack thought for the first time, of the close parallels between the members of the two teams.

"Next touchdown wins!" Jack announced as they reclaimed possession.

"That's right. Make up the rules as you go along, Uncle Jack," Marty retorted.

On first down, Jack spotted Tommy in the center of the field after he had faked a block. Jack scrambled and threw on the run only to see, at the last minute, Timmy step in and intercept the pass. He stumbled over Tommy and was immediately tagged, but now the tide had changed.

Marty spent an extra few seconds in the huddle, diagramming the play. Bobby snapped him the ball and raced straight downfield, taking Jerry with him. On target, Marty threw a short pass to Timmy only three or four yards beyond the line of scrimmage. Both Jack and Tommy converged on the receiver, but just before being tagged, Timmy lateraled to Marty, who had raced to the outside of Tommy after he had thrown the ball. The two defenders were totally committed toward Timmy with no chance to adjust. Game over.

Whoops of glee and hollers of triumph filled the air. Jack had not seen that particular play in a tag football game in recent years. Not since he had tried it unsuccessfully one day on Laundry Hill.

Bobby Latimer climbed the steps of the Twelfth Street Baptist Church to pay his last respects. He had dressed conservatively, both to demonstrate his regard for Lonnie Woods and as a sign of his new status. The old fool had finally died, Bobby thought, after stuffing his face and clogging his arteries for years. A do-nothing from the old school who had kissed the white man's ass for crumbs.

In recent years all Woods had going for him was his age, Bobby thought. The Black tradition of venerating the elderly had sustained him, but his weakness as an organizational leader had led to splinter groups all over Roxbury and Dorchester both before and after his recent retirement. Maybe I should be grateful, he thought. Bobby had successfully built a base of support from Mission Hill and Mission Main toward

Washington Street and from Cass Boulevard to the Southeast Expressway. Woods, Johnson, Hollins, some of the other Black leaders had occasionally slapped his wrists, and called him to task for intrusions into other people's territories, but he had been careful. He had never interfered with Woods' or Virgil Johnson's or Henry Hollins' personal interests, being content to position himself as the man among the various splinters.

Now was the time to act, he thought, as the choir burst into a spirited rendition of "Rock of Ages." He glanced across at Virgil Johnson, who nodded to him. Dorchester was next, he thought. Virgil was a fat cat ready to be had, and Hollins was even softer. Johnson would already assume that Lonnie Woods' son, Kenny, would continue in his father's place and, therefore, as usual would be asleep at the switch. Assholes, Bobby thought. They would be dead within the month.

At the conclusion of the service, Bobby stood at the bottom of the steps to offer his condolences to Mrs. Woods. The dignified woman followed immediately behind the coffin, weeping uncontrollably. Beside her Kenny Woods assisted his mother. Tall and angular, he would fit quite easily into a coffin like the one just a few feet in front of him, Bobby thought.

He stepped forward to embrace Rhonda Woods. "I'm so sorry, Rhonda."

"Oh, Bobby, what am I going to do?" she wailed.

He extended his hand to Kenny. "I'm sorry, brother. He was like a father to me." He backed away to allow others to approach the family. At his sleeve his lieutenant, Roland King, whispered in his ear, "You the man, Bobby. You the man."

The sight of the apartment house in Chelsea depressed Vinnie Sullivan. A dilapidated three story building with asphalt-shingle siding, it was located on Orange Street, just off Route 16. There were two front doors, and next to the mail box a small wooden sign announced that a number of apartments were for rent. He rang the bell for Apartment 4A and waited for the signal that would gain him entry. Maybe the fuckin' IRA could place a bomb over here instead of at Harrod's and strike a blow for urban renewal, he thought.

At the buzz he entered the musty corridor, walked down the center to the last room on the right, and knocked on the door. The smell of urine hung heavy in the area, and he almost gagged as Quinn opened the door.

"Jesus Christ," he said to Quinn, "how can you guys live like this?"

"Taxpayer money, Vinnie. We have to be sensitive to the citizens you guys are ripping off."

"Fuck you, Quinn," Vinnie responded, entering an apartment completely devoid of furniture except for a small conference table in the middle of the room.

"And a cheerful good morning to you, too, Vinnie," Matt Folan smiled from his position at the table. Before him lay a telephone, a tape recorder, and the remnants of their latest venture to Kentucky Fried Chicken. Matt flicked the ashes from his cigarette into the empty coffee cup at his elbow. "Have a seat, Vin. Want some coffee?"

"Let's just get to it, huh, Folan?" Vinnie responded.

Folan shrugged his shoulders. "I'm fine with that, Vinnie. Let me be sure the recorder is working. Testing 1, 2, 3; Testing 1, 2, 3." He played it back, satisfied with its quality and the volume.

He spoke into the small microphone. "The date is June 1, 1982. The time is 10:00 A.M. Present are FBI agents Matthew A. Folan and William F. Quinn. Following is our first interview with Vincent Joseph Sullivan of Boston, Massachusetts, who is also present.

"Your name for the record, please."

"Vincent Sullivan."

"Your address."

"290 Monument Avenue, Charlestown."

"Occupation?"

"Supervisor, Boston waterfront, Longshoreman's Union."

"Mr. Sullivan, to begin I want to go over some of the material we've discussed, this time for the record. For a period of thirty-five years you have been an active member of the Jimma Flaherty - Jack Kelly crime family. Is that true?"

"Yes," Vinnie replied, fidgeting with the makeshift ashtray before him.

"You were recruited to the family by Jimma Flaherty in 1947?"

"Yes."

"In 1962, with the demise of Jimma Flaherty, Jack Kelly of Lynn assumed his leadership position?"

"Yes."

"Mr. Sullivan, did Jack Kelly murder Jimma Flaherty?"

"He said he did."

"Were you with him on that occasion?"

"No."

"What caused Kelly to move against Flaherty?"

"Something about a fight fix gone wrong back then. I can't remember the details. It was fuckin' twenty years ago. But the tension between them was getting worse anyway. Jimma was jealous of Jack, and Jack felt Flaherty didn't protect his brother from the fight mob."

"Mr. Sullivan, you've told us that on July 1, 1955 Mr. Kelly murdered John Latimer, also known as the Chocolate Drop, on orders of Jimma Flaherty. Am I correct?"

"Yes."

"And were you present on that occasion?"

"No."

"Mr. Sullivan, were you ever physically present on any occasion when Jack Kelly committed felony murder?"

"Yes. On August 29, 1956, Jack Kelly and I waited in a stolen car on Huntington Avenue to assassinate Frankie O'Neill of New York City."

"Would you describe the incident, please?"

"We parked on the corner of Huntington Avenue and Mission Street and waited for our target. As he walked from the top of Mission Street, Jack Kelly stepped from the car and executed Frankie O'Neill."

"Have you ever been present when Jack Kelly has committed any other crime?"

"Yes. Any number of times since 1953."

"And the nature of these crimes?"

"I've been in his presence when we extorted money from businesses, unions, bookies, restaurant operators, drug dealers over the years. In the early days, I ran numbers with him."

"Are you willing to testify to these incidents?"

"Yes, I'm willing to provide descriptions of the incidents to the best of my recollection. The dates may be a problem."

"Mr. Sullivan, let's turn your attention for the moment to Mr. Kelly's younger brother, Tommy," Folan said. "For the record, would you describe to us your knowledge of his involvements with his brother in the crime family?"

"Tommy ended his boxing career sometime in the early sixties due to a serious injury to his eye. He was told by doctors that he couldn't fight again. Shortly thereafter, Tommy joined our family, and became an enforcer, like me, for the family."

"Did you ever see Thomas Kelly commit felony murder?"

"No."

"Have you any knowledge of his having done so?"

"Once or twice I heard others comment about Tommy icing some target, but I have no direct knowledge."

"For the record, are you willing to describe time and place situations involving Thomas Kelly and his violation of federal racketeering statutes in a court of law?"

"Yes."

"Mr. Sullivan, you've indicated to us that you are a member of the inner circle of the Kelly crime family. Where do the meetings of the group occur?"

Vinnie laughed into the microphone. "Here, there, and everywhere."

"Let's be more specific," Folan said.

"Jack is too smart to sit still in any one place. He rotates the meetings. He worries about surveillance, wiretaps, bugs and constantly has Ray Horan screen for any potential listening devices. He thinks the Italians are stupid, always meeting on

Prince Street in the North End. He believes that eventually they'll pay for their arrogance."

"Give me the most frequent places for your meetings."

"Over the years? An old warehouse in Charlestown on Medford Street. The Fantasia Restaurant near Fresh Pond Circle in Cambridge. Dini's Restaurant on Tremont Street in Boston. His home on Lynn Shore Drive. The Tides Restaurant in Nahant. The Powerhouse in Southie."

"How is business conducted?"

"What do ya mean?" Vinnie asked, bewildered.

"How does Jack Kelly pass on orders to you and to the other members of his inner family?"

Vinnie laughed. "You guys have never had any luck catching him because he's a thinker, the son of a bitch. No use of phones at all. None. Nada. He forbids any phone calls except social calls."

"How, then, do you receive your marching orders?"

"At the meets in those rotating settings in part, but largely through one-on-one personal communication. For example, he'll ask Tommy and me to meet him for a pizza at Monte's in East Lynn or he'll ask Ray to take a walk around Red Rock on Lynn Shore Drive, or he'll walk with Chris Kiley near Carson Beach in Southie."

"Anything put in writing?"

"Nothing. Happy birthday cards is all," Vinnie laughed.

Folan turned off the recorder. "End of session for today, Vinnie. Thanks."

"How many more of these fuckin' questions will there be? We're just going over the same stuff."

"On Wednesday I want you to meet with Quinn here and detail the incidents regarding Jack and Tommy where you were personally present. So go home and start thinking about major crime violations, the victims, the time, the place, and be ready to respond."

"You're not answering my question, Folan."

The FBI agent pushed away from the table. "Probably two or three more after that, Vin. Next, I want to concentrate on the

338

business side. What happens to monies collected from the 'business lines' as Kelly calls them? Who does the laundering of the cash? How do you guys get paid? Who does the accounting? Questions along that line. Be thinking about it, huh?" Folan stood, flexing his muscles.

"I'll tell you what I'm thinking about, Folan. This is taking too fuckin' long. I've worn a wire in Jack's presence twice now, and he can probably smell the fear in my fuckin' body."

"Vinnie, Vinnie," Folan said slowly, "relax, please, relax. We need just a few instances of his discussion of racketeering initiatives. You said it yourself, he's clever. We need your personal testimony in court, and we need examples of plans to violate the law, particularly a direct charge to one of you to take out a target or take some other action."

"You know, Folan, this guy's smarter than all of you. You think he knocks off a guy a day, like you take pills once a day? Even when he gives an order like that, it's not done in front of six or seven of us. It ain't going to happen, and I'm wearing a fuckin' coffin maker taped to my chest."

"Vinnie, listen to me. Just a while longer is all I'm asking. We'll pull you out very soon now."

"You have enough with my testimony, Folan. The fuckin' tapes aren't even admissible, are they?"

"Let me worry about that, huh, Vin? The more information we have the better our case. We'll go for the arrest very soon now, Vinnie."

"Hey, Vinnie, the man said, relax," Quinn grinned. "Remember what the poet said, 'Cowards die many deaths; the valiant only die once.'"

"Fuck you, Quinn."

"And you have a nice day,too," Quinn said, as Vinnie headed for the door.

<u>52</u>

The afternoon sun streamed in over their shoulders as they walked toward the Tavern on the Green. They planned to enter Central Park near the restaurant so very popular with out-of-towners. Holding Courtney's hand, Jack was eager to leave the noise and frenzy of Central Park West behind and to enter into the quiet world of the Park itself.

As they turned into the parking lot of Tavern on the Green, they dodged the automobiles and hansom cabs discharging tourists for lunch. From there they crossed into the Park itself, turning north toward the softball diamonds. Ever since his first visit twenty-six years ago, he always returned to the Park whenever he visited New York. It was a place for reflection, a much simpler world within a world where problems always seemed more soluble and life much less complex.

Lining the benches along the walkway were the faces of the life cycle itself. Old men lost in their newspapers, nannies pausing with their strollers and their little charges to catch the sun's rays, young business types absorbed in their own importance, the down-and-out looking simply to be left to their misery, little children licking popsicles holding fiercely to their mothers' hands. Bikers and roller-bladers flew down the roadway, taking care to steer clear of pedestrians or slow-footed joggers. Unlike their colleagues on the city's streets, vendors, too, respected the peace of Central Park, never raising their voices in search of a sale.

"I'm glad you could take the time, Courtney," he said, guiding her through the green grass to a pathway leading down to the softball fields.

"The fact that you convinced Jerry and Sheila to come made it very easy for me. What time do we meet them?"

"Cocktails at the St. Moritz at 6:00, a little something to eat, and then we see the play at 8:00 over on 45th Street."

"Perfect way to end the summer," she said. "One of my favorite cities, a beautiful day, and enjoying them both with my favorite man."

He slipped his arm around her waist. "There's a price for all this, you know," he said.

"Yeah, I can guess."

"Remember the signs during the gas crisis back in '73? I remember one of them read 'Gas: credit cards, cash, or ass!' That applies as well in the summer of '82, you know."

"I'm surprised you even give me an option. Somehow I thought you were only interested in the latter."

"I love you," he said, brushing her face with his lips. "You always going to be my girl?"

"For always and in all ways," she replied, squeezing his arm almost too mechanically, despite the words.

"Let's sit for a minute," he said, leading her to a long wooden bench just above the array of softball fields, the azure blue sky above them, tall trees blotting out the larger tall buildings on all sides of them.

"You all right, Courtney?" he asked as soon as they sat down.

"The running back and forth to San Francisco has me a bit down," she responded, averting his stare. "The doctor has Mother taking antidepressant pills, but she doesn't seem to be responding well. But she'll be all right. It's just taking a little time, that's all." She smiled at him as he moved to kiss her cheek.

"If you need anything..."

She pressed her hand into his. "I'm fine. Come on, let's go see him."

As they descended the hill, they spotted Bobby taking grounders at second base and waved to him. He wore blue shorts and a white T-shirt, the words "Hurley's" emblazoned on the front. On the other side of the backstop members of "O'Neal's" team surveyed Bobby's group. Many of the players obviously had something to do with the theater, the names of various restaurant sponsors displayed on their chests. So many aspiring actors and actresses survived with that steady check earned as waiters and waitresses.

How do two brothers from the same womb become so different, he thought? He knew that was a question that parents all over the world asked. This friendly young man before him, focused on his goals, uninhibited, joyful, at ease with himself and all others. His brother only one year younger and so different. He caught himself. There had been highly positive changes in Timmy in recent years, changes he attributed largely to Tommy's taking a hand.

Now twenty-four, Timmy was far different from the callow youth of eighteen who fought first and asked questions later. At strategy sessions he now offered thoughtful opinions, and chose correctly more often than not when offered alternatives. He now understood when to take risks and when not, to hide his true feelings and think before he spoke. The foolish arrogance of youth had been replaced by a reflective contemplation and a concern for the group and for its individual members.

Timmy is me, he mused, at a similar age. I'm as proud of him as I am of Bobby, he thought. And, through his work with the Corsicans, Tommy had become more focused and more relaxed. Theirs was a bond of love as strong as his love for all of them and for Courtney.

From their seats in the lounge at the St. Moritz they could look across Central Park South to the hansom cabbies. On this late summer night one agitated cabbie dickered with a group of tourists, fighting off their attempt to sit an even dozen in the horse-drawn cab for the price of one.

"While you two were strutting around the Park, I made a call to the Raytheon people," Jerry announced, sipping his scotch and soda.

"And?" Courtney asked.

"And you and I have a date to see them tomorrow afternoon."

"Hey, I thought this was a pleasure trip," Jack laughed.

"Just a little sidebar call back home."

"My brother, the multimillionaire," Jack said, lifting his VO and ginger in salute.

He raised his glass toward Sheila, who was always quiet in his presence. He sensed her fear, not of him, but of the life he led. He saw her regularly, but ever since that night in February, 1962, she had never been the same with him. The shock of the attack on Jerry coupled with her inability in later years to cope with Marty had scarred her. Yet she remained very close to Marjorie, and the friendship of the cousins made her a constant presence at family gatherings. On those occasions she was always friendly toward him but never very relaxed.

Jack sensed her conflict, both wanting to talk and not wanting to talk about the life. She knew her son as a car salesman, and yet wore on her face a mask of worry about his hidden life. Frequently she seemed on the verge of asking him about that life in quiet small gatherings such as tonight's, but instead she would bite her lip and keep the conversation centered on social chatter and innocuous small talk.

Tonight, for some reason, he sensed the question would come just seconds before she spoke. "Jack, how is our son?"

"Sheila, this isn't the right time..." Jerry began.

"There's never a right time, Jerry. I see my son the car salesman regularly, Jack. I just need to know something about his other life. I guess I need to know that he's all right." She began to sob quietly, tears welling from her soft brown eyes.

Courtney opened her pocketbook and handed her some tissue.

"Thank you, dear," Sheila smiled as Courtney placed her hand on top of Sheila's.

"Sheila..." Jerry began again.

"No, Jerry, it's all right. We can talk about it," Jack said kindly.

"You know, Jack," Sheila said, composing herself, "I think you believe I hate you."

"Sheila!" Jerry bellowed.

"Well, nothing could be further from the truth. I'm eternally grateful that you've cared for him. He idolizes you, as he does his own father. When he visits, he can't talk enough about your business acumen, about sales at the agency, about the methods you use to beat the competition."

"He's a natural salesman himself, Sheila," Jack said.

"I just see what you've done to shape an extremely hostile young man into a charming, caring individual. He reads now, Jack, constantly and he's interested in things. So you see, Jack, I don't hate you. My concern is with what I don't know. I need to hear something about this other life he leads."

Jerry started once again to interrupt, but Jack's body language stopped him as he opened his mouth.

"I have a mother's concern, Jack. I just need to know. Is he in danger? What kinds of activities is he involved in?" She started to sob again.

"Sheila," Jack began calmly, "let me tell you about Marty." He could not tell her there was no more natural leader or more ruthless avenger than her son.

"Isn't that funny, Jack? You have to tell me about my own son. You know Jerry and I did everything we could to keep him out of trouble from grade school to high school to college. We didn't succeed, Jack, but God knows we tried everything."

"Jesus, Sheila, it's not doing us any good to go over old ground," Jerry said calmly.

"Forgive me. I'm not saying this right," she said, working hard to compose herself. "I'm trying to express my gratitude, Jack. If you and Tommy weren't there for us, we would have lost him for sure. Perhaps to prison. Perhaps to something far worse. I'm not angry, Jack. I'm just very afraid of what I don't know."

He reached his hand across the table, placing it on top of hers.

"Sheila, Marty's now a member of a small circle of advisors to me, as are Tommy and Timmy. He supervises our numbers operations in Boston and in some of the cities. He takes quite naturally to those responsibilities. He's in little danger principally because he's dealing with gamblers, people who bet, not hardened criminals. Sheila, he's not out robbing banks."

She nodded, partially reassured by his words. She smiled at him.

"Sheila, I watch him, believe me. Tommy is with him constantly -- especially if there's any possible danger. I can't assure you..."

"I know, Jack. I know that. Don't even say the words. Just watch out for my baby, please."

He leaned across the table and brushed his lips against hers. "You know I will, Sheila."

After the performance they waited for Bobby at the stage door. As he walked through, three giddy young girls in their late teens shoved autograph books toward him. "Hey, good looking! Sign for me right here," a thin girl with an empty face nearest to the door yelled.

Obligingly, Bobby signed for them, and just to keep his ego in balance, they turned their attention very rapidly to the stage door as a second young actor ambled through.

"Success is fleeting, huh, Bob?" Jerry teased.

"You sign autographs after speaking only five or six lines?" Jack asked.

"Let's be nice, Dad," Bobby responded.

Looking back at him, the empty-faced girl asked, "Hey, you're the guy on 'The Golden Dawn' on television, right?"

"That's right," Bobby smiled.

"Can you say something about that in my book?" she asked.

"Sure. Let me have it again." He scribbled something quickly and handed it to her.

"Yeah, that's right. You're Dr. Tom Palmer. I watch it every noon," she said.

They walked up to 55th Street to the bustle of the Carnegie Deli. Over pastrami sandwiches and slaw, Jack and Jerry unmercifully ragged on Bobby about his small role in the play and his larger role on the soaps.

"She didn't know you from Adam until you told her you were in the soaps," Jack teased.

"I didn't tell her, Dad. She just knew," Bobby laughed.

"Don't pay any attention to him, Bobby," Sheila said. "I watch the soaps every day, and you're getting to be one of the best recognized young people on television. Your mother and I sit and watch every noontime."

"I can vouch for that," Jerry said.

"Have you seen the show, Courtney?" Bobby asked.

"Every time I'm home, and I tape it when I'm not. Tell me, Dr. Palmer, exactly which one of those three young ladies will you marry?"

"Probably Elizabeth," Jack said.

They all stopped talking for a moment, and all up and down the long family style table they looked at one another, wondering if they had heard what they had heard.

Jack smiled. "Well, I watch it as often as I can."

Bobby slapped his father on the back as the table erupted.

Over coffee, Bobby announced that at the end of the year, he would be leaving the play. With production of "The Golden Dawn" moving to Culver City, he would be relocating to Los Angeles, where he also felt he would have the opportunity to obtain stronger roles in upcoming movies. His agent was confident that he was on the threshold of stardom.

"I know I can get there. Right now, all I need is a break, and I'll have a better chance out there."

"You'll get there, Bob," Jack said.

"Yeah, if you don't marry Elizabeth," Jerry grinned.

53

Bobby Latimer peered into the trunk of the '78 Chevy Impala. "What do you have here, Roland?" he asked his lieutenant.

"We got a 9MM automatic, a MK-ten, a .22, a shotgun. Pick your poison. I like the shotgun," Roland King responded.

"You got it," Bobby answered. "The twenty-two have high velocity rounds?"

"Yes. Low noise factor there too," Roland answered.

"You're gonna fire a fuckin' shotgun and you worried about the noise from a twenty-two?"

"Oh yeah, I forgot."

"Dumb fuck," Bobby said. "Give me the nine millimeter. Where'd you boost the car?"

"Behind the Museum. Suckers line up there rather than pay for parking at Fenway. Easy pickings."

"You changed the plates. Right?"

"Of course!" Roland replied, indignant.

"Let's roll then. You drive."

After passing through Adams Square in Dorchester, they watched for the sign indicating Verdun Street on their right. The rain continued to mist down. "There it is," Bobby spoke softly. "Down there. Easy. Past the house and park on the right."

He searched the darkness around the three-decker cream colored tenement on his left. At midnight the only lights came from the first floor apartment.

"Bradley sure they play here every Friday night?" Bobby asked, as they pulled to a stop and cut the lights.

"Absolutely guaranteed. Virgil Johnson be in there with the young Woods kid, Henry Hollins, too. Their poker's like a ritual. They never miss on Friday night. Old Lonnie used to join them till he ate himself to death," Roland said.

"Anyone else?"

"What you think? I got x-ray eyes?"

"You better shut the fuck up or you'll have no eyes," Bobby said angrily. "Come on. Let's go do it. Pop the trunk."

Roland placed the shotgun down along the side of his leg and jammed the twenty-two into his waistband. Bobby kept the nine millimeter at his side, and together they crossed Verdun Street and ascended the wooden steps to the first floor front door. If Bradley had done his job right, the front door would be slightly ajar.

Bobby pushed lightly at the door with his left hand. In the background he could hear the laughter of a small group coming from the kitchen. Just a few steps and a few seconds. They had the element of surprise with them.

He walked inside the front hallway and turned toward the living room, pausing for a second to be sure that the rhythm of the talk emanating from the kitchen stayed constant. Other than the blaring of the television to his left, he heard no new signals of sudden change.

With Roland following, he quickly advanced toward the kitchen, just beyond the living room. To his left Bradley stood at the sink mixing himself a drink. At the round kitchen table to his right, Virgil Johnson dealt cards to Henry Hollins and Kenny Woods.

Johnson, facing the living room, was the first to see them. He rose from his chair, "What the fuck is..." Before he finished the sentence, Bobby shot him twice in the head, sending Johnson sprawling backward toward the cabinets. Bradley hurried to his left, as far away from the table as he could get.

"Good evening, gentlemen," Roland said, squeezing the shotgun once, its impact opening a gaping hole in Kenny Woods' head. As Henry Hollins scrambled toward the back

350

door, Roland raised the shotgun and shot him in the back, sending Hollins forward into the back door.

"Jesus!" Bradley yelled. "A home run. You got them all. I told you they would all be here," he smiled.

"You did everything right, Bradley," Bobby said, raising the nine millimeter.

"Bobby, what you doin', man? You crazy? I set this up for you," Bradley screamed.

"You know, Bradley. I've been thinking. You just demonstrated your loyalty to old Virgil there. You being his right-hand man and all. I don't think I'll wait the test of time for your next sign of loyalty." He shot Bradley in the stomach, and then twice in the head.

They raced from the apartment, their heads low, aware now of the noise of neighbors awakening and lights beginning to brighten the night. In a minute they were away, their car bathed in darkness, the misty rain now more like a steady drizzle.

Michael Forelli picked up the first edition copy of <u>Catcher in the Rye</u>, crisp and beautiful in its original jacket. He walked along the perimeter of his library, scanning his collection. Here in East Islip he guesstimated his book holdings at $20M conservatively. He found Allan Drury's <u>Advise and Consent</u>, personally autographed by the author himself and placed it on the desk, along with Salinger's classic.

His stable of four bookscouts all pros, scoured New York and the East Coast and even traveled to California whenever they heard of opportunities to purchase rare books, fine modern firsts, or specialty books that interested him. He paid them well to find suckers who thought they knew more than he or they about books. Many antique dealers would place a $50 value on a worthless book of manners from the eighteenth century and let a rare find, a true gem go for $5. When that happened, Michael or his stable members would be there to pay the fiver with a poker face and a gay heart.

The elaborate security systems encircling the estate were there as much to protect his valued collections as to prevent another Apalachia disaster. Throughout the house mounted video cameras allowed him and his staff to observe the comings and goings of all. Within the library itself each book had been electronically tabbed so that an alarm would go off if someone attempted to leave the estate with it.

He sat at the huge oak desk and began flipping the pages of Advise and Consent. How best to respond to Gianelli's request, he thought. He had long ago learned to let sleeping dogs lie. Both through his beloved books and through his ascendancy to power, he recognized such a course was usually best. Why then was Gianelli so insistent on resurrecting the past?

He leaned back and savored his expensive cigar, slowly inhaling as he considered options. And why was Gianelli pushing so hard for a non-Italian? He probably owes Ryan big time for some business deal the Irisher had put him on to.

It would not be difficult to deny Gianelli his request. After all, the Council had decided this particular matter years ago, and Gianelli knew that. He could just refuse the powerful Manhattan boss. Bur if he agreed, he would personally hold Gianelli responsible if something went wrong, thus weakening his position with the other heads.

He stood and walked to the security pad adjacent to the door. He activated the alarm and then snapped off the lights. He now knew how he would respond.

Driven by an unrelenting wind, the warm light rain blew along Second Avenue, unusual weather for the second week of September. Connie Ryan arrived early as he needed a little more time to collect his thoughts before meeting Don Michael Forelli, the Don of Dons and his own boss, Don Mario Gianelli. So he had asked the cab driver to leave him on Second Avenue, near 46th Street.

The Scoop Restaurant was perfect for such an important meeting, he thought as he walked along in the rain. It lay halfway between Second and Third Avenues, on 43rd Street. Quiet, atmospheric, it would not be busy on this Monday evening. The food would be superb, the wine first class, the service impeccable. Based on his conversation earlier with Mario, Connie was optimistic that the meeting would go extremely well. After all, Mario had already spoken to Forelli. Yet Connie wanted everything to be correct in every detail.

He shed his soaked raincoat in the lobby, passing it to the maitre d' and stepped to his right into the bar area. He needed a drink, maybe even a boilermaker before they arrived. Scattered about the bar were four or five reporters from the nearby New York Herald Tribune, half drunk, talking loudly about newsroom policy, visibly concerned with the health of the once great newspaper.

He chased the whisky with the beer in his usual quick fashion, an event that caused the reporters to look up and study him. He felt like asking them what their problem was, but thought better of it. Fucking pansies drinking their wine, like Goddamn women.

Behind him the door opened, and Forelli entered, Mario at his side. Ryan stood to greet them effusively. They looked like polar opposites, Ryan thought. The Don of Dons aristocratic in his bearing, his thin frame and hawkish features in sharp contrast to the diminutive, portly Manhattan boss. Mutt and Jeff.

"Michael, Mario, my good friends. Good evening. Let me take those wet coats for you."

"Connie, it's so good to see you again. It's been some time," Forelli smiled. "What a night, huh? When Sinatra sings of 'Autumn in New York', he is not referring to a night like this."

"Connie, my friend," Gianelli said warmly, extending his hand.

"We have a reserved table in the rear. Please follow me," Ryan said, handing the coats to the maitre d'.

They stepped down two stairs to a large room marked by comfortable booths and wall to wall, blood red carpeting. Near the stairs a young couple stared dreamily into each other's eyes, oblivious to the surroundings, unmindful that the two most influential crime leaders in New York City were among the few other customers at this early hour.

Connie sat on the right edge of the L-shaped booth at the rear of the room, allowing Forelli to take his rightful place in the middle. Immediately, a tuxedoed waiter approached, filling water glasses and taking drink orders.

"Thank you for allowing me this audience, Don Forelli. I express my appreciation for this opportunity, as I know your schedule is full and many matters demand your attention," Connie was particularly careful not to rush his words. He wanted to appear respectful but not obsequious.

Forelli smiled broadly. "We all must find time to eat, Connie. It is I who appreciate your kind invitation and thoughtfulness."

Connie knew, that despite the Don's words, he needed to make his request early. There was no doubt Mario had prevailed on him to attend and that the Don would not feel the particular issue was worth too much of his valuable time.

"Don Forelli, I'm sure that Don Mario had made you aware of my request," Connie began. He paused to see whether Forelli wished to discuss the matter now or later.

"You have a loyal friend in Mario, Connie. He constantly praises your work on behalf of his family. Your contacts with judges, the police, the union leaders, particularly those of Irish heritage, have greatly enhanced our position in Manhattan." He paused and changed course. "I'm interested in your opinion of our family situation at the present time."

Ryan sat back and thought. "We live in difficult times, godfather. Too many people seek only materialistic value. They zap their food, they buy on credit, they bank in the streets. Having abandoned the notion of patience rewarded and pleasure delayed, they live only for the moment. As a society we have turned our backs on the notion that one generation has a responsibility to provide the foundation for the next generation. In this time we run valueless as a society and so the principle of loyalty is easily compromised. Allegiance to one's self transcends everything else," Ryan answered emotionally. "In my mind we offer stability and a set of values that all America needs to adopt."

"What you say is true, my friend," Forelli said. "More than ever, we are needed. More than ever, we must insist on loyalty, on devotion to our set of values. And, unfortunately, more than ever in these difficult times, we must act aggressively against those who would cause us harm."

"A perfect segue into our friend's request," Mario interjected.

They waited for the waiter approaching their table to lay out the antipasto, the thick minestrone soup, and a basket of breadsticks and sesame seed rolls. Connie signaled him for another round of drinks.

"Proceed, Connie," Forelli said.

"Don Michael, twenty years ago my brother Johnny was murdered on these Manhattan streets by Jack Kelly of Boston. All this time I have been asked by the Five Families to turn the other cheek, due principally to our business interests in the Boston area. I hope you see I have been patient. But time goes by. My good mother, God rest her soul, passed away two years ago, still wondering, still inquiring until her death, about her youngest child. 'How did this happen?' she asked repeatedly. 'Who took my baby from me?'

"I'm growing older, godfather. My request is for your intervention in this matter. I ask that Don Biggio in New England and, through him, Don Cardoza in Boston, be prevailed upon to allow me to seek revenge for this loss that I live with each day of my life."

Forelli nodded his head, whether in agreement with the request, or in understanding its thrust, Ryan could not readily determine.

He allowed time to pass before responding, assuring their attention. "I will grant your request, my friend. At our next Council meeting Mario and I will recommend its acceptance. The vote will be perfunctory."

"Thank you, Michael," Gianelli beamed.

"Godfather, you will forever have my complete loyalty," Ryan said.

355

Forelli nodded. "I'll arrange things in Boston. The matter will be concluded to your satisfaction."

"Godfather, I seek vengeance. I wish to handle the matter myself."

Forelli glanced at Gianelli. "You're in agreement?" Gianelli nodded. "Then all right. I ask only that you give me time to inform Don Biggio of this decision."

"Be careful, my friend. Kelly is a most dangerous man. To have survived this long, to have been so successful, the man is no fool," Gianelli cautioned.

Smiling effusively, Ryan extended his hand to the dons. He relaxed, the tension slowly leaving his body.

"Now, my friends," Don Forelli said, beckoning the waiter, "enough talk of business. Let's enjoy good food together, and the company of good friends above all else."

54

Greg Morris described the incident to his high school classmate over drinks at the Shawmut Grill in Lynn. "Where is justice in this fuckin' world of ours?" he asked Timmy.

"A young flower beaten to within an inch of her life, her jaw fractured, left for dead, for Christ sakes," he said. "Luckily, two ten-year-old boys wandered into the woods trying to find some secret place where they could smoke their pot. They happened onto Ellen, and then ran to the entry to Lynn Woods to get help. One of the runners they met was a doctor. That in itself probably saved her life."

"Jesus, Greg, I read about it in the Lynn Item, but I didn't make the connection to you," Timmy said.

"She's my half sister, Tim. Her name's Ellen Gannon. Can you imagine the fuckin' predators out there today? Battering a twelve-year-old girl who's walking home from junior fucking high school."

Timmy stirred his drink slowly. "How did it happen?"

"She left Pickering Junior High alone after staying for some extra help. She took a short cut through the Lynn Woods. About a day or two later she recovered enough from the shock and pain to recall that a young white blond man, twenty or so, suddenly appeared on the pathway. He started groping her and when she resisted his advance he beat her. He stole half her clothing as well. He hurt her real bad, Tim."

Timmy nodded in understanding. "What did the police do about it?"

"They showed Ellen pictures of known assholes here in the city, and she fingered a guy named Alden Hathaway who she

357

thought might be the one. Then they moved fast, too fast. She wasn't 100 percent positive but thought he might be the guy. One of the Lynn cops failed to get a proper search warrant for the creep's apartment and even though they found Ellen's clothing there, the D.A. refused to press the charges."

Greg pounded the table in frustration, describing his sister's present condition, her face distorted, her beauty destroyed, her confidence shattered.

Timmy downed the straight whiskey and followed it with a water chaser. He listened carefully, contained his anger, and focused on Greg.

"Jesus, Greg, I didn't know."

Greg glanced around the room. "What could you do about it anyway, Tim? What can any of us do against a system of justice that allows scum like this guy to run free. He's got an arrest record a fuckin' mile long. He hangs around with the worst fucking creeps in the city."

Tim tried to change the subject. "How are things at the Y?"

"Hey, you haven't been down for hoops with Marty for a while. Everything's fine. We're getting lots of new memberships and are planning on some expansion in the next year. They might even enlarge my responsibilities to include a couple of the district Y's as well."

"That's great, Greg. You've given a lot of yourself. You deserve it."

"You selling a lot of cars these days?"

"Pretty good, but the Jap cars are hurting us."

Greg placed his hands to his face. "Ellen's facing some operations to correct the bone structure in her face."

"How much is involved?"

"Probably $25,000, our part alone."

Timmy studied his watch. "I need to head out, Greg. I'll be down with Marty in a week or so, see if he can go one on one with me. Okay?"

"Call me when you know you're coming in. I'll take care of the arrangements."

Tommy listened to the story while sitting in the living room of his home near Goldfish Pond. When Timmy had finished, he looked up. "It's a sad story."

"That it is, Uncle Tom, but I'm telling you about it for a reason."

"I'm listening."

"I want to take action against this pervert," Timmy said.

"Well, at least we're making small progress. A couple of years ago you and Wild Bill Hickok over there wouldn't have even asked." Across the room Marty raised his glass toward Tommy and smiled.

"What do you care about this Y guy? What's his name again?"

"Greg. Greg Morris. He played football at English with me, Tom. You remember when I dove off Forty Steps in Nahant and hit my head on the rocks on the way down? He pulled me out of the surf. Marty was there. He'll tell you."

"What action are you talking about?" Tommy asked.

"We won't kill him if that's what you mean," Timmy replied. "But he's going to look a lot worse than she does."

Tommy nodded. Two years ago, that would not have been the response.

"One other thing, Tom," Marty spoke for the first time. "Could you and Jack put in $5,000 each to go with ours to help the girl?"

Tommy raised his glass and drained the remainder of the beer. "Absolutely. Tell your friend it's a gift from the agency."

Two nights later, Timmy and Marty cornered Alden Hathaway walking from City Hall Square along Essex Street toward his home. As he ascended the sharp incline, he listened to the boom box he held in his right hand, its noise level filling the area. He never heard the car easing to a stop adjacent to him until the driver signaled to him. Curious, he lowered the volume a bit and walked toward the Ford Mustang.

"Yeah? What?' he asked belligerently.

"You Alden Hathaway?" Timmy asked.

"Who the fuck is asking is what I say."

"Calm down pal. If you're Alden Hathaway, we want to do some business."

The stringy-haired blond nodded. "I'm Alden. You came to the right place."

"And you, my short peckered friend, are at the wrong place. You remember Ellen Gannon, asshole?"

"Who the fuck are you? Heat?" Hathaway replied, startled.

Marty exited the car, turning quickly in front of the headlights. As Hathaway stepped back from the window, he raised the .38 and fired once at his kneecap. Hathaway sprawled foreward, his boom box shattering in pieces as it hit the sidewalk. Timmy picked up the baseball bat from the rear seat, opened the door, and swung it directly into Hathaway's face, sending him onto his back.

On most Sundays they spent the hour attacking each other, playing each other fairly evenly, trading jump shots and drives, long range perimeter shots, and lay-ups in the kind of spirited competition that they both enjoyed.

"That's twenty-one, cousin," Timmy yelled out on the last Sunday in September, 1982. "Three games to two, you lose," he laughed.

The sun slanted through the high windows, brightening the still green leaves on the tall trees. Outside the Lynn YMCA the wind rattled the windows, harbinger of the season to come. Inside, they sat under the basket, breathing hard, perspiration dripping from their faces, exhausted yet invigorated, the tension of competition now behind them.

"How do you read my father on this Cardoza-Rizzo shit, Marty?" Timmy asked.

"I read your father as being two steps ahead of those two guineas, whatever he says publicly. He won't sit still for any further erosion of his territory. He knows he can't. My guess is that he won't even go along much longer with what's already been agreed to."

"What do you mean?"

"He told us to cooperate with Salvy and that lackey, Rizzo, right? Your father is the master, Tim. A master strategist. He'll appear to be responding positively to Cardoza, but he knows if he does, the next step is further intrusion or, more probably, they ace him out completely. He's buying time, that's what he's doing now. He's letting Cardoza and Rizzo think they have the upper hand."

"But what options does he have? We can't move against Cardoza."

"Don't be so sure of that. I think he's planning something. And if Cardoza moves against him again, he'll definitely act. He can't sit still. We go to war. But even if Cardoza leaves him alone, he'll find a way, some way to regain those territories."

"But Cardoza acts for Biggio," Timmy countered.

"Yeah, but both may have troubles with New York. The dons in New York won't go along with an outright war between us and the Mafia. They might even think that Biggio pushed us too hard, causing an unnecessary fight. Remember Rizzo is his wife's relative."

"Jesus, we don't stand much chance against Biggio and Cardoza."

"You really believe that? That old man of yours had a big advantage over them all, you know."

"What's that?"

"The old Mafiosos want to live and enjoy the good life. Jack's a fuckin' warrior, and he's emotionless. He doesn't give a shit, and that's the most dangerous opponent anyone can have."

Bobby Latimer was surprised that Lonnie Woods' widow wanted to see him. He had paid his respects at Kenny's wake, sympathizing with her loss of both husband and only son in such a short span of time. Why did she want to see him? Could she possibly have heard rumors of his involvement?

"Send her in, Roland," he said moving from behind his desk in the back room of the Social Club on Dudley Street.

The overweight woman walking slowly toward him looked as if she had aged twenty years in the last twelve months. Laughing eyes had lost their luster and her perpetually smiling face was creased with small worry lines and the clear signs of advancing age.

"Bobby, thank you for seeing me. I appreciate this very much," she said warmly.

"Please sit over here in this comfortable chair, Mother Woods," Bobby said, directing her to one of the two large green leather chairs in front of the desk. "Can I get you some coffee?"

"No, Bobby. I'm fine. Well," she stammered slightly, "I guess I'm not so fine. I need to pass on some information to you that's been bothering me for weeks now. I've been beside myself, Bobby. My man and my son both gone in such a short time." She began to cry.

Bobby removed the white pocket handkerchief from his green sports coat and leaned forward to press it into her hands. She quivered, dabbed at her eyes, trying hard to compose herself.

"I miss them both terribly, especially Kenny. It's a horrible thing to lose an only child, Bobby. You never really think you will outlive your child, you know. I'm confused now. Lonnie used to handle everything for me."

"You need any money, Mother Woods?"

She looked admiringly at him. "You are very thoughtful, Bobby. So kind. No, Lonnie provided for me. I can get by just fine."

"I came to tell you something and ask you about something," she said. "Bobby, do you have any idea who could have killed my boy?"

The question slowed him for the moment, but he recovered quickly. "No, Mother, I've asked around the city, and I'll continue to do so. But so far, we have no answer."

"Do you suppose those Irish brothers could be responsible?"

"You mean Jack and Tom Kelly, the Lynn guys? No. I don't hear anything like that," Bobby responded. "Why do you ask?"

"Bobby, before Lonnie died he acted as if he were afraid they might come after him. Said they were angry because Lonnie and you others were pushing into their areas."

"Well, that's right. We did sit down over in Lynn with them some years back. Nothing changed because of it though. We didn't take any shit from those honkies. Some minor disputes followed is all."

"He feared them more than the Italians, Bobby. He said they killed your father, Bobby. And so I wondered if they killed my baby, too."

"He said what, Mother?" Bobby riveted on the woman beside him now.

"What do you mean?" she asked, confused.

"You said Lonnie said the Kellys killed my father?"

"Yes. Years ago, Lonnie said the Flaherty Irish gang was responsible for your father's death. He was working with George Jackson at the time. The rumors were Flaherty had Jack Kelly kill your father. Never proved, mind you, but Lonnie said Flaherty was responsible."

Bobby sat motionless in his chair. Jack Kelly had killed his father. Jack Kelly had left him fatherless. He stared at Mrs. Woods for a long minute, then stood.

"You walk here?" he asked. She nodded. "Let me give you a ride home."

55

The call from New York City came just as Don Gennaro Biggio was admiring his appearance in the hall mirror of his luxurious home in Bristol, Rhode Island. In another five minutes he would start toward Federal Hill in Providence. He did not want to keep Maureen waiting. There is nothing better for an old man's health than a young mistress, he thought. A quiet dinner at Angelo's Civita Farnese on Atwells Avenue to satisfy her appetite, and then the short walk to her apartment to satisfy his.

He smiled at his image in the mirror. Not bad for a gentleman of seventy-one. The silvery white hair was all his own, with little sign of recession. He could afford to lose some weight, maybe fifteen pounds, but his height helped hide the problem, and he made extra efforts to stand erect, to compensate for his arthritic right leg.

The phone screamed from the living room, breaking the silence. His stupid wife had probably forgotten her pocketbook or maybe even her ass, if it hadn't been wrapped around her. She had left a half hour ago for the movies with their divorced daughter.

"Hello."

"Gennaro, this is Michael. I ask that you call me back. Would that be possible?"

He meant it had better be possible, Gennaro knew.

"I will call sometime," Gennaro said and hung up.

He snapped the hall lights off and locked the front door, descended to the circular driveway and entered his new El Dorado. Long ago they had arranged signals in full anticipation that federal agents could be monitoring their communications. "Call me back" was the code for returning the call from pay station to pay station, each station within ten minutes of both their homes. At least the pay station was on the way to Providence. He hoped Michael Forelli could state his business promptly. Maybe he had a mistress to keep happy this Saturday evening, too. He dialed the New York number from a convience store about a mile from his estate.

"Michael, Gennaro," he said as soon as Forelli answered. "How are you?"

"Well, my friend. If we could keep the fucking FBI off our case, even better."

Gennaro knew that the extortion rendered from the new deal with the truckers' union and the lucrative sports betting nationally were beginning to drive profits upward once again for New York. Soon, the money coming in from sports buffs around the nation would equal the drug profits.

"And you, Gennaro. All goes well in New England?"

"Same problems you have. I yearn for the 50's and 60's when we were left alone to do our business."

"Gennaro, I have to ask your indulgence in an extremely important matter," Forelli spoke softly.

"Of course, Michael."

"You remember our friend Connie Ryan? He now works closely with Mario."

"Yes?"

"Do you remember his desire to take action against Jack Kelly back in the 1960's?"

"Yes, I do."

"We would not allow such an act back then, principally due to your intervention and concern, and that of Salvatore, as well. You needed Kelly, you told us."

"Yes, all that is true," Biggio responded.

"What can you tell me about Kelly today?"

"Kelly? An old Irish warhorse. A survivor, Michael. Involved in the business for almost thirty years. A natural leader. To have survived this long, he is also careful, cunning.

You always feel he is thinking ahead or along with you. Unlike most of the Irish, he keeps his head. As good or better than anyone we have."

"How has he reacted to the recent cutbacks in his territories?"

"Cardoza reports he's not happy, Michael. We, of course, have little choice. We face pressures, with profit margins falling and the desire of our own family members to assume a greater role. I believe I have explained much of this to you previously."

"What's your plan for the future, Gennaro?"

"Cardoza's assistant, Nick Rizzo, has assumed certain territories from Kelly. We hope to expand this action soon."

"And Kelly just sits and waits?" Forelli asked.

"Yes. I recognize he is dangerous, but I believe we can control him."

"I don't think so, Gennaro. If he is what you say he is, we have trouble ahead. Gennaro, I have authorized Connie Ryan to extract the revenge he seeks for the death of his brother. Ryan's services to Gianelli have been invaluable. It appears to me that our agendas are coinciding. You desire to enhance our position in Boston, and we desire to accommodate Ryan's request. Then let's get it done."

And so, Jack Kelly was dead, thought Gennaro. Too bad. He had served them well. Along with providing stability, he had controlled various splinter groups, particularly the Blacks, most of them out of control attempting to infringe on all of them.

"Michael, I'm in agreement. His day has come and gone. There are no longer any opportunities for mutually accommodating arrangements."

"Then let's move ahead." Forelli paused for a moment. "Gennaro, one other matter. Ryan wishes to act on his own. I ask that you have this Rizzo available to back him. If Ryan succeeds, everyone is pleased. But if he fails, we need to be sure. Have Rizzo ready to move, if necessary."

"I'll make the arrangements, Michael."

"Good. I should allow you to get back to your evening, Gennaro. I am sure you have plans."

"Thank you, Michael. Yes. My wife and I plan a trip to Providence for dinner."

"Well, enjoy, Gennaro. Please give her my regards."

"And mine to Maria," Gennaro responded. "I look forward to seeing you soon."

He hung up and glanced at his watch. With luck, he could still make Providence and find Maureen waiting. He would be at least a half hour late. Why was he worrying? he finally asked himself. The bitch would be sitting there, feeding her face with shrimp and wine. God forbid she pay the bill herself. She would wait all night for him rather than do that.

56

"You telling me the fuckin' smokies aren't out of control, Ray? Because if you are, I say to you, you ought to cut down on the fuckin' tea, maybe go to one of those AA places where you bare your soul. Tell them you found salvation before your brains burst," Chris Kiely said, pointing his paper cup in Ray Horan's direction.

Ray Horan raised his coffee cup toward Kiley and laughed aloud. "Chris, all I'm saying is that Bobby Latimer is not to be underestimated. Look at what he's done, for Christ's sake. Grew up in the Mission Hill projects. Started out as a small-timer right there. Now, both of the Woods are gone. Hollins is gone. Johnson is history. And where's Bobby? King of the hill. All competition eliminated. Out of control? I don't think so."

"You know, Ray, you ought to link up with the fucker. You admire him so much," Chris Kiely said derisively.

"I admire competence, Chris," Ray said. "He's an increasing danger, and we need to understand that."

They sat on the usual box crates at the warehouse in Charlestown, awaiting Jack and Tommy's arrival. Chris Kiely, Paulie Cronin, Ray Horan, Vinnie Sullivan, Marty and Timmy. In about an hour they would all attend the funeral of a former South Boston ward boss.

"What do we give a shit about the fuckin' Blacks?" Vinnie interjected. "What are we going to do about Nick Rizzo and the other greaseballs pushing our faces in the sand? That's the real question."

Marty walked around the perimeter, sipping his coffee, exchanging glances with Timmy as Vinnie continued. "What's

Jack thinking, anyway? Pretty soon we'll be out of business turning areas over to the Italians."

"Why don't you tell him how you feel directly, loudmouth," Marty said evenly.

"Who do you think you're talking too, you little fuck. I was cutting my teeth on punks like you before you were born."

"Shut up, Vinnie, or we'll shut you up so you won't have any teeth to brush, never mind cut with," Timmy retorted.

The loud knock on the glass door called them all to attention. Ray Horan rolled the door halfway up so that Jack and Tommy could move under it.

"What's going on here?" Jack asked. "I could hear voices screaming halfway down Medford Street."

"Tell him, asshole," Marty said.

"You know, Jack, I don't have to take this guff from this guy. Relative or no relative, he keeps pushing me he's going to regret it," Vinnie stood and stared at Marty.

"Calm down, Vin," Tommy said, putting an arm around his neck and leading him to his seat.

"We don't have enough outsiders to worry about, you guys have to now threaten each other?" Jack asked.

"That's what we were talking about, Jack. The Blacks. The Italians," Chris Kiely offered.

"What about them?" Jack asked, discarding his gray cashmere sports coat and placing it on an empty crate.

"You think Latimer knocked out the competition, Jack?" Ray Horan asked.

"I don't know for sure. Probably. But what do we care? He's not making moves against us. I don't spend any time worrying about him until he does," Jack said, sitting down.

"Bobby's a dangerous guy, Jack," Ray said. "First guy in decades to consolidate operations in Mattapan, Dorchester, Roxbury. We need to watch him."

"Agreed. But for now we leave him alone."

"That's my position, too, Jack," Vinnie broke in quickly. "But what about Rizzo? Why are we sitting quietly while he moves into our territories?"

Jack grimaced, his facial expression indicating his displeasure with the question. "Vin, I've explained before our friend's request of us. Our friend's request comes from on high, right from Providence. We have been asked to cooperate because of the times. I'm honoring the request."

"Honoring the request, Jack?" Vinnie asked incredulously. "Honoring the request? Those guys aren't ever going to give us back any territories. When they're gone, they're gone."

"Calm down, Vin." Tommy flicked an ash on the floor.

"Jack, can I review some history with you, with a man I respect?" Vin asked. "Do you remember how we handled intrusions in the old days? Remember the time you took out the Chocolate Drop back in the '50's? You remember that? You made your bones that day for Jimma.

"And remember the time you caught Paul Lamana selling drugs big time to little kids in our terrain over in North Cambridge? You took care of him yourself. Shot him twice in the head, you told me. And him a connected guy. You sent them a message, then, Jack. Remember?"

Jack sipped the steaming coffee Ray had handed him slowly. What was causing Vinnie's agitation, he wondered. Why the recitation of the past and Jack's role in it?

Vinnie waited for Jack's answer. Jack thought about Vinnie's normal caution in discussing family business. It was unusual for Vinnie or anyone to discuss crimes committed in front of the group. If they needed to eliminate a mark, Jack would assign the problem individually to one of them. It was an unspoken rule, particularly subsequent to the FBI's greater involvement in crime fighting, to avoid open discussions of actions taken, past, present, or future. His initial assessment was probably correct. Vinnie was an old soldier frustrated with the new situation. Unable to adjust, he yearned for action and was simply reminiscing in his frustration. Was that it? He hoped so. He paused. Something else clicked in his memory. It had been Vinnie who had brought the IRA phonies forward. Had he actually been duped, or was he part of the potential sting? Had they turned Vinnie? But that was years ago. And he remembered that Vinnie was always Flaherty's man, Jack thought. Yet he had seemed to adjust to the change of command.

"Remember, Jack?" Vinnie asked again.

"Look to the future, Vin. That's where opportunity lies."

In frustration, Vin shook his head. "There won't be any fuckin' opportunity we don't show the guineas we're not going to be pushed."

"Stow it, Vinnie," Tommy ordered.

"What time does the Mass start?" Jack asked Ray.

"In half an hour."

"Let's all go pay our respects to Jimmy Doyle."

On the drive to St. Brigid's Church on East Broadway in South Boston, Jack sat quietly, lost in his thoughts.

"What's the matter?" Tommy asked as they sped into the South Station Tunnel, the traffic lighter than usual on a Saturday morning.

"Vinnie. Something's wrong there, Tom."

"Oh, don't worry about Vinnie. He likes to hear himself talk half the time. He means no harm. Like the rest of us, he's growing older and yearns for the old days, that's all."

Jack thought for a moment. "You're with him more than anybody. You haven't noticed any changes in him?"

"No, Jack. What are you saying?"

"I don't know exactly. Something's funny. All that talk about what crimes I committed was forced, unnecessary."

"He was just trying to show you the difference between then and now. He's just impatient with these times, Jack. That's all."

"Maybe. Maybe not. He's the one that brought us those two IRA guys years ago."

"Jack!" Tommy raised his voice. "He was duped is all. You smelled it out. How was he to know? That was years ago, for Christ's sake. I vouch for Vinnie all the way."

"Let's check it out, Tommy. He may be wearing a wire."

"Wearing a wire?"

"Next time you're alone with him, check him. In the meantime be careful what you say around him."

"You know something, Jack. Maybe Vinnie's right. Maybe you're running scared, becoming too cautious."

"Yeah, and maybe I'm right, Tommy. You going to look into it, or do I ask someone else?"

"I'll be glad to prove you wrong, big brother."

57

On Sunday he and Courtney drove down Route 6 toward Dennisport, one last trip to the Cape before the winter season was upon them. Courtney sat sideways facing him, one leg crossed over the other. She wore dark blue jeans, a light blue polo shirt topped by a dark blue sweatshirt thrown over her shoulders. Her hair was pulled back into a ponytail.

Looking ahead to closing the cottage for the winter, he relished this drive and the opportunity to leave the fast pace of city life behind for just a while. When you crossed the Sagamore Bridge, the gateway to Cape Cod, it was as if you were leaving one world and entering another, he felt. Most people loved to tour New Hampshire these first weeks of October, but he enjoyed those weeks following Labor Day when the Cape stopped to breathe, when families and tourists returned to jobs and school, and the difference between city and country living became even more pronounced.

Once in Dennisport, he pulled into the Glendon Beach parking lot and turned off the engine. Two hearty old men swam together ever so slowly through the choppy green water while an elderly couple held hands and walked the small beach, pausing occasionally to study shells of different sizes and colors. A slight breeze caught the sands, bringing with it the strong smell of the sea. Dirty white sea gulls swooped to the beach in a vain search for the food remnants no longer available.

"Hungry?" he asked.

"Not really."

He studied the gray horizon for a moment. "I better get to our business. It should take me about an hour, and then we'll get something to eat."

"Okay," she replied. She had been short with her conversation for most of the trip, unusual for her. On second thought, he had noted her generally quiet demeanor for over a month now. He had attributed it to her rigorous schedule, the consistently long hours devoted to business matters, her frequent traveling, partly for Jerry, partly to visit her parents in San Francisco, especially since her mother's bout with depression had escalated.

It took him close to an hour to turn off the water, gas, and electricity at his place at 40 Glendon Road. While he made sure the tri-level cottage was secured, she packed toiletries and the small amount of food left in the cupboards. Afterward, they headed toward the small Italian restaurant on Lower County Road that they both enjoyed just as the overcast day opened up and a spatter of rain came on them.

In the dark restaurant a candle flickered on top of a Chianti bottle in the middle of the white and red checkered tablecloth. They hadn't said much to each other for the last two hours, but that, he felt, was the language of true love. Good friends and ardent lovers never really do have to say much to one another.

He curled the spaghetti around his fork, noticing her playing with the manicotti, moving it around the plate. "Hey, lover, what's the problem? You seem far, far away today," he said gently.

She looked at him, as if deciding on a strategy, a small tear beginning to form in the corner of her eye.

He reached across the table, placing his hands in hers. "Hey, come on. Whatever it is, it can't be that bad."

"It's as bad as it can get, Jack."

"Just tell me, honey. Let me help."

"I'm confused Jack, and I just don't know how to tell you. God knows I don't want to hurt you."

And that was the beginning of the end of life, he later thought. Sitting in a small restaurant on the Cape, his whole world pulled out from under, not having ever seen it coming. As she spoke he only half heard the words, reflecting back in his mind to that day his mother had left him, to the time that Jimma Flaherty had turned against him, to Marjorie and her inability to stand by him, and now a new betrayal from someone he loved.

"I believe there's a number of factors, Jack, some of which I frankly don't understand myself," she was saying, her voice coming to him as if from an echo chamber. "Work has caused me a lot of tension, for one thing. I can't seem to relax anymore. I'm constantly on edge. I thought I had what I wanted, but now I'm not so sure."

He put aside the spaghetti and signaled the waiter. "Let me have another VO and ginger," he said as the young man approached their table. Maybe five or ten, he felt like adding.

"With my mother's illness, you know I've been spending more time in San Francisco. That's where I met him. He's a psychiatrist at the medical center where she's being seen. He's divorced, about my age, with two young girls. He asked me for coffee once or twice, innocent enough I thought, while Mother was being seen by someone else. I liked him right away, Jack. He's a good man who cares about people.

"He asked me out about four months ago. I accepted. And now I can't seem to wait until the next time I go back home. And that's also a factor. I want to go home. I miss San Francisco. And then there's us, Jack. Your age and my age, the worry about you, the kind of work..."

"Jesus, Courtney. Hold it there. The Lord himself only had ten points. I think I get the picture."

"I can't eat anymore," she sighed, pushing the food aside. "Can you get me another drink?" She wiped her eyes with her white cloth.

He raised his hand, pointing to Courtney. The waiter nodded and moved toward the bar.

"I love you, Jack. I do. But I guess I love myself more. I'm being selfish, I know, but..."

"Courtney, I love you more than life itself."

"Don't say that."

"Let me finish," he said gently. "Because I love you, I want you to be happy. If you want out, I don't want you around counting up all the reasons why you should stay or go. Let me make it easy for you. You want our relationship to end? Then it will be over, Courtney."

She touched his hand. "I'm so sorry to hurt you."

The ride home was similar to the drive down. They again mostly sat in silence, occasionally commenting on some minor matter while listening to the radio. But now the strong silence reminded him only of growing distance. He never thought of trying to convince her against her will. He concentrated instead on the scenery: the orange sunset that followed the light rain in the western sky and the changes of colors in the trees to his right. Browns and yellows, reds and greens co-mingled. In the autumn of his life he never felt more alone than on this day. Although these strong emotional encounters marked him deeply, they also gave him strength. They forced him to rely on himself. In truth, he prided himself on his ability to adjust. He felt tremendous hurt, and yet he did not. She would always be there in his memories, and yet she mattered much less to him now than she did three hours ago. And that would never change.

"I'll meet you in three hours along Memorial Drive. I'll be sitting on a bench halfway down. Don't dress."

Vinnie pondered Tommy's phone call. An individual meet was a signal that something important was to be conveyed. Usually Tommy would indicate an action that Jack had ordered for his key enforcer. "Don't dress" was code for do not come armed. That, in turn, usually meant they would not move directly to action, whatever Tommy's message.

Vinnie taped the wire to his body, making sure it was secure. He became increasingly agitated each time he affixed it. It had been two months now since Folan's promise to call him in for his own protection and still he was in the field. With each passing day he felt increasingly vulnerable. Jack was no fool. Just the other day in Charlestown he sensed Jack's concern when he had ranted and raved about the Italians. Folan had asked him to lure Jack into speaking of past crimes, and he had tried his best through his reminiscing about the past. He hadn't failed to note that Jack had not joined in the conversation.

He first chose a T-shirt and then a heavy green sweater to cover the tape. Then he selected a dark brown sports jacket, a perfect complement to his light brown slacks. Looking into the living room wall mirror, he patted himself down, assuring a reasonable fit. The wire lay compactly against his stomach, and he observed no uneven contours.

Folan was particularly adamant that he wear the wire to individual meets with Jack or Tommy, having realized some time ago that nothing of substance was conveyed at the group meetings. To date, he had worn it to three meetings with Tommy, and Folan had seemed delighted with the results.

He snapped off the light and walked out to a beautiful fall day. October in New England. Nothing could compare to it, he felt, as he started toward Memorial Drive. It made him think of the importance of being free and remaining free.

Tommy looked across to Boston, the sun hovering in the eastern sky practically blinding him as he stood at the rail. Bobbing white sailboats skirted over choppy waters, their owners intent on prolonging the season for one more run. A long shell with college markings flew across the Charles, its coxswain urging greater efforts, the crew responding to the increased cadence count.

"Hey, Tommy," Vinnie greeted him effusively. "What's going down?"

Tommy grunted at him and offered his hand. "You dress?"

"You said not to so no I didn't."

"Good. Just checking. Let's sit over on the bench."

"So what do we have?" Vinnie inquired, sitting to Tommy's left.

"Vin, there's a problem we need to resolve."

"A mark?"

"No, Vin. I don't know how to say this right. Jack's worried about you."

"Jack's worried about me? What the fuck's he worried about me for?"

"You seem different lately, Vin."

"Different? Different like how?"

"Vin, you seem nervous, agitated over something. I notice it, too. You and I spend more time together than any of the rest of us. Is there something you need help with? Something you're not telling us?"

"Jesus Christ, Tommy. You fuckin' guys now qualify as shrinks do you? I'm fine, Tommy. Few things at home got me down a bit, that's all."

"Like what?"

"Like my dumbass wife running up bills at every mall in eastern Massachusetts, and my kid's taking to the juice at thirteen years old. I get less trouble from the marks we whack around, for fuckin' sure."

"Jack's worried about something else, too, Vin," Tommy said, staring straight ahead.

"Now what? Maybe your brother ought to worry about the Italians breaking our balls a little more if he wants to spend his time worrying."

Tommy turned toward him slowly. "Vin, I'm telling my own brother he's wrong. I know you. I..."

"Tommy, what are you driving at?" Vin asked, trying to hide his fear.

"He thinks you may have turned, Vin. He thinks you're wired."

"You know, I don't have to listen to this bullshit," Vin said, starting to stand.

Tommy shoved him down. "Open your jacket, Vin," he ordered, his right hand gripping the .38 in his pocket. "I told him I'd check it out. I hope he's wrong, Vin. For the first time in my life, I hope my brother's wrong. Open the fuckin' jacket."

He placed his left hand inside the jacket under the sweater and felt the bandages and the wire itself. As he yanked at the tape, the recorder fell into his hands. A lone elderly walker sauntered by the bench lost in his own reveries, paying scant

380

attention to the two men who sat in silence for a long minute, one looking straight ahead, the other dabbing at his eyes with a white handkerchief.

"Jesus, Vinnie, what happened?"

"The feds caught me straight on, Tom. A murder one rap with two feds as eye witnesses. I had no choice," Vin said, panic in his voice.

"No choice, Vin? You could have come to Jack or me. We've got people who..."

"Your brother would have had me iced, Tommy."

"You're wrong." Tommy shook his head from side to side.

"No, I'm not, Tom. I was never his man. I was Jimma's guy. I transferred the loyalty, Tommy. You know that. But your brother's a funny guy. I would always be a question mark to him. Then to bring this problem to his doorstep, calling attention to the family, I would have been a dead man, no question."

"I would have spoken for you, Vin. He would have listened to me."

"Stop trying to convince yourself."

"Who reached you?"

"Two feds, Folan and Quinn. The two who posed as IRA guys years back."

"Jesus, Mary, and Joseph."

"They caught me taking out a bookie I owed big time."

"How much they know?"

"Enough. They've been talking to me for a few months now. They asked me about the times I've been with Jack and you. What I actually saw, you know? I had to tell them how we operate. The wire is to mainly catch the one-on-ones, the direct transfer of orders. They also hoped I could get Jack to talk about his own hits. Then they expect me to testify later on."

Tommy stood and walked to the rail, his hand gripping it tightly. He felt Vinnie approach and stand next to him, on his left. The morning sun streamed into their faces and made it difficult for him to focus on the silhouette next to him.

"What now, Tommy?"

"You would have testified against us, Vin?"

Vinnie threw his hands in the air. "In the end I don't think I could have. I was trapped, Tom. I had no choice. What now?"

Tommy stared straight ahead. "You're wrong, Vin. There're always choices. You testify against us and you're a dead man. All bets are off. If we can't find you, then we'll find your two brothers. There'll be no protection for family members. I promise you that. No one gets away with informing on us." He paused long enough for Vinnie to absorb his words. "And even if you don't, it's gone too far. We're going to have to take action against you, Vin."

"Tommy, can't you help me? Can't you get me out of this?"

"There's another choice, Vin," he said slowly, turning toward him, trying to catch his eyes through the glare.

"Think about a mutually accommodating solution that satisfies everyone. And think about it fast. You remember those World War II movies we used to see? Remember the Japanese general who failed at Okinawa, Vin?" With that, he turned and walked toward his car, never once looking back.

Diagonally across the street from O'Neal's at Sixth and West 57th, Marty and Timmy sat in a booth at Wolf's Delicatessen waiting for Bobby's arrival. At a few minutes after midnight, a surprisingly large number of customers filled the multitude of booths.

The warm October day had turned dark in the late afternoon, and in the evening hours sheets of angry rain had deluged the city, causing havoc with taxis, forcing pedestrians to seek shelter. It was close to midnight before the storm had abated.

"He should be here any minute," Timmy said, fingering his coffee cup.

Bobby paused near the cash register looking for his brother and cousin. He spotted them, near the rear and looped toward them, smiling broadly.

"Hey, the Corsican Brothers," he teased. "How did you guys ever find your way to the Big Apple?"

"Sit down, Warren Beatty. It's a wonder you still talk to us," Timmy said, sliding over to make room.

"So what did you guys think?" Bobby asked, shedding his wet trenchcoat and hanging it on the hook next to the booth.

"About which one?" Marty asked. "First I have to watch your sorry ass on the soap opera in my hotel room in some crazy plot about your being in love with your own sister, and then at night watch you in person singing and dancing in tights looking like some fag."

"Your depiction of and appreciation for the arts is something else, cousin," Bobby said, laughing. "When I'm a big star in Hollywood, you guys will wish you treated me with more respect."

"Everything going Okay for you, Bob?" Timmy asked.

"Couldn't be better. I received some big news yesterday. I want you guys to be the first to know. I'll call Mom tomorrow morning."

Marty waved to the waitress, indicating coffee for three with his gestures.

"I flew out to Hollywood about two weeks ago looking for a place to stay? One of the major studios that's been scouting me asked me to test for a part in a new crime movie. You guys are looking at the second lead."

Timmy threw his arm around his brother. "You really are Warren Beatty!"

Marty extended his hand across the table. "You're really something, cousin. I'm awfully proud of you."

"A movie about crime?" Timmy asked.

"Yeah. It takes place in the 1930's."

"You think they're in need of any technical advisors?" Marty asked. "Like real life gangsters?"

"Wiseass," Bobby responded. "Amadeus closes in a month and then I'll be relocating. The movie starts production in about six weeks. Things are really coming together now. How's it with you guys?"

"Things are a little quiet, Bob," Timmy replied. "The cops are much more sophisticated. We're being careful."

"I hope so, guys," Bobby said a frown appearing on his forehead. "How's Dad?"

"I think he's a little down since Courtney left, but you wouldn't know it from him. He won't talk about it," Timmy answered.

"I talk to Mom every week. She's coming down next week to see the play again for the fourth time. Your mother's coming with her, Marty. What's new with Aunt Sheila and Uncle Jerry?"

"Dad's business is doing great, so she's kept busy with the social life that's part of it. I see them regularly, but there's always that strain between them and me. Sometimes I catch her looking at me like she may never see me again."

Bobby sensed it was time to change the subject. "Well, come on you Irish Corsicans. Let's go out on the town for a few drinks. We'll see if you can take the late hours," Bobby said engagingly. "By the way, try not to shoot any of the patrons at the disco. I'd like to keep my friends, thank you very much."

"Maybe we'll just wound them," Timmy replied. "Either way you can learn some techniques for the crime movie."

At close to 1:00 A.M., at exactly the same time the cousins entered the disco at Seventh and 55th Street, Vinnie Sullivan sat alone in his car on Day Boulevard just down the road from the L Street Boathouse. The rain rushing in from New York drummed against the window, beating a rhythm, making it nearly impossible to see Boston Harbor and Thompson's Island in the distance. He rolled down the window for a minute, just to observe for the last time the outline of the South Boston tenements behind him, and the white capped waters of the sea before him.

What a night to die, he thought. He pushed the button to close the window and sat for a minute as the wind hurled rain against the glass. The straight whiskey had made the evening much more palatable. He picked up the bottle of Canadian Mist, now half empty, and took one last long swig.

Flipping open the glove compartment, he took out the .38 and placed it in his left hand. Curiously, in these last minutes he thought of the Catholic Church, of the nuns who had taught him, rather than of his own family. Suicide was the major mortal sin against his Catholic faith, but he could see no other option. Although the Church could never accept his choice, he was now personally content. Better to die in sin, he thought, than to be labeled an informer. Jack would see to his family, that would be a part of this accommodation.

He took off the safety catch and placed the weapon against his temple. His last thought was of Sister Maria lauding him in fourth grade because of his improved penmanship. It had been the highlight of his academic life. How many other left-handed people could learn to write right handed with their left hand tied behind their backs? Sister had insisted that no one was to write left-handed.

He could not sleep so he got up with the sun. While coffee brewed in the kitchen, he glanced at himself in the mirror, studying the deep lines under his eyes. First the body blow from Courtney, and now Vinnie, he thought.

There was a crisp chill in the October air, but he took his black coffee to the back deck and stood, inhaling the smell of the marine fog layer filling the neighborhood at dawn. He had been right about Vinnie. When Tommy had reported on his meeting with Vin, Jack had indicated that such treachery meant decisive action had to be taken right away.

Now Vinnie had saved him the trouble. He should have seen it coming because he had never fully trusted him. As he leaned against the railing, he thought long and hard of the potential damage. If Tommy was right, it was minimal. The tapes were probably inadmissible, and even if they were, key to any indictment and conviction was Vinnie's personal testimony. But the sons of bitches were on their case. No doubt he would feel increased pressure in the time ahead.

He threw the remainder of the coffee over the rail. Vinnie had compromised them, leaving their entire operation vulnerable. Two days ago he had offered his sympathy to Ann Sullivan, assuring the grief stricken widow that she would be taken care of financially. In the near future, he would visit Vinnie at Forest Lawn Cemetery and piss on the traitor's grave.

Larry Bird caught the ball along the base line and in one smooth motion hit nothing but net. The frustrated Knicks forward muttered to himself and bounced the ball in play without noticing Bird's position. The Celtics star streaked between the forward and the intended receiver, intercepted the ball and quickly jammed it through the hoop.

"Will you look at that guy!" Jack exclaimed. "Isn't he something?"

Danny nodded in agreement, but his body language connoted a mind far, far away from the raucous Boston Garden crowd and the final minutes of the Celtics easy victory over their hated rivals.

"You're awfully quiet tonight, kid," Jack said. "Something wrong?"

"I need to talk with you, Jack. Let's get a drink at the Iron Horse afterwards."

"Fine with me. Let's go now. This is all over anyway."

Below the Garden they sat in a rear booth as far removed as they could get from the crowd beginning to congregate at the bar. They both ordered boilermakers from the too quick waiter and looked occasionally at the big television screens above them as they waited his return.

"So what's up?" Jack asked.

Danny downed the whiskey and winced. He looked at Jack then back at his glass.

"Whatever it is, how many more of them do you need before you tell me?" Jack winked at him, as he downed his own shot.

Danny pulled at his tie and scanned the crowd. From behind him a number of the celebrants crowded around the long bar, becoming boisterous and rowdy, embellishing what they had observed at the game with each new drink.

386

"My mother feels I should let you know what's going on, Jack."

"Your mother feels?" Jack responded. "Catherine wants you to tell me something?"

Danny nodded.

Jack sipped his beer and glanced at the crowd. "I respect Catherine, but I'm a little concerned that you begin by telling me what your mother feels, Danny Boy. Why don't you just tell me what you want to tell me straight on."

"Ha. There's the rub," Danny said faking an Irish brogue, trying too hard to relax. "I feel conflicted, Jack. She feels..."

"Never mind for the moment what she feels, Danno. You tell me what you want to."

Danny flinched and sat more erect. "Jack, you've done so much for me, ever since my dad was killed. And for Mom as well. Always. But I work for the FBI, and I feel loyalty to..."

Jack raised his hand in a halting motion. "Danny, your mother is my very special friend, and you're like a son to me. I'm as proud of you as I am my own sons and nephew. Now you listen to me carefully, because I can guess the rest, what causes you this trouble..."

"No, you listen to me, Jack. They're on to you, on to you big time. I can..."

"Don't you think I know that? Listen, boyo, and listen good, just for a minute, will you please?"

Danny sighed and looked around for the waiter and signaled a second round. "Go ahead," he said.

Jack held his eyes. "Feel no conflict. No conflict at all. I want no favors from you. Your loyalty must be to the FBI, as the loyalty of my people must be to me. I'm just happy you're not stationed in Boston."

"But, Jack, besides Sullivan, I hear they have tapes and..."

"Danny, you stay straight on this. Stay on course. I'll handle my own problems. I don't want any record that you and I ever discussed Vinnie Sullivan, tapes, witnesses or anything else. Have I ever asked anything of you?"

"No," Danny said.

"That's right. I don't ask, and I don't need to know."

Danny shook his head. "I should help you."

"I want you clean. I want you to be able to stand up to your bosses in court -- if that's ever required -- and take an oath that you had no contact with me regarding the life. None whatsoever. You with me on this?"

"But I can tell you..."

"There's nothing you can tell me that I want to know. Remember what you said earlier? I've done for you. But you've done something for me as well. You're my special redemption, Danny. Something good that touches my life. I want to keep it that way. For me and for your father."

"They'll close in on you. They'll..."

"Then they better have a hell of a lot more than I think they have. Relax, Danny. Don't be conflicted; just be the best fuckin' agent the coppers have -- for me and for your mother and your father."

Connie Ryan disembarked at Gate 3 of the Eastern Airlines shuttle at exactly 2:10 P.M. As he walked briskly through Terminal A at Logan Airport, he looked at the various message boards hoisted by a variety of well-dressed drivers. He spotted the sign "Mr. Arthur Roberts" easily and moved toward the square-jawed, mustached bearer.

"I'm Roberts."

"Come with me, sir."

They strolled into the main lobby and took the down escalator to the basement area. "Any luggage, sir?"

"Just one piece."

They waited at the carousel for five minutes before the baggage appeared. Ryan lifted the very first bag, a light tan Hartmann suitcase, but before he could set it down, the messenger stepped in. "I'll take that, sir. Please follow me."

Leaving the building, they crossed to the parking lot. Nick Rizzo followed them in the rear view mirror as they approached his Cadillac. He slid out from behind the wheel to greet Ryan.

"Mr. Ryan? Nick Rizzo. Welcome to Boston. We're very pleased to have you here," he said, too obsequiously.

Ryan looked at the extended hand and offered his own. "I appreciate your picking me up."

They sat together in the back seat as the driver placed the luggage in the trunk. "How long will you be with us, Mr. Ryan?" Rizzo asked, as the driver backed up.

"If everything goes well, just a few days. Can we talk?" he asked Rizzo, pointing to the driver.

"Yes."

"You have any merchandise for me, Nick?"

Rizzo handed him a large brown paper bag from under the seat. He opened it and smiled. He placed his hand on the .357 Magnum. "Perfect, Nick. Now let me tell you about the plan."

"Now where the fuck are we?" Quinn asked Folan as they sat parked in front of the Orange Street apartment in Chelsea.

"Where are we, Billy? We're fucked. That's where we are. What the hell could have happened?" Folan asked, not expecting an answer.

"The medical examiner, the autopsy people all agree it was suicide. No question about it."

Folan stared out the window. "Why did he do it? We had him covered. He had a clear future, a pathway out. I don't get it."

"He obviously didn't see it that way," Quinn said, squashing his cigarette into the ashtray.

"He saw something we're not seeing, Billy. Maybe it was that boyo bullshit about informing. He was becoming increasingly apprehensive recently. I should have pulled him earlier, Billy. I was going for the whole ball of wax. I put too much pressure on him."

"Don't punish yourself, Matt. We needed the one-on-ones. What did we really end up with?"

"Not enough. Not after the months we've put into this set-up. Our key witness is in the ground, we have his testimony, and we have three tapes where Sullivan and Tom Kelly are talking some leg breaking or battery on some marks. We went for a home run, hoping to catch them talking major league hits. We're on the scoreboard with two or three singles, that's all."

"You know what fuckin' amazes me, Matt? The guineas have the reputation for being business-like. That Irish prick is ten miles ahead of them. While we can't put a case together on him yet, the Italians are rattling on at Prince Street telling our guys on tape the last time they took a piss as well as who they knocked off last week."

"They're all going down in the end, Billy. We have something else working for us," Folan said.

"Yeah? What's that?"

"Time. Come on, let's clean up the apartment and close it down."

58

Two days after his arrival in Boston, Connie Ryan was ready to set his plan in motion. From the Beachmont Social Club in Revere, Nick Rizzo made the call.

"Tommy, Nick Rizzo."

"Yeah, Nick. How goes the battle?"

"We're hanging in there, champ. But I need to get a message to Jack."

Tommy lowered the volume on the television set next to the bed and sat up. It was not unusual for Rizzo to pass messages through him. He didn't like Rizzo, dismissing him, as did Jack, as a gofer completely dependent on Biggio and Cardoza. Since he had assumed control of the new jurisdictions, profits had slowed, largely because of his inability to instill discipline or provide leadership to his family. Three or four times, his own people had ripped him off, and it had taken months for Rizzo to discover the infractions. If he weren't connected by blood to Biggio, he would have been replaced months ago.

"Sure thing," he responded to Rizzo.

"I need to see him here tonight. Important message from the big man. Can he make it at midnight?"

"I don't know his plans, Nick, but I'll pass the message. Ray or I will get back to you by seven if it isn't all right."

"Perfect, Tommy. Keep those gloves high, kid. See you soon."

He hung up, turned and smiled at Ryan. "He'll be here. Like clockwork. We meet occasionally. He won't think anything of it."

"What time is it now?" Ryan asked, looking at his own watch. "Five o'clock," he answered his own question. "I'm going to catch some sleep for a few hours. I'll see you here around ten."

Jack pulled the knot of his tie tight and put on his light blue sportcoat. He snapped off the hallway light just as the phone rang.

"What's on the docket tonight?" Tommy asked.

"I was just going out for a bite to eat," Jack responded.

"Want some company?"

"Sure. Meet me at Anthony's Hawthorne in Olympia Square. I'll be there around six."

From the beach Jack drove past Tommy's house at Lafayette Park, one area of Lynn that had come back strongly in the 80s. The Lafayette Park Neighborhood Association had dredged Goldfish Pond, painted the benches surrounding the area, and planted flowers in spring and summer. Located halfway between their former house on Fayette Street to the west, and the beaches to the east, the Park reminded Jack of the true middle-class neighborhoods of his boyhood. It was 1947 revisited, an attempt at urban sanity in a sea of neglect.

He decided to drive across Laundry Hill to Fayette Street. It at once stimulated and depressed him to view the old neighborhood. Very positive memories flooded his mind as he descended Laundry Hill to Fayette Street, but the signs of decay on the street irritated him. Apartment dwellings were now neglected, their paint peeling, garbage strewn about the buildings, small lawns left untended. If the Blacks and Hispanics living here now had inculcated the values in their young that his parents had in him, they wouldn't be in this predicament today.

He corrected himself almost immediately. If crime families like his weren't peddling drugs, prostitution, gambling and loans in cities like Lynn, then maybe urban America wouldn't be in the situation he observed. Maybe. Just maybe. Nobody was twisting arms to have them buy.

From Fayette Street he circled the block in order to make a right turn down Union Street. He headed toward Central Square, passing the burned out stores, the site of probably the only failed McDonald's in America, the closed Connelly's candy shop, that had been operational since the 1940's. Middle-class America had long ago emigrated to the suburbs, selfish people unwilling to live near minorities, another part of the problem, he felt.

He pulled into the parking lot close to Anthony's Hawthorne and killed his lights. He noted Tommy's car among the very few in the lot. From the 1940s, into the 1970s, you could not have found a parking space in the area near Central Square.

He walked through the small alleyway adjacent to the bank toward Olympia Square. As a small boy, he, Tommy and Jerry would walk back from the Auditorium Theater through this same alley from Andrew Street, just off Olympia Square, after watching John Wayne fight Randolph Scott in "The Spoilers," or "The Perils of Nyoka" or some other fifteen segment serial.

As the oldest brother, he had chased the other two down the alley, playing the part of the white-hatted hero, bringing the black-hatted villains, the evil gold mining commissioner, or any assortment of scary Indians, to justice. When they had been caught, they had been pummeled. Justice had prevailed. In those days, black was black, and white was white. That is, until Tommy had gotten too big for him to handle.

Tommy waved to him from a booth in the bar. On a Saturday evening, the restaurant was only one-quarter filled, like the city itself, its middle-class clientele having deserted it.

Anthony's food was still outstanding over all these years, he thought, as they both ordered scrod with Caesar salad and waited for the restaurant's signature popover rolls and the cheddar cheese and crackers that would accompany their drinks.

"You handled Vinnie perfectly, Tommy, and he did the right thing." They had talked about it previously, but Jack sensed Tommy's uneasiness.

"Jesus, who would have suspected him turning. He was our friend, Jack. I thought I knew him."

393

"He was a traitor, Tommy. That's all he was. A disloyal traitor. Don't think on it too much. What we should think about is those FBI guys and what they have. We're going to have to be more careful. They're not going to drop it."

Tommy nodded.

"I passed by the old neighborhood on the way here tonight. Jesus, what would Ma and Dad think if they were alive today?"

"Every time I come out of my home to the pond I think of the time you pushed Jerry's tricycle into the water."

"I didn't push him, Tom."

Tommy laughed out loud. "So you say. Those were good days. Well, not that particular day," he added sheepishly.

"I remember carrying your sorry ass home from King's Beach when you stepped on the broken Coke bottle. That's what I remember," Jack said.

Tommy grinned at him. "I was only a featherweight then. No problem for you."

"It's good to be out with you, Tom. I debated about even going out tonight. I'm a little tired lately."

"You okay about Courtney?"

"Fine. She's gone. That's it," he said, raising his glass. "Anything new?"

Now was the time to tell him about Rizzo's call. A message from the big man meant a communication from Biggio himself. Tommy looked across at his older brother. He's had enough problems the last few weeks, he thought. Let Jack enjoy the dinner and go home early. He would go to Revere himself.

"No. Nothing at all."

The incessant pounding seemed to come from far away. Was he dreaming? His head cleared a bit, enough for him to realize that the noise was real. He snapped on the lamp and tried to focus on the alarm clock hands. 4:10 it read.

Walking slowly, getting his bearings, Jack found his robe at the foot of the bed and placed it over his T-shirt and shorts. He studied the alarm system buttons next to the door and cut the switch. Then he walked toward the front door, cursing under his breath at whatever was causing this intrusion at such an ungodly hour. He peered through the living room window toward the porch where Ray Horan stood alone, alternating between ringing the bell and hammering at the door, breathing in small, sudden foggy spurts.

On opening the door, he directed his anger at Ray. "Ray, what the hell's the matter?"

"Jack, I..." he paused, standing in the hallway.

"What's wrong?"

"Tommy's dead, Jack."

Jack stopped in his tracks. Was he dreaming? Yes, for sure. He simply had to wake himself up. Yes, that would stop the nightmare from overwhelming his thoughts. He had to come awake and analyze why he would be dreaming such terrible thoughts.

But he was awake, he slowly understood. The cold air that followed Ray into the hall worked on his consciousness, and his friend's words penetrated through the last remnants of his subconsciousness.

"Jack, I'm sorry. I don't know what to say. I..." Ray hesitated, unable to finish the sentence.

"What are you telling me, Ray?" What happened?"

"An hour ago we received a tip from one of the Boston locals you helped in the past. You know Rocco Landetta. He told me that Tommy's body was found in the trunk of a car abandoned on Northern Avenue, near the waterfront."

Jack walked toward the living room, stabbing at the light switch, beckoning Ray to follow him. He sat on the couch, his body thrust forward, now visibly alert. Ray positioned himself in the chair adjacent to the couch, shedding his trenchcoat and placing it on the other chair.

"Tell me what you know, Ray."

"Landetta said a patrol car noticed a Ford Maverick parked in a deserted area near the Massport properties. The plate check indicated it was stolen from some kid over in Arlington a few days ago. The patrol guys observed blood stains around the trunk and popped it."

"He tell you anything about how Tommy looked?"

"Jack, don't ask me that. You don't want to know."

"Answer the fuckin' question, Ray."

Ray sighed deeply. "He had two gunshot wounds in the back of the head. Shot execution style, Landetta said. There are some welts on his face, as if he were punched a few times. He was hog-tied, Jack. His hands and feet together with a rope around his neck."

"Jesus, Mary, and Joseph," Jack said, tears welling in his eyes. He wiped at them with his forefinger. "Anything else?"

"There was a note, Jack."

"A note. Who would leave a note?"

"It was pinned to his sports jacket."

"What did it say?"

"Remember MSG."

"Remember MSG?"

"Cops have no idea what that means so far. Some guy's initials they think. It makes no sense to me."

Jack thought for a moment. "It's not anyone's initials, Ray. The cops could look forever, and they won't find anyone. MSG means Madison Square Garden. It's Connie Ryan, Ray. The message is intended for me. Son of a bitch."

"Jack, I'm staying with you the rest of the night. Just in case..."

"Ray, I had dinner with Tommy earlier tonight. Where was he tonight? I thought, like me, he was going directly home?"

"You came directly home?"

"Yes. Right after dinner."

"He didn't tell you about Rizzo's call?"

"What call?"

"Rizzo called during the day. Said he had a message from the big man. Wanted to see you around midnight to deliver it."

"Tommy never mentioned it. He must have decided to go there himself. Find out what Rizzo knows. Did Tommy ever show there? We need to know."

"Now, you mean?"

"Yes, now. Get to him," Jack commanded.

"I've got Paulie out front and Chris Kiely's out back. I'll be back as soon as I can."

"Ray, what am I going to tell his mother?" Jack suddenly asked. "She'll wonder why I didn't take care of him."

Ray looked at him, surprise registering on his face. "His mother?"

Jack suddenly refocused, coming out of the fog as quickly as he had entered it. "I've got to make preparations for him, Ray. As soon as the sun's up. I need to go to Jerry and Marty and Timmy. And call Bobby." He stood slowly. "I've got to dress, Ray. I thank you for coming by. I know this wasn't easy for you." He embraced Ray and then turned toward the kitchen, envisioning that the longest day of his life was about to begin.

59

The funeral home on Maple Street in Lynn was located just down the street from Manning Bowl, the site of some of Tommy's greatest athletic accomplishments. He lay in a closed casket in a large room just to the right of the front doors. Outside on a beautiful early November evening, a double line snaked along the walk for a distance of over fifty yards as friends from a variety of life situations stood ready to pay final respect at the one-day wake. Football teammates and high school friends mingled with the fight crowd from Boston. Fellow car dealers and customers, neighbors from the Goldfish Pond area stood patiently with strangers from Boston, Somerville, Cambridge -- waterfront workers, loan sharks, gamblers -- all friends of Jack and Tommy Kelly and the cousins.

Inside, Jack stood next to the bier, Marjorie to his right, and in the family greeting line, Jerry and Sheila, Marty, Timmy and Bobby. He listened attentively to each sorrowful expression of condolence, engaged the visitor in conversation and thanked each individual personally for his sign of respect.

Banks of flowers surrounded the oval room on three sides. Directly in front of the coffin ten rows of small wooden chairs were filled, their occupants curiously avoiding the chatter so common to such an event.

It was in the last hour that Father Dolan appeared in the hallway with the new pastor from St. Joseph's, Father Keefe. Moving slowly behind his walker, Father Dolan held on to the young pastor's arm with one hand while advancing the walker with the other. He looked around, seemingly confused, until he saw Jack crossing the room.

"Father Dolan, it's good of you to come," Jack said, extending his hand. "Come sit here with me for a minute," Jack said, pointing to the first row of chairs.

"I must say a prayer for Thomas first, John," Father said, pushing the walker toward the bier.

"Thank you for bringing him, Father Keefe," Jack said.

"He lives with his sister Ellen in Roslindale now, Jack. He seldom leaves the residence, but he called me this morning, asked if I might be able to send transportation. I picked him up myself."

"Will you say the prayers this evening?"

"No. I asked Father Dolan to lead us, and he's pleased to do so."

The old priest made the Sign of the Cross and slowly turned toward them. Father Keefe agilely stepped toward the walker, guiding his predecessor to the seats.

"I'll rest only for the minute, John. Then you must introduce me to your family." He glanced at the receiving line, his hands quivering. "And which of those good looking young men are yours, John?"

"My sons Bob and Tim are next to Jerry, Father."

"And the handsome lad in the dark blue suit?"

"Jerry's son, Marty."

"It's been so many years. I hardly recognize them. They're a fine looking lot, John. I hope they provide you solace in this most difficult time," he said slowly. "Jerry's son reminds me of you, John. Do you remember when I asked you to consider the priesthood? You must have been twelve or thirteen years old. And you had some interest, I recollect."

"That I did, Father. But you know how events can change the course of our lives."

"I know how events changed the course of your life, John," the old priest replied wistfully. "But I'm sorry that you could not stay close to the Church."

"Father..."

"No need to say anything, John. I'm not here to resurrect the past. God loves all his children. Particularly the lamb who went astray. You remember that story from catechism class, John?"

Ray walked toward them from the hallway, his hand extended in greeting to a number of those waiting in the line moving toward the coffin. As he reached Jack, he leaned down to whisper in his ear. "Cardoza and Rizzo are in the hallway."

Jack nodded in acknowledgment and turned to Father Dolan. "Father, please excuse me for five minutes." He signaled Jerry, who stood waiting for the couple kneeling in front of the coffin to stand and approach the line.

"Jerry, would you please introduce Father Dolan to the family?"

"Gerald, my boy." The old priest greeted him warmly.

"Father, thank you for coming," Jerry said embracing the priest as he stood.

Jack crossed into the hallway, nodding his recognition to those waiting. He observed Cardoza and Rizzo halfway back to the front door, whispering to one another, unmindful of his approach.

"Salvy, Nick, thank you for coming," he smiled, offering his hand. "Join me across the hall for a moment," he said, pointing to the small room.

"Jack, my friend, I don't know what to say," Cardoza began as they entered the room. "Such a tragic happening. I only hope that the memories of the wonderful times you shared with him can help sustain you in this time of loss."

"Thanks, my friend," Jack replied. "Please sit with me for a moment." He pointed to the blue velvet couch and accompanying chairs.

"Do you need anything? Anything we can do?"

"Thank you, Nick. No. We haven't had much time to even think with all the necessary preparations for the funeral and all. At the moment we're fine."

Two days ago Ray had called Rizzo as soon as he left Jack's house. Rizzo claimed to know nothing about Tommy's whereabouts that evening. Yes, he had phoned Tommy, and yes, he had a message for Jack from Gennaro Biggio, but neither Jack nor Tommy had shown. Like them, he was shocked to hear of Tommy's death and would immediately enlist all his sources to seek information. He had called back late Sunday. No one reported seeing Tommy that Saturday night, and no one knew anything about who might have committed the murder. He would continue to push hard, but to date, nothing was forthcoming.

Jack studied Rizzo carefully. What did he know of the message pinned to Tommy's chest? Jack guessed that he probably knew nothing about it, or else he would never have appeared here tonight. Ryan probably left it without anyone else knowing he had -- a message for Jack's eyes only. Did that mean that Ryan had acted alone? He doubted it. And what was it Gennaro Biggio had wanted?

"What about the message for me, Nick?"

There was not a glimmer of light in Rizzo's eyes. Messages were clearly not on his mind.

"Message?"

"From Gennaro, Nick."

"Oh, yeah. He wishes to see you sometime soon. He wants your take on the FBI's recent activities. He's asking a number of us the same question. Wants to be sure he has everyone's best thinking as to where we are with them."

Jack nodded, "Tell him I'll call him as soon as I can after all this is over. Ask him if he can give me just a few days."

"Of course."

Ray gestured to him from the doorway. "Please come in and join us for the prayers," Jack asked them. "They're waiting for me."

In the early morning heavy dark gray clouds scudded across the sky. A light rain began to fall as the funeral procession pulled away from Maple Street on the way to Union Street and St. Joseph's Church. Jack, Marjorie, Jerry, and Sheila sat together in the rear of the limousine, directly behind the lead car bearing Tommy's body.

Jack insisted that they follow the convoluted route he had mapped to the church. From Maple Street they climbed the hill toward Manning Bowl so that Tommy could pass by, for the final time, the huge stadium. They turned left down Western Avenue over to Chestnut Street, heading into East Lynn, following Chestnut to Fayette Street and their boyhood home. Finally, they filed slowly down Union Street to the high steepled brick church.

The long line halted in front of the church, the rain now coming in renewed force, whipping the faces of the large throng as they climbed the steps. As the family members followed the casket down the long central aisle, Jack surveyed the packed pews carefully. Cardoza sat on the aisle about halfway down, Rizzo beside him. Bobby Latimer, sitting three rows in front of them, nodded silently as Jack met his gaze. To his right, near the front, Petey Santangelo and Gus Regan sat. He saw newspapermen everywhere.

The newspapers had treated the murder in different ways. The local papers played up Tommy, the Lynn businessman and former great city athlete, victim of an unknown assailant. In Boston, emphasis had been placed on Tommy's boxing career, but there were also strong suggestions of his criminal association, and a life led on the edge.

He summoned Ray to his seat just before the Mass began. "Have Timmy and Marty meet you and me tonight at six at my place."

"Tonight, Jack?"

"Tonight. That's what I said," Jack eyed him sullenly.

He tried to listen to Father Keefe's eulogy, in particular, but he could not concentrate. He drifted between memories of Tommy and the plan that he had been formulating for the past two days. Whatever words of comfort the young pastor intoned meant little to him. There was no veil of comfort to be found here. His brother was dead. He would comfort himself through

403

his own loving memories in the months ahead. He would heal himself as he had in the past.

When the service ended, he took his place alongside the coffin. He had refused the use of professional pallbearers. His brother would be escorted to his final resting place by Jerry, Timmy, Marty, Bobby, Ray, and himself. Hoisting the casket on their shoulders, they moved slowly down the aisle and the long descent to Union Street. How often he and Tommy had bounded down these same steps, racing out of Sunday Mass to run home and change clothes for the football game on Laundry Hill. Today, for this final race, they would go forth slowly, savoring their final moments together.

At the cemetery, as Father Keefe delivered the final prayer, Tommy's body was lowered into the ground beside his mother and father. The craftsman had completed his assignment on time, having worked day and night to finish the new gravestone. The inscription was now perfectly framed on the slab.

"Thomas F. Kelly
October 28, 1937 - November 3, 1982
A Champion Always and in All Ways"

60

"Tonight, Dad?" Timmy asked quietly as they sat in the living room of his father's home on Lynn Shore Drive.

Marty stood against the fireplace, still dressed in the dark blue suit he had worn to the funeral Mass that morning. Ray Horan peered out the window, observing Paulie Cronin in the car across the street and Chris Kiley in the deepening shadows on the front porch.

Dressed in a white turtleneck and blue trousers, Jack studied his son, his mind completely focused on this evening's work. "That's right. Tonight. Their defenses will be down. They would never assume that we would take any action tonight."

"There's no better time than tonight," Marty agreed, tossing his cigarette into the fireplace.

"Who's they, Dad?" Timmy asked.

Ray turned from the window. "Ryan acted alone, Jack. It's personal all the way."

Marty shook his head. Observing him, Jack asked, "What's your take, Marty?"

"Ryan had to have help from two directions. First, someone in New York had to give permission for him to move against Tommy. Probably the Don -- Gianelli -- that he works for in Manhattan. Then on this end, someone -- Biggio, Cardoza, somebody -- had to give an okay. And I don't think they were looking for Tommy, Uncle Jack. I think it was probably you, and they settled for Tommy."

Nodding his agreement, Jack looked admiringly at his nephew.

"What about Rizzo, Dad?" Timmy asked.

"He's in it up to his teeth. He set it up for Ryan, thinking I would show to hear what Biggio wanted. Tommy was there all right, and Ryan..." He stopped himself, not wanting to think about that evening.

"What's the plan, Jack?" Marty asked.

"We pay Rizzo a visit tonight."

"What about Cardoza?" Ray asked.

"He's in this up to his eyebrows is my guess. But we'll find out for sure tonight. Above all, we need to find out where everybody is, especially Ryan," Jack replied.

"Jack, you sure of this? A move on Rizzo...we're talking about Biggio's nephew?" Ray asked.

Jack nodded. "That we are, Ray. And we're talking about my brother. You with me in this?" he asked gently.

"You know I am, Jack," Ray replied.

"Then all of you -- let's sit at the dining room table, and I'll lay out the plan."

Marty elbowed Timmy as they entered the dining room. "Didn't I tell you he'd have a fuckin' plan?" he whispered.

Nick Rizzo felt the effects of the long day. That never ending fucking funeral mass for that Irish pug followed by the visit to his invalid mother in the nursing home in Beverly and then the drive back to the North End for dinner with his lieutenants. He had enjoyed that part, the camaraderie of close friends at the European Restaurant, the manicotti, the vintage wines. He had finally relaxed. Unfortunately, he had drunk too much. Better to be aware of the fact and drive cautiously, he thought, as he turned off the Northeast Expressway in Revere to Sargent Street, just under the main highway. The rain had stopped in the early evening, but the roads were slick now that the temperature had dropped.

He turned into the semi-circular driveway of his one-level ranch, cursing the fact that every fuckin' house on the street looked alike. He always worried about driving into someone else's carport some night when he had too much to drink. The clicker to raise his carport door probably opened half the fuckin' roll-up doors on the street.

He made sure the engine was killed before he lowered the door. Another worry with these fucking one slabbers. Some night he might fall asleep at the wheel with the door down and the engine still running.

Stepping out of the car, he entered the kitchen through the small door on the side wall of the garage. Feeling for the kitchen light switch, he almost stumbled over the entryway. At his touch light flooded the kitchen, and he walked more confidently toward the living room. He discarded his topcoat over a kitchen chair as he turned the corner and hit the switch.

"Hello, Nick," Jack said from the living room chair, the .38 in his right hand, pointed at Rizzo.

"Jack! What the fuck are you doing here?"

"Sit down, Nick. Make yourself comfortable," Ray said from the edge of the dining room, making sure that Nick observed the .38 in his hand as well.

As he sat, Rizzo looked at Jack. "What the hell is this?"

Jack leaned forward in the chair, his eyes completely focused on Rizzo. "What is this, you ask Nick? I'll tell you. You're going to die tonight. That's what this is. We're not going to be able to reach any mutual accommodation on that matter. So don't even think about it. The only issue before us is how you die."

He stood up, walking slowly up to Rizzo's chair, hovering over him, his gaze never once leaving Rizzo's eyes. "Let me explain the options. You answer my questions honestly, and I assure you a quick end, a head shot, no suffering, and that's the end of life. Screw around with me, Nick, and we'll do it the old-fashioned Irish way. We'll take off your sticks first and while you're down, I'll shoot your balls off. Then we'll move to your gut and leave you here, bloodying up this pretty carpet, taking a good half hour to die. You with me?"

Nick tried to regain his composure. He fought to shake the fear, feeling that he could play hard ball with anyone, and there was no way this Irish prick could outthink him. He needed to calm his nerves, to gain time, to use his wits.

"Jack, I'm asking you to be reasonable. What are you talking about? I know you're upset about Tommy's death, but you turn against your friend? I don't want to have to tell Gennaro..."

Jack stared him down. "Fuck you and Gennaro, too, Nicky."

"I don't really think you mean that," Rizzo replied, trying to remain calm.

Jack continued to stare at him. "Let me tell you the difference between you, Gennaro and me, Nick. The two of you want to live. There's nothing Gennaro, Salvy, you or any other Mafioso can do to me. You see, Nicky, I don't give a shit. One way or the other -- life or death -- I don't care. And when you don't care, you have absolutely nothing to lose. Follow me, Nicky?"

"Then think about your family," Nick answered slowly. "You think you can kill me and there won't be repercussions?"

"But that's not for you to concern yourself with, Nick," Jack responded.

It was at that precise moment that Nick Rizzo realized he was going to die.

"So answer me carefully, Nicky. I'd much prefer to end your life the Irish way."

Rizzo sighed. "What do you want to know?"

"Who killed Tommy?"

"Connie Ryan."

"Where is he now?"

Rizzo hesitated for a very long moment before answering. "He's here. He's at the hotel at Logan Airport. The Ramada. Under the name of Richard Fallon."

"Tommy was the target?"

"No," Nick shook his head. "You were. But Tommy showed. Ryan decided to go ahead anyway."

Jack nodded. "So far, so good, Nicky. Why is he still at Logan?"

Rizzo answered now more rapidly, trying to demonstrate his newly found spirit of cooperation. "He's staying in the room for a few days. He never leaves. Room Service only. He's letting some time pass. He still wants you, Jack. Unless the New York dons call him off, he's coming after you."

"I figured New York set Ryan loose. Is Biggio involved?"

Nick looked to the ceiling, as if it might provide him with a response.

"Can I smoke, Jack?" he finally responded.

"Give him a cigarette," Jack said, motioning to Ray.

Ray walked forward, tapping a cigarette from his pack, his eyes riveted on Rizzo, as if daring him to make an untimely move.

"Yeah," Nick replied. "It's coming right from the top. Mario Gianelli of Manhattan, Ryan's sponsor, requested the go-ahead. Forelli called Gennaro. He passed on the instruction to back-up Ryan. Provide him with whatever he needed."

"Whatever he needed?" Jack asked, his voice rising.

"Meaning weapons, a place to stay."

"What about Cardoza?"

Rizzo nodded quickly. "Cardoza's always wanted you gone. He thinks Gennaro's taken too long to move on you."

Jack leaned forward into Rizzo's face. "Nothing else you can tell me, Nicky?"

Rizzo inhaled the cigarette and held the smoke for a few seconds before exhaling. "I've told you all I know! How about a fuckin' break here, Jack! Give me a chance, for Christ's sake," he pleaded.

"I appreciate your cooperation, Nicky. I really do. But now I need you to make two calls. Call the hotel at Logan. If Ryan answers, tell him you're sending someone with important information from New York and Biggio. Something that can't be relayed over the telephone. The person will knock four times on the door at exactly 10 P.M., using his alias."

"What else?" Nick asked.

"Let's take care of the first one, Nicky. And Nicky," he paused, "do this very carefully. Remember what I said earlier."

Rizzo stood and walked to the wall phone in the kitchen. He dialed and waited for the ring. Jack approached him, positioning himself at Rizzo's shoulder. "Yes. Room 403. Mr. Richard Fallon."

A long pause.

"Richard, I have some instructions from our friends in New York and Rhode Island. My person will be there exactly at 10 P.M. He'll knock four times on the door. He'll use your name."

Another pause.

"Yes. 10 P.M. Good-bye."

"That was perfect, Nicky," Jack said. "Now one more call."

"To?"

"Your cousin in Bristol. Rose Biggio."

"Now wait a minute, Kelly!" Rizzo exclaimed.

"Nick, I only want to know where Gennaro is tonight. Is he home, or is he off visiting his whore in Providence? That's all I need to know. Either way you have my word no harm will come to his wife."

Rizzo moved to the phone once again. "How do you know about the girl friend?" he asked as he dialed.

"I make it my business to know, Nick."

"Hello? Rose, how's my favorite cousin? Fine. I'm fine. Everything is all right. I have a little cold, is all."

A pause.

And then he spoke almost too rapidly. "Rose, is Gennaro home tonight? Do you know where he is? No, No. Don't worry. Let him know I called. I'll try again tomorrow morning. Fine. See you."

Rizzo placed the phone in its cradle and turned toward Jack. "He's away on business in Providence. He won't be back until early morning he told her."

"You did real good, Nicky." Jack pulled the .38 from his shoulder holster and attached the silencer to its barrel.

Sweat broke over Rizzo's upper lip. "Jack, please. Don't do this. I was only following orders."

Jack shook his head. "You lured my brother to Beachmont, Nicky. You as good as killed him yourself."

"Don't do this, Jack. I can square everything with Biggio and the others. I can. You need me. If you don't want that, give me a head start out of here. I'll get lost, I promise!" he half screamed.

"Nicky, remember I said earlier that if you cooperated I'd make this quick?"

"Yes, you did," Rizzo sobbed.

"I lied," Jack said, aiming for his right kneecap and shooting. Rizzo staggered, clutching for his knee so that he didn't see the second shot coming. It hit him in the left kneecap, causing him to fall forward to a fetal position groaning in pain. Ray stuffed a handkerchief into his mouth, gagging him.

Jack stood above him. "Did you hog-tie my brother, Nicky? No? But you stood there and watched him die. Didn't you?" He fired again, this time toward the groin area where Nicky's hands moved as soon as the pistol erupted.

"Take a look at the street," he instructed Ray. "Make sure there's no neighborhood activity."

Ray parted the living room blinds and studied the scene. Turning away, he shook his head at Jack. "Just Timmy sitting out there in the car. Nothing else."

Leaning down toward Rizzo, Jack lifted the .38 again and shot him in the head. He stepped away, Rizzo's body now perfectly still, a small trickle of blood meandering down his temple.

They exited the house through the front door one at a time, a minute apart. As Ray walked toward the car, Timmy stepped out and moved around the front to the passenger seat side. Ray sat behind the wheel and started the car. Jack exited from the garage, leaving the carport door up. He looked back to be sure that the house lights were off and then walked down the asphalt driveway.

"Everything go all right?" Timmy asked as Jack sat in the back seat.

"Couldn't be better. Number one down."

"Marty should have reached Rhode Island by now," Jack said, as he leaned toward Timmy. "Remember he'll call you

411

from Providence at exactly 10:30 P.M. You have to be back to your place by then. You have to have taken care of your end by then. Let him know Biggio is in Providence, not Bristol. Tell him I'm depending on him."

Ray kept the lights off as he waited to pull away from the curb. Timmy turned toward his father as Jack handed him the keys. "Remember -- leave the gun, right Tim?"

"I'm all set, Dad," he said as he exited the car.

Ray waited until they were halfway down Sargent Road before he turned on the lights. As they headed toward Logan Airport, Jack studied the road ahead. "He won't recognize you, and that will be to our advantage," he said more to himself than to Ray.

61

Turning into the Central Parking Garage at Logan, Ray snapped the ticket from the automatic dispenser and entered the ground floor. He cruised around for a minute or two before locating a spot in the corner nearest the Ramada. He cut the lights, and they sat looking around in the dark for a moment.

Moving to the trunk, Ray lifted the lid as Jack watched for any intrusion by pedestrians on their way to the various terminals. Ray picked up the two Glock nines and placed one in his topcoat pocket and passed the other to Jack along with a silencer. Together they exited the garage, walking diagonally east toward the Ramada. They quickly separated, Ray crossing to the west, intending to loop around to the front entry, Jack continuing east.

Jack entered the crowded lobby, avoiding eye contact with the convention revelers, acting every bit the part of a businessman on his way back to his room. Proceeding directly to the bank of elevators, he pressed the button for the third floor and stepped inside quickly as the doors slid open. A young couple, lost in each other's eyes, entered with him, but scarcely noticed him. He stepped out to the third floor and walked confidently down the corridor, his topcoat over his arm, just another visitor returning from a night on the town. He observed the pattern of the room numbers and then turned at the end of the corridor, walked back toward the elevator, and the stairwell adjacent to it.

As he climbed the stairs, he glanced at his watch. 9:57 P.M. He opened the door leading to the fourth floor and he looked both ways. From the extreme right, far down the corridor, Ray motioned to him. Jack walked at an even pace past the elevators, noting the room numbers descending door to door as he approached Ray.

Ray pointed to the last door on the left side of the corridor. Good, Jack thought, not too many people would be entering rooms at the very end of the corridor. He pressed back alongside the wall as Ray faced the door and knocked four times.

"Yeah, who is it?" a familiar voice from within asked.

"Mr. Fallon, I'm here for Nick Rizzo," Ray answered, his Glock in his right arm behind his back.

No doubt at that moment Ryan was observing Ray through the eyelet. "Wait a minute," finally came the reply, as the noise of locks turning and a chain rattling filled the air.

As the door opened, Jack eased himself along the wall. When it was a quarter open, Ray smiled disarmingly and advanced. Jack smashed his shoulder heavily against the now half open door causing Ryan to fall backward just enough for Ray to gain the advantage.

They stormed into the room as Ryan froze in front of them. "Sit over there," Ray ordered, as Jack entered behind him, his Glock in hand.

"Check the other rooms," Jack ordered.

Ray moved to the bathroom and then to the small bedroom beyond. "Nothing," he said evenly.

From the lone easy chair Ryan stared at Jack, hatred in his eyes. He was dressed in an open necked white dress shirt and dark brown slacks. On the couch behind him lay his light brown sports coat. He glanced furtively toward it, obviously having been lulled to sleep by Rizzo's call. He said nothing.

"I received your message the other day, Connie," Jack said.

"Fuck you, Kelly," he finally spoke.

"Let's make it quick, Jack," Ray said. "There's too many people around here."

"You couldn't let it lie, could you, Connie?" Jack said. "Even after all these years."

"No, I couldn't and neither would you have in the end. There's no difference between us, Kelly."

Jack stood with his back to the door, facing Ryan. "Yes there is, Connie. You're dead, and I'm going to be pissing on your grave for years to come."

He raised the Glock and shot Ryan twice in the stomach. Reeling forward, Ryan broke his fall with his hands. Advancing quickly, Jack motioned to Ray to help him lift Ryan, not noticing Ryan's hand moving to the ankle holster. Crossing the room, Ray yelled, "Look out," in time for Jack to raise his knee and smash it against Ryan's face. He fell backward, moaning, his hands trying to cover the flow of blood from his stomach.

Together they lifted him, walking swiftly toward the sliding glass door at the rear of the room. With one hand Ray released the lock and slid the door open, the cold and the wind overwhelming them.

"Have a nice trip home to Hell's Kitchen, Connie," Jack said. "This really is the only way to fly," he added, as he and Ray pitched Ryan over the rail to the roof three stories below.

They quickly closed the door and rearranged the curtain. "Let's get out of here quick, Jack," Ray said. They left the room together, Ray continuing to the stairwell, Jack waiting by the elevator bank. In fewer than two minutes, that seemed more like an eternity, he was descending alone in the cab. At the lobby level Jack headed toward the front door, walking straight ahead. He had long ago learned that if you averted your eyes from others', they would not focus on you. He walked back to the Central Garage, entered the car, and placed the Glock under the driver's seat.

At the toll gate, he waited in line, being sure to stay in the busiest of the three lanes, intent to avoid talking with the attendant if at all possible. "Three dollars, please" a grizzled old veteran collector requested. He passed the correct change and proceeded along the exit road toward the Ramada. Just beyond the hotel, he stopped near the sidewalk for Ray.

"Two down, two to go," he said to Ray as he drove out of the airport, heading north toward Revere and Lynn. He glanced at his watch. "Marty must be at Federal Hill by now."

Timmy remembered what Tommy had said about creatures of habit. They had been spending a summer weekend on Glendon Beach at the Cape, just the three of them -- Marty, Tommy, and him. It had been part of that long period of time in the '70s when Tommy had taken them under his wing, when he had posed difficult problems to them and had guided them to right solutions. So often he would talk to them about life, about the complexity of decision making and make the answer seem so simplistic when you took the time to think about options.

As he exited the Callahan tunnel and drove Nick Rizzo's car into Boston, he remembered they had been sitting on the deck drinking Cokes, Tommy having weaned himself from the booze, winning the battle of his life by becoming absorbed in teaching them.

"You have to avoid regular routines," Tommy was saying as they sat in the long-backed newly painted wooden slat chairs. "You take Jack now. You guys notice him -- how he absolutely never regularizes his routines. Where does he meet people? Here, there, and everywhere, right? Where does he eat? No special place. Have you observed that?

"Above all, avoid being a creature of habit. Don't let anybody pinpoint you like we can those fuckin' wops who sit every night in the same clubs drinking their wine and peeing it out the same time every night. Change it up, guys -- don't throw all fast balls, or they'll eventually take you and I don't mean downtown, I mean just plain fuckin' down."

Timmy turned into Prince Street and parked forty yards up and across from the Social Club. He looked up and down the street, but there were only a very few pedestrians about, the usual bustle of the North End greatly subdued on a weekday evening at 9:50P.M.

A creature of habit. For sure Salvatore Cardoza fit that description. Every weekday night at exactly 10P.M. he would exit the club, walk either alone or with one of his many accomplices back toward Haymarket Square toward his apartment on Tremont Street. Jack had planned that he would be here because the old guinea was into rituals and would conduct his business and any social amenities on schedule.

Timmy tugged at the white elasticized gloves and very carefully picked up Rizzo's .38 from the passenger seat. If Jack were right, Cardoza would be leaving any minute now. He started the engine, then lowered the window, keeping the lights off for the moment.

Across the street he saw no signs of activity outside the club, and then suddenly the front door opened and Cardoza appeared with another person on the top step. As they descended the three steps, Timmy donned the ski mask and then turned on the lights, being sure to give a left directional as he pulled away from the curb. Just another customer leaving one of the restaurants.

He drove slowly down the street, watching to see if anyone else would be in the vicinity. Now coming up on the two pedestrians, Cardoza closest to the street, he stopped, but not abruptly. As Cardoza glanced toward the car, Timmy shot him three times in the head and then dropped the .38 out the window. The old man accompanying him ran into the shadows of a storefront, and as he did Timmy stepped on the accelerator.

He smiled to himself as he approached Atlantic Avenue. If only Tommy had been here to see his work.

Naked in bed, Gennaro Biggio sipped the red wine slowly, savoring its flavor. He lay there pleased with the wine and more pleased with himself. That cow at home could not excite him enough to cause an erection, but Maureen, as always, had been patient with him. Granted it sometimes took a half hour to get it hard, but he attributed that to her not rushing nature, to her wishing him full enjoyment, to her obvious pleasure in stimulating him. He had then mounted her quickly, spending himself within ten seconds.

He placed the glass on the bedroom table and glanced at the alarm clock. 12:35. In a few minutes he needed to dress and prepare for the trip home. Should he wake her for another round or let her sleep? He turned and rubbed his penis on her back side. She seemed in deep sleep so he decided to defer.

He stood beside the bed, stretched, and walked across to the living room window. Two stories below he spotted his '82 El Dorado across the street. Good, still intact, too, he thought. With the way teenage crime was going in Providence, he considered himself fortunate. The young people today had no respect for authority, not even for the head of the New England Mafia. If he roasted a few of their balls on a skewer, they would shape up, he thought.

He suddenly felt old, but was seventy-one really old? How many men his age could keep up with him? Not many, he thought. He smoothed down his white widespread collar and tugged at the plain green tie. His new black suit had cost him a fortune, but clothes made the man, and he must always dress impeccably.

Walking slowly toward the bed, he leaned over to kiss Maureen on the forehead. She flinched, but did not awaken. He moved through the living room, proceeding to the hallway where he found his traditional cashmere outer coat and his cane. Bracing himself for the cold night, he turned off the lights, darkening the entire apartment.

From the street Marty had stared at the lights in the second floor apartment for almost two hours now. Tonight he was riveted on his assignment and on nothing else. He was cold, but there was no way he would start the engine and call attention to himself. In the last hour, only an occasional vehicle had come down the street.

He thought back over the last few hours. Paulie Cronin and he had left I-95 in Pawtucket at School Street and cruised down Pond Street in the area around McCoy Stadium looking for an isolated car. Luckily, they found the '79 Pontiac Bonneville in the shadow of the ballpark. It had been easy for Paulie to boost the car. He had then followed Paulie back down Pond Street to the Memorial Hospital of Rhode Island visitors' parking lot, where he parked directly behind the Bonneville so that Paulie

418

could replace the Rhode Island plates with the clean Massachusetts plates.

From there they had returned to I-95, Marty now driving the Bonneville, Paulie following in his Ford Mustang. At Providence they took the Atwells Avenue exit, turning left back over the highway, and drove into the center of the city, heading for the public bank of phones across from the Fleet Bank at Kennedy Plaza. Marty parked and waited the five minutes until 10:30, Paulie positioned directly behind him, and then rang Timmy's apartment in Marblehead.

"Hello."

"Which road leads to Rome, cousin?"

"Providence."

"See you later." He hung up quickly and signaled to Paulie, pointing to the ground.

When they arrived at Federal Hill, Paulie swung in front of him, parking a hundred yards beyond the 40 Federal Street address. For close to two hours, then, Marty had waited in the cold at the corner of Federal and Bradford, memories of Tommy intersecting with his emotional high and his attention to the moment. He thought of Tommy's tutelage of his nephews. "Head shots always, unless you want to slow things down. Too many wear vests today, but no one's invented a cover for the head yet. Go for the head 99 percent of the time."

He remembered the time when he had been drinking heavily, both he and Timmy right after high school in the days when they were rebellious, unfocused, itching for recognition. Tommy had understood that, having conquered his own problems with alcohol. On what Marty remembered as a perfect summer night in the '70's Tommy had sat with his nephews in Dennisport, explaining the harm liquor had caused him, advising not insisting, cajoling not ordering, making his point without lecturing.

Suddenly, from above the lights went out. He watched the front door for what seemed an eternity before a slow, shadowy figure moved down the front steps, heading for the Cadillac across the street.

419

Urging the car to life, Marty waited until the elderly man had stepped into the street before edging away from the curb, his lights on. He closed the distance rapidly, the old man in the brown cashmere topcoat curiously looking toward him, a look of horror slowly spreading across his face as he realized the intent.

He was halfway across the street before he tried to run back toward the building. By then, it was too late. The Bonneville smashed full force into him, lifting him on its bumper, throwing him some ten yards from the point of impact. Marty then drove ahead past the point where Paulie waited.

They were both careful to stay within the speed limit as they drove around the block back to Atwells Avenue. In the early morning hours only two or three cars were parked along the nearly deserted street. Marty parked the stolen Pontiac in a legal spot under the Pineapple Archway spanning the street and stepped out just as Paulie came abreast.

62

Don Gianelli loved his morning constitutional, especially whenever he was at his apartment near the Park. Although aware that a Mafia boss should make every effort to vary his routine, he, nevertheless, thoroughly enjoyed the half hour walk along Central Park West. He had just returned when the telephone rang.

"Mario?" a soft voice asked after he had answered.

"Yes?"

"Is this line safe?"

"Absolutely. It's checked by our technicians once a week, just yesterday as a matter of fact," he responded confidently.

"Have you heard the news?" Michael Forelli inquired calmly.

"What news?"

"It has come apart, Mario. Do you remember my concerns in the Boston Irish matter?" He paused, waiting for a response.

"Kelly?" Gianelli answered. "But Ryan said he would handle it."

"He handled it all right, my friend. Ryan is dead."

"Connie Ryan dead?" Gianelli sat down in the leather chair beside the telephone, shocked at what he was hearing.

"He was shot and thrown off a building at Logan Airport. Read the morning papers, Mario. Unfortunately, this ugly vendetta has spread its wings. Gennaro Biggio is also dead. In Providence last evening, struck by a hit and run driver."

Gianelli pinched his nose between his thumb and forefinger. His head throbbed. "I don't believe it," was all he could say.

"There's more, Mario. Salvatore Cardoza, Biggio's man in Boston, is also dead, and his associate was murdered outside of Boston -- Rizzo, the relative of Biggio's. Four people in one night, Mario. On the evening of Kelly's brother's funeral."

"I don't know what to say, Michael," Gianelli responded. "We'll retaliate."

"No, my friend. There will be no retaliation -- at least not for now. We need to learn exactly what happened. There are many questions yet to be answered. For one, Cardoza may have been shot by Rizzo. His gun was found at the scene, and an observer identified his car at the scene."

Gianelli sat stunned, listening to the calm words of the don of dons. His manner belied the inferences behind them. He, Don Mario Gianelli, had advanced the cause of his associate, Connie Ryan. He, therefore, was responsible for this chain of events. If there was to be retaliation, he could conceivably be the target.

"The arrangements went wrong from the beginning. When Ryan killed the wrong brother, I should have called an end to the whole matter then," Forelli continued.

Again, the words muted the real message. He, Don Mario, should have called off Ryan when Tommy Kelly was killed.

"And now, my friend, we have called much attention to ourselves in what is already a difficult period for us. Our colleagues won't be pleased."

"We cannot handle one stupid Irisher, Michael?"

"You didn't hear me, Mario? The matter is concluded. I'll call a mutual friend in Boston and arrange for Kelly to meet with me personally. It's now my problem to correct. 'The stupid Irisher,' as you call him, appears to be much brighter than some of the dim light bulbs that would pull him down. Hopefully, we can end these long-standing animosities and return to business."

Gianelli felt a massive headache forming. "I'm sorry for all of this, Michael. Yes, that's the way to proceed. Is there anything I can do?" he pleaded.

Forelli responded coldly, without feeling. "Nothing, Mario. It's my fault, you know. I should have been more cautious in agreeing to your initial request. I did not follow my natural instincts. You've done enough already," the ominous voice said. And then he hung up.

Three days later, Pete Halloran sat back in his chair blowing smoke rings into the air, his eyes riveted on his creations, his attention these last few seconds far removed from the two FBI agents sitting across from him.

"Well?" Billy Quinn asked.

"Well, I'm not positive and we don't have all the evidence analyzed yet," Halloran finally said. "Look, with Rizzo, the Revere locals found nothing at the scene. Nada. No evidence. He or they -- the killers -- wore gloves. The place is clean."

"Jesus, are they fuckin' blind or what?" Quinn said. "The fucker was shot in each kneecap, in the balls, in his head. Did they need to leave a bottle of Guinness before the fuckin' locals can determine an Irish signature? It was Kelly, all right."

Halloran cast a disgusted look at Quinn.

"Well, they could go out and arrest every Irishman they come across, but maybe, just maybe, Cardoza's people took revenge and made it look like an Irish hit," Halloran responded.

"Bullshit," Quinn said. "And what about the New York guy at the airport? Who's handling that hit?"

"The State Police have jurisdiction at Logan, but we were on the scene as well. Connie Ryan is connected to La Cosa Nostra. He's high up in the Gianelli family, according to our New York sources. Former Westie from Hell's Kitchen."

Matt Folan paced the second floor room at police headquarters on Berkeley Street, listening to the exchange. He stopped for a moment and focused on Halloran.

"What's a New York hood doing at Logan holed up in a hotel?"

Halloran shrugged his shoulders. "How should I know? Waiting for a plane, maybe."

"He could have done Rizzo for Cardoza's people. Remember Rizzo's gun was found at the scene of Cardoza's shooting," Folan conjectured. "What were the times of death -- approximately?"

"We think they all occurred -- Ryan, Rizzo, Cardoza -- between 9-11 P.M. It's very difficult. We're all trying to figure out what happened first and who did what to whom," Halloran replied.

"What do your Providence guys say about Biggio's death?" Halloran asked.

"They don't see any connection to the three here," Folan replied. "They theorize some kid stole a car in Pawtucket, went joy riding to Providence, and ran the old prick over as he was leaving his girl friend's home on Federal Hill. They arrested a kid who claims he boosted the car at Atwells Avenue, not in Pawtucket. Claims he had nothing to do with hitting old Gennaro. The car has plenty of dents to prove otherwise."

Quinn fished in his pocket for the pack of Camels. "We're just not adding this up right. Three mob guys don't die on the same night, for Christ's sake! In some way, they are all connected to Kelly, no fuckin' doubt in my mind. There's too much coincidence here."

"On the same night he buries his own brother? Bullshit. It's a New York - New England Mafia beef, Billy is what it is. That's my best guess at this point. Ryan's Irish, but he's right up there high with the guineas. Kelly's smart, not stupid. He depends on the Mafia to let him run. In that case, you don't arrange to kill the New England Mafia head and the local Mafioso. Not if you want to live, that is," Folan said emphatically.

"Well, there's one sure thing," Quinn offered.

"What's that?" Halloran asked.

"Someone's doing some good work for us good guys."

Two days later, Jack Kelly prepared for the most difficult meeting of his life. He had asked Timmy and Marty to come by for dinner. He had to prepare them, although, if he was correct, they would have some inkling regarding the purpose of the meeting.

He stirred the spaghetti sauce, assuring an even simmer, and then placed the small salad plates on the kitchen table. Everything looked in good order. He opened the refrigerator door, making sure there was plenty of beer and soft drinks.

When they arrived together, he brought them into the kitchen. Mixing a VO and ginger ale for himself at the counter, he pointed to the refrigerator. "Help yourselves."

"How you doing, Dad?" Timmy asked, placing an arm around him as Jack sat down.

In his nervous state, Jack really didn't hear the question. "Sit down here, Tim. Marty, you just want the Coke? Your brother go back to Hollywood?"

"Yesterday, Dad. He stayed with Ma for a few days, but he's about to begin that new movie, and the soap's being produced out there now. Didn't you see him yesterday?"

"Yeah. In the morning," Jack replied nervously, not looking at either one of them.

"Something the matter, Jack?" Marty asked.

"Not really. I just want to review these last few days with you two. Talk a little bit, too, about our next moves."

Marty grinned across the table at his uncle. "That was some plan, Jack," he said with admiration in his voice. "Some plan. Four of the bastards down in one evening."

"The newspapers aren't making much of a connection among the four," Timmy said. "They make Biggio out to be an accident while giving him the strongest play. They..."

"I heard from New York, from the don of dons, Michael Forelli," Jack interjected.

"From Forelli?" Marty couldn't believe his ears.

"That's right. He wants to meet me in New York next week. He says this can all be resolved amicably."

"You believe him, Dad? Why would the big man get involved in this?"

"He said something about errors having been made, and, of course, to protect business investments as well. But there could be other reasons. We need to prepare, that's why I wanted to see you two."

"You going?" Timmy asked.

"There's no choice, Tim. Forelli calls you to a meeting, you go."

"You always have some choices, Jack," Marty said.

Jack stood and moved to the stove. Stirring the sauce, he then used the tongs to place the steaming pasta on a large oval plate. He poured the sauce over the pasta. "Let it cool for a second."

"What choices?" he finally asked Marty, although he knew the answer as well as Marty did.

"Where does he want to meet?" Marty asked. "You could have some control of that."

Jack smiled at him. "He wanted to meet on Long Island, someplace I never heard of. I told him I would prefer the Staten Island Ferry."

"And he agreed?" Timmy asked, astonished.

"He would agree to show his good faith. It's also a very positive sign," Marty said.

"Yes, it is. There's a good chance everything's on the up and up," Jack replied.

"What about Biggio's people? Cardoza's?" Timmy inquired.

"If Forelli is now involved, then they've all been neutralized, at least until after the meet. But we have to keep our guard up anyway," Jack said.

"Did you tell him you're bringing someone with you, Jack? That's another choice you have," Marty said.

Jack stood and placed the cooled dish on the kitchen table. "You're right. Help yourselves."

"I'm going down there on Thursday. I'm telling no one else about my plans or how I'm getting there, but I'll meet with Forelli at the Ferry in the afternoon. Now, there's some contingency plans I need to go over with the two of you."

And now to the part he had been avoiding. To help himself along, he first mixed another VO and ginger ale. "You should know, because I know, that there's a chance I may never come back from this meeting," he stated as he sat down. "The signs are positive, but you never know. Marty, you and Ray come with me. I want to surprise him, just in case there's any problem. You and Ray will position yourselves in some way in which I'm always in your sight. We'll talk more about it tomorrow. Bring Ray here tomorrow morning for breakfast."

Marty nodded, acknowledging the instructions.

"Now, one other matter. Something could happen to me before the meet. Forelli could feel we're relaxed, vulnerable at this point. I don't believe that, but we need to anticipate any eventuality." He paused making sure he had their attention. "If I go down, what are you two going to do?"

The cousins looked at each other for a moment.

"We still want the meeting with Forelli," Marty answered.

"That's right. It's our only chance to come to a mutual accommodation. You'll need the face-to-face under any circumstances. You must meet to put an end to it all, to ensure all our security."

How to make his most important point? Just be direct, he thought to himself. "Now if something were to happen to me..." he began tentatively.

"Dad, first of all, that's not going to happen. But God forbid something ever did, don't you think Marty and I have talked about it?" Timmy interrupted. "We know what to do."

Jack turned, then reached for the spaghetti plate, just to have something to do with his hands. "Is that right? So how about letting your father in on it?" he said, forcing a laugh.

"Marty will head the organization, and Ray and I will back him up," Timmy said emphatically. "We've agreed on that."

Jack knew he looked surprised, particularly with his fork suspended halfway between his dish and his mouth. He did not know what to say. Prior to Tommy's death, he had devised the plan to eliminate his enemies. Only one more piece to be implemented he thought; and that would be taken care of and very soon. But for the last week he had dreaded the thought of this topic. He had spent hours thinking of ways to introduce the matter. His concern lay largely with Timmy. Should he pull him aside and let him know of his decision? Should he wait until they were all together? He had decided on the latter course. He loved his son, took immense pride in his achievements, but knew deep in his heart that Marty was the better choice to both lead his organization and deal with their enemies.

He now realized he had underestimated both of them. Easy to do, after all, they were his son and his nephew. In his mind, therefore, they would never be ready to assume command. They were more than ready, but he simply hadn't been able to accept that fact, that is, until now. For a year Tommy had been indicating what all the others around them had perceived -- Marty was a leader to rally behind. And now, like real leaders, they had taken the decision upon themselves, anticipating this moment, alleviating the tension for him.

"You two have discussed this?" he finally said.

"Marty's the right choice if we have to come to that point, Dad. I know it, and I accept it. I love him like a brother."

The Irish Corsicans, Jack thought. Inseparable, fiercely loyal to one another, their youthful irrational tendencies now subdued, tempered by their newfound ability in the last year or two to care about those dependent on them. For a quick moment he thought of Tommy. They were both fortunate, he thought. Through the Corsicans, both he and Tommy would have life extended.

Jack stood and moved to a position between them, bending forward so that he could place an arm around each. "You have two brothers, Tim, and I have three sons." He first kissed Tim on the cheek and then Marty.

They both rose to embrace Jack. They stood there together for the longest time, relishing a moment in life unknown to most, when love combines with fealty to forge a bond that even death cannot sever.

On Monday night the handsome young man with the cropped black hair and the contrasting pale features walked confidently into the bar on Blue Hill Avenue. He had about him that look peculiar to Irishmen new to the country -- a grin for one and all, a general heartiness coupled with a basic shyness. He noted that ninety percent of the clientele were Black, and that all ninety percent would know his purpose in walking into the smoke-filled room.

From the rear Roland looked up from his poker hand -- two fives weren't going to take him too far anyway -- and whispered softly to the table in general and no one in particular, "Look what just rolled in."

Bobby Latimer turned to look back at the bar and stared for a long moment at the tall, muscular youth dressed in gray sweats. "Deal me out," he said to Roland as he pushed away from the table.

"What will it be?" the bartender asked.

"Give me a shot and a bottle of Bud," the Irisher answered as Bobby Latimer approached him.

"Charge that round to my account, Stevie," he said.

"That's real generous of you, Mister."

"Name's Bobby Latimer. This here's my place," he said extending his hand.

"Patrick Regan, Mr. Latimer. And I thank you for this."

"You new to Boston, Patrick?" Latimer asked as he signaled to the barkeep.

"Now how could you have guessed that?" Patrick asked, his brogue coming through strongly.

"I'm a mind reader, Patrick, is what I am."

"Then you know I want to return the favor and pay for that one," Patrick said as Stevie set down the scotch and water.

Bobby Latimer smiled at him and hoisted his glass. "Patrick, you have any idea what kind of place this is?" he asked, studying him.

"Indeed I do, Mr. Latimer. I've been told it's a gay bar by friends."

"Just wanted to be sure you weren't some turnip falling off the truck, like you Irish say," Bobby grinned.

"Far from that, far from that."

"Where you from?" Bobby asked.

"Dublin."

429

"Just off the boat, if not the truck, huh, Patrick?"

Bobby eyed their reflections in the long mirror behind the bar. He glanced over at Roland who winked back at him. "You comin' back to the fuckin' game or not, Bobby?"

Latimer stared at him for a long second but didn't answer. Some day soon he would have to kick that dumb nigger's ass around a bit so that his brain could start functioning.

"Another round, Patrick?" he then asked, placing his hand on top of the Irisher's.

An hour later they entered Bobby Latimer's place on Columbus Avenue. As Bobby searched his pocket for the keys, he anticipated the pleasures awaiting him. Patrick was both young and willing, a perfect combination.

"Make yourself comfortable, Patrick, while I hit the head," he said as they entered the condo.

Bobby left the bathroom door open and moved toward the toilet. Unzipping his pants, he began to urinate into the bowl continuing to fantasize about the hours ahead. He neither saw nor heard Patrick Regan at the doorway. And he neither saw nor heard the Glock nine that ended his life.

<u>63</u>

It had been eight days since Tommy's death. From the day of the funeral itself he had planned a return to the cemetery, to be alone with his parents and Tommy, to speak with them silently. On Sunday afternoon he parked just within the gates of St. Joseph's Cemetery and walked the half mile to the gravesite. The early coolness of November had given way the last two days to sunny, cloudless skies, with temperatures stretching into the fifties. Autumn's last effort to ward off the long season to follow, he thought.

He often came here alone in the years after his mother had died, just to speak with her, to assure her that Tommy and Jerry were cared for, eating well, and receiving their education. In later years he came just for himself, to be alone with his most trusted friend. He did not cry that day she had passed away, but in his most difficult or exhilarating moments he had come by to cry tears of frustration or tears of joy, to share the events of his life with her.

He stood before her gravesite, offering a Hail Mary to begin as he always did. Then he silently told her of Tommy's death, of his having substituted for him at the very last moment. He hoped that she already knew of these events, because Tommy was with her now. Stooping to touch Tommy's headstone, he offered a prayer, and then spoke to him of the acts of vengeance that he had committed.

From the distance he first heard rather than observed the approach of the solitary figure. He looked up to see Jerry walking toward him, waving as he closed the gap between them.

"Timmy told me you would be here," Jerry said.

He knelt down on one knee, made the Sign of the Cross, and for a minute prayed silently. Standing, he repeated the Sign.

"I need to talk, Jack. Are you all right?"

"I miss him terribly."

"Jesus, Jack, when does it all end? Tommy, now Ryan. And those other deaths. Are they related to Tommy or Ryan?"

Jack cast a furtive glance at his brother and then focused his eyes on the headstones. "You don't need to become involved in any of it, Jerry. It's best you never know."

"Jack, do you know how much never knowing tears Sheila and me?" He raised his voice. "Do you?"

Jack kept his eyes directly on the stones.

"You at least are living the life. Do you understand how difficult it is to have a son -- a son you love deeply -- who does not, cannot, share his own life with us? We worry all the time, Jack. How is he? Is he safe? Is he involved in this crime or that crime that we read about or hear about?

"Is he a murderer, Jack? Isn't that a great question to have to ask about your own son? Not many families ask that one of each other, do they?" He stopped, wiped a tear from his eye and blew his nose into his handkerchief.

Jack placed his arm around Jerry's neck, embracing him.

"Listen to me, Jerry. It's near over now. I'm meeting in New York next week with the Italians. They want an end to it all, as do we. We'll get it done. I know we will."

"I hope so, Jack. For all our sakes. But when it's over, what does that really mean? We wait a year or three for the next vendetta to break out? It's like Northern Ireland and the troubles, isn't it? It's the Irish way. It's never over."

"Come on, Jerry. Let's go home. It's getting colder." Jack kept his arm draped over Jerry's shoulder as they turned and walked toward the entrance.

Three days now before the meeting in New York. Dressed in a dark blue suit with a white shirt, Jack adjusted his maroon tie and turned toward Marty, who stood in the doorway watching him. "Pretty good shape for an old man," he teased.

"You want to try me, son?" Jack smiled.

"No thank you. I'll pass."

"Where's Timmy?"

"At the dealership. I'm the assigned baby sitter."

"That will be the day."

"You're stealing lines from a John Wayne movie," Marty laughed.

"You ready? Let's get going," Jack said.

They had taken more than the normal precautions over the last week. Paulie Cronin stood beside the car while Chris Kiley walked around the outside of the house. As he and Marty entered the car, he began running events through his mind.

The end was in sight, he thought as they pulled away from the curb. If he was correct, in this time of increasing police pressure, Forelli understood the need to stabilize relationships, to protect investments. He was excited about the upcoming meeting. If past reports were accurate, Forelli's word was golden. If he guaranteed the security of a meet, then you could go to the bank with his assurance.

He had already formed his strategy for the meeting. He would ask for the return of the lost territories. Could Forelli agree to that? He wasn't sure. Above all, Jack understood the don of dons could never appear weak or be perceived the loser in any negotiations with an Irish leader of much less importance than he.

He tried to put himself in Forelli's position. What could he be thinking about the recent chain of events? The don could not be absolutely sure that Biggio had not been the victim of a hit and run driver. If he believed Biggio had been murdered, he could never justify letting the murderers of the New England crime family's leader go free. Forelli might have his suspicions, but he would never have absolute proof.

If Forelli truly wanted to set the peace, he could explain away the Cardoza and Rizzo deaths on the evidence alone. Something had gone wrong in Revere. Rizzo had turned on Cardoza and then had been killed in turn. And did he really care what had happened with Ryan? Could he really believe that

Jack has been responsible for them all -- on the night his brother had been buried? Unlikely.

But he had long ago learned never to underestimate an opponent. As they approached the dealership, he remained silent, absorbed in his thoughts, Marty and Paulie respecting his mood.

64

He remembered the call from Forelli, and his own attempt to learn from the tone behind the words. He had dialed the number provided to him while standing in his kitchen.

"Hello," replied the agreeable voice from Long Island.

"Hello. This is Jack Kelly. I've been asked to call this number."

"Jack. Thank you for honoring my request. This is Michael Forelli."

"How are you, Don Forelli?" Jack replied, an edge of respect in his tone.

"I'm doing well, Jack. I want to personally express my deep sadness at the death of your brother. I have heard from many sources of your closeness to Tommy. I know this must be a very difficult period for you."

"You're very kind, Don Forelli. Our entire family deeply appreciated your flowers and your note."

"Is there anything else you need at this time?" Forelli had asked kindly.

He must not appear aggressive, Jack thought. Let Forelli take the first step and then he would counter. "Not at this time, Don Forelli. But your concern is very meaningful to us."

There was a long pause, Forelli no doubt weighing the responses from Jack, gauging the person with whom he might or might not negotiate.

"Jack, I would appreciate your meeting with me down here. Would you be willing to accommodate me?"

Stated politely by a very powerful and dangerous man, Jack thought. He paused to convey his thoughtfulness across the line, but for days he had practiced his reply.

"Don Forelli, like you, we want the peace, to place behind us the unfortunate events of recent times. But if we're to discuss the matter, I need your assurance regarding my safety."

Without hesitating, Forelli had answered. "If I wanted you dead, Jack, you would already be dead. My word is my bond. You will come and go from any meeting with me safely. My word on it."

"Name the day, Don Forelli."

"Next Thursday afternoon at St. Patrick's Cathedral. Is that possible for you?"

"Yes, I could be in New York next Thursday."

"Bring people with you if you like."

He surprised Jack somewhat with the comment. But Jack had long ago learned to take important phone calls on his feet, to pace the room, to think. Don't ever let down your guard. Be alert to every nuance.

"That won't be necessary," he had responded without hesitating.

"Then I'll meet you..."

Before he could finish, Jack interrupted him. "Don Forelli, with all due respect, I would prefer meeting somewhere other than St. Patrick's Cathedral. I have a place in mind."

A test. What flexibility was there?

"Then name it, Jack," the calm voice had responded.

"I'll be on the Staten Island Ferry on Thursday, the one leaving at 2:10 from Manhattan."

"Fine. I look forward to a positive meeting. Good-bye."

Jack had stared at the phone for a moment, surprised at the abruptness with which Forelli had concluded the conversation. But he had thought then and still felt now that it had gone well.

On Sunday afternoon he rang the doorbell at 34 Copeland Road, as he had virtually every Sunday for over ten years. He enjoyed the Sunday get togethers with his mother and father.

436

Although always there hung in the air the issue of his involvement in the life, over the years they had all learned to stay principally with safe subjects. Marty particularly liked to hear of Jerry's business successes, and, in turn, would discuss the vagaries of the car sales business with his father. His mother just loved him there, and would dote on him as only women brought up in the '40's and '50's would. She insisted that he bring his laundry by each week, that he eat every morsel of the expertly prepared dinner she would serve, that he take home any leftovers. If he were serious about a particular young woman, Sheila would urge him to bring her along.

But he dreaded today's meeting, so quickly following on Tommy's death and so close to the Thanksgiving holiday. He sensed there would be no avoiding the subject of the life today. All of his mother's fears would be there to be read, her struggle to introduce the topic consuming her. And he guessed that today his father, weighed down by sadness, would be more likely to introduce the subject when they were alone.

Jerry answered the doorbell dressed in a white shirt and red tie topped by a blue coat sweater. He gripped Marty's hand firmly, hugging him as he moved through the entry. From the kitchen his mother greeted him warmly, and together with his father Marty walked into the sparkling clean country kitchen complete with an island cooking station in the middle of the room.

Sheila leaned into him as he embraced her, raising her face to accept his kiss. "Smells good, Mom. What's on?"

"Duck. Duck L'Orange. How's that sound?" she replied happily.

"Great. Just great. Are you two doing OK?"

Jerry's eyes showed the burden of the events of recent weeks. The loss of his brother, the visits from the police inquiring about the murder, the escalating publicity in the Boston and Lynn papers. Black circles newly formed under his eyes, contrasted with the white pastiness of his face, gave him the appearance of a tired, older man. And despite her cheerful words, his mother appeared edgy and stressed.

"It's been difficult, son. Very difficult," Jerry replied. "For all of us."

"Come sit at the dining room table," Sheila interjected nervously. "Everything's ready."

Throughout the dinner they spoke sparingly, trying hard to avoid the issue on everyone's mind. Sheila jumped from topic to topic, settling down only when she spoke about Bobby.

"Did you notice the young teenagers clustered outside the church at the funeral mass?" she asked. "There must have been close to two hundred of them on Union Street, trying to catch a glimpse of him."

"He doesn't let success go to his head. He hasn't changed much at all, has he, Ma?" Marty said.

"His mother is very proud of him," she said too quickly. Then, fearful that Marty would misinterpret her intent, "I mean...what I meant to say was..."

"Ma, I know what you mean. We're all proud of Bobby," he said gently. "That new feature movie is going to make him a big star and soon. Did I tell you he'll be in New York for a day next Thursday? I'll see him when I'm down there."

"No, you didn't," she replied happily. "Oh, I'm so pleased for him. Give him a big kiss for me, won't you?" She stood to clear the plates.

"Ma, please sit down. That duck was delicious. I'm all set for now."

"I just want to cut you some cake and get us some coffee. I'll leave the plates," she compromised. "Be right back."

Staring across at his father, Marty dabbed at his mouth with his napkin. "You and Ma going to be all right, Dad?"

Jerry glanced toward the kitchen, assuring himself that for the next few minutes Sheila would be preoccupied. He pawed at his water glass before responding.

"Let me answer a question with a question, Marty. If you lost a brother, and had another brother, a son and a nephew still involved in this shit, would you be all right?" he asked calmly.

Marty did not answer. He stared at his father for a moment, then lowered his eyes.

438

"Son, is there any chance that you can leave?" he asked anxiously. "Get out of it all? You know I always have a position for you with me. You're a natural salesman, a leader. We could..." In mid-sentence he stopped, partly in frustration, partly because a new thought had come to mind.

"When's it all going to end, Marty? Can you tell me that? Your mother sits here worrying every night. When is it ever over, Marty?"

"Dad, Jack and I will be in New York on Tuesday. As I see it, it's very possible we can end it all."

Jerry looked at him for a very long moment. "What does that mean? You'll be in New York with him? You're that close to the top now, Marty? Jesus!"

Marty picked up his water glass and sipped at it, deciding then and there to answer his father directly. "That's right, Dad."

"Then there's no hope for it to end for you, is there? You're the number one guy behind Jack now, aren't you, Marty?"

"That's right, Dad. But it will end, Dad."

"Maybe, Marty. Maybe this time. But what you're saying is that for your mother and for me, there's no end. Not until some night some cop knocks on the front door and tells us that our son is dead. Don't you see, Marty? It's an Irish thing. It's an Irish tragedy. There's not ever going to be a happy ending."

Marty knew it was fruitless to answer. He could not allay their concerns with words, and there was no sense even trying.

"You know something, Marty? You're so much like your Uncle Jack. I swear to God I'm sitting with him. You even look like him when he was twenty-five."

"He's a very special person to me, Dad. As you are."

"As I am," Jerry answered dejectedly. "You believe your own bullshit, do you, Marty?"

"What I believe, Dad, is in myself. You have a business, and a number of people believe in you. They expect leadership. I now help run a business, too. And my people believe in me. They depend on me, as your people depend on you."

"And there's no difference son? No difference between business efficiency in the food services industry and murder?"

439

Marty stared at him without expression before standing. "I have to go. There are some things I need to attend to."

Sheila appeared in the doorway with a small tray of cake and coffee. "Where are you going?"

Marty took the tray from her and placed it on the table. "I'm sorry, Mom. I really do need to run. I'll see you on Thanksgiving. Thanks for a wonderful dinner." He leaned to kiss her.

Recognizing the importance of not upsetting Sheila, Jerry stood and smiled. "We'll see you then, son."

65

Ray Horan and Christine Wall walked along the Battery Park promenade, holding hands, two lovers engrossed in each other. The sky was slate gray, with ominous clouds lurking on the far horizon. A few tourists braved the chilly November day to stroll the area. Occasionally Ray and Christine stopped to observe the ships sailing in New York Harbor as they casually closed the distance to the Staten Island Ferry.

Ray estimated over two hundred people were in the many groups gathering to board. Near the front he spotted Marty, alone, wearing a navy blue peacoat and a New York Yankees baseball cap. In the middle of a contingent of elementary school children Jack could have passed as one of their teachers, the adults around him scurrying to keep their young charges together in some semblance of order.

It was Ray's job to spot the don of dons -- to see him early and to stay close to him at all times. But he did not see Michael Forelli anywhere in the crowd. He looked back down the corridor where another fifteen to twenty late arrivals walked aggressively toward them. On the edge of that group, Michael Forelli walked alongside a hulk who might as well have worn the lettering "bodyguard" across his front. Dressed in a navy blue cashmere topcoat and a soft gray fedora, Forelli held a rolled up newspaper in his left hand which he gently tapped against his side.

The hulk surveyed the large assembly now as they all moved forward at the voice command to board. He looked slightly bewildered, unable to find anyone fitting Jack's description in the throng. Forelli joined him in looking about but seemed much less concerned.

Staying close to the middle of the crowd, Ray walked with his arm around Christine. He noticed Marty, among the very first three or four to board, moving straight ahead through the deck doors into the heated area. He was to take a position on the second deck initially in order to observe and study all boarding parties. As Ray stepped from the gangplank onto the ship itself, he directed Christine to the rail where they faced the huge skyscrapers, pointing out the various sites to one another.

Jack walked past them, through the doors and onto the heated deck, his blue trenchcoat open, the holster concealed, but within easy access for him. He had not worn a suit jacket so that he could locate the weapon quickly if needed, but he had not forgotten to place the bulletproof vest under his white dress shirt.

Ray watched Forelli and the hulk board, walking, like Jack, directly into the first deck seating area to escape the cold and the moderate wind. When they were seated alone, just inside the doors and to the right, Forelli said something to the hulk who then nodded, stood, and wandered slowly through the crowd staring at each passenger. Once everyone had boarded, Ray and Christine stopped their gawking and pointing, opened the deck doors to the heated area, closing the portal behind them. Meandering arm in arm, they took seats diagonally across from Forelli.

As the ferry disengaged from its berth, Marty watched Ray and Christine enter the inner area and walked quickly to the doors at the stern and moved the length of the outer deck back to the same doors through which Ray and Christine had entered.

From a seat near Ray, Jack rose, turned the corner, and moved toward Forelli, Ray watching him close the ten yards.

Expressionless, Forelli concentrated on the newspaper. Just another businessman interested in the market, as far as the world could see, Jack thought.

"Mr. Forelli, I'm Jack Kelly," he said, standing directly in front of the don.

"Jack, it's so good to meet you. Please, sit here next to me," Forelli said warmly. "I very much appreciate your coming to New York."

"It is my honor to be asked, Mr. Forelli," Jack said, sitting to the left of the don.

From out of nowhere the hulk appeared, his face showing his chagrin that Jack was seated with his boss. "Jack, please meet my associate, Anthony Moriello." The hulk extended his hand, and Jack, to the surprise of both, stood to accept it.

"Anthony, do you think it's possible to get some good coffee for all of us? Coffee all right with you, Jack?" Forelli asked. Jack nodded his agreement.

Anthony moved toward the refreshment area, his hands jammed in his topcoat pockets, through habit looking carefully at each face in the crowd. He walked directly past the two middle-aged lovers who could not keep their hands off each other.

"Jack, I'm very sorry for your recent troubles. It's a great sadness to lose a brother. I'm truly sorry," Forelli said sincerely, never taking his eyes from Jack's face.

"Thank you," Jack replied, locking eyes with Forelli, looking deep into them, searching for nuances, for treachery, for the slightest sign of sincerity or a lack of sincerity, for betrayal if it were there.

"Could you indulge an old man's curiosity, Jack?" Forelli asked, setting the newspaper on the bench next to him.

"Of course."

"Are you alone on this ferry?"

Jack smiled at him, his own eyes alive and flashing. He was positive Forelli already knew the answer, and, like an expert trial lawyer, would never ask a question to which he did not already know the answer.

"No," he replied. "I have someone with me."

Forelli smiled back at him. "I like that. Honesty. If we're to establish a working relationship, it's critical that I be completely honest with you and, in turn, you be the same with me."

"I always appreciate honesty," Jack replied.

"Then let me begin by showing my good faith. Let me try to answer any concerns you have regarding these unfortunate recent events, Jack. What do you want to know?"

"Who ordered my brother killed?" Jack asked calmly.

"Indirectly, I'm responsible. Ryan approached his don, requesting permission to end the long standing truce, to fulfill the vendetta he felt against you. You were the target, not your brother Tommy. Ryan specifically asked to handle the matter himself. Due to his good works for Don Gianelli, our council granted his request at my recommendation.

"We made a mistake, Jack. Or rather I made a mistake. I should not have listened to Mario Gianelli. Later, I learned something else. You faced simultaneously the gluttonous desire of Gennaro Biggio to move you aside to provide more territory for his worthless cousin by marriage. In time, the leaders there would have moved against your family."

Anthony Moriello returned with three steaming cups of coffee, handing one first to Forelli and then to Jack. "Anthony, things are fine here. Would you excuse us for a few minutes?" A kind form of dismissal, Jack thought, as Anthony strolled about fifteen yards from their spot and took another seat. Jack glanced across the deck, observing Ray and Christine engaged in quiet conversation. He couldn't see Marty, but he knew he would be close.

"Now would you be willing to answer a question or two for me, Jack?" Forelli asked, sipping the hot coffee.

"I'll try."

"Who killed Ryan?"

"I did. I found out where he was staying, and I paid him a visit."

Forelli sat, silent for the moment, gazing across the deck, seemingly looking directly at Ray and Christine.

"And Rizzo? Cardoza? What do you know about them?" he asked, shifting his eyes toward Jack.

"I know nothing."

"There are those who think otherwise, Jack," Forelli responded.

"Then they give me too much credit, Don Forelli. I take my revenge on those who have injured me and mine, and on them alone. Are you aware Connie Ryan left me a calling card so that I would know who was responsible for my brother's death?" He pulled a copy of the "Remember MSG" message from his pocket. "You can very easily check with the Boston police, who will confirm the original was attached to my brother's body."

Forelli studied the message carefully, pondering more than the message, Jack suspected.

Now close to Staten Island, the ship slowed as the navigator looped the vessel across the windy surface to ease its passage between the twin stanchions and its eventual berth. Anticipating the end of the half-hour crossing, individuals and small groups began to close on the deck doors and the point of disembarkation.

"You bought a return ticket, Jack?"

"Yes."

"Good. We have more to talk about. Let's get off and get back on."

As they exited to the Ferry terminal, Jack followed Forelli's lead, as he commented now only on mundane topics, such as the weather, a face in the crowd, or the city itself. Jack knew Ray would be directly behind him, looking for any sign of a problem, protecting his back. And Marty would be off to the side, watching the perimeter and the area before them. As they walked along, Jack stayed to one side of Forelli, the hulk on the other.

It took almost fifteen minutes for them to re-enter the ship, a new crowd of travelers joining with those sightseers returning to the city. They positioned themselves directly inside the deck once again, virtually in the same area as before. The ship banged against the stanchions as it manuevered itself for the round trip. From the deck a few passengers braved the increasingly stronger wind to observe the departure.

There seemed to be fewer people for the return. Anthony now sat thirty feet away from them, almost directly opposite Ray and Christine. He seemed more relaxed now, less anticipatory of trouble. On the deck, just outside the doors, Jack spotted Marty walking back and forth, engaging in conversation with the other observers but never for long.

Forelli leaned back in his seat, turning his eyes toward Anthony. He said nothing for a time, and then turned to Jack. "Let's walk out on deck, Jack," he finally said. "The view approaching the city always fascinates me." He stood, opened the door to the deck and held it for Jack. Anthony never moved, his eyes following Forelli and Jack to the exterior.

Ray wanted to stay with the hulk, but he needed to cover one other base. Was there some threat above them? "Christine," he whispered in her ear, "just sit right here. I'll be right back." He walked quickly to the center of the ship and climbed the steps.

On the outer deck Forelli pointed toward Ellis Island and to the Statue of Liberty, twin sentinels in the distance. "Look at that, Jack. Imagine what our forefathers felt seeing that great lady for the first time," he marveled. "My grandfather came from Palermo in the late 1890's. What a country. You believe in this country, Jack?"

"I believe in me, Mr. Forelli. And I depend on three people -- me, myself, and I."

Forelli laughed into the wind. "You Irish are too cynical, Jack. No appreciation of history? No sense of the American dream?"

"I do think of what this country has meant to my people," Jack replied. "But my loyalty is to people, Mr. Forelli. Never to dreams."

"Do you read much, Jack?"

"Yes."

"What kind of books?"

"Fiction. Biography. Biographies about leaders such as Roosevelt, Churchill, Kennedy. Books about military history, like the Battle of Midway."

"Take the latter -- Midway. What did you learn from it?"

"That you can plan, strategize, as both the Japanese and the Americans did in 1942. Yet in the end circumstances beyond your control -- fate, luck -- often determine outcomes. We can only control so much. We kid ourselves if we believe too much in our own skills. We then become arrogant and make more foolish errors."

Pondering the reply, Forelli gazed at the Statue of Liberty as they passed by. "Let's talk of the future? What do you want from us?"

"I consider it an honor that you have sent for me, Mr. Forelli. All my family wants is the opportunity to continue the relationships of the past. I can work with Salvy Cardoza's successor and provide all of us with a greater profit than you've seen with Salvy and Rizzo. I ask that you consider returning the territories Don Biggio and Cardoza took from me. I'll assure you a profit line ten percent more than what they and Rizzo provided."

"And how would you accomplish that?"

"Rizzo was an incompetent. Look at the results you had with me before. I'll guarantee you and the New England family the new margins."

Forelli stared at the approaching coastline. "I'm willing to return the disputed areas to you, Jack, but there is a condition."

Marty stood at the rail opposite them, his body half turned toward them, the massive skyscrapers looming larger as they neared Manhattan. On each side of them small craft mingled with large ships, all of them hurrying to and from the great Port of New York.

"There is to be no more killing -- for any reason. I do not intend to justify a hit and run, or anything else in the future. With some biting of my tongue, I can justify to others the events to this point including Biggio. We made a mistake with Ryan, and you've paid and we've paid. We write if off as the price of doing business. But it's over now, understood?"

"Understood."

"I want stability in our business. Here in New York, and in the country as a whole, we see a resurgence that will benefit us.

The real estate market is booming. Reagan is pushing policies favorable to our interests, but the police are much smarter now, Jack. They're everywhere now and utilizing new strategies and new technology. We have all we can do to hold them off. No more personal vendettas. We can't continue with personal grudges that call attention to us."

"You have my word, Mr. Forelli. There will be peace."

Forelli extended his hand. "Then we have an agreement, Jack."

Jack shook his hand vigorously.

"I'm sure I'll hear more about you in the years ahead, Jack. And about him, too," Forelli added, pointing at Marty.

Jack tried to hide his surprise.

Forelli grinned at him. "Do well by your people, Jack. Despite Midway, skill in leadership will still surmount circumstance most of the time. But know something? I think you know that already."

Jack smiled and grasped his hand. "Take good care of you, don of dons. I thank you for your wise counsel."

"I'm going to run along the beach. The weather's just beautiful. Can you believe this? Sixty degrees on December 1?"

"Where will you be?" Marty asked.

"Right across the street. I'll run from the first staircase leading to the beach to the last one, toward Swampscott and back. Do that four times that's got to be four miles," Jack said, standing and stretching.

"You still averaging five days running out of every seven?"

"Yup," Jack said, bending to touch his toes. "I'll be back in half hour or so," he said, putting an arm around Marty's shoulder as he moved to the doorway.

He crossed Lynn Shore Drive, descending from the street level to the sidewalk, and then, via the first staircase, to the beach below. Jogging toward the water, he turned to look back at the long staircase. He loved the beach at low tide on days like this, but nothing could beat the high of diving from that stairwell

448

at high tide on a hot summer day. He still enjoyed watching young teens jump into powerful bluish-green waves, the most skilled among them always being sure to time the jumps so as to not be pulled back into the seawall by the incoming tide.

He turned and ran close to the water where the sand was firm. Moving now at a good pace, he observed the walkers in the distance coming toward him. At this time of year anything goes, he thought. Some wore shorts and T-shirts; others were bundled in long pants and heavy fall jackets. Of the dozen walkers, at least half held leashes in their hands, their dogs running free along the sand chasing the sea birds at the water's edge. A runner's delight, he thought. Dogs shitting all over the beach, after chasing down more joggers than they did birds.

Occasionally, a young runner would overtake him, waving as he or she ran by. And from the opposite direction, a young couple ran together, laughing gaily, enjoying each other's company. There were now as many runners as walkers, something you just did not see before the '80s. In the east, beyond the horizon, the sun poured its riches onto the beach, partially blinding him, making it a bit difficult to concentrate. He looked down, studying the ground, running events through his mind.

He had won. All enemies and traitors had been accounted for. He had regained his territories and achieved a peace through Forelli that the new leaders in Providence and Boston would be obliged to honor. He could relax for the first time in a long time.

He ran hard the last one hundred yards of his third lap, pausing parallel to the first stairwell to rest before setting off for the final stretch. Bending to pick up a sea shell, he thought of Marty and Timmy. He was immensely proud of them. Perhaps in the near future, he could even retire from the life. In recent weeks he had thought about it. Could he ever give it up? He wasn't sure. The action, the men, the camaraderie fueled him, made life worthwhile. Yet he would then have more time to visit with Bobby in California and New York. And perhaps there was still time for him and Catherine. He might be able to give more of himself then, to a woman as loyal to him as he would be to her.

Looking toward Swampscott, he planned on jogging the half mile there and then sprinting all the way back the length of the beach to complete the run. He ran effortlessly, the sun now over his right shoulder flaring down the beach. On reaching the last stairwell, he turned for home, accelerating his pace, his legs churning, the sun now almost blinding him from his left.

Halfway back, he first felt the pain. It started small, and like all runners he knew his body and was very sensitive to changes, any change at all. It ran up his arm and crept toward his chest. He stopped in his track and walked for a few yards. A cramp that would pass he thought. He started to perspire more profusely than his norm, but his legs felt strong. He increased his gait, walking a bit more quickly. The pain receded and so he broke into a run once again.

And then it came again, only this time it was searing, invading his stomach and chest, causing him to stop completely. He fell on his left side about five yards from the waterline. He tried to right himself, leaning on his left elbow, the low tide now moving tighter to him. Then suddenly the sun seemed to fade, and he felt very cold. In the distance he could see walkers accelerating their pace toward him and behind him someone who looked like Marty sprinting in full flight toward him. He lay back on the sand, trying to stay conscious.

From the water itself he saw his mother approaching, hands extended to help him up. But why was she wearing a cotton dress and a full apron? He hoped she was no longer angry about Jerry's vaccination. As she came closer to the shore, he noticed she was smiling.

Then, just as suddenly, behind her he saw himself, as a young boy deep in the water body surfing with the waves toward the shore where Tommy stood yelling frantically for him. He swam rapidly, urging his body forward until he could stand and run toward the sand. Tommy's foot was cut. How had that happened? He would have to carry his brother home.

But he couldn't get up. How then could he help Tommy? From far away he could barely hear Marty's voice, as someone turned him on his back. At least his stomach and chest did not hurt anymore. He tried to remember the words of the Act of Contrition, but could not. What was it that the Jesuits used to say? Something about give me the child for the first seven years and he will be mine for the rest of his life. Well, he had proven that wrong.

Then she was there again. She lifted him to her bosom and carried him toward the sea and the horizon beyond. For the first time in so long he felt contentment and peace. He was with her once again.

Two weeks before Christmas 1982 Marty and Timmy watched the workmen place the new headstone above Jack's recently dug grave. It was sized exactly like the other two. Carved into the granite was the lettering:

"John Anthony Kelly
  1936 - 1982
  Father to Us All"

"It look all right, Tim?" one of the workmen asked.

"It is fine. Very well done, Dan. What do you think, Marty?"

"He would be very pleased," Marty responded.

"Leave us alone now, would you, Dan?" Timmy asked.

The three workmen picked up their tools and walked slowly toward the roadway. In the east the sun slanted through the barren trees, bathing them in bright light.

"Let's pray," Tim said, kneeling on one knee. Marty joined him, each quiet for the moment, then making the Sign of the Cross before rising.

About the Author

John Curry is President Emeritus of Northeastern University in Boston. He was born and raised in Lynn, Massachusetts and is a graduate of Northeastern University with a degree in history. He earned his doctorate in education from Boston University. He has taught writing at Northeastern and is the author of numerous educational articles. From 1989-96 he served as president of Northeastern University, elevating its academic status to that of a research institution. He lives on Boston's North Shore, where he is now at work on his second crime fiction novel.

Printed in the United States
1012400001B

9 781587 210976